the
orpheus
deception

the
orpheus
deception

DAVID STONE

G. P. Putnam's Sons | New York

G. P. PUTNAM'S SONS
Publishers Since 1838
Published by the Penguin Group
Penguin Group (USA) Inc., 375 Hudson Street, New York, New York
10014, USA • Penguin Group (Canada), 90 Eglinton Avenue East, Suite 700, Toronto,
Ontario, M4P 2Y3, Canada (a division of Pearson Canada Inc.) • Penguin Books Ltd,
80 Strand, London WC2R 0RL, England • Penguin Ireland, 25 St Stephen's Green,
Dublin 2, Ireland (a division of Penguin Books Ltd) • Penguin Group (Australia),
250 Camberwell Road, Camberwell, Victoria 3124, Australia (a division of Pearson
Australia Group Pty Ltd) • Penguin Books India Pvt Ltd, 11 Community Centre,
Panchsheel Park, New Delhi–110 017, India • Penguin Group (NZ),
67 Apollo Drive, Rosedale, North Shore 0632, New Zealand (a division of Pearson
New Zealand Ltd) • Penguin Books (South Africa) (Pty) Ltd, 24 Sturdee Avenue,
Rosebank, Johannesburg 2196, South Africa

Penguin Books Ltd, Registered Offices: 80 Strand, London WC2R 0RL, England

ISBN 978-0-399-15463-8

Printed in the United States of America
1 3 5 7 9 10 8 6 4 2

Book Design by Paula Russell Szafranski

This is a work of fiction. Names, characters, places, and incidents either are the product of
the author's imagination or are used fictitiously, and any resemblance to actual persons, living
or dead, businesses, companies, events, or locales is entirely coincidental.

While the author has made every effort to provide accurate telephone numbers and Internet
addresses at the time of publication, neither the publisher nor the author assumes any responsibility for errors, or for changes that occur after publication. Further, the publisher does not
have any control over and does not assume any responsibility for author or third-party websites or their content.

For Catherine Stone

. . . the Serbs reconquered Kosovo in 1912 and committed atrocities against the Albanians, who sided with Germany in 1914 and oppressed the Serbs, who regained control of Kosovo in 1918 and tyrannized the Albanians, who sided with the Germans again in 1939 and crushed the Serbs, who recaptured Kosovo in 1945 and persecuted the Albanians, who rioted in 1981 and beat and robbed the Serbs, who . . .

—P. J. O'Rourke, *Peace Kills*

I would rather be the hammer than the anvil.

—Erwin Rommel

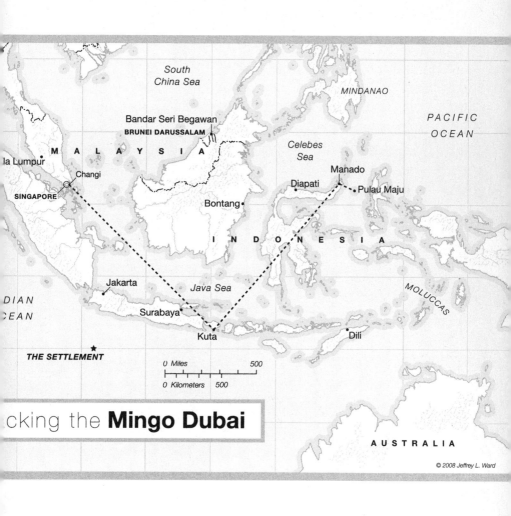

South
China Sea

MINDANAO

PACIFIC
OCEAN

Bandar Seri Begawan
BRUNEI DARUSSALAM

Celebes
Sea

Manado

la Lumpur

M A L A Y S I A

Changi

Diapati

Pulau Maju

SINGAPORE

Bontang

I N D O N E S I A

Jakarta

Java Sea

DIAN
CEAN

Surabaya

MOLUCCAS

Kuta

Dili

★
THE SETTLEMENT

0 Miles   500

0 Kilometers   500

cking the **Mingo Dubai**

AUSTRALIA

© 2008 Jeffrey L. Ward

the
orpheus
deception

prologue

After the killings, Dalton went to Venice, where the rain fell for two days and three nights, a hard, slicing torrent, and, under it, the threat of worse things coming, the deep, hard cold of the Venetian winter. At first light, unable to sleep, he had watched as a swirling mist rose up around the boats out on Saint Mark's Basin. By noon, the Palladian façade of the San Giorgio Maggiore across the lagoon was little more than a formless white blur. Dalton stared at his own reflection in the window of the suite—colorless eyes deep-set in a haggard face, his long blond hair limp, and gray in the half-light, his cheeks sunken and seamed. He drew in a lungful of acrid smoke, breathed it out in a harsh exhalation, erasing his reflection in a cloud of blue smoke.

Cora. Cora Vasari.

She kept a little study in the Museo Civico, overlooking the Piazza San Marco, where she liked to revise and sharpen her lectures before going back to the academy in Florence in late November. He'd called her number from a pay phone next to the equestrian statue of Garibaldi only thirty minutes ago. She had answered the phone herself. He had listened to her slow and steady breathing for thirty seconds, knowing that anything he said in the clear could trigger a voice-recognition relay at Crypto City. But her . . . *closeness* . . . her presence, held him fast. After a full minute, Cora had spoken, in a whisper, only six words:

Micah, do not come to Venice.

Too late for that, Cora, he thought. *I'm already here.*

Dalton poured a final glass of champagne, drained the crystal flute, and set it carefully down on the window ledge. He stubbed out his cigarette, shoved the Ruger into his shoulder holster, gave the suite one last look, and went out onto the crowded quay, pushing through the milling crush of oblivious tourists. The city was full to overflowing, even this late in the season; everyone had come to watch the Venice Marathon. They'd put a wooden boardwalk across the Grand Canal, a novelty and therefore an atrocity. Venice had its air of jaded carnival in place, although the streets were running with gray water, and the sky was low and sodden. He had to butt and shoulder his way through the cheering crowds lining the marathon route, moving right along the edges of the runners' lanes, heading west along the Riva degli Schiavoni—the Quay of Slavs—toward the Piazza San Marco.

Reflexively, automatically, he searched each face in the throng, scanned every roofline, looking for something *wrong;* a fixed glare, a look that was a little too intense, eyes suddenly averted, a half-seen figure stepping back into a doorway as he bulled his way along the quay. But there was nothing: just the rain, the rank sewage smell of the flooding canals, the purring murmur of vaporettos and water taxis out on the fog-shrouded basin, the pressing crowds, the crush of runners pelting past his left shoulder.

In the middle of the crossing near the Bridge of Sighs, his attention zeroed in on the faces of the people streaming toward him, he was struck suddenly, forcefully, from behind; struck hard enough to knock him, reeling, into the balustrade, almost hard enough to send him over the edge and into the canal below. He slammed into the stone banister, turned and saw a skinny blond girl in runner's shorts and a dripping tunic with a number on the back: 559. She was glaring at him, her hard, red mouth twisted. She hissed something at him in a language he could not understand—not Italian—and he opened his mouth to say something equally stinging in reply, but no sound came, only a bright red spike of agony deep in his rib. He fingered the area and doubled over when he found a sharp, searing pain.

The bitch had cracked his ribs.

Dalton, whose temper was never far from the surface, began to stumble after the blond runner, breathing through thinned lips, indignant outrage driving him, but she was quickly lost in the crush of a hundred other runners flowing around him, their feet pounding and thudding, the air thick with the animal reek of their sweat and their urine, their rapid panting breaths, and now Dalton was caught up in the flow of the marathon, carried along the quay like a leaf in a flood, staggering, his ribs sending jagged bolts of pain up into his chest. As the press of runners turned the corner by the Palazzo Ducale, he was finally cast out of the stream and into a narrow cloister. He put a hand on a pillar and rested there for a moment, his chest heaving, his cracked rib burning in his side, cursing, miserable—he looked angrily around for the blond runner . . .

. . . and there was Cora. Tall, her black hair flying in the wind-driven rain, her long blue trench coat flapping: she was hesitating by the steps of the Basilica, a sheaf of papers in her arms, watching the runners flowing around her, the pigeons swirling up like leaves. The piazza was packed with thousands of people and filled with a vast, roaring, thunderous cheering, wave after wave. He could hardly hear his own voice calling her name.

Cora heard a call, turned, searching the sea of faces. Finally, she found him, a flash of recognition—a fleeting smile—and then her expression changed into shock as she looked down at his hands . . .

IT WAS THE morning of the next day; Cora Vasari and Micah Dalton were in Cortona, for Porter Naumann's funeral. The same cold, slanting rain that had drowned Venice the day before was beating against the shuttered houses along the Via Berrettini. Cora Vasari was a little way ahead of him, going up the steep hillside between the overhanging roofs, the tilting walls of medieval villas lining the narrow, cobbled street. She was walking with the Carabinieri major, Brancati. She was wearing a wide-brimmed black hat, a black silk coat, very long—she seemed to be in mourning, but her head was a fraction too close to Brancati, and her hand was on his arm, an intimacy that Dalton found just possible to overlook. Farther up the street, a group of men in black stood waiting—pallbearers, from the look of them—grouped around a huge rosewood casket.

Naumann's casket.

Dalton turned his collar up, pulled his coat tight, and plodded doggedly upward in a file of solemn carabinieri, rain dripping down his face; funeral weather, and the streets of Cortona breathing of the grave.

The column of men passed an open laneway, and, glancing to his right, Dalton saw through a curtain of dripping laundry the stone parapet that ran beside the Via Santa Margherita: beyond the parapet, in the cold, gray distance, he could see the faint outline of Lake Trasimeno. A familiar figure was leaning on the parapet, screened by a wall of rain, arms folded, white face staring. Dalton looked at this figure for a time, and then he called up the hill to Cora, but the rain drowned out his words, so he turned aside and stopped. The man standing there was Porter Naumann.

To be precise, it was the *ghost* of Porter Naumann. Naumann's ghost raised a hand, beckoning him down the lane, and, in spite of the rain and the wind, Dalton could hear Porter calling his name, a faint sound, lost in the hissing of running water. Dalton glanced up the street, saw Cora turn and look back, her broad black hat glistening in the downpour.

He waved to her, lifted his wrist high, tapped his watch, and then stepped into the alley, hurrying away under the lines of dripping laundry. Water ran down his neck, but, oddly, the pain in his rib had suddenly disappeared. He reached the broad lane of the Via Margherita and crossed over to Naumann, a tall, elegant figure, leaning there with his arms crossed, smiling at him. He was wearing a pearl gray single-breasted suit over a pale pink shirt, a flaring charcoal tie held with a gold collar pin, and, over it all, his signature long blue Zegna overcoat. His face was as it had been in life, sharp, hard-planed, a great beak of a nose, pale blue eyes, bright and full of wry humor.

"Micah, how are you?"

"I'm fine, Porter. You're going to miss your funeral."

Naumann shrugged, grinned.

"I'm there in spirit. Walk with me a minute, will you?"

Dalton looked at Porter Naumann's ghostly face for a time, trying to read his expression. There was something in his voice . . . a warning note?

"Can we do this later, Porter? Cora will be waiting."

"What are they going to do? Start without me?"

A valid point, thought Dalton, as they walked off down the hill, the flat Tuscan landscape stretching away on their left, Lake Trasimeno barely visible through the mist, Naumann striding ahead, Dalton a little behind, his thoughts moving between the funeral and the Agency, what Deacon Cather may be planning for him, what little future he had left to worry about in the first place. In the front of his mind, he was also idly wondering what had conjured up this final visitation from an old, dead friend. Naumann was carrying something in his hand, Dalton could see, a slender, shining thing, colored green, some sort of long glass bottle, and he was fingering it as they walked down the hill, wrapped in his own silence.

"Where are we going, anyway?" asked Dalton, finally.

"Just a few blocks down. How's the rib?"

"It's fine. Hurt like hell yesterday, but I seem to be okay now."

Naumann received the news with an absent nod, and they walked on. The gloomy sky was breaking up and the air around them was now glowing with diffused light. The broad valley below them was opening up as the mist burned away. They could see the distant lake, see pale sunlight glimmering on the water. Down at the bottom of the hill there was a large square: Dalton knew it very well, the Piazza Garibaldi, its broad stone pavilion surrounded by ancient oaks and cypress, extending far out over the cliff with the entire valley laid out before it, a medieval tapestry of green and amber and golden squares that stretched away into the purest smoky blue infinity. The square itself seemed to be full of people, a gathering or a reception of some sort. Naumann slowed his pace a few hundred feet from the plaza and turned to look at Dalton, his face showing affection, solemnity; an uncharacteristic display for Naumann.

"Look, Micah, do you know what this is?"

He held his hand out. In his palm was the slender green glass bottle.

"No idea. Looks like Murano glass."

"It is. The old Venetian assassins used to use these."

"I know. I've heard about it. They say that Murano glass is so fine that a single drop of poison will shatter the bottle."

"That's right. But that's not what this is. This isn't a bottle."

"What is it?"

"It's the hilt of a dagger. A dagger made out of Murano glass."

"Yow! Nasty. Where's the blade?"

"Well, that's the thing."

"The *thing?* What thing?"

Naumann stopped, turned, and looked him full in the face, his expression grave, his eyes gentle.

"The thing is, the blade is in *you,* Micah."

Dalton looked skyward, sighing theatrically.

"In me? The blade is in *me?* Oh for chrissakes, Porter. What the hell are you trying to say?"

"The marathon runner, in Venice, the blond girl who ran into you near the Bridge of Sighs? She used this on you when she ran into you."

"Used it? On me? How . . . ?"

"You've been stabbed with it."

"Stabbed? She broke a *rib,* Porter. A rib. Don't go all blithering hysterical on me now. I broke a rib. I got better. I'm fine now. I'm . . ."

Naumann shook his head.

"No you're not. The wound is *mortal,* Micah. You're dying. Now. At this moment. Can you understand?"

Dalton stared down at the long green glass hilt.

"Stabbed? She *stabbed* me? With this?"

"Yes. The dagger is made of Murano glass; the blade is very long and very thin. It goes in deep, but it leaves only a narrow mark. The hilt breaks off, leaving the blade in the body. In *your* body, Micah."

"The runner? She stabbed me? Why?"

"I don't know. Maybe the Serbs, for what you did to their people in Venice. Or maybe the Company. Cather. I don't know why you've been stabbed. They don't tell me these things. They just send you off on your mission. It seems that once you're dead, you're sort of out of the loop. But you *have* been stabbed. The blade went deep. The wound was mortal."

"Mortal?"

"Yes. They tell me the blade cut an artery near your liver. Sliced it open."

Dalton felt his heart beating, a rapid, fluttering impulse in his neck and throat. Naumann's pale eyes were kindly. Behind him, the sun was burning, and the day was now as warm as a summer afternoon.

"They? Who the hell is *they?*"

Naumann shook his head, shrugged.

"The people running the . . . running wherever it is I am now."

"Okay. Let me get this straight. You don't know where you are and you don't know who's running Hell or Heaven or . . ."

"There's no Hell, Micah."

"Great. Heaven either?"

"So far, no sign."

"Jolly. John Lennon got one thing right, dipshit hippie moron. So you don't know about all that afterworld stuff, but you do know I'm . . ."

"Dying."

"Jeez."

"You're bleeding to death. Inside. That's what I'm here for. I'm here to explain this thing to you. To help you . . . adjust. Do you understand what I'm saying?"

"No. I sure as hell don't. This is just some nasty dream. A nightmare. Anyway, dammit, no offense, Porter, but you're *dead.* Over a month dead, not to put too fine a point on it. Cashed in your chips. Bought the farm. Vertically deployed into the terrain. Deceased. You're now ex-Porter. A goner. Like the parrot. You follow? That sort of impeaches your credibility."

In spite of the circumstances, Naumann smiled.

"You're starting to get on my nerves, kid. Here I am on a mission of fucking mercy, and you're giving me these old Monty Python riffs."

"Well, Jesus, Porter. You're the corpse and *you're* telling *me* I'm dead! How do you know you're not just dreaming that you're alive?"

This concept seemed to give Naumann something to think about.

"Jesus. I see your point. Maybe a drink will help clarify the—"

"Micah!"

They both turned. Someone was calling Dalton's name, a woman's voice. It was Cora Vasari. She was standing a little way up the Via Santa Margherita, holding her wide black hat with a gloved hand, her hair blowing in the rising wind off the valley.

"Micah," she called. "Where are you going? They're waiting for you."

"That's Cora," he said, turning to Naumann.

"I know who she is," said Porter. "I've seen her before, remember? Stunner. Reminds me of Isabella Rossellini. If I'd known about *her* when I was still alive, you wouldn't have stood a chance."

"Look, Porter, setting aside the queasier aspects of you being both feet in the grave and still having a sex drive, I happen to have a life to go and live. I should go back."

Naumann's face became solemn, unreadable.

"Think about that. Do you really *want* to, Micah?"

Cora's voice carried down the hill, calling his name again.

"Micah . . . ?"

Dalton's face became set, his expression conflicted. Naumann looked up the laneway at Cora for a time, his face marked with longing.

"You know you can't stay with her, don't you?" he said, the wind plucking at his coattails. "Clandestine will send a team. Cather won't back off until you're dead. And if you're with her when they find you, they'll kill her too. That's just policy. You might have told her. They can't take a chance. Don't pull her into this one. If you're dead, it's all over with. Let it end here."

Dalton hesitated. Naumann pressed the point.

"Grief is coming, Micah. More than you know," said Naumann, his eyes sharp and his face hard. "You could miss it all. Just let go. Come with me. We'll go down to the piazza and have some wine. There are people there waiting for you."

Dalton looked down at the crowd in the piazza. He could hear music playing, a string quartet, and the soft murmur of voices.

"People I know?"

"A few. You're kind of hard on friends."

"Any enemies?"

"None invited. Too many of them to fit on the piazza. How about it, Micah? 'Home is the hunter . . . home from the hill . . .'"

"'And the sailor home from the sea,'" Dalton finished. His throat was closing up. For a moment, he wondered what it would be like to just let go, not struggle for another breath, another pointless day.

"I'd like to, Porter," he said, after a time. "I really would. But . . ."

"Not yet?"

"Yes," said Dalton, with a thin smile. "Not yet."

"Saint Augustine said that. They tell me it's what everybody says."

"Do they? Well, if it was good enough for Saint Augustine . . ."

"You sure?"

"Yeah," said Dalton, with a sudden grin. "Dead sure."

Naumann's hard face changed; he flashed the same lunatic grin, and then his expression became solemn again.

"Then run along, kid. I'll be seeing you."

Dalton looked at his dead friend's face. There was friendship there, as well as a kind of affectionate envy. His eyes were calm and his skin was very pale. It seemed that a light was shining through him. Dalton looked back at Cora. She was standing there in the rain, her hat in her hands, her black coat blowing around her legs, her dark eyes fixed on him.

Waiting.

Dalton turned away from Cora to say good-bye to Porter but Porter Naumann was gone. Where he had been standing a few dry leaves fluttered up in a spiraling swirl, carried away on the back of the rising wind. Faint music was coming from the Piazza Garibaldi, and the sound of many voices. The wind out of the valley grew much stronger, carrying away the music and the voices, pulling at his coat— leaves flew into his eyes and he closed them.

The sighing of the wind changed into the sound of cheering, thousands of people cheering. When he opened his eyes again, he was no longer in Cortona. He was still in Venice, lying on the steps of the Basilica in the Piazza San Marco, and the crowds were roaring like the sea as the marathon runners swept around the square. Cora was kneeling beside him, and, for some reason, a young Carabinieri trooper was holding a folded cloth against Dalton's belly. Cora was saying his name, her voice low but urgent. He tried to get up but she pushed him down. He lifted his hand to touch her face and saw bright blood on his fingers.

"You've been stabbed, Micah. We think the blade is still inside you, so you must not move. You must lie very still. Do you understand? The boat is coming. I can hear the siren. Don't go away, Micah. Please stay."

The light grew stronger around her, and the low, charcoal-colored clouds beyond her shoulder changed to a fiery opal. He closed his eyes, and the sounds of the piazza faded away, and, for a timeless interlude, he was aware of nothing but the fluttering beat of his heart and Cora's cool hand on his forehead. Then the feel of her hand faded, and there was only the hissing of his blood in his ears and the beating of his heart, like the half-heard murmur of a ship's engine churning away in the darkness beyond the outer reef, and, soon afterward, there was nothing at all, and he was gone.

The *Mingo Dubai,*
Strait of Malacca,
the South China Sea

Chiddy Monkut was a good-natured seventeen-year-old Thai kid with a lot of charm and a ton of potential and fifty-three minutes to live. Chiddy's only failing, as Father Kevin Casey back at the Jesuit school in Chiang Mai saw it, was a poor work ethic. On Father Kevin Casey's advice the skinny, henna-haired boy with the outrigger ears had taken a break from his studies at Loyola. "Go off to sea for a year. Learn something about life," said the leathery old priest, "and think hard about your potential," meaning it kindly, because Father Kevin Casey had a real affection for the boy. So young Chiddy Monkut went off to sea for a year to learn something about life and to think hard about his potential and it killed him.

On this windy November evening on the far side of the world Chiddy was pulling watch duty on the stern deck of a five-hundred-foot-long tanker named the *Mingo Dubai.* The tanker had just cleared the southern end of the Malacca Strait and was entering the Java Sea off Sumatra's north coast when the long gray shadow boat glided smoothly into her wake.

It was Chiddy Monkut's job to notice precisely this kind of thing. Unfortunately, Chiddy was, at that moment, too busy getting himself outside a large jug of the Hindu cook's potato-peel whiskey to notice the steel-gray cigarette boat that was now cruising along in the white V of the *Mingo Dubai*'s wake at a range of about six hundred yards.

In his defense, the light was failing. A pomegranate sun was setting behind the jagged green crest of Sumatra, and the shadow of the big island was spreading out across the Java Sea, cloaking Singapore and Kuala Lumpur in the fast-falling tropical night. Chiddy waved at the tiny people lining the rail as the *Mingo Dubai* swept ponderously by the Kepulauan Lightship and cruised out into the broad reaches of the South China Sea. The heel and pitch of the big tanker increased dramatically, and Chiddy honored the transition to wide-open water with another pull at his plastic jug of pilfered screech. In short, and from his rather narrow point of view, Buddha was in his heaven, and all was right in Chiddy Monkut's world.

Chiddy stood and stretched out a cramp in his left thigh. As he did so, he heard the big prop change its rhythm, begin to drive deeper, harder. He reached out to brace himself on the stern rail as, sixty feet above him on the towering bridge, the captain gave orders and the wheelman increased the speed of the *Mingo Dubai* to twenty knots. The deck began to heave as the ship butted hard into a broad, big-shouldered ocean that was running very high, with a jagged, white surface chop that looked like shark's teeth, tips wind-whipped and streaming with yellow foam. Seabirds—mollymawks, terns, and frigate birds—shrieked and wheeled over the waves, riding the gusts like surfers carving a run out of the Pipeline.

Underneath the chop, there was a rolling groundswell that lifted the *Mingo Dubai*'s bow, and the tanker began to heave slowly from port to starboard, her hull plates audibly groaning with the strain.

Thirty thousand tons of liquid caustic soda and Bunker C oil began to roll in their holding tanks. Sixty feet above her waterline, the Malay seaman on the rusty bridge fought the wheel to hold his course.

The captain, a sixty-three-year-old mainland Chinese named Anson Wang, stood in a wide-legged brace behind the elderly Malay at the wheel with one hand on the binnacle and watched the *Mingo Dubai*'s high-flaring bow as it lifted up to meet the oncoming swells. The steel decking rose and fell ponderously under his feet. As the bow slammed into a wall of glassy green water, a torrent of white spray rolled over the starboard rail and spread out across the forepeak, foaming and churning around the rectangular steel hatches lined up along her deck.

Bracing a hip on the back of the pilot chair, Wang turned his binoculars onto the shining spires of Singapore City nine miles off his port side, thought briefly of his ex-wife and his ex-children who lived there and whom he had not seen in six years.

Then, as always, he put them out of his mind. When he looked eastward again, he could see the darkness rising up out of Borneo, the leading edge of a large tropical storm coming in out of the South Pacific. He glanced at the weather radar long enough to watch the luminous green line sweep through three hundred and sixty degrees, filling ninety degrees of the screen dead ahead of the ship with a shapeless mass of red light. The Malay at the helm gave him a nervous glance.

Wang put a prematurely arthritic hand on the old man's bony shoulder, patted him gently—they were longtime shipmates—and turned on the intercom. Three decks down, in the cluttered wardroom, the eleven men of the evening watch—a mixed crew of Malays, Dyaks, Filipinos, Thais, and a few rookie Serbians making their first passage—were watching a bootleg DVD of *The Poseidon Adventure* remake for the twelfth time and sipping tin mugs of tepid green tea when the intercom buzzer cut through the floating blue clouds of clove cigarette smoke. The third mate, Vigo Majiic, a tall, rail-thin, and rather gloomy Serbian with a skimpy black goatee that failed to strengthen an underslung jaw, picked up the receiver.

"Vigo, Captain."

"Let me talk to Mr. Fitch."

"He isn't here, sir."

"Where is he?"

Vigo didn't want to answer that question. Brendan Fitch, the first mate and the current front-runner in the *Mingo Dubai*'s informal competition for the Most Dangerous Drunk of the Voyage award, had put away a fifth of lukewarm sake and gone staggering down the companionway toward the sleeping cabins a half an hour ago. He was now snoring in the dim red light of a barracks with the other nine stateless men who made up the ship's off-duty watch, and it was Vigo Majiic's devout wish that the very large and very unpredictable British expat would stay snugly abed until very late into the next century.

Vigo looked around the steel-walled wardroom at his shipmates as if he might find some sort of inspiration in the scruffy figures slouched listlessly on tattered sofas in front of the ancient television or grouped around the card table, cigarettes hanging limply from their mouths. The narrow room was filled with smoke and the hot-house smell of unwashed and sweaty men in a steamy climate.

Captain Wang knew what Vigo's hesitation was all about. By now, he was almost comfortable with it, the way he was resigned to the way the ship's hull groaned and moaned like a cart horse whenever the seas set up ugly. He sighed to himself, watching the storm rising up and the rollers marching in.

"Go wake him up, Vigo. Pour some hot black coffee in him, clean him up, and have him on my bridge in fifteen minutes."

"Yes, sir," said Vigo, into a dead phone.

Anson Wang put the intercom back on the hook and stared out at the oncoming rollers, bracing himself as they crashed over the plunging bow of the tanker. He could feel her hull working, feel the grinding of her plates in his own belly. He turned to look out the stern portholes at the receding mouth of the Malacca Strait. The mile-long, arrow-straight wake of the *Mingo Dubai* looked like a highway paved with broken glass, as the last of the twilight glimmered along it. He thought for a moment that he saw a long dark object in that pale field of light, possibly a small craft. He stared out into the falling night, trying to find it again. No, there was nothing there.

If anything, it was a whale surfacing. Or, more likely, a deadhead hardwood log, broken loose from a forestry boom somewhere along the Java coastline. He looked up at the sky.

The last of the light was slipping into the west, and the ship was steaming at twenty-two knots into the Java Sea, with Borneo three hundred and eighty miles to the east, and the reef-filled archipelagoes of Indonesia to thread through before they reached their destination port of Port Moresby in Papua New Guinea, almost two thousand miles away. If this storm building out in the southern Pacific turned into a hurricane, they'd have the ironbound coasts of Flores and Timor as a lee shore. There isn't a captain alive who doesn't wake up at night sweating from a dream of a lee shore in a tropical storm, the booming of the surf on the shoals and the wind screaming in the rigging, the breakers flashing white in the blackness, the sickening wrench as the hull strikes the reef and her steel plates start to crack. He thought about changing course to the northwest and making a dash for Singapore. There were moorings there, and a good holding ground.

They could batten down the ship and ride out whatever was coming. But his owners—whoever they really were, back in Belize and safe in their beds—had zero tolerance for what they called spineless, stick-by-shore skippers, knee-deep navy slackers with four eyes for the weather and no balls at all. He'd already been docked six months' pay for a storm-delayed arrival in Bombay last year. Since his divorce six years ago, money was a pressing issue for him. He was looking at the compass and waiting for the next weather fax to print out when the cabin door flew inward on a gust of wet wind and all six foot three, two hundred–odd pounds of Brendan Fitch developed unsteadily into the pilothouse.

Wang looked at Fitch with a mixture of resignation and affection, assessing the red-faced and slowly weaving tower of bone and muscle that was smiling back at him through a five-day growth of black beard, his wide-set green eyes vivid against his sunburned face. Wang took in Fitch's stained and wrinkled summer whites, the missing epaulette, his bare feet, his sausage toes splayed out, and sighed again, this time more heavily.

"We are sorry to wake you, Mr. Fitch."

"Not at all, sir," said Fitch, grinning back at him. "I find a wee nap midwatch keeps me at the top of my form."

Wang caught the scent of mint toothpaste and, under that, a strong whiff of sake.

"A nap or a nip? I hope you are sober?"

Fitch straightened his spine and attempted a crisp salute.

"Painfully, sir."

Wang shook his head and raised an arm, pointing to the east.

"You see this?"

Fitch looked out the forward windshield and then down at the weather radar. His weathered, roast-beef face hardened, and he looked at Wang carefully, sobering visibly.

"I do, sir. Have we a warning?"

"Gales only. But I am concerned. I am considering turning around and making for Singapore to ride it out."

Fitch's grim expression changed to one of polite interest.

"Are you, sir?"

"I am. Would you support such a decision?"

"You mean, sir, will I cheerfully partake of the traditional shot glass of potassium cyanide the owners will require us to chug down if we get to Moresby even one day late?"

Wang nodded briefly, smiling a weary smile.

"Serve it up, sir. If that's your call, I'll back you all the way."

Wang studied Fitch for a time, weighing him. He'd keep his word; that much Wang knew. But how much weight would the word of a twice-cashiered professional inebriate carry with the owners?

Fitch, the soft-focus lens of his attention wandering a bit, had turned to look back at their wake. He stiffened, and stepped over to the windshield, staring out into the darkness. He tapped the glass.

"What's that?" he asked.

Wang stepped up beside him.

"Where?"

"In the wake. I thought I saw something."

"So did I," said Wang, peering out into the darkness. The lights of Singapore were now little more than a dim glow on the far horizon, but there was enough of an afterglow to make out what might be a low black shape in the phosphorescent wake. A second later, it was gone.

Both men watched the pale glimmer of their wake with ferocious attention for a full minute. They saw nothing at all, but they were thinking the same thing: the Malacca Strait was the most dangerous passage in the world, with more than fifty large freighters and tankers taken by pirates in the last three years alone. Although the navies of several local countries patrolled the Strait, half of these naval gunboats moonlighted as pirates themselves, and not one of them could be trusted within a thousand yards of your ship. As for self-defense, the gun locker on the *Mingo Dubai* held several antique Lee-Enfield rifles and a wooden crate of dubious World War II .303 ammunition. This crate was currently half empty, since it was the consoling pleasure of their morose and chronically seasick Hindu cook to get himself weeping drunk on his own homemade screech and then stagger out on deck to blaze away at the terns and mollymawks. So far, he hadn't hit a single bird, but he had managed to blow a fist-sized hole through one of the starboard lifeboats.

"There anything on the narrowband radar, sir?"

Wang went back to the ship's radar and turned the gain down, reducing the arc but raising the strength of the return. They watched as the green line swept across their wake. Nothing. Just a smooth green emptiness. Wang and Fitch stood side by side and stared out into the night, seeing only their red reflections in the porthole glass.

"Who's got the stern watch?" asked Wang.

"The Thai kid. Chiddy Monkut."

"He's not answering his radio," said Wang. "Go see how he's doing."

"What about that?" said Fitch, nodding at the storm.

Wang shrugged, put on a stoical mask.

"I must make Port Moresby by next Friday. I have no choice."

Fitch looked at Wang for a while, real sympathy in his face. Wang was a good man, and Fitch, who had once been a good man himself, liked and admired him. Since both men understood each other completely, there was nothing to say.

"Very good, sir. I'll go do a walkabout."

Brendan Fitch pushed through the wheelhouse door and stepped out into a forty-mile-an-hour gale that was quartering across their port bow. The ship was lifting up and falling rhythmically; under the boom of the swells and the gusting wind, Fitch could hear the hull groaning. The ship's running lights were ringed in misty halos and beyond their pale light the black night pressed in all around, a pall of darkness that seemed to weigh the ship down. He padded unsteadily down the gangway, his bare feet slipping on the ridged plates, and stopped for a moment at the middeck locker, fumbling with a key attached to a lanyard around his neck. He braced himself against the ship's roll as he worked the dead bolt, got the lid off, and took out a small parcel wrapped in oilcloth. He unwrapped the stainless steel Colt Python, checked the cylinder, and shoved the huge revolver in his belt. Then he reached deeper into the locker and extracted a sterling silver hip flask with the phrase DEEDS NOT WORDS engraved on the sides.

The battered old flask was reassuringly heavy with the last of his Southern Comfort. Fitch slipped it into his back pocket, remembering to button down the pocket flap. When he reached the main deck, he lifted a Maglite out of its sheath by the gangway gate, walked over to the starboard taffrail, and leaned out into the shrieking night. Thirty feet below him, the sea was running wild along the hull, a hissing tumult of broken black water and mountainous swells. He looked forward, his shaggy hair flying, and then aft, along the hull: he saw nothing but wild black ocean, and heard nothing but the sea howling back at him, a shrieking wail over the bass-organ groaning of the *Mingo Dubai*'s hull. The wind stank of sea rot and decay.

Fitch worked his way around the stern, holding on to the rain-slick railing with his left hand, shielding his face from the spray that was flying back from the bow. He blinked away the salt tears and strained to see anything at all through the storm and the darkness that was out there.

About a mile off to starboard, he could barely make out the pale blue pulse of a waypoint buoy—the Ten Mile Light—the buoy that marked Kepulauan Lingga Island. Beyond that, there was only the booming sea and the black vault of the sky.

He came around the corner of the bridge and made his way out onto the stern deck, cantilevered out over the rudder. Thirty feet below him, the ocean was being churned into white foam by the ship's twenty-foot-high propeller. The rumble of the ship's wake was deafening, like standing too close to Niagara Falls. The air reeked of diesel and the sewage trail of the ship's leaking bilge. It looked like Chiddy Monkut was nowhere around.

And it was too damn dark back here.

Fitch looked up. The stern light that was supposed to be shining at the top of a twenty-foot pole was out. He moved to check the in-line fuse box and his foot struck an object lying in the gangway—a plastic bottle. He picked it up and shook it; it was almost empty.

He unscrewed the top and sniffed at the neck. The bitter smell of potato screech made his eyes weep. He considered the remains of the bottle for a while, trying to decide if the sticky black substance on the side of it was blood or grease. It smelled like a bit of both.

He thought about taking a quick slug of the screech and decided against it, tossing it into the maelstrom of the wake below him. Fitch turned the Maglite on and swept it around the semicircle of the stern deck. It was empty. He started to get a very bad feeling about Chiddy Monkut's welfare. He pulled his radio out of his shirt pocket and thumbed the CALL button.

"Chiddy, this is Brendan Fitch. Come in?"

Silence.

Fitch stared at the empty deck and felt a stony-cold sobriety welling up inside him. He backed up against the wall of the bridge tower and pulled out the Colt Python, pressing the radio CALL button again.

"Captain, this is Fitch. Chiddy's nowhere—"

The handset popped and crackled, as a burst of lightning sizzled across the night sky far astern, briefly illuminating the ship's wake and showing him a long matte-gray shape running fifty yards off the stern, riding inside the ship's wake. A yellow face with a thin black beard—frozen in the lightning flash—was staring up at the deck. Then it was gone, as the dark came rolling back and a peal of thunder shook the night. Seconds later, a torrent of rain swept across the deck, drenching Fitch to the bone and bringing the visibility down to a few feet. Fitch took out the radio handset, thumbed CALL.

"Captain—we have boarders! Boarders! Lock down the wheelhouse!"

Barely audible in the storm, Anson Wang's voice came back on the handset, shredded in the driving rain, drowned by the steady churning of the prop. "Boarders? Where—?"

Wang's voice was cut off abruptly, but Fitch heard the eerie banshee wail of the ship's siren winding up, a ghostly shriek that increased in volume and intensity until it was almost louder than the storm. Fitch heard the thudding of steel doors and the clatter of feet on the interior gangways as the crew ran for their stations, and muted voices calling out. Then a deep, rhythmic chatter that drove the last of the sake out of his head; semiauto fire—from the sound of it, an MP5—and the muffled screams of men.

The siren shut off a second later.

Light flickered from the bridge, and Fitch shoved himself back into the dark as a shape came tumbling down from the upper deck, arms flailing. The shape struck the taffrail with a dull clang and lay there—broken-backed and obscenely twisted—and Fitch stepped forward and saw the bloody face of the old Malay wheelman. Under the old man's chin his slit throat gaped wide, ripped muscles still twitching like the mouth of a hooked trout.

Fitch sensed movement to his left, turned, and fired into the mist, the muzzle flare of the big Colt reflected in the rain droplets, the sound slamming off the steel decking. A dim, plaid-shirted figure fell back into the dark, and something came clattering across the decking plates, a large parang with a wooden handle wrapped in bright green silk.

No telling how many pirates were already on board. Fitch had only five rounds left. If he kept using the Colt, he'd be out of rounds in four seconds. He tossed the Maglite against the wall, shoved the Colt into his belt, and scooped up the long wickedly curved machete just as a second figure rounded the other corner and ran at him, shrieking in Tagalog—an angry, falsetto howl—right arm raised high, holding a parang.

Fitch parried the downstroke with the flat of his own parang and stepped in under the slicing horizontal return cut, feeling the thrumming rush of the parang as it passed through the air above his left shoulder. He caught a fistful of the figure's shirt in his left hand and felt the swelling of breasts under the thin material. He jerked the slender girl sideways and she smacked down hard onto the steel decking, the air puffing out of her, as she twisted, snakelike and very fast, trying to regain her feet, her machete slicing sidelong at his left ankle.

Fitch blocked the strike, and his automatic riposte split the young girl's chest wide open from her chin to her belly, the force of the blow shuddering up Fitch's arm all the way to his shoulder.

She screamed and dropped the parang, bringing her hands up to her chest, her exposed ribs pink in the half-light, her body twisting and writhing as she hissed with pain and fear. Fitch brought the heavy blade down hard on her forehead, splitting her skull open, the tip of his parang striking red sparks off the decking underneath the girl's head.

Fitch turned away from the ruin of the girl, fumbled in the dark for the Maglite, found it but did not turn it on. He patted his waist belt to make sure of the Colt but did not draw it. If he was going to kill enough of these people to take the ship back, he was going to have to do it in silence.

He kept the Maglite in his left hand, to parry with, and held the parang in his right as he walked barefoot along the deck and took a very cautious look around the corner. In the misty glow of the ship's starboard running lights he saw a naked man dashing forward along the deck, closely pursued by three skinny figures, barefoot, in tan shorts and plaid shirts, wearing bright red head scarves. The glitter of their knives showed through the rain. The figures caught up with the naked man by the forward hatch plates and he fell to his knees, raising his hands in front of him—it was the hapless Hindu cook. The figures formed a tight circle around the cook as he knelt there. A brown arm went up and a silvery blade flashed down. Under the howl of the storm, Fitch heard a cry and the coconut crack of the man's skull being split open.

Fitch rounded the corner of the deck and went silently up the gangway as the figures on the foredeck set to work on what was left of the Hindu cook. At the turning of the third flight, he ran straight into a broad, squat, toadlike figure racketing down the stairs—the toad man bounced off Fitch with a breathy grunt, fell back against the steel stairs, and lifted a black pistol, which flew outward into the rain, along with ten inches of his forearm, as Fitch took the man's lower arm off with the parang.

He opened the man's throat wide with the returning stroke, cutting off his hoarse cry, stepped over the man's body, and went up the rest of the stairway in grim silence, his breath rasping in his chest, his lungs burning, his now-quite-sober mind filled with stone-cold murder. If these people got control of the ship, every man on board would die exactly like the Hindu cook. Brendan Fitch did not value his own life very highly anymore, but he had no intention of being butchered like a hog.

He stopped just below the bridge deck and flattened against the steel wall as he heard voices—Malay? Dyak? No. It was English, but heavily accented—Serbian? Croatian? Two men at least, standing on the bridge deck just outside the cabin. A flare of red light as the wheelhouse door opened and closed again, and now only one man remained on the upper deck.

The motion of the ship changed as the storm increased in force—

Fitch felt the engines power up and the deck shifted under him—they were turning the ship out of the eye of the wind, turning her off course, veering her to port in a long, dangerous turn that would expose her entire starboard flank to the incoming seas. If the ship failed to come all the way about and take the storm on her stern, the seas would roll right over her exposed foredeck and drive her under in seconds. No real seaman would have put the old tanker through such a turn. Which meant Anson Wang was no longer at the wheel.

But perhaps not dead. Not yet. They'd need Wang to tell them the ship's private transponder codes and the location of her EPIRB emergency beacon. If they were taking the ship off course, they probably intended to do more than just off-load her cargo to another tanker. They'd dump the EPIRB in the sea, kill the transponder. The Singapore Coast Guard would think the ship had sunk. They'd stop looking when they located the EPIRB and come back for survivors when the storm subsided.

But how many hijackers were on the ship?

If they had all come from that single cigarette boat trailing her stern, not that many, and he had already killed three of them. Another three were down there on the forepeak four hundred feet away, still senselessly hacking the Hindu cook into curried chutney. Two more up here on the deck, one man outside, and another who had just stepped back into the wheelhouse. That meant two inside the wheelhouse, perhaps three.

Someone on the stairs above him stepped up to the forward rail of the bridge and called out to the three men still mutilating the corpse at the bow, raising his voice to a hoarse bellow, to carry through the wind howling out of the night and the boom of the swells crashing over the ship's side, speaking Tagalog with a European accent. An answering shout came from the bow: the three men crouched over the spreading puddle of flesh got to their feet and began to make their way back toward the stern of the ship.

Brendan Fitch climbed the last of the stairs and stepped softly out onto the bridge deck just as the man at the railing turned around, a large white man in a black watch cap, a blue jean jacket, and military-looking pants.

The man had a small gray pistol in his right hand and he pointed it at Fitch as soon as he saw him. Fitch threw the parang straight at the man's head, as he drew out his Colt, and missed him completely, but, as the man ducked, his own first shot went wide. Fitch fired the Colt, the revolver bucking in his wet hands—a wild shot that spanged off the steel wall of the bridge house, struck the staircase railing a glancing blow, and slammed right back into Brendan Fitch's rib cage.

The impact of the slug threw Fitch backward against the pilot-house wall, a cold numbness spreading out from his rib cage, but, by then, he had fired the big Colt twice more, the weapon kicking like a mule in his right hand. The man in the watch cap lurched toward the pilothouse door, firing as he stumbled across the wet decking, the little gun popping like a toy and tinny rounds ticking off the steel plate next to Fitch's head and zipping away into the darkness. Fitch fired the Colt again—that was four rounds out and one to go—and the watch-cap man flattened against the wheelhouse door with a large black crater in his temple.

Fitch pivoted as he heard the slice-and-dice unit clattering up the gangway stairs, looked back toward the wheelhouse again, saw another white man inside the wheelhouse—short, black-haired, pale-eyed, with a well-trimmed black goatee, his narrow, sharp-featured face vividly defined by the red cabin light. He was shouting something at Fitch, but it was muffled by the glass and then carried away by the wind.

The man with the goatee raised a black weapon—in the heightened intensity of the moment Fitch recognized it as an MP5. The man aimed it at Fitch through the glass. Anson Wang was standing at the wheel behind the man, his face battered and bloody, his mouth slack. And on Anson's far side, holding one of the ship's .303s, its muzzle hard up against Anson's temple, was the third mate, Vigo Majiic.

Fitch, in rage and desperation, fired his fifth and last round at the sharp-faced little man at exactly same time that the muzzle of the man's MP5 filled up with sparkling blue fire and the glass window between them shattered into a blizzard of shards. When the broken glass fell away, the little man was still standing, but Anson Wang and Vigo Majiic were gone. Wonderful.

Six rounds out, and Fitch had managed to shoot both himself and Anson Wang with two of them. Brilliant. No rounds left in the Colt and caught between an MP5 and the salad chefs from Hell with only his hip flask to throw at them. Time to bail.

Fitch stepped over the taffrail and launched himself outward into the storm just as the bearded man in the wheelhouse fired the MP5. Several rounds plucked at his billowing shirt as Fitch hurtled through the air, hoping he had enough arc to clear the main-deck rail and reach the open water sixty feet below him. The wind tore at him as he fell through the rain and the corrugated black wall of the ocean rose up before him. He sliced into the flank of a great sea roller as another spray of machine-gun rounds punched into the foamy chop all around him. Fitch sank rapidly, for a strangely silent time, dimly aware of the great wall of the ship's hull sliding ponderously by him in the deep, and the rhythmic pounding of the ship's propeller, a dull, concussive booming that was coming closer every second. He felt the salt ocean around him moving in perfect time to that terrible churning prop, so near now that he felt the pull of the undertow and the ocean pulsing like jelly all around him.

He heard a muttering burble very close to his head and a long shape moved across the waves a few feet above him. His lungs aching, Fitch kicked hard for the surface, broke into the streaming air; his flailing hand struck a hard, slick surface. An angry face appeared in the air over his head, a staring yellow face with a black beard.

Fitch put a hand on the ridge of the boat's gunwale as the yellow face leaned over to hack at him. Fitch caught the man's wrist and jerked him over the side into the ocean. The man slashed out at Fitch one last time, even as he slipped under the waves, missing Fitch but hacking a chunk out of the gunwale right next to his head. A gasp, a cry cut off in a choking bubble, and then Fitch was alone in the black water.

The gray cigarette boat yawed crazily. The engine snarled and muttered as the long craft turned in a slow, driverless circle. Huge waves washed over the side, and the boat took on water. The storm rolled above him with a sound like a freight train crossing an iron bridge, but Brendan Fitch held on to that slick, hard ridge of the gunwale for a very long time.

In a while, the black hulk of the *Mingo Dubai* slipped away into the storm, until her running lights blinked out and he was lost in blackness, unable to see his hand in front of him. Above the roaring of the sea he could still hear the pounding of the tanker's prop and the volcanic throb of her diesels: after a time, the noise faded, and then died away entirely and all Fitch could hear was the mutter of the cigarette boat's engines and the wild wind howling over the South China Sea.

2

SINGAPORE DESK: XR266GT—EYES/DIAL

Singapore Coast Guard confirms that a 500-foot tanker (MINGO DUBAI) disappeared from radar (presumed sunk) 6 miles off the Kepulauan Lingga Lighthouse after clearing the Strait of Malacca and entering the South China Sea. The vessel, registered in Belize to a numbered corporation (298767 CR) based in Mexico City, was en route to Port Moresby, Papua New Guinea, with 30,000 tons of caustic soda aboard. The prevailing conditions were gale-force winds and extremely heavy seas, and indications are that the vessel experienced a rogue wave that raised the stern and bow sections, causing the ship to break in two. No emergency message was received by Singapore Maritime Patrol, and a subsequent helicopter overflight observed extensive caustic spill in the water with attendant fish kill and three corpses that could not be recovered. The ocean depth in this part of the South China Sea is 3,000 feet. A sonar scan is pending the subsidence of the storm and the availability of a ship properly equipped. No lifeboats were observed from the flyover, and it is not known whether the vessel's EPIRB beacon was not activated or malfunctioned upon immersion.

Out of a crew of 28, composed of Malays, Dyaks, and Serbian sailors, only 1 man was pulled from the water, a British national serving as first mate aboard the MINGO DUBAI and carrying ID as one BRENDAN MICHAEL FITCH. FITCH reported to his rescuers that the ship did not in fact sink and was instead hijacked by crew members aided by unknown assaulters who boarded from a high-speed craft during the storm. This allegation cannot be confirmed, and is contradicted by the presence of the caustic soda spill and debris sightings. FITCH claimed to have overcome the pilot of the assault craft and taken possession of it, but, when found, was adrift on a section of fiberglass hull of unknown origins. It is the preliminary conclusion of the Singapore investigators that the MINGO DUBAI was sunk through rogue wave action that may have been exacerbated by the fact that FITCH, the Officer of the Watch at the time, was drunk at his station in the wheelhouse. FITCH was examined by a Coast Guard medic in the chopper en route to Singapore and was found to have a blood-alcohol level equal to the level of complete intoxication, according to Singaporean authorities. A gash in his rib cage that FITCH contended was a bullet wound was found to be inconclusive, since no round was discovered in the wound. FITCH was held, pending a full maritime inquiry by the Singapore Police, and local sources say he is being interrogated by Singaporean officials at a secure facility in an unknown location. This incident was tagged and forwarded to Langley HQ for further action by our staff at Singapore Sub-Station HALO because an intake body scan conducted by Singapore SID revealed an Agency tracing implant registered to a contract employee (6064-988C) of the Agency at LONDON STATION (seconded from the SAS) (real name RAYMOND PAGET FYKE—operational code IBIS) and was at the time of his disappearance in November of 2002 under a DETAIN / SEQUESTER / DO NOT INTERROGATE order filed with INTERPOL and related agencies, which raises the issue that the debriefing of IBIS by Singaporean Intelligence officers may constitute a serious security risk for the USA. MESSAGE ENDS.

CLASSIFIED UMBRA DNC

CLANDESTINE SERVICES

EXECUTE/ADDENDUM re xr266gt EYES/DIAL

Preliminary HumInt received from agents on site in Singapore has been evaluated by this office and it has been concluded that the unilateral and unrestricted interrogation of <u>IBIS</u> by Singaporean SID agents or their official proxies is an unacceptable risk to national security.

Therefore London Station, as the last station of active service for <u>IBIS,</u> will take such immediate action as is necessary to remedy the situation and neutralize the vulnerability by any means available and without restriction. Results only will be recorded. Zulu time initiates immediately. Operational Protocols appended:

DIAL/EYES—DG/CS—CATHER

3

Kotor, Montenegro

Branco Gospic, a heavy-bodied, slope-shouldered bull of a man with cold gray eyes and a bald skull distorted into a chestnut shape by a near-miss mortar round, was sitting stiffly upright—his bullet-pocked belly would tolerate no other position—on an iron bench on the pillared balcony of his villa overlooking the Montenegrin coastal village of Kotor. The ancient fortress spread itself out below him, a stirring prospect if the man had cared to care—which it was not in his nature to do—a sweeping view of a fjordlike, craggy coast, the huge slab-sided mountain walls rising up to meet the parapet of the medieval fortress on the peak, built by the Venetians in the years of their naval power to stem the northward tide of the Ottoman Turks. The great triangular fort overlooked a blade-shaped deepwater inlet filled with pleasure boats and trawlers, and out to the far west the slate-gray sea churned with shards of glassy light as the pale winter sun slid down into Italy on the far shore of the Adriatic.

Two hundred feet beneath his balcony, a broad, stone-paved seawall stuck out into the water like the prow of a battleship. Although fall was dying in the air and the first snowflakes of winter were feathering the stones of Venice, on the eastern side of the Adriatic the evening was still just warm enough for the people of the old town to be out walking the seawall; pretty girls in Parisian dresses, gliding along on shell pink clouds of self-esteem, watched by roving packs of sharply dressed young men, sporting huge mustachios in the latest Serbian manner; sagging old men, burned out by the eternal ethnic wars, staring out to sea with glazed, dead eyes; feral children, running wild on the stones, calling out with harsh voices, their green kites trailing in the salt wind.

Gospic, a tactical, self-directed man with no eye, and less time, for beauty of any sort, noticed none of this: his ferocious attention was fixed on the Sony digital camcorder he held in his large callused hands. A few feet away from him, three small boys were kneeling in a cluster around a large, gray-muzzled gundog with a withered hind leg. The ancient dog was lying on his right side, stretched out, one blind eye ringed in white, panting heavily. The boys were prodding the feeble dog with a wooden spoon and laughing. Like the wolfish sounds of the children down below them on the seawall, their laughter was harsh, cruel, taunting—the piping yelps of little jackals.

Gospic found their laughter an annoying distraction and he would have kicked them away, or had one of his women do it, if it were not for the fact that one of them was the current sexual amusement of the man sitting beside him on the bench; a stiletto of a man with an air of dissipated elegance, blue-lipped, of indeterminate age, wearing a beautifully tailored gray silk suit. This man, Stefan Groz, a senior capo in the Serbian mafia that controlled most of Montenegro, was also watching the little LCD screen on the Sony camcorder, where a video was playing.

In the video was a view of a large, private swimming pool set out on a terrace overlooking a tree-filled valley with olive groves in the middle distance and what may have been a tall, wrought-iron gate down at the bottom of a long, curving drive paved in terra-cotta stones. The villa next to the pool was built and furnished in a style its owners mistakenly imagined to be Château French, opulent and deeply vulgar, and reeking of criminal money, the way these villas do, from Baghdad to Boulder. A party of some sort seemed to be in progress, several hard, hoggish, heavily tattooed men in far-too-tiny Speedo swimsuits, swilling some clear liquid from glass bottles—perhaps vodka or slivovitz—and many younger women, wearing little more than uneven tans and frightened smiles, were gathered around the pool.

In the video, their voices could be heard, braying and drunk, but the sound was poor, and the film appeared to have been taken by a concealed camera. The men urged the women to drink from the same bottles, looked resentful until they did. Everybody was getting loose and crazy. A woman was pushed into the water by one of the men, an immensely fat, towering, bald-headed hairy goon with a large tattoo entirely covering his pork-white chest—an American eagle with its wings outspread and pierced straight through the breast by a lance bearing the flag of the Kosovo Liberation Army—this man was then shoved by a drunken friend, and soon they were all in the water, laughing, splashing. The half-naked women were being roughly handled, but they endured it. A young woman in the deep end began to cough. She looked up, and a thin ribbon of mucus was running from her nostrils. A girlfriend moved to help her, but she became distracted by the sight of a man who was holding his hand over his eyes. This man—the bald-headed goon with the dying American Eagle tattoo—began to convulse and vomit. The camera never wavered; within six minutes, all the young women were floating lifeless in the water, and only two of the stronger men had managed to climb out of the pool.

There they died, in apparent agony, on the white marble. The video ended, the screen glowing blue. Gospic leaned back against the bench and closed the screen with a snap.

His face was flushed and his breathing a little fast. Groz closed his hooded eyes and wiped his wet lips with a lace handkerchief. Both men sat and stared, unseeing, out at the narrow fjord beneath the balcony.

Nothing was said for a few moments. The boys had the dog pinned against the stone pillars now, and it was baring its old brown teeth at them, a humming vibrato deep in its barrel chest.

"Well, well," said Groz. "That was Dzilbar Kerk, wasn't it? DoDo?"

"Yes. It was."

"I thought I recognized him. Of course, that ridiculous tattoo."

"I was with him when he had it done. In Trieste. It took eleven hours. He drank five bottles of Stolichnaya, one after the other."

"He was always a drinker. The other big one, that had to be JoJo. It was always the two of them, DoDo and JoJo."

"Yes. Josef Perchak."

"I know I shouldn't ask, but why them? Of all people?"

"Two birds. I wanted to show you what could be done. And it was necessary for Kerk and Perchak to be retired from the project."

"But they were good men. Hard to replace. And the villa . . . it cost a lot of money. I've been there myself. What will you do with it?"

"Nothing. It's yours, if you want it. Larissa will send you the papers. Why them? Because they were *embarrassing*. The way they were living there—the people of the town hated them—they were behaving like drunken clowns, throwing euros around, making scenes in the cafés. Sooner or later, the police would start wondering about them. It was better to be safe, and, as I said, I needed a demonstration."

"Well, it's very impressive, Branco. But . . . too fast . . ."

"It was in an undiluted form. Contained. In the—"

"This . . . substance . . . once it is released, how is it to be contained? It will multiply, will it not? Exponentially?"

"No. It is neutralized by salt water."

"You are certain?"

"Korshunov was. And Langford confirmed it."

"Both are dead," said the man in gray silk, his tone mildly accusing.

"All are dead," grunted Gospic, dismissing the point. "Benito Que, in Miami. Then Wiley, Pasechnik, Schwartz, Set Van Nguyen, in Australia."

"His wife . . ."

"She was reached in November of that year. As you know."

"The papers said she was killed by anthrax. On the subway."

"Yes," said Gospic. "That's what they said."

"Then, in Moscow, Glebov and Brushlinski?"

"And Victor Korshunov, also in Moscow. And Langford, in England. And, of course, the plane from Tel Aviv, with Berkman, Eldor, and Matzner."

"Impressive. I am amazed. All this by Kerk's own people?"

"Not all. The Australian end was done by freelancers from Jemaya Ismail. They had no idea why. Just did it. And the American work was done by our associates in Matamoros. Also freelancers. JoJo had the Tel Aviv job done by the Chechyns."

"You trusted the *Chechyns?*"

"I trusted them to do the job and make it look like the Ukrainians, who are famously incompetent, did it by accident. I did not trust them with why."

Groz shook his head, his expression solemn.

"DoDo and JoJo were our old comrades-in-arms, Branco."

"Yes. As I said, it was necessary for the integrity of the project."

Groz showed his long yellow teeth again, his face creasing in a smile.

"I suppose so. Such a long . . . time frame, in this matter."

"We were not in at the beginning. We came in after the breakup of Yugoslavia. There was an opportunity, after the Soviets dropped the Biopreparat project."

"You picked it up."

"I picked up some of the people. They were scattering everywhere. Looking for work. Iraq. Iran. North Korea. Some went to America. Some came to us."

"You saw a use?"

"Poppa felt that the *discoveries* would be useful. Someday."

"The long view," said Groz.

"Yes. That is what Poppa is good at."

The gray man nodded, pursing his lips like a Mother Superior; he opened his mouth to say something more when a burst of shrieking laughter erupted from the three little boys. They scattered across the balcony as the old gundog writhed to its feet, baring its blunt teeth, its red-rimmed eyes wide with fright. It began to bark, its hackles bunching up in folds.

One of the boys struck out at it with the handle of the spoon. The old dog seized the handle and wrenched it away, snapping the spoon in two. Another boy, the one belonging to Stefan Groz, kicked out at the dog.

The old gundog dodged away from the kick and then charged suddenly forward, sinking its blunt yellow teeth into the boy's calf. The child began to shriek, and Groz, rising, tried to intervene, dancing around the pair, fluttering his hands uselessly. Gospic set the camcorder down carefully on the bench and, in two long-legged strides, was on the bitten child, the dog now shaking the boy's leg, blood bubbling up around its teeth.

Gospic took a fistful of the dog's neck skin, jerked it high in the air, holding the big dog aloft, the animal rigid now; the old hound rolled a yellow eye filled with glassy defiance at him, its gray tongue hanging, the vibrato in its chest growing into a kind of purring snarl.

The dog, who knew his man well enough, didn't bother to struggle.

Gospic twisted his muscular body and hurled the dog over the edge of the balcony. It fell, turning in the twilight, yelping, a splay-legged, pinwheeling starfish shape clear against the shimmering water, seeming to fall forever, and then smashing with sudden force onto the seawall below, breaking apart, a brown heap of guts, a broken pile of flesh and hide, running blood.

Down on the quay, people begin to scream in tiny voices, ant figures scurrying, and a young girl in a blue sundress pointed up to the balcony. Gospic glared at the little cluster of pale boys in front of him, who stared back at him with their wet red mouths gaping, tiny, round teeth showing, the green light of sadism fading from their flat-brown eyes. Gospic, breathing heavily, shrugged once and turned away. Stefan Groz sat back down on the bench, sighing, his face as gray as his well-cut suit, his small black eyes bright with glittering attention, a thin, hard smile playing on his blue lips.

"Well?" said Gospic, looking at the man.

Groz lifted his hands, palms up, spreading them apart in a gesture of acceptance, showing Gospic his too-white, too-large, too-even teeth.

"You have the . . . means to deliver this?"

"We are in the process of acquiring it."

The question hung in the air, but Groz knew better than to ask it. Gospic's methods were none of his business. It was better not to know. He lifted his hands again, let them fall limply into his lap. The bitten boy, silent until now, began to grizzle, a reedy, whining snuffle, his stubby nose running with snot. Groz made a pinched, disapprov-

ing face and handed the boy his lace handkerchief, putting a decep-
tively soothing palm up against the child's cheek. Then he looked
back at Gospic.

"We will need to know the timing. To the day."

"Of course," said Gospic, letting his impatience show. The timing
was the only thing that mattered. Everything depended on the timing, and they both knew it. The question was irrelevant; Groz was
stalling.

"And the people? You have people who can do this? People who
are . . . capable? Reliable people?"

Gospic didn't answer that. His face, without any visible change,
altered indefinably, hardening, becoming stonelike, and his eyes emptied of expression. Groz, no fool, took the point. He indicated the
Sony with a withered finger.

"What will you do with the video?"

"It needs to be seen. We will post it on the Internet."

"People will know where it came from."

"No. There are ways to strip it. The video will be posted, and
reposted, until no one will ever know where it came from. Many will
think it a hoax."

"What about the Americans?"

Gospic showed his teeth.

"That's the point."

Groz considered that for a time and then nodded.

"Okay. Yes. I see. What will you need from us?"

"The money."

Groz inclined his head, smiling; there would be something else.
With Gospic, it was never just the money. Besides, he was pleased to
have been given Dzilbar Kerk's expensive villa, so he was in a mind
to cooperate with Gospic. He waited.

"And I need to know something from Venice."

"But you have your own people there."

"Right now, my people are being ridden by the Carabinieri. The season is ending. Most of our people get out of Venice in November. To stay would make them conspicuous. There is a Carabinieri major. His name is Brancati. He is pressing my business pretty hard right now and I need him to stop."

"Stop?" asked Groz, his eyes closing slightly.

"I need him distracted. Killing him would only intensify the war he is making on us. He has this Jew—from the Mossad?"

"Issadore Galan."

"Yes. This Jew. He is more dangerous than Brancati. His only loyalty is to Brancati. I want to have him distracted."

"Even here?"

They looked out at the medieval fastness of Kotor.

"Yes. Even here."

"Distracted, then. In what way?"

"He has put it out officially that a man—an American tourist—was stabbed in the Piazza San Marco two weeks ago. They say he is dead. I need to know if this is true. I need the inquiry to be noticed by Galan."

Groz nodded.

"The distraction. This dead man. We have heard this story too."

"Do you know if it's true?"

Groz studied Gospic's face for a while in silence.

"No. We do not."

"You have a source in the Carabinieri." A statement.

"Perhaps," said Groz.

Gospic raised an eyebrow. Groz got the message.

"So you ask me to . . . reach out, Branco . . . to this possible source of ours and have this question asked. Asked in such a way that Galan is *distracted*."

"Yes," said Gospic, his tone as lizard flat as the look in his eyes.

"If such a source existed," said Groz, slowly, "one would be reluctant to activate him for a reason such as this unless one knew the purpose."

"The purpose is that I am interested in the answer."

"A favor, then?"

Gospic nodded, implying a reciprocal favor in the future.

"So, this question of the dead American, then . . . And the money, of course?"

"Yes. This question. And the money."

Groz closed his eyes. The muscles in his face went slack, and he ran a pale white tongue around his thin lips, considering the risks contained in saying yes and comparing them with the risk of saying no to Branco Gospic in his own town. Gospic looked out across the fjord at the setting sun, his blunt face rocky in the sidelong light, his eyes hidden. Something buzzed in his shirt pocket, and he pulled out a small BlackBerry handset.

There was a terse message on the screen.

ARRIVE PMI

Tarc

Gospic's face did not change. He flicked the screen off, returned the machine to his shirt pocket, and looked back out to the fjord again. Groz stirred and sighed. Gospic turned to him.

"Yes," said Groz, his thin voice carrying a slight quaver. "We will do this. The question."

"And the money?"

"And the money."

Groz nodded, looked around vaguely at the pillared balcony and the sparkling fjord beyond it as if he had just awakened from a dream. He sighed, pushed himself to his feet. Gospic remained sitting, gesturing to a short, blunt man with ridiculous sideburns wearing a pale blue suit and no shirt who had been sitting a careful distance away.

The man stood and waited. Groz nodded, pulled the little boy to his feet and shoved him at the man in the bad blue suit, turned back to nod once at Gospic, and the little group shuffled off the balcony and into a shaded hallway beyond.

Gospic sat alone, holding the Sony camcorder in his hard hands. The remaining boys looked up at him and, one by one, padded away into the hallway, whispering to each other. Far above his head, a cloud of swifts wheeled in the dying light, their thin cries falling down through the chilly air. Beyond the breakwater, the tide was turning and the sea was moving, a vast, shapeless surging, as if something huge and ancient living beneath the surface was rolling in its long sleep. A wintry old man in worn corduroy pants, wearing a tattered olive-drab sweater and thin leather slippers, shuffled out from the shadowed hallway and stood beside Gospic, looking out at the water. Finally, he spoke.

"It was a mistake to ask for the help of a man like Groz. He will find something to his advantage in Venice and use it against the family."

Gospic nodded.

"I agree, Father."

"Then why?"

"Our man in the Carabinieri wishes to know who Groz has turned."

"Our man?"

"Yes."

"Why?"

"This Brancati, he is running a search for moles within his Venice office. He is doing a very good job of this, and his security man, Galan, he is . . . subtle. Skilled. Our man inside wishes Brancati to find his mole."

"I see."

"If Groz uses his mole to find out about the American, and conveys it to us accurately, our contact thinks he will be able to identify Groz's man. This mole can then be exposed to Brancati . . ."

"How will our man do this?"

"Apparently, there is some element in the data that would allow him to determine the source. So, the man working for Groz is exposed—"

"Suspicion passes over. Groz loses a source. Our man remains."

"Galan is a professional, Poppa. He will remain vigilant."

"But not quite so acutely. Still, Brancati is a problem for us. He has done us some damage. I looked at Larissa's books, and we have lost some income. This American? Do we already know about the dead American?"

"Yes. He is alive. Our source says he is badly injured."

"Saskia failed?"

"Yes. She failed."

"Is she back yet?"

"I sent for her. She . . . lingers . . . in Venice."

"Hoping for a way to redeem herself?"

"Yes."

"Will you let her?"

"I will let her think so."

"So we have Galan and Brancati and the American. Will you send Radko? Or Emil?"

Gospic sent his father a look of concern. His father's grip on the business was tight, but, in recent weeks, he had been forgetting things. It was troubling to Gospic, because, in the limited capacity he had for love, he loved his father and would dislike the bloody business of putting him aside.

"No. Remember, Poppa? Last month? That Vasari woman shot Radko Borins in the face. And Emil's in Indonesia. Remember?"

Gospic watched, with a sudden, piercing sadness, as his father struggled for the memory. Then his father brightened, and smiled down on Gospic.

"Indonesia! Of course. Then who . . . ?"

"Kiki. He is in Venice now."

His father smiled, his shrunken face breaking into cracks and seams.

"Kiki Lujac," said his father. "You sent Kiki?"

"I did."

"Well," said Poppa, looking out across the fjord. "That will be interesting to watch."

4

Venice

For a while, the young priest, like the pain, kept a civil distance, as if unwilling to intrude on Dalton's privacy. All in black, broad-shouldered but not tall, with a violet sash around his neck, the young man stood with his arms folded in front of him, his back to Dalton, staring out a thick casement window at a view that Dalton, from his position on the hospital bed, was unable to see. When Dalton tried to raise his head to look past the priest's shoulder and see what he was looking at, the white plaster-walled room faded and his bed began to roll, slowly, sickeningly, to Dalton's right.

So Dalton did not do that again.

He lay there for a time, breathing gently, staring up at the heavy wooden beams that supported the slate roof. The floor smelled of timeless age, old granite and limestone blocks, with an overtone of pine and polish. The narrow bed was hard, the pillow badly placed under his neck, but he was unwilling to move enough to make himself more comfortable because of the awful rolling that would certainly follow.

He was afraid he would vomit if the bed rolled again and he was unsure how he would then get himself clean, whether the silent priest would help him or if someone would come in through the heavy oak door. He wasn't even sure there was anyone or anything beyond that oak door, any more than he was able to say where this room actually was, in what building, in what country, in what time of year.

So, for the moment, he felt that the best course before him was to lie there quietly on his back and stare at the ceiling and breathe as slowly as he could because if he started to breathe too fast, then the pain—which was still keeping a polite distance—would come surging back.

He found that he appreciated the discretion of the young priest, whose face he could not recall as he lay there trying not to let the pain come back. His memory of the last few days was uncertain and filled with blank spaces and fleeting impressions: Cora Vasari's tear-stained cheeks, her dark eyes wide; Major Brancati's reassuring presence in a darkened room, recognizable only by the deep, purring rumble of his voice as he spoke to a subordinate; a high, white light and the sound of steel instruments clattering on a tray. Of course, the pain was constant and clear, a chain unlike his memories, a chain unbroken. Always, the pain was there. He was reasonably certain that it was now just possible to maintain a degree of equilibrium, of perfect balance, between pain and unconsciousness. It was just a matter of controlling his breathing. If he did not breathe too deeply, or too shallowly, then the pain would stay at a discreet distance, like the young priest at the window whose face he could not quite recall and whose name had also, it seemed, slipped his mind, although the man was familiar, someone he had met not too long ago.

But he felt no sense of urgency to remember the man's name. The important task here was the management of pain.

Managing the pain required concentration, as he had been taught at the Farm, and the fact that he was now becoming dimly aware of faint noises at the outer edges of his mind was interfering with this effort. He felt a surge of anger run through him. He wished the noises in the hallway would stop. He began to hope that the silent young priest at the window would do something about the noises in the outer hall: women's voices, perhaps, and the sounds of carts or trolleys being trundled about, the clatter and clang of plates coming through the heavy planks of the door.

Now that he was actively listening to the sounds in the outer hallway, he had lost the necessary concentration, the balance, and soon the pain was no longer at a polite distance. It had come closer. He could see it quite clearly, standing now at the side of his bed, the pain, staring down at him with a look of compassion.

No. It wasn't the pain, Dalton realized, that was standing by his bed; it was this nameless, silent priest. The priest was looking down at him, his rough-cut, dark-skinned face and black eyes sharp, a thin-lipped mouth with a black mustache and a duelist's goatee. Dalton tried to understand how he had come to confuse the priest with the pain, but, then, he was aware that his mind was not working quite right, so he closed his eyes for a time . . .

When he opened them again, the young priest was still there, his face closed and his expression unreadable.

"Do you remember me, Signor Dalton?"

Dalton, flat on his back, unable to move, swallowed twice, silently wished for water, and finally found both his memory and his voice.

"You're Father Jacopo. You were in Cortona. At the chapel."

The young priest showed his teeth then, strikingly white and even against his deeply tanned skin, his narrow black mustache.

"Yes I was. With old Paolo, the verger. Only, a while ago. So much has happened. Remember, he found your friend's body, huddled in the doorway of our little church? A terrible thing. So much blood and ruin. Such . . . *savagery.* Poor Mr. Naumann."

Dalton had nothing to say to that. He blinked and swallowed. The priest must have known he was thirsty, but he did not offer any water. He had the air of a man who had come to Dalton's hospital room to say one important thing and was now about to say it.

"Do you remember what Paolo had to say? About the dead man, who was calling your name? By the Via Santa Margherita?"

Dalton nodded, opened his mouth to speak, feeling his dry lips cracking. No words came, but he began to feel a little afraid of this young priest. The man seemed to sense this. He reached out a long-fingered hand and laid it on the crisp white sheet over Dalton's belly. The gesture may have been intended as a comfort. It was not a comfort. Dalton's belly muscles tensed, and now the pain, which had been gradually increasing, spiked and sharpened. The priest showed no sign that he was aware of this.

"Paolo said you should not answer that man, that you should not go with him for a walk along the Via Margherita. That he was a ghost who had been standing by the parapet along the Via Margherita for almost a year, calling your name. The ghost of your murdered friend Mr. Naumann. But you did not listen to Paolo, did you?"

Dalton shook his head.

"No, you did not. And now here you are, in this place. With this . . . thing . . . inside you. Right under my hand. Can you feel it? I can."

Dalton watched as the priest closed his dark eyes as if about to begin the Eucharist, raised his hand slightly, extending a strong, thin index finger, making a spike of it, which he drove sharply down through the white sheet, ripping through that and through the skin and the muscles beneath and inward, deep, deep into Dalton's belly. Purple blood flowed upward in a gout around his muscular hand and blue-red fountains of it sprayed out across the rest of the sheet. Dalton watched in paralyzed horror as Father Jacopo dug his hand in deeper, brutally searching Dalton's belly.

"Yes, here it is," he said, his eyes still closed. "I have it."

Dalton felt the man's probing fingers in his entrails, felt something hard being moved around by the priest's finger. Father Jacopo curled his fingers around whatever it was and started to pull. Pain flowed out from Dalton's belly and ran through him like a spreading fire.

Through half-closed eyes, he watched as Father Jacopo plucked his hand out of the gaping wound he had made in Dalton's belly. Gripped in his bloody fingers was a long, jagged sliver of bright green glass. Father Jacopo opened his eyes and turned the shard in the light from the window, his face flushed, his breathing short and rapid.

"You should have listened to Paolo, my son," he said. "This is only one piece. We must be sure to get them all. Try not to move."

Father Jacopo leaned forward with a look of renewed concentration, his bloody hand poised again above the gaping wound in Dalton's belly, his eyes fixed and full of hard purpose. The ghost of Porter Naumann appeared on the other side of his bed. Father Jacopo looked up at Naumann's ghost without changing his fixed expression.

"*Cancrenato,*" he said, with dismissive contempt. "This is no place for you. You are expelled. Leave us."

Naumann ignored the priest's command, looked down at Dalton.

"Micah," he said, "now would be a good time to make some noise."

DALTON TOOK PORTER Naumann's advice immediately to heart and, although he was only able to utter some strangled croaks, help did come running, in a black habit and sensible shoes, a nursing sister, with a stiff white cowl and an air of resigned irritation, who stiff-armed the big oak door and squeaked a rubber-soled streak to his bedside, where she leaned over Dalton as he moaned and thrashed, trying hard in his nightmare state to activate his screaming gear. And then, quite suddenly, he was wide awake and fully present in a room without either Father Jacopo or the ghost of Porter Naumann. He blinked stupidly up at the nun as she pressed her hands against his chest to quiet him. She had soft pink cheeks and cold gray eyes and she smelled of soap and lemons—her scent was very familiar, although her name refused to come to him. She placed a cool, dry hand on his forehead and then ran it down the side of his cheek to press an icy fingertip against his right carotid artery.

"You were dreaming, Signor Dalton—you are okay. You are safe. The morphine drip has come loose here . . . you must be still."

Dalton made the mistake of trying to sit up again. The pain in his gut snapped him backward and he hit the pillow hard. As he did so, the fragments of his memory came together: the blond runner by the Bridge of Sighs, the ghost of Porter Naumann with the green glass hilt of a broken dagger in his hand, the pigeons going up like blowing leaves in the Piazza San Marco as Cora begged him to be still . . . the opal sky burning above.

"Jesus *Christ*—how long have I been out?"

The sister's face closed, her seamed lips puckering.

"Do not blaspheme, Signor Dalton. Jesus protects you here."

"Does He?" said Dalton, mainly to himself. "Well, He's doing a really crappy job of it, then, isn't He? Am I still in the Arsenal?"

"Yes. Good. You remember. You are in the clinic of the Arsenal."

"So, I'm still in Venice?"

"Yes. With the grace of God, the Arsenal remains in Venice, so of course you also remain in Venice," she said in a soothing voice, "and you must try to lie still. You will open your . . . *dei punti*? Your stitches."

Dalton, tensing, could feel them pulling in his lower right side, like fishhooks in the flesh. He arched reflexively, the pain spiking again.

"What day is it?"

"Today is *Sabato*. Saturday. You came here two weeks ago, on *Mercoledi*."

"Chri— I mean, really? Two weeks? I've been out for two weeks?"

She straightened up and looked down at him. She was ageless, anywhere from thirty to sixty. *What life could you lead,* thought Dalton, *that would leave you so beatifically unmarked?* If the sister's body was a temple of peace and tranquility, apparently his was an arena.

"Cora? Is she here?"

The sister's face cleared, sunlight coming out from behind the clouded aspect of her eyes . . . She nodded, her ageless smile spreading.

"*Sí. La Signorina Vasari.* She has been here *many* times."

"Many times?"

"Yes. Many times. You have been sedated, put into a sleep, so you would not tear at the incision. This morning at dawn we begin to bring you back to life. Your lips are dry. Would you like some water?"

Dalton nodded. She moved away, a dry rustle of her habit and her rubber shoes squeaking on the stone floor, and then she was back with a tall glass filled with ice water, an angled straw; she put a hand under his back and lifted him—she was quite strong. Dalton pulled at the water and felt its cooling rush down his throat. She lowered him gently back.

"There . . . you should go to sleep again, now."

Sleep.

Sleep and dreams, and Father Jacopo with his surgical fingers.

"No. I've slept enough. Too much. I need to sit up."

"You are sure?"

"I am."

She gave the request her professional consideration for a time while Dalton lay there and tried to pull himself fully into the here and now. He knew the Arsenal, the big military citadel next to the old naval basin in the eastern end of Venice. It belonged to the Carabinieri, the military police. It was off-limits to civilians. It was also sometimes used as a secret prison for high-security detainees. Was he now one of them?

If he was in the hands of the Carabinieri, then it was likely that they would have already notified the Agency in Langley. Keepers would be here now, out in the hall, waiting for him to come out of the sedation. He was as good as in shackles, on his way back to Langley. Or he might never reach it. The sister's expression changed as she saw a series of strong emotions run across his face. Her words indicated that she was more than just a nurse and that she knew at least something about his situation.

"You are under the protection of Major Brancati, Signor Dalton. You must not be afraid. I am Sister Beatrice, the Director of the clinic here. No guard is waiting in the hall. No one is coming for you today. Here. Let me help you to sit."

She managed to get him more or less upright, stacking pillows behind him for support. The room rolled only a little as she did this, and the nausea stayed under control, but he was weak . . . boneless. He could barely hold the glass she handed to him. She stepped back again, folding her hands across her waist, her face in repose and considering.

"Are you hungry? Some soup, I think, would be possible now."

"Yes," said Dalton, feeling the emptiness in his belly.

"You are in pain. Would you like something for it?"

"Yes. No, no I would not. No morphine. But soup, yes, please."

He could not afford to be drugged any longer. If the price of being awake and ready for what was coming was to be in pain, it was a reasonable exchange. He glanced around the room and saw a large leather chair, some sort of narrow wooden armoire, doors open, with nothing inside it but a blue terry-cloth bathrobe and a pair of thin cloth slippers. A half-open door in the end wall that probably led to a bathroom. There were no guards in the room. There could be guards in the hall, in spite of the sister's assurances, but in here there was also a window.

So anything was possible, if he was awake and ready for his chance. Sister Beatrice saw the direction of his thoughts and gave him a conspirator's smile, but all she said was, "Major Brancati is now here. He has been waiting for you to wake up. He has been called. Are you ready to see him?"

"Yes," he said, pulling in a deep breath and riding out the consequences with as blank an expression as he could manage. "Of course."

She nodded, leaned over to straighten his sheets, and to push his long blond hair back from his forehead, letting her fingers move through his hair with a less-than-virginal touch. Then she turned and glided out of the room.

As soon as the door closed, Dalton pulled back the sheets and tried to get out of the bed. He got his feet down onto the stone floor, feeling faint, braced himself, and pushed himself to his feet, swaying, seeing the room go pale as a mist rose up in his vision.

He was wearing some sort of striped pajama bottom and nothing else. A broad surcingle of pale blue gauze was wrapped tightly around his lower torso. He touched his belly with caution, feeling for the stitches underneath, and found a row of them, perhaps eight inches long, running from his hip almost to the middle of his belly. He stood upright with an effort and tried to walk, found that it was just possible to attempt a few uncertain steps in a kind of old man's shuffle.

The door to the bathroom was half open, a tin shower stall visible beyond it. It cost him a great deal to cover the eight feet between the bed and the bathroom, but he managed it, closing the door and leaning his hands against the broad ceramic sink, with its rust-stained drain, while he gathered himself. He looked at his reflection in the stainless steel mirror; dark rings under his pale, colorless eyes, his cheeks sunken, long hair in limp, greasy strands.

He badly needed a shower and a shave, and he was very aware of the fact that a light breeze could knock him down, but he was still alive, and if the Company was trying to get to him, they hadn't done it yet.

He shuffled carefully to the barred window and looked out at a long canal that ran northward between low stone walls, the Canale delle Galeazze, the surface of its placid gray waters pebbled with a light rain that made it look like a sheet of hammered tin. Shreds of mist drifted across the canal. The wind off the Adriatic carried the smell of fish, a hint of garlic, and the graveyard reek of Venice in the fall. Just visible out in the sea mist was the low tomb-filled cemetery island called Isola di San Michele. The bars of the little window were thick and set deep into the stone casement.

The distance from the bathroom window to the roof of the buildings below looked to be about forty feet, with nothing but sheer stone wall between the casement and the roof. He reached up and tugged at one of the bars; he might as well have been trying to pull the sword from the stone. He heard the sound of amused laughter and turned to see Alessio Brancati, a major of the Carabinieri, wearing his formal navy blues, boots gleaming black, his leather harness shining, a holstered Beretta at his hip, leaning against the doorway, his dark, craggy face wearing a sardonic grin, his piratical leer set off by a black mustache, his strong yellow teeth showing.

"Awake for only a minute and already you are plotting, Micah."

Dalton could not help but return the smile, although his satisfaction at seeing Brancati again was, under the circumstances, rather muted.

"Alessio . . ." Dalton swayed a little, and Brancati's expression changed to grim concern. He stepped forward and took Dalton's right arm in an iron grip. He smelled strongly of the same Toscano cigars that he had been smoking when they first met in the little courtyard of the church of San Niccolò in Cortona, where an old verger named Paolo had found the bloody remnants of Dalton's friend Porter Naumann huddled by the gates. Brancati was the officer in charge of the murder investigation, and, although his part in it had remained in Italy, he had been an unlikely ally in the pursuit of Naumann's killer during the following days, a chase that had taken Dalton from Venice to London, to Washington, D.C., and finally to a violent collision in a stand of cottonwood trees by the Little Apishapa River, in southeastern Colorado.

Brancati led Dalton gently across to the wooden chair and helped him down into it, making odd little soothing sounds as if he were leading a lame horse. When Dalton was safely settled, Brancati went across to the wooden armoire, retrieved the threadbare blue robe, and arranged it with rough but careful hands across Dalton's shoulders. Then he stepped back and looked down at him with an expression on his strong Tuscan face that was a curious amalgam of sympathy, strong official disapproval, and residual affection.

"*Cretino!*" he said, not unkindly. "You came back. *Perché?*"

Dalton opened his mouth to answer, but Brancati raised his hand, palm out, shaking his head. "No need. You came back for *her*. And now look at you. Stuck like a *bistecca,* and all the Americans in an uproar. This is ridiculous. You are ridiculous. And you have placed her in danger too. You are a professional, a trained man. And yet you do this?"

"I just wanted to . . ."

Dalton's voice trailed off, bitterly aware that there was nothing to be said in his defense. Brancati nodded once, as if satisfied that on this point at least—on Dalton's state of sentimental idiocy—there was to be no argument.

"Yes. No defense. At least you still have your honor. She has been here many times. Not ten hours ago, she sat in that chair, love struck, with a face as white as Palladio's paint box."

"Cora?"

Brancati shrugged and made a hard face, his hands upraised.

"There is no reason in it. I tried to reason. No chance. She is down below now, waiting. Sister Beatrice, who is a romantic, called her at the Museo Civico. At least she has accepted having a guard, so there is that to be grateful for. It is not much, but I will take it. Now, I have to ask you, what are your intentions?"

"About Cora?"

Brancati waved that aside with the gesture of a man dispersing a cloud of cigar smoke, which seemed to remind him of his Toscanos. He patted his uniform tunic, his harness creaking, and extracted a rumpled pack of cigars, offering one to Dalton as a reflex and then jerking the pack away as Dalton reached for it.

"No. No cigar for you! Your intentions about Cora will be what I tell you they are. They are to have nothing to do with her. You know this is true."

"Yes," said Dalton, eyeing the pocket into which Brancati had shoved his Toscanos. "I do. I would like to tell her so myself."

Brancati nodded as he set his cigar burning with a heavy gold lighter and drew the smoke in deep, exhaling a blue swirling cloud.

"We have not found her yet, you know."

"Found who? Cora?"

"No. The girl who stabbed you."

"How do you know who to look for?"

Brancati puffed out his cheeks and glared at Dalton.

"But the description you gave—"

"I gave a description? To whom? When?"

"In the ambulance. To the medic. A young blond girl, short hair, a hard, red mouth, one of the marathoners. Number five-five-nine. You don't remember this?"

"No. Some of it. Not much."

"Well, there was video of the runners, taken by a news channel, as they came into the piazza. We were able to identify a girl wearing that number. Even a photograph. We have placed a watch on every ferry, all the ports, the airport, the Giudecca—everywhere."

He drew a small photo out of his breast pocket and handed it to Dalton. In the shot, a blowup of a camera capture, was the blurred and foreshortened image of a young woman, in a crowd of other runners, her top and shorts soaked, the number 559 plastered to her sexless, bony body, her white face harsh with strain, as she worked her way through a crowd on a wooden bridge across the Grand Canal. The girl had an underfed and somewhat-feral look, with the cheek-bones and color of a Slav or a Swede.

"It is her?" asked Brancati.

"I think so. What about the marathon number? She must have given a name."

"No. No name. The number was made up; the shirt, a fake. She must have joined the runners at some point. There were six thousand of them, wandering all over Venice in the hours before the race began. She may already be out of Venice, but, as I say, we keep the watch very close. If she is here, we will find her. Of course, you, being an idiot, made it very easy for *them* to find *you*. Back at Mr. Naumann's old rooms in the Savoia."

"The company had resources in Naumann's suite. A Ruger, and cash, and some travel documents. I needed to get at them. The concierge is a friend. He let me in without registering. I had watched the hotel for hours before I surfaced. No one was on it. I figured, because it was so obvious, it would be the last place they'd expect me to show up."

"We are speaking of *they* as if we knew who they were. Do you know who is this *they?*"

"In my case, Clandestine Services."

"Yes, Clandestine Services of the CIA . . . the Special Action men. When we met, a month ago, you were much caressed by the Agency, and now, I see, not so much. I wonder why this is so. But we will come to that. For now, for what immediately concerns me as an official of the Carabinieri, we have the attempted murder of an American visitor and the suspect an elusive blonde. So, now is the time to speak."

Dalton stared up at Brancati for a time, his mind working. In this brief, tense interlude, Sister Beatrice found it convenient to arrive with a broad silver tray piled high with cakes and biscotti and a china bowl full of soup—*straciatella*. There was even a pot of coffee, along with a series of colored pills that she insisted Signor Dalton take while she watched him.

She also glared so ferociously at Major Brancati that, sighing theatrically, he went into the bathroom and flushed his cigar down the toilet. Then he emerged, appropriating three of Dalton's biscotti, flopping himself down on Dalton's bed and waiting with clear impatience until Sister Beatrice drifted back out of the room on her squeaking rubber shoes.

She paused at the door to send an over-the-shoulder farewell glance at Dalton freighted with an earthly warmth that struck both men as rather more carnal than was quite right in a nursing sister, even an Italian one. Brancati managed to allow Dalton to eat almost half of his soup, and they both took long sips of what turned out to be *caffè corretto*—coffee with Sambuca—before Brancati, sitting up on the side of the bed and leaning forward, returned with his usual force to the lines of inquiry before them.

"So . . . *aspetto* . . . talk to me! Explain."

Dalton, sighing, said, "What do you want to know?"

"You have been stabbed. The weapon was a medieval Venetian assassin's blade. We have examined the fragments taken from your body. The knife was an antique, over three hundred years old, obtained by theft from a museum of Murano glass in the Ghetto. It was valued by its owner at over six thousand euros. Quite a price to pay for an object that is to be stuck with great force and no reasonable hope of recovery into a man's vitals. This act from beginning to end was . . . cinematic. Implausible. So unlikely that it suggests someone wishing to *appear* Venetian, which raises the possibility that the killers are not, as you say in America, *from around here.*"

"Have you thought about the Serbs?"

"Yes," said Brancati. "Your little dancing lesson on the Quay of Slavs. This has occurred to me, I admit."

This was reference to a late-night collision near the Palazzo Ducale between Dalton and two Serbian thugs from Trieste—Milan and Gavro—an attempted mugging that Dalton, feeling the effects of at least two bottles of Bollinger, had resented so extremely that he had kicked Milan into a state of quadriplegia and pounded the hapless Gavro into a permanent coma.

This had happened over a month ago, during the early days of Dalton's pursuit of Porter Naumann's killer; an unrelated off-ramp in the investigation that had nevertheless resulted in the arrival in Venice a while later of two Serbian enforcers in the employ of one Branco Gospic, a Serbian warlord based in Split, and, as it happened, a close relative to the now-comatose Gavro. The enforcers, Radko No Last Name Given and an unidentified male accomplice, had traced Dalton's movements to Cora Vasari's town house in the Dorsoduro district of Venice, where they had broken in by force and terrified the woman for a few moments before she was able to produce a pistol—her grandfather's, a famous flier assassinated by one of Mussolini's agents during Il Duce's adventure in Abyssinia. Cora shot Radko in the face, which ended the ugly interview at her villa but not, quite likely, the grudge between Dalton and Gavro's Serbian godfather, Branco Gospic.

"You think Gospic sent the girl?"

"It's a theory. I would be more in love with it if Mr. Gospic and his associates were the only people expressing an interest in your location."

"What does that mean?" said Dalton, knowing damn well.

"Now we come to it, my friend. The Agency. Your fall from grace. What happened in America? You found Mr. Naumann's killer; this we have been told?"

"Yes."

"And did it end there? In Colorado?"

"There were complications."

This obviously came as no shock to Brancati, as his wry smile indicated.

"*Complications,*" he said, savoring the word. "I begin to see that *complications* follow in your wake as seabirds follow the fishing fleet. Do you wish to enlarge on these *complications?*"

Dalton lifted his hands, winced, and shook his head, his face hardening.

"Alessio, I can't. I can't tell you a damn thing."

Brancati shook his head sadly.

"If you wish my cooperation, Micah, you have no choice."

"I *can* tell you that the Company wants to find me. I can tell you that they have a good reason to find me. I know that sounds . . ."

"Cinematic?"

Dalton laughed in spite of his pain.

"Yes. Cinematic. But it's true."

Brancati's face became a little stonier, showing Dalton the hard man he had seen before, the soldier-spy under the courtly façade.

"These are difficult times, Micah. This terror war, the forces at play in Europe now. These jihadis are a virus in the blood of the West. Wherever they are found, they must be exterminated. They are a death cult. There is no reasoning with them. Even the Dutch and the French have stiffened themselves. You cannot have a *truce* with such people. It is a cold war, and, like the Cold War, we are forced to descend to brutal tactics, even when we have a strong distaste for it. Methods are used now that Il Duce would have liked, and even good men are stained by what must be done. I cannot give comfort to someone who has become an enemy of his own country."

"I'm not an enemy of my country. Or of the Agency."

"Then why are you running from your own men?"

Dalton studied Brancati's face and saw no room for games in his cold, dark glare. Hell, he deserved at least a sense of what was at play in his own city, if only for his own safety.

"Okay. I can give you the situation, but I can't tell you what the central matter really is, other than to say that it relates to a Company operation. Run out of Clandestine Services, under Deacon Cather."

"A . . . *black op,* is that how you say it?"

"Yes. A black operation."

"And you can't tell me the name of this . . . op?"

"No."

"No? Then maybe I tell you. Was it something called Orpheus?"

Dalton's face seemed to harden up, close down, like concrete setting. Which of course told Brancati, a trained interrogator, all he needed to know.

"I see that it was," said Brancati, not without sympathy.

"It was called that, yes. I suppose I talked . . ."

"I'm considering the application of morphine in all our future interrogations. So much happier for all concerned than a beating. Everyone smiling. Dreamy. Much happy talk."

"What did I say . . . about Orpheus?"

"Everything! Like a chattering cuckoo. I know all, Micah. *Tutti.*"

Dalton looked at the man for a while, his breathing constricted, and then he remembered that Brancati was also a cop.

"Like hell you do. I don't believe you."

Brancati held a sharpened glare for a while and then broke into a grin.

"No, of course you don't. But you *did* say the name. So now that we know the name, will you tell me what is behind the name?"

"I can't, Alessio."

"Okay. *Allora.* Whatever Orpheus is, is it a threat to any Italians?"

"No. Not at all. It's not a threat to *any* civilian anywhere. It's not even something I *disapprove* of. I don't think you would either. My problem is, I found out about it. It was handed to me by . . . a dead friend—"

"Mr. Naumann?"

"Yes. But indirectly. Through an intermediary."

"And the intermediary . . . ?"

"His secretary. In London. A woman named Mandy Pownall. She was also his lover, I suspect. But now that I know about Orpheus, it can't be unknown, and it's quite plausible that some men connected to the operation will do whatever is necessary to make sure I don't talk."

"Are you likely to talk?"

"Hell no."

"Then say so. Tell the Company. What did Le Carré say . . . 'come in from the cold'? Reassure them. You're a trusted man, a proven man."

What Brancati was saying made sense. Maybe it was still possible to come in from the cold. In the CIA, the tricky bit about being a prodigal son returning was surviving your welcome-home party. In the meantime, Brancati's restless mind had run on to his own official concerns.

"Micah, what you cannot tell me about Orpheus—this thing that's apparently fatal to know—would it cause the CIA to send someone to kill you in Venice?"

"Possibly."

"Like this blond girl?"

"Possibly. But I don't see them using a stolen glass blade to do it in the first place. If the Company wants you dead, most of the time it happens so quietly that no one ever thinks of it as a murder. We don't like attention. This stabbing, right out in the open, in front of thousands of witnesses, it looks more like a revenge thing, a *demonstration*, a point of honor. It just doesn't *feel* like an Agency stunt."

"Yes. I agree. Which brings us back to our Serbian friends. About the CIA, I should tell you that we have unofficial inquiries from the Americans here. At the Consulate. And in London. They wish to know if you are here, in Venice. Even in the Arsenal. They are being very aggressive."

"What have you told them?"

Brancati said nothing for a time.

"So far, we are officially uncommunicative. We admit to holding the corpse of a murdered tourist and that we are making inquiries. For the time being, we will tell the CIA nothing more than that."

"Why?"

"An excellent question . . . I myself find it hard to answer. Of course, the relations between America and Italy are not good—have not been good since your own Clandestine Services people kidnapped Abu Omar off the streets of Milan a few years ago. The government has chosen to resent this, and there has been a trial—in absentia, in Milan—a trial of twenty-five American citizens. All convicted. There has been an official demand for their extradition. This, of course, has been farted upon by the Americans."

"Farted upon?" said Dalton, laughing in spite of his stitches.

"Yes. Farted. As one would blow out a candle?"

Brancati made a pursed-lips gesture, puffing his cheeks out.

"I think you mean *blown off?*"

"Blown off?"

"Yes. Dismissed. Ignored."

Brancati repeated the phrase in a whisper, considering.

"I think I like my word better. Anyway, after Milan, when the American Consul raises her voice with the Director of the Carabinieri, this does not make us tremble quite so much as it used to."

Here he broke off, going inward for a time.

"So, I have a problem. It affects you."

Dalton waited.

"In the last few weeks, there have been breaches. Information has been given to the Serbian mafia."

"How much Serbian mafia is there?"

"Effectively, the whole of Serbia and Croatia and Montenegro is divided up between two outfits that have agreed to share the territory. There is Stefan Groz, an aging *ermafrodito* who collects little boys—a Pantaloon in that area but a viper in his business—and there is your friend Branco Gospic. They are the two houses. For the rest, they are freelance *brigante* who operate on the fringes. No, Gospic and Groz, they are the only ones with the organization for this kind of *spionaggio.*"

"Where's the information coming from?"

Brancati shrugged, his eyes hardening.

"From here. This office. In Venice."

"You have a mole?"

"Perhaps. Perhaps not a mole but someone with divided loyalties."

"Divided between . . . ?"

"Between his duty and the euro, I suppose."

"Do you know who he is?"

"No. I am looking. But the information that has been leaked, it is of a specific nature. Of use to only a few men."

"So you're trying to identify the mole by defining the buyer?"

"That is one method. We are employing others."

"We?"

"My security chief, Issadore Galan."

"And I'm concerned?"

"Yes. Very. You are officially dead. Your murder was a public sensation. We have circulated digital pictures of your corpse to various departments—"

"How did you do that?"

Brancati grinned.

"We made you up to look dead. While you were sedated."

"Son of a bitch. May I see them?"

"Sweet Christ no! Very gruesome. Very disturbing."

"Jesus . . ."

"And the digital photos—"

"Contain hidden text files identifying each version."

Brancati nodded.

"So if the shot surfaces, we will know where it came from."

"How will you know if it surfaces?"

Brancati touched the side of his nose.

"I am not just a pretty face."

"So what I am is bait. You're after Gospic yourself, aren't you?"

"He has my attention, yes."

"For sending people to attack Cora Vasari last month?"

"For that. Also for drug running. Weapons traffic. Bribery. Corruption of officials. Manipulation of the stock markets. Being a . . ."

"Pain in the ass?"

"Yes. A very big pain in the ass. I have had enough of him. Venice has had enough of him. I have made him a personal project."

"And his vendetta with me . . . ?"

"If it truly is Gospic who sent the girl, then it makes you useful. To Venice. To the people of Venice. To me. You are not offended?"

"No. It explains a great deal. It explains your amazing hospitality, and why you've protected me from the Agency. Where does this leave me?"

Brancati raised an eyebrow, gave him a twisted grin.

"It leaves you here, in the Arsenal, until you are stronger. Then perhaps you will do me the honor of staying a few weeks with me at our villa in Arezzo. My wife is there now, with the girls. I am a bachelor in Venice for two weeks now. I have my little apartment upstairs, with a view of the lagoon. So, you will stay with us here for a time, and we will have some more talk about this trouble you are in and what we should—"

A knock at the door, soft but firm, and the sound of boots on stone; both men looked up from their separate seas of trouble and saw a woman standing in the open door, tall, with a shining bell of long blue-black hair, deep-set hazel eyes in a strong handsome face, prominent cheekbones and a wide sensual mouth, red-lipped. She was wearing a long black leather trench coat over a black leather skirt, a severe white silk blouse buttoned to the neck over her full breasts, her long legs encased to the knees in black leather riding boots. Her features were made for kindness, for wit and playful talk, but the expression they were carrying at this moment was not in any way a loving one. Both men got to their feet in a reflexive convulsion, but only Brancati managed to stay upright. Dalton collapsed back into the chair, his face whitening rapidly as the pain burned up from his incision.

"Cora . . ."

"Signorina Vasari . . ."

Cora Vasari ignored both greetings, stalking forward into the room, her boot heels hitting the old stones hard, her face set and accusatory.

"Alessio! You have been interrogating him!"

Brancati did not have the appearance of a man capable of stuttering, but he managed it.

"I . . . I have *NOT* . . ."

Cora Vasari leaned down and kissed Dalton on the cheek, her hair falling forward and enveloping him in the scent of her perfume, a strong, complex aroma composed of citrus and spices. Her lips left a mark on Dalton's cheek. He tried to reciprocate, but she straightened up again and turned on Brancati with a grim intensity.

"*Alessio—bruto! Minacciare un infermo! Che cosa—*"

"I am not browbeating an invalid, Cora. We were—"

Cora's face colored as she prepared a rebuke that was not to be heard—perhaps just as well—since it seemed to Dalton that the stones of the floor underneath his feet were rising to meet him. He had the illusion of effortless flight over a countryside made of various square fields in shades of blue and gray, toward which he was descending . . . turning . . . turning . . . Brancati caught him just before he hit the floor, and that pretty much made it a day, as far as Micah Dalton was immediately concerned.

5

Somewhere in the
Indonesian Archipelago

In the half-light of a veiled moon, the tanker eased her way through a narrow passage flanked by steep hills covered in dense jungle growth. At quarter slow, her prop was barely turning, just enough to keep a little headway against the ebbing tide. In the black mountains to starboard, the sound of her engines was like a low murmur of distant thunder, and the villagers who were awake to hear it put it firmly out of their minds. The Babi Rusa Brigade owned this island, and all the oceans between Papua and the Lembah Strait in northern Sulawesi. The Babi Rusa Brigade did not encourage curiosity about the movement of ships in and out of its secret dry dock at the end of the passage.

The tanker was running without lights and was being guided by a pair of outrider Zodiacs. The outriders communicated with the man on the bridge with short-range radios. The man on the bridge, Vigo Majiic, felt the wheel fighting in his sweaty hands. Without real headway, the ship would yaw and veer as the tides worked along her flanks.

His attention was rigidly fixed on the depth-finder screen in front of him. The bright, full-color screen showed an undersea canyon with sharp sides and a vicious turning only a quarter mile ahead. The ebbing tide was running down the canyon like a flash flood down a dry wash. It was trying to force the tanker into the jagged reefs only a few feet off his starboard side. Majiic was trying very hard not to let it win this battle, because, if the ship so much as brushed the sides of this narrow channel, the fox-faced, black-bearded young man named Emil Tarc, standing behind him and watching the bow of the ship as it moved against the starry sky, would bring up the muzzle of his pistol and put Majiic's brains all over the control panel. Emil Tarc was here as Branco Gospic's enforcer. So, of course, Majiic's attention was rigidly fixed.

"Slow, now—slow," came a crackling message from the radio handset in the leading Zodiac. Majiic picked up the handset and answered in a taut growl: "I can't slow her any more—she's already losing steerageway!"

He clicked off, and looked at Tarc.

"They should have provided a pilot."

"They're tribesmen, Vigo. Not sailors. Just do the job."

"We should have kept the Dyaks on board. At least they could help."

"Like they *helped* by trying to shoot down that chopper that buzzed us off the coast of Borneo? We're better off without them."

Majiic had nothing to say about that. In Tarc's world, the phrase *better off without them* had included cutting them all down with his MP5 while they were gathered on the bow decks to receive their share of the spoils and then tossing their bloody corpses into the shark-infested waters of the Sulawesi Strait, a few miles southwest of Diapati. Emil Tarc stepped forward and peered into the enveloping dark, as if he had night vision. His posture was tight, and his face, pocked with shrapnel fragments from a tour in Kosovo and lit up in a red glow from the control screens, looked slightly satanic. In his left hand was a Tokarev pistol taken from the body of a Russian Major. It was fitted with a suppressor, and he held it a little apart from his body as if ready to place it against Majiic's temple and squeeze the trigger.

"They say slow, Vigo."

In spite of his fear, Majiic snarled back at him: "You want the wheel?"

"No. But be careful."

"Then be quiet, Emil. Please."

Tarc grunted and fell silent. The deck plates hummed with the contained power of the ship's engines. A bat flickered past the windshield, a red flutter with a green spark in one eye. A single green-and-white light showed like a star on the distant bow. The ship's wheelhouse still reeked of dried blood, and a plywood board had been screwed onto the shattered starboard window where the man Majiic knew only as Brendan Fitch had fired his last two rounds before leaping into the dark. Part of the FLIR screen showed brittle clumps of some unidentifiable matter, perhaps some of them containing the neurons that had held Anson Wang's last thoughts of his family in Singapore before Emil Tarc had blown all of Wang's memories out through his forehead. In Majiic's hands, the wheel fought him, and his sweat slicked the green metal.

Tarc and Majiic looked up as the stars were slowly blotted out by a dark cloudlike screen; the Babi Rusa Brigade had rigged a camouflage net across the narrowing entrance to the dry dock. Large enough to hide an entire ship, it stretched out like a fan from pylons drilled into the cliffs on either side of the fjordlike inlet. On the netted surface, the shapes and colors of jungle growth had been laboriously hand-painted, months of work carried out by the entire population of the entire island under the guns of the Babi Rusa. From the air, the inlet looked like a shallow bay on the eastern edge of an insignificant island lost in the immensity of the South China Sea. The whole five hundred feet of the bamboo-and-wood scaffolding was hidden by the overhead netting. The Babi Rusa leased the facility out to anyone with enough money and the right connections with the international terrorist brotherhood that had sprung up in the middle nineties, while America had amused itself with far-more-pressing questions, such as the exact legal meaning of the word *is*.

The channel's left turn was on them now, and Majiic eased the wheel to starboard. The ship slowed even more as the light on the bow moved across an arc of black night. A range of hooded lights became visible in the distance, an opening V like a double string of landing markers on an airfield. Majiic lined up with the markers and felt his chest and belly muscles easing. Steering a five-hundred-foot tanker through a narrow passage in absolute darkness while a socio-pathic lizard stood ready to kill you for the slightest error had Vigo Majiic regretting his career choices.

"We're under the netting," said Majiic. "May I put on the bow lights?"

Tarc grunted again, as if he had to pay for words expended. Majiic flipped a breaker and the waterway in front of the boat sprang into sharp relief. Hard-faced, brown-skinned men stared back into the glare of the halogens, red pin lights in their eyes. Many were armed.

"What if they try to take the ship?" said Majiic.

"They won't," said Tarc. "At least, not until it's ready."

"And then?"

Tarc turned to look at Majiic, his eyes two tiny red lights in the shadowed wheelhouse. He smiled, showing small, uneven teeth that were painted bloody red by the binnacle glow.

"By then, we will be ready too."

6

The Arsenal, Venice

Brancati, whose wife and three daughters were spending the fall in his mother's villa near Citerna in Tuscany, had turned his office in the tower of the Arsenal into a kind of private apartment, with a kitchen and a spartan bedroom connected to his official quarters. There was also a small, terraced balcony that looked north over the ship channel—crowded with the bulkheads and the hydraulic machinery of the Moses project, which was somehow going to save Venice from the rising waters of the lagoon—and, beyond that, the graveyard island of San Michele across the lagoon. The weather had turned in the last few days and now was unseasonably warm for this late in November, so warm that a long white-over-blue Riva cruiser was idling across the lagoon, trailing a lacy white wake across the deep-blue water. The sun on the water was sending shimmers of golden light onto the plastered ceiling as Dalton sat in a beach chair, nursing a glass of pinot grigio and watching the afternoon gliding dreamily toward the evening. He heard Brancati's phone ring on his desk inside the main room and Brancati's muted baritone as he answered. He spoke a few words, set the phone down, and walked out onto the terrace.

"Cora is here, Micah."

Dalton shifted in his chair to look up at Brancati's lined face: his dark eyes were filled with judgment, but his expression was warm, even sympathetic. Brancati had insisted, and Dalton had given his word, that there could be no more contact between Cora and Dalton. Dalton had nothing to offer and no future in which to offer it. Cora was leaving for Florence this evening, returning to the university. She was here to say good-bye.

There had been little opportunity for the two of them to be together in the last week. Brancati had seen to that, and Dalton had no real inclination to fight the circumstances. It would have been pure selfishness, and dangerous for Cora. He had come to Venice to see her one last time and been duly stabbed for his troubles. So, it was done. Both understood that clearly. It was a condition of Brancati's continuing protection. And Dalton had long ago made career choices that cut him off from the simple dreams of normal men.

Dalton had told Cora nothing of Brancati's covert campaign against Branco Gospic and Dalton's role as bait. As far as Cora was concerned, Dalton was leaving Venice as soon as he was healed. They would very likely never see each other again. There was a light knock at the glass doors that led out onto the terrace, and Cora stepped out into the afternoon light.

She was wearing the same knee-length black leather skirt and the emerald green cashmere twinset that she had been wearing when Dalton first saw her in the stairway of her family's apartments in the Dorsoduro, and, over that, her long black leather trench coat. Tall, full-breasted, and long-legged, her blue-black hair shining, her handsome face sharp and slightly tanned, her hazel eyes troubled, she flashed a brilliant smile at them both, kissed Brancati on both cheeks, and then leaned over to kiss Dalton rather more warmly on the lips, her long hair falling over his face in a sensuous, aromatic tumble. Dalton, whose libido had recently awakened from a nine-year coma, found her nearness magnetic, an irresistible pull.

She broke away—too quickly—and looked out at the canal, and the Adriatic beyond, spreading her arms expansively.

"A lovely afternoon, Micah."

Brancati gave Dalton a warning look, and looked as if he were about to speak, when the phone on his office desk rang, a shrill beeping.

"Okay, I leave you two for a moment. Micah . . ."

Brancati withdrew, and Cora turned to look down at him, the wind off the water fluttering her hair around her cheekbones. Six hundred yards away, in the pilothouse of the idling white Riva, a deeply tanned, muscular young man, with long black hair and a rough-cut but striking face with wide-set Moroccan-green eyes, bared his teeth as he side-tapped the butt of a Hungarian-made Gepard M1 sniper rifle. The scope image shifted by a hairline, moving from a spot just below Cora's right elbow to the center of Dalton's forehead. The image rose and fell with the slow movement of the water, but, by lifting the butt in rhythm with the gentle motion of the hull and using the forward bipod as a pivot, the man was able to keep the sixty-inch-long weapon zeroed in on Dalton's skull. It was a skill that could be learned, but it helped to have a gift. This young man had the gift.

"Is it him?" asked his companion, a skeletal blond woman with Slavic features and a sour expression on her thin-lipped face. She was wearing a long indigo silk scarf, and nothing more. Kiki loved that scarf.

"It is," said Lujac. "Very alive. You fucked up, Saskia."

"No. Gospic did. The weapon was ridiculous. A toy."

"You tell him that," said Lujac, keeping his eye to the scope.

"You are going to shoot?"

"No," said Lujac.

"Why not? What are you waiting for?"

"I enjoy . . . watching."

Saskia looked upward, her shoulders rolling, as she steadied the ship against a sudden rising swell.

"Everybody knows you like to watch. But there he is. Kill him."

"Perhaps," said Lujac, centering the crosshairs on Dalton's nose. He thought the man looked . . . interesting—like a Roman statue of some barbarian captive, the marble surface weathered by time and storms. Dalton had long blond hair and a lined face that looked battered but retained an aspect of wry humor and a mouth that looked willing to smile if given the right reason. *He's beautiful,* thought Lujac, moving with the seas underneath him, keeping the image steady. It would make him sad to kill something that beautiful. Gospic had been vague about killing him, saying only that he needed to know if the man was still alive. He had left it up to Lujac to decide. Saskia, who was bitter at her own failure, wanted the man dead, so she could put an end to her discomfort. But Saskia had no eye for beauty.

Lujac steadied the butt and pulled in a long slow breath, let it out slowly. Becoming still. His finger tightened on the trigger. Maybe he would kill him, anyway. Killing was a little like sex, after all, although with the killing there were no uncomfortable mornings with strangers. The woman moved in front of Dalton, hiding him from Lujac. Lujac lifted his eye from the scope and sighed. Fate. Destiny. Cora stood looking down at Dalton, her back to the sea, her face in shadow.

"You look well, Micah. Are you well?"

Dalton stood and walked over to lean beside her on the railing, his motion abrupt, forcing Lujac to shift his position. He reacquired

Dalton in a moment and settled in again, watching, considering. At the wheel, Saskia sighed theatrically. Lujac ignored her, centering the crosshairs on Dalton's right cheekbone. *Like a kiss,* he thought. Dalton stood close to Cora, close enough to smell her perfume, a spicy, Eastern aroma.

"Yes, Cora. I'm fine."

She studied the lines in his face, the parchment skin.

"Liar. You should not have come to Venice."

"No? Why not?"

"Look at what has happened to you."

"I'm standing on a balcony in Venice with a beautiful woman."

She frowned at him, but there was a smile flickering around her lips.

"You are ridiculous. You got yourself stabbed. For what?"

"I did what I wanted with what I had left."

"And now . . . ?"

"And now here we are."

"And that's enough?"

"Not in the slightest. But it's all I'm going to get."

Her expression grew solemn.

"E'vero. Alessio has protected you."

"And you. When do you leave?"

"Soon. An hour. Alessio has insisted on a driver, so I will have a young carabiniere to keep me company all the way to Florence. And you?"

"Me?"

"Yes. When do you leave? Where do you go?"

Dalton looked at her face, seeing the emotions there.

"I don't know. Brancati thinks I should try to reconnect with the Agency. To come in from the cold."

Cora's face hardened a little, her full lips thinning.

"That was in a book. This is life. They have already tried to kill you once. You cannot go back. It was very bad for you. The lying. The violence. You were poisoned. Drugged. You saw ghosts. Hallucinations. That terrible man. Pinto? What happened to him?"

"He changed his ways."

"You killed him, I suppose."

"Not at all. We reached an understanding."

Cora didn't smile.

"A liar still. And a killer. And now a *hunted* killer. No. Enough. Your life in that world? It is over. Look what that life has already done to you. You have done enough for America. America does not deserve you."

Dalton smiled at her.

"I have limited talents, Cora—"

She waved that away.

"My family has connections. My uncle owns the Capri Palace Hotel in Anacapri. A wonderful man. You could be his security . . ."

Her voice trailed away into a whisper as Dalton placed both hands gently on her shoulders and drew her toward him. He kissed her, gently at first, and then more strongly as she stirred and moved into him. Her arms moved up the small of his back and she pulled his hips into her, and then they were moving together and the heat was rising up between them.

Out in the Riva, Lujac watched, his mouth half open. Saskia could only see two tiny figures on a distant balcony, but there was something in their posture that made her smile down at Lujac.

"Not on your team, Kiki."

"I don't have a team," said Lujac, his throat slightly constricted as he watched the couple embrace. "I am . . . adaptable."

Saskia smiled again, because this was very true, and Kiki had proved it quite definitively only a few hours ago. Dalton and Cora broke apart, Dalton breathing hard, his belly hurting and heat racing all along his chest and shoulders. Cora's cheeks were flushed and her eyes unfocused, inward, her lips wet and open. Although she had stepped away from him, her dark eyes on him, a little stunned by the sudden visceral rush of it, Dalton could still feel the pressure of her hips, her thighs, her belly, her breasts, the scent and the warmth of her skin and the steady pulse of her carotid at the side of her neck. Heat. Brancati stepped through the curtains, his face hard.

"What is it?" asked Dalton, seeing his expression.

"There's a woman. In the piazza. Sitting at Florian's."

"A woman?"

"Yes. She came in on one of the Minoan cruise ships this morning. From Trieste, Galan thinks."

"Issadore?" said Cora.

"Issadore Galan," said Brancati. "My security man."

"Your Israeli?"

"Yes," said Brancati, shifting his glare to Cora, and then softening it as he realized that he had put Issadore Galan in charge of Cora's protection detail after Radko and No Name had attacked her in the Dorsoduro.

Galan was a short, crumpled man with a large round skull and too many features crowded into the center of his face to make for much in the way of looks. The fingers of his hands had been broken many times during the course of his captivity with the Jordanians in the late eighties. Broken with hammers. They had healed badly. Other atrocities had been performed, taking away any hope he may have had of ever being given or returning physical love. Perhaps as a result, Issadore Galan's spiritual force was ferocious. It flared out at life through small dark eyes wreathed in spidery pain lines. His feral smile was sudden and brilliant. Passionate and cold. He adored Cora, and had said so several times to Brancati.

Of course Cora would remember him.

"Who is she?" asked Dalton, although he felt he knew the answer. Brancati held out a color photo, taken from a short distance away, a flight of pigeons blurring in the foreground, the woman luminous in a long pale linen dress, a wide-brimmed black straw hat with a pink fabric gardenia shading her face, her age indeterminate but not young, her lean and graceful body conveying an air of contained languor as she sat at a small round table near the bandstand, looking down at a copy of the *Herald Tribune* that lay on the table in front of her. She was holding a turquoise cigarette with a gold tip between the middle and index finger of her right hand. Dalton looked at the shot for a time while he contemplated his answer, deciding finally on the truth, if only for the novelty of the choice.

"Mandy Pownall," he said, looking up at Brancati.

"Who is *this* Mandy Pownall?" asked Cora, with a definite tone. Both men heard it and exchanged wary glances.

"She is a business associate," said Dalton.

Cora made a face, her expression closing down.

"One of *them?*"

"Mandy was Porter Naumann's assistant at London Station."

"She is with the CIA, then?"

"Yes," cut in Brancati. "Galan has her on a list."

Dalton, sensing something in Brancati's tone, looked at the man.

"Are you arresting her?"

Brancati shook his head.

"For Milan? No. She's not on *that* list. But she is CIA."

Cora watched the exchange, sensing what was not being spoken.

"She is from London? Why is she here?"

Dalton was looking at the picture. The last time he had seen her was in his Agency flat on Wilton Crescent in Belgravia. She was showing him a file, and in that file was the reason Porter Naumann had been killed, and Dalton's response to what Mandy Pownall had shown him was why he was on the run in Venice right now.

"She's trailing a wing," he said, finally. Brancati grunted, his attention pulling away. He shaded his eyes, staring out at the lagoon.

"How long has that boat been out there?"

7

Piazza San Marco, Venice

A pale winter sun was just touching the roof of the Museo Civico on the western end of the square when Mandy Pownall looked up to see a short gnomelike figure standing in the last of the sunlight, a stunted, slope-shouldered shadow man, oddly bent, as if he had been injured and had healed badly. She set her wineglass down and looked up at him, waiting.

He bowed—a short, sharp bob—and spoke.

"Signorina Pownall?"

His accent was strange, a hoarse, croaking rasp that sounded like a cross between Italian and Hebrew. Mandy smiled brightly up at him.

"Mr. Galan. How delightful. I was hoping you'd come. *Do* sit."

Galan ducked his head, enfolded in an embarrassed air that did not affect his eyes, which were as hard and sharp as a crow's. He took the chair opposite and folded his ruined hands in a clasp under the table, as if to spare Mandy the sight of them. She picked up the iced decanter and filled the second glass that had already been waiting there. Galan watched her fill it, thinking that she looked a little like Cora Vasari—the English version; chilly, composed, a fine, aristocratic face. She did not have Cora's tropical fire. But she had *presence,* a strong, sensual air. There were delicate lines around her eyes and her lips; her neck was long, and, beneath the dry, crepey skin, there were blue veins showing. Mandy felt his oddly carnal appraisal, as she re-filled her own glass. She sat back, raised hers in a toast.

"To Venice," she said, and they both drank.

Galan set his glass down with regret—he loved cold Chablis far too much, especially when in the company of an elegant woman. He leaned back in his chair, said nothing more, and seemed content to wait out the remainder of the afternoon with the same serene calm. Mandy smiled to herself. She had been *brought up to speed* on Issadore Galan's formidable talents by Stennis Corso, their Italian specialist at London Station.

"Well, to business," she said, setting her glass aside.

"Of course," he said, smiling.

"We'd like to talk to Micah Dalton."

"We . . . ?"

"I'm here for Deacon Cather."

Galan closed his eyes slowly and opened them, a reptilian tic. He said nothing at all, but he seemed to gather into himself, as if coiling.

"Please convey to Mr. Cather my best regards. We met once, at Camp David. During President Reagan's era. I found him most . . . professional."

"I will. About Mr. Dalton . . ."

Galan was shaking his head. It turned smoothly, as if on an oiled pivot, but his eyes stayed locked on Mandy's pale pink face.

"Regretfully, it is my sad duty to inform you . . ."

Mandy was reaching into her purse. Galan's voice trailed off, as he watched her retrieve a small silver Canon camera. She held it out to Galan, who accepted it with the fingertips of his left hand, as if he expected it to carry an electric charge.

"It's a digital," said Mandy. "Open the stored pictures section."

He did, and found that he was looking at a photograph of a man's face. He shaded the LCD screen from the sidelong sun, and set a pair of thin, gold-wire-framed glasses onto his nose, squinting at the screen.

"Yes. This is a photograph of Mr. Dalton."

"Taken at your morgue, so we gather."

"Yes. It is a picture of him that we used to identify his body."

"So, he's dead, then?"

"As I said . . . regretfully. We did all that could be—"

"Are you at all curious as to how we came by this picture?"

Galan shrugged his shoulders, lifted his clawlike hands skyward in a ghastly imitation of divine supplication. He smiled—showed his tiny yellow teeth, at any rate—although he did not return the camera.

"You are with Clandestine. The CIA. I suppose you have your ways."

Mandy offered him some more Chablis—he accepted it—and shone upon him a smile he would remember for days afterward, in the silent rooms of his gloomy little backstreet villa near the Tempio Israelitico in the Ghetto.

"This picture was circulated internally. Within the Carabinieri. It was not shared with the municipal police. Or with any other of your agencies."

"Yes. That's true."

"We had it analyzed by our forensic people in Maidenhill. It was compared with file photos of Micah Dalton, and they came to the intriguing conclusion that the subject of this photo was not quite reliably dead at the time the shot was taken."

Galan smiled, inclined his head, and lifted his eyebrows.

"Fascinating. A marvel. And how did they determine that?"

"As it was explained to me, when a man dies, at the moment that his body begins to undergo the various processes, there are immediate changes in such things as muscle tissue, skin cells. Nothing that would be obvious to an untrained observer but present nevertheless."

"For example?"

Mandy gently took the Canon back and slipped it into her purse before she replied. She lifted her glass, placed her red lips against it, looking at Galan over the rim, her eyes bright, her expression one of teasing enjoyment.

"You're going to make me run through the whole silly thing, Mr. Galan. How boring."

"Call me Issadore."

"Issadore. You may call me Mandy."

"Mandy, then. You were about to explain . . ."

"The muscles of the face begin to tighten. They lose flexion. Density. Cohesiveness. The expression changes. Life, as an animating force, an organizing principle, releases the tissues, drifts away, and the face assumes what we call the death mask, a certain rigidity. This is why morticians have such a difficult time making the dead look as if they were merely asleep. Our people did a graphic overlay—some computer thingy they have; bores me to tears—but somehow it showed them that Dalton's face in this photograph is not the face of a Micah Dalton in real death. Actually, they feel he may have been heavily sedated, drugged. But he was not dead when this photo was taken."

Galan said nothing. His hooded eyes studied the glass of Chablis before him with perfect stillness, as if he were a wizened Buddha contemplating a disappointing lotus. Mandy reached out and pinged the side of his glass with the lacquered nail of her index finger.

"Really, Issadore, love. We *know* he's not dead. You might want to ask me why we think you'll admit this eventually."

Galan lifted his eyes and fixed her with a look. Mandy resisted the reflexive desire to sit back, to disengage from the force of that glare. Galan ran a dry, white-tipped tongue over his lower lip, took another sip of his Chablis. A flight of pigeons fluttered overhead, making a noise like flags snapping in a strong wind. The sun was now well below the roofline, and there was a damp chill rising from the old stones of the square. If the day had been mid-September, the evening was late November.

"It was resented, you know?" he said, after a silence.

"What was . . . resented?"

"The taking of Omar. In Milan. In 2003. It was arrogant. A slap in our faces. Collectively. We—I personally—resented it. As you would resent it if we came to"—here he searched for a place-name that would convey the American heartland—"to Topeka. Came to *Topeka,* and took a man off your street there? In front of your own people?"

Mandy held his look.

"We—London—had nothing to do with that. You know that."

Galan was gracious enough not to pull the lie apart, there and then. Perhaps, he thought, Anthony Crane, the calculating Oxford aristocrat who was the current chief of London Station, had not told Mandy Pownall about their involvement in the operation. If he had not, there may be other things she did not know. For example, that many of the CIA's Clandestine operators involved in the rendition had actually used their own personal credit cards to book hotel rooms in Milan. Why? To get the air miles. And that two of these people had come directly from the London office. This was an extraordinary breach of tradecraft, but the CIA had been a shadow of its former self ever since Clinton had ordered a thirty percent reduction in its overseas staff. Clinton had effectively gutted the CIA, just in time for September 11. Now Galan had respect only for a few members of the

Clandestine Services, and most of them were ex–Special Forces. Like Dalton.

"As you say," he said, simply, letting the entire complicated issue pass, "I am curious as to why you think we would *admit* that your Mr. Dalton is not dead."

"The camera I gave you is a digital camera."

"So I observed."

"Why would I bring the camera when I could simply have brought a printout of the photograph?"

"I'm sure you will enlighten me."

"The photo is a digital photo. It contains an encrypted text file. Like a digital watermark. We call it steganographic encoding. The boffins at Maidenhill decrypted it and found a random-number identifier. In effect, the file hidden in the digital matrix of this shot could be only one of two things."

Galan lifted his glass, turning it in the dying light. Mandy took the glass from him, refilled it, continued talking.

"It could be a message. Or it could be a marker. Maidenhill ran some clever little program on it and determined that there was no message. So, a marker, then, something that made the shot unique."

"Not at all," said Galan, smiling. "We sent many copies of the shot—"

"You sent many *versions* of the shot. To all of your departments. In the expectation that one of the versions would be leaked."

"Leaked?"

"Issadore, dear man. You have a mole."

Galan said nothing.

Mandy snorted, pulled out a gold cigarette case and a heavy, well-worn Cartier lighter. She snapped the cigarette case open and held it out to Galan, a small golden tray full of long, slender cigarettes in deep turquoise, with dull-gold filters. They were ridiculous, and Galan was delighted to accept one. Mandy leaned forward and lit it for him, and then took one for herself, leaning back into the chair and regarding him with a grimly amused expression. She turned her head to one side, showing Galan the side of her neck and one delicate pink ear, and blew out a cloud of blue smoke. It coiled in the last of the light. The sound of a cello being tuned floated out onto the square from somewhere inside the dark-wooded cloisters of Florian's.

"We will give you your mole, Issadore."

"And in return?"

"Micah Dalton."

Galan inhaled the cigarette, savoring it, took it from his mouth and held it on the tabletop between two crooked fingers heavily stained with nicotine. He shook his head, as if he were feeling genuine regret.

"Even if this . . . speculation . . . were founded on anything but the fertile imagination of your Mr. Crane at London Station, my chief will never agree to such a bargain. Even for a dead man."

"We are prepared to show you an expression of our good faith."

"In what form?"

"You know a man named Stefan Groz?"

"Of course. A Serbian businessman."

"This digital shot was e-mailed to him through a local server. At just after midnight last night. We monitored the transmission—"

"One message in a *million*? A very lucky break?"

Galan was fully aware of the Agency's latest program, targeting Internet cafés all over Europe. Agency personnel would simply circulate through hundreds of different Internet cafés and in each one they'd download an e-mail-monitoring program called Digital Network Intelligence. The Americans were probably monitoring Internet cafés all over Europe and the Middle East. Again, Galan had no reason to betray this knowledge to Mandy Pownall. So he let that pass as well.

Mandy Pownall smiled at the compliment.

"Well, not so lucky. Groz is of interest to us."

Galan chuckled, a deep rumble in his bony chest.

"Stefan Groz is of interest to most of the Intelligence agencies in Europe."

"Yes," said Mandy. "My point being, we know the source of this e-mail to Stefan Groz. We have the computer IP address. As a gesture of goodwill, we're prepared to give you the precise location of this computer."

"Some Internet café, most likely?"

"Yes. The Café Electro in Campo San Stefano. You know it?"

"Of course."

"Then find out who used this particular computer at"—she hesitated, recalling the details she had painstakingly memorized under the judgmental consideration of Stennis Corso and Tony Crane—"precisely six minutes and eleven seconds after midnight last night, local time. The IP of the computer is . . . Do you wish to take this down?"

Galan shook his head. Mandy looked around the plaza.

"Issadore, you bounder. You have a mike on us?"

Galan bowed, offered a gnomic smile.

"Yes. We also have a camera in the Café Electro."

"You do?"

"We have cameras in every Internet café in Italy."

Mandy thought this over.

"Of course. A reasonable security measure."

"Yes. Well, this is much appreciated—"

He had started to rise; Mandy placed a restraining hand on his arm.

"Look, Issadore. Do you know about Micah and Porter Naumann?"

"Of course. The bizarre affair of the red-skinned man."

"Do you know that Porter and I were lovers?"

Galan looked away, not out of any sense of discomfort. Perhaps only to hide a momentary betraying glitter. He had several telephoto shots in his own filing cabinet, surveillance shots of Porter Naumann and this splendid woman in an intense embrace outside a car-rental office in the Piazzale Roma. Galan was no one's lover and never would be again. Which was why he was living in Venice and had never gone home to his wife in Haifa after the Jordanians traded him back to the Mossad for six of their own spies. Galan had also read the Naumann file. He nodded.

"Then you know that I would never hurt Micah. I give you my word, Issadore. If Micah will only come in . . ."

"This is not a decision that I am qualified to make. Such a determination would have to come from Major Brancati."

"Is Micah Dalton alive, Issadore?"

There was a look in her face that reached him deep in his desiccated core. Friendship, affection. Love. There was no room for that sort of thing in this business. He knew Mandy Pownall was not a street agent. Tony Crane had sent her because she had a personal stake in Micah Dalton. Crane knew Galan would sense this. He was banking on it. The kindest thing he could do for this splendid woman would be to send her away with her hopes shattered and her loving heart broken. But Micah Dalton had become a card, in an unknown game being played by London Station and therefore by Deacon Cather himself, and for a card to be useful the card must be kept in play.

"Yes, he is alive."

"Will he come in?"

Galan shook his head.

"Not to London Station."

"Then where?"

Galan looked up toward a suite of windows in the offices above Florian's, raised his hand. Then he looked back at Mandy, his black eyes glittering but his expression not unkind. If he had pity in him, he might have been feeling that, but he did not. It was closer to mild regret, and he was very familiar with regrets. He had many of them, but there was room in his damaged heart for a few more.

"He's here?" said Mandy.

Galan nodded.

"Yes. Come with me."

AROUND THE SAME time that Galan was sharing a decanter of icy Chablis with Mandy Pownall, Alessio Brancati was having his marine unit run down the white-over-blue Riva—the name SUBITO on the stern was done in glittering gold letters—the pursuit boat managing to intercept it after a confused, ambiguous, slow-speed, stop-and-start chase on the way to the ship channel north of the Lido. The man at the wheel, a lean, foxlike young man with vaguely Arab features and amazingly clear green eyes, was only too happy to bring his sixty-foot cruiser to a slow crawl—he had long lines in the murky water, running on downriggers. They trailed behind the boat as the marine unit pulled in closer.

"I was fishing," said the man at the wheel—there was something wrong with his radio, it seemed—while the Carabinieri crew in the long mahogany speedboat puttered to the gangway. He stood by the gangway to greet the young officer and his men as they came up the ladder, their faces set and stern, carrying HK MP5s at port arms.

"Papers," said the young officer, his voice not quite as deep as he would have wished. The young man, very tan, barefoot, in clean white slacks and a powder blue V-necked cashmere sweater with a long indigo scarf tied around his neck, gave the young officer a decidedly carnal once-over and then led the little boarding party around to the fantail and along into the pilothouse. The boat was obviously expensive, done in brass and teak and hardwoods, uncluttered and elegantly appointed, and the young man—the *owner*, according to his papers, was Kiki Lujac. *"The photographer!"* blurted one of the junior carabiniere.

"Yes," said *the* Kiki Lujac, showing a brilliant smile, his face opening like a sunny dawn. "The same—"

They searched his ship. They found nothing at all; he was quite alone, fishing idly and without any real desire to catch anything, it seemed, the downriggers still and untended. The officials thought there may have been a girl at some point in the past; the captain detected some lingering female scent in the master cabin—of course, this was only to be expected, as the man had this reputation. At any rate, they left, after many autographs and some chilled prosecco and then much more laughter, pulling away from the long, low, sleek Art Deco cruiser in a purring growl, powering up flamboyantly to impress Kiki, the mahogany chase boat carving a golden arc of spray through the dying glimmer of the setting sun on the broad lagoon, the youngest soldier explaining in detail to his captain just who Kiki Lujac was—the many photo spreads in *Vanity Fair*, the glamorous fashion sessions in Ibiza, seen in Capri with Tom Cruise, seen in Cannes with Lauren Hutton. "Lujac," he said, in a hushed tone. Kiki Lujac, the globe-trotting, jet-setting nephew of a Montenegrin *Duke*. Kiki Lujac, the world-famous shooter.

GALAN LED MANDY through the dimly lit, polished wooden labyrinth of Florian's inner rooms, which smelled of cedar incense and wood polish and garlic, down a long, narrow, seventeenth-century hallway lined with Venetian-glass sconces. He stopped her a few feet short of a private booth, covered by a faded tapestry, turned to look at her in the flickering light of the candle sconces. When he spoke, his voice was low but contained an electric charge.

"Miss Pownall . . ."

"Mandy."

"Mandy . . . it is very important that you understand one thing."

"Yes?"

"Mr. Dalton has been wounded. He has recovered—he heals like a young dog—but he is not . . . invincible. He is damaged. By the blade, and also by the drug he was exposed to last month. The doctors feel his hallucinations may reoccur without warning. The drug has saturated his limbic system, they tell us. I have no idea what that means, but now he is . . . almost a Venetian himself. He has become close to an old Venetian family, the Vasaris, who have much influence here and in Tuscany. Also, and this is the part you must understand, he enjoys the protection—and remains effectively in the *custody*—of my chief, Major Brancati—"

Mandy began to speak, but Galan held her with a look.

"Major Brancati has objected to this meeting. But he left it to me to decide if you should see Mr. Dalton. So this meeting is happening. Major Brancati has no problem with you personally, and Mr. Dalton says you were a help to him in his last investigation for your agency. But you are connected in this to Mr. Crane, whom, after Milan, we do not now trust, and through Mr. Crane to Mr. Cather, your Director of Clandestine Operations in Langley, and Mr. Cather is well known to anyone in our business, right across Europe and into the east. His reputation is for subtle ruthlessness and for cruel intelligence. So, we—Major Brancati and I—wish to make this known to Mr. Cather—if you would be so kind, Mandy—and the thing to be known is that we—I speak of the Italian Intelligence arms—will resent *very* bitterly any harm that may come to Mr. Dalton as a result of our trusting you this evening. We will not hold you responsible, but Mr. Cather and Mr. Crane may take it as a certitude that in whatever ways that may be open to us in the future we will . . . reply . . . to such a perfidy in coin. In coin. Am I understood? Mandy?"

Standing in this dark hallway and staring into Galan's small black eyes, Mandy had no trouble at all in understanding and believing everything that Issadore Galan was saying to her.

"You are quite crystalline, Issadore. Now, may I see Micah?"

Galan led them a little farther down the hallway, stopped, and pressed a mother-of-pearl button hidden by a fold of the tapestry. On the other side of the tapestry, he heard a muffled voice. He pulled back the curtain.

Dalton was sitting at a low, round marquetry table, with his back to a banquette padded in golden silk shantung, lit from above by a dark-red-shaded lamp that cast an amber glow on the tabletop, on the silver tray that held a bottle of Bollinger and two tall flutes, on the Murano-glass bowl filled with figs and grapes, on the dull-blue Ruger that lay on its side next to the Murano bowl, on Dalton's skull-like, deeply shadowed face, his blond hair glimmering in the downlight and on the hostile glitter in his pale eyes as he looked up at Mandy Pownall with a killing face.

Dalton showed her his teeth, half rising. She stepped into the booth, dimly aware of Galan drawing the curtain behind her, conscious of Dalton's scent in the room—Toscano cigars and under that something like soap and citrus. *In this booth at Florian's,* she thought, *he looks like a Medici prince.* She held him, feeling the muscles under his white shirt, the bones under the muscles. He kissed her on the cheek and let her go.

She slid into the booth opposite him, placed her broad-brimmed hat on the seat beside her, keeping her eyes on his death mask of a face.

She was surprised to find she was a little afraid of him.

"Micah. I'm so happy to see you."

"Surprised and happy?"

"No. Just glad. You look . . . terrible."

"And you look lovely, as always."

"May I smoke? I mean, are you healthy enough to . . . ?"

"Only if you share."

She brought out her Cartier case, extracted a long turquoise cigarette, offered another to Dalton, and lit both with her heavy gold lighter. As she set it down, Dalton, now half hidden in a cloud of coiling smoke, reached out and picked it up. His hand looked like a leathery claw, the tendons standing out clearly and the muscles in his wrist writhing like snakes under the skin.

"Porter gave you this, didn't he?"

"Yes. In Corfu. Two years ago. It was his father's. How are you, Micah? Forgive me. You do look like hell. What kind of shape are you in?"

Dalton shrugged, set the lighter down.

"They picked nineteen pieces of Murano glass out of my guts. If the blade had nicked an artery, I'd be dead, and we wouldn't be having this drink together. Other than that, and the fact that I've still got untold quantities of assorted hallucinogens fizzing around in my blood, I'd have to say I'm . . . peachy."

"*Fucking* peachy?" she said, mimicking Porter Naumann's voice. "*Fucking* peachy" was one of his favorite expressions.

"Yeah. *Fucking* peachy."

"Have you . . . seen Porter lately?"

One of the side effects of his last mission had been a massive exposure to a high-potency mix of powdered datura and peyote. It had nearly killed him, and had kicked him into a series of vivid hallucinations, some of which included long and very complicated discussions with the ghost of Porter Naumann. Naumann's ghost had worn a pair of emerald green silk pajamas throughout several appearances in the days that followed.

Except on one occasion.

"The last time I saw him was in Carmel. The day Laura died. He was wearing a navy blue pin-striped suit. Other than being dead, he looked splendid."

He didn't tell her about seeing his ghost again, in a dream of Cortona, while he was lying bleeding on the steps of the Basilica in the piazza. Nor did he tell her that in the dream his old friend Porter Naumann had tried to talk him into dying.

"Porter always knew how to dress."

"Yes. Taught me everything I know."

Mandy smiled, put the turquoise cigarette to her red lips, inhaled, the tip of the cigarette flaring into a yellow cat's-eye in the half dark. The scent of tobacco—rich, dark, Turkish—filled the room, and the smoke drifted upward into the shadows, writhing gently. They sat together in silence, watching the smoke. After a time, Mandy spoke.

"It wasn't us, you know."

Dalton's face got rockier, his mouth hardening.

"I hear you telling me."

"That's why I'm here."

"I was wondering."

"Cather wants you to know that."

"Gosh. This eases my mind wonderfully. I was fretting so."

"Stallworth lied to you, Micah. I believe him. At the end, Stallworth was lying to you."

Jack Stallworth had been Dalton's boss, the head of the Cleaners Unit in Langley, a subgroup run under Clandestine Services, essentially a cadre of covert *fixers* whose brief had been to go wherever someone in the Agency had left a dangerous bloody mess and clean it up. Dalton and Stallworth had disagreed about a Clandestine operation called Orpheus. Their disagreement had ended Dalton's career and Stallworth's life.

"How do we know this?"

"Cather told me himself."

Dalton grinned, a sardonic rictus that chilled her.

"Well, that's a relief. Hugs all 'round, then?"

"I believe him."

"I'm sure he thinks you do. You're here."

"And not dead?"

"Not yet. Try going home after you've accomplished whatever it is you're here to accomplish."

"For God's sake, Micah, I'm the one who told you about Orpheus. If Cather had wanted you dead because you knew about Orpheus, why am I still alive?"

"Perhaps you reached an understanding?"

Mandy's face went white. She said nothing for a while, but her anger was making the air crackle.

"You're a mean-tempered, sanctimonious little prick."

"Little?"

"Fuck you."

"If you'd like. Let me move these dishes."

They glared at each other for a time. The ice around the Bollinger bottle cracked with a silvery tinkle. Dalton saw a motion in his left eye and turned, half expecting to see Naumann's ghost leaning back in the banquette, a cynical smile on his dead lips. But there was nothing there. Mandy reached for the Bollinger and refilled her flute, her eyes down and her nostrils flared over thin white lips.

"Crane said you'd be a prick. And Stennis Corso said you'd listen."

"So they're both right. I'm listening."

"Tony Crane has a problem. In Singapore. Cather wants you to fix it."

"Me?"

"You."

"And if I fix this problem in Singapore?"

"Cather says you can come in."

In spite of his cynicism, Dalton felt his heart rate jump.

"Back to Langley?"

Mandy looked down and away and then sharply back.

"No. Not right away. The story they told State about you and Stallworth, it would have to be undermined. And it couldn't come from us."

"Why?"

"Cather says the only way to rehabilitate you is to sink Stallworth's reputation. It could be represented then . . ."

"To the DI?"

"Yes. And to the Secretary. They'd be able to tell her that your collision with Jack was based on information you had about his financial dealings."

"Around Orpheus?"

"God no. Anything but."

"Okay. Say Cather manages to rehabilitate me by slanging a dead man. I'd be back in the Agency? Officially?"

"Yes."

"Reinstated? Record cleared? Pension? Benefits? The key to the pool room?"

"It's a serious offer, Micah. What else have you got?"

Dalton lifted his hands, made an inclusive gesture.

"I have Venice. The mad love of a dangerous woman."

Mandy waved that away like smoke.

"Bosh. Utter bosh. You? Permanent exile? A stateless man? Without meaningful work? You'd rot in two seasons. I know you too well. We think it was Branco Gospic who tried to kill you."

"Hardly a leap. File under *Stunningly Obvious.*"

"What do you plan to do about it?"

"Something massive."

"We could help. With that."

"How?"

"Logistics. Information. Travel assistance. People to help you."

"Ducky. Sounds like a travel ad. Why would Cather offer that?"

"Gratitude. Inducement. Motivation. He's pretty worried about this thing in Singapore. He thinks you're the ideal man to fix it."

Dalton lifted the flute, drank. Savored it. He set it down.

"Okay. Tell me what Cather wants."

"Do you remember a contract agent named Ray Fyke?"

Dalton laughed out loud.

"Fyke! That fucking lunatic? How could I forget him?"

"Tony Crane said you two had a history."

"Oh yes. We did. He tell you what it was?"

"The Horn? Then Kosovo? The Grand Hotel Pristina?"

Dalton went inward, seeing the Soviet-style hotel, the beefy, bullet-headed men with gold chains around their greasy necks, while, outside the hotel, the bloodstained rubble lay piled in the streets, and, in the middle distance, the endless, half-felt rumble of the heavy guns, the thudding chatter of a machine gun, the popcorn crackle of small arms, the dark shape of Ray Fyke a few yards ahead, down a sewage-stinking alley, staggering under the weight of a fat man's corpse, both of them drunk on slivovitz and giggling like loons, Fyke's snaggletoothed grin lighting up his black-bearded face, his shadow huge against a neon sign that read KOZY'S KRAZY KIT-KAT KLUB, Fyke reeking of sweat, blood, cheap brandy and cheaper cigars.

In November 2002, Ray Fyke had gone dark on what was supposed to be a routine trapline job—running a string of midlevel sources and trolling for workable HumInt somewhere in Southeast Asia. Fyke dropped off the grid, as if he had stepped off a bridge into the abyss, leaving behind a fog of ugly rumors and the reek of failure vaguely connected to his binge drinking and a subsequent Clandestine Ops cluster fuck, the exact nature of which was never openly discussed at Dalton's pay-grade level.

Dalton had never seen him again.

"IBIS. Fyke was IBIS," he said, more to himself than to Mandy.

"And you were SHRIKE. Tony says they called you *the Birdmen*."

"Ray Fyke's dead. Or he's gone so native we'll never find him."

"Apparently not. Someone answering his description is sitting in Cluster C at the Changi Prison right now."

"Jesus. Poor bastard. Who's got him?"

"The SID."

"Holy Christ. Then he'll never get out. Even if he does, he'll be . . ."

"Ruined?"

"Yes. Ruined. Worse than dead. What is he accused of?"

"As a pretext, the Home Ministry has him on dereliction of duty. He was first mate of a gypsy tanker called the *Mingo Dubai*."

"Was?"

"It was reported sunk. In a storm. Off the Kepulauan Lingga lighthouse. Eastern outlet of the Strait of Malacca."

"How'd Ray Fyke get blamed for the sinking?"

"Probably because he was the only survivor. Singapore thinks the ship was steered into a rogue wave in the middle of a nasty storm. Broke in two and sank with all hands. It's happened to tankers before."

"All hands except Fyke."

"Except Fyke. They fished him out of the South China Sea. He was drunk as a lord, and laid it all on pirates."

"Pirates? Sounds just like him. Did he have any proof?"

"Not a jot. They put a chopper over the site and found a massive, caustic spill and lots of bodies. Wearing life jackets. Debris all over."

"What about the EPIRB beacon? It's water-activated."

"Never came on. Considering the state of the ship, it was probably out of whack, anyway. Fyke claimed they were overrun by a crew of Dyaks and Malays, who assaulted from a speedboat. Said they were helped by some of the crew members."

"He say who?"

"The SID's not releasing anything at all about his interrogation. One of our stringers in Singapore managed to reach the pilot of the chopper that pulled him out of the water. The guy remembered Fyke raving on about somebody named Magic."

"What, like Magic Johnson?"

"Who's he?"

"Did you run it against the crew manifest?"

That brought a wry smile to Mandy's face.

"Crew list? Micah, this boat didn't have a working EPIRB beacon, and the only lifeboat they found was shot full of bullet holes."

"Machine gun?"

"No. They pulled it out and found a bunch of .303 slugs from an old Lee-Enfield rifle. They figure somebody on the crew was using it for target practice. At any rate, there was no manifest."

"How'd they ID Fyke?"

"He still had his implant. Singapore ran him through a scanner and the casing showed up."

"His trace tag? Why the hell would he keep that? I had mine taken out after the Horn. It was too much a telltale. Not worth the risk."

"Tony says they tried to use it to locate Fyke back in 2002, but the signal was too weak for a fix."

"And the SID removed it? How'd they know it was one of ours?"

"We've been sharing low-level hardware with them for over a year now. Remember? The Minister Mentor's New Partnership Against Terror?"

"And how'd *we* find out about all this? Like, how'd Langley come up with the serial number on a tag that is currently in the hands of the SID?"

Mandy gave that some thought.

"That's a hard one. Cather never told me."

"We'd have to have somebody inside the Home Ministry."

"I have no idea. Does it matter? They've got him and we want him."

"I'd like to know how we got wind of the serial number. That's an important bit of data. We need to know how Langley got it."

"I'll ask."

"If they won't tell you, or they shine you on, I want to know."

"Know *why?*"

"No. Just *if.* Just tell me if Langley won't reveal the source of that tag info. If they won't, it means they're protecting somebody close to the SID."

"If they've got somebody inside the SID . . . why this mission?"

"Good question, Mandy. Very good question. In fact, it's *the* question. So make sure to ask. Jesus, you know, Fyke, all this, it's self-inflicted bullshit. Ray went dark. He knows about going dark. He should have had it removed. If I recall, didn't we put out a DSDNI order with a lot of our allied agencies? That would have included the Singaporean Intelligence guys. Protocol would have been to simply give us back our guy. I know those orders get ignored all the time. But why didn't we insist?"

"Maybe Cather doesn't want the SID to know we care that much. The official Agency position is, who the hell is Ray Fyke?"

"Stupid, stupid, stupid. Fyke should have had that thing removed."

"Well, it's stuck pretty deep into his back."

"He never took that stuff seriously enough. The mook."

"You liked him?"

"Yes. Yes I did. He was a good fieldman. For a Brit. The SID knows he's a spook, then?"

"That's right."

"Jesus. Those guys will take him apart just for chuckles."

"That's what Cather thinks."

"Why does he want me to help?"

"He told Tony that since IBIS is one of ours, it's a London Station problem, and you were London Station too."

"And Fyke was a friend of mine . . ."

"That was a consideration."

"What does he want? Specifically?"

"You're a Cleaner, aren't you? Cather wants the problem *cleaned*."

Dalton was silent. The sound of the Florian's string quartet, playing its first set of the evening, drifted back from the piazza outside, something lilting and regal by Offenbach. *Tales of Hoffmann*. The candles guttered in a random breeze and golden smoke swirled upward into the dark.

"Why? Ray Fyke's been dark for years. Whatever he knew back when he was operational, it's of no tactical or strategic use to anyone now."

"Tony told Cather that you'd ask that. Cather said to tell you that he can personally confirm that Fyke has indirect knowledge of an Intelligence asset that is of ongoing strategic importance to national security and that to have this asset compromised would be very damaging."

"To whom?"

"Tony didn't ask, of course. You know the drill."

"I see. Not very persuasive, is it?"

"I guess everybody feels that you have no choice. And you've done this kind of thing before, haven't you?"

"If you're talking about Calixto Obregon, he was in Matamoros. That was a Mexican prison, full of terminally stupid American dopers and drunken guards addicted to *La Mordida*. Fyke's in Changi Prison. In Singapore. They don't take bribes in Singapore. There's no way in hell anyone can get to him there. Not if the SID is holding him. It can't be done. It's an operational impossibility, even for one of our best extraction teams. And they're not going to let *any* American in to see him. The only way to—"

"Cather knows that. He has a solution."

That stopped him.

"And the solution is . . . ?"

Mandy lifted her hands, made an inclusive gesture that took in the room and somehow invoked most of Venice as well.

Not here.

"Fine. I'm going to be taking that on faith, am I?"

"Cather wants you to commit before we tell you. The thing is, he needs you to get Fyke out *alive*. Talking and walking."

"Which means Cather wants to know if Fyke got dismantled enough to have him compromise this mysterious *ongoing asset?*"

"Yes. He'd have to be debriefed. In person."

"Setting aside the complete impossibility of extracting Fyke from Cluster C . . . unless Cather has something deeply brilliant in mind—"

"He does."

"Even so, Fyke's not going to be debriefed by *us*. Unless Cather's going to let us know what he's trying to protect. Fyke would have to be handed over to an Agency team that knew precisely what it was looking for."

"Yes. Exactly."

"Hell, Fyke may not even *know* what he knows. It could be anything—some insignificant event that Fyke had a glancing connection to. The SID could put him feetfirst into a wood chipper and he wouldn't know why until he screamed it out at the very end. Poor bastard. This is as ugly as it gets."

"Yes. Nasty."

"Very."

"So, if this mission goes south . . . ?"

"Three muted cheers in the bubble, coffee and doughnuts all around, and another nameless star goes up on the Wall. What if the SID develops an interest in *me*, Mandy? I know all about Orpheus. The SID could get it out of me if they had enough time. Why would Cather risk that?"

"An excellent question. My guess is that whatever Fyke knows is at the very least of equal importance—"

"I fail and they have us both. Fyke *and* me."

"You're to have a microsurette."

"Not a chance. One wrong move with those inserts and you're a three-line obit on page sixty-two of *The Sentinel*. Anyway, if the SID took me in, they'd scan me just like they scanned Fyke. They'd see it."

"One would assume that by then you'd have activated it, and the point would be rather moot."

"All this just to get Ray Fyke out of Changi so the Meat Hookers can gut and flay him themselves. To protect an *ongoing asset* somewhere?"

"That's what our business is, Micah. So. Will you do it?"

Dalton considered her red lips and snow-white neck while he worked out the odds. Mandy, waiting, knew what he was thinking. He had few other options, and most of them would likely either ruin him slowly or kill him outright. Dalton lifted his glass to Mandy, who raised hers and waited.

"Fine. I'm in. *Morituri.*"

"*Te salutas,*" she replied, finishing an old joke, and they both drank. Mandy put her glass down, stood up. Dalton rose with her.

"How am I traveling?"

"I have papers in my room. Everything we'll need."

"*We?*"

"I'm going with you."

"To Singapore? Like hell you are. And I don't need a minder."

"Yes you do, actually. Anyway, that's the deal."

"You knew I'd say yes, didn't you?"

"We hoped."

"Who's in charge of this op, then?"

"Why, Micah. Darling. Of *course* you'll be in charge."

"Yeah. I see that."

"Knew you would. You're a dear boy."

"If we're going to go flying off the grid into darkest Southeast Asia, we'll need buckets of hard cash."

"We'll have it. Whatever we need."

"Where are you staying?"

"I have rooms at La Giostra. We can go there now?"

An invitation?

Dalton shook his head.

"No. In the morning."

Mandy gave him a meaningful look.

"Are you still in Porter's suite?"

"Yes."

"I see," she said, with an uneven smile that did not light her eyes.

The buzzer at the entrance to the suite chirped twice.

"Yes?" said Dalton, giving Mandy a warning look.

"It's me. Alessio."

Dalton set the Ruger down as Brancati pulled the tapestry back, filling the entrance with navy blue and gleaming black leather, his seamed face set and stony. He nodded to Mandy Pownall.

"Please excuse me, Signorina Pownall."

Mandy, who had seen surveillance pictures of Brancati but had never seen the man in the flesh—especially not in the striking uniform of a major in the Carabinieri—had a look of frankly sexual delight on her face. She did not exactly *sparkle* at him, but Brancati's face colored just a little and he gave her a brief, predatory once-over before turning back to Dalton, who was now on his feet and wary.

"You need to come," said Brancati. "I have a boat waiting."

"Where?"

"The Lido beach. Near the *ospedale*."

"Now?"

"Now," said Brancati.

8

Cluster C,
Changi Prison Complex,
Singapore

Fyke had been here—wherever *here* was—for either the last four weeks or since the Rape of Nanking, during which time he'd been beaten so often—they wore padded leather gloves and cheerfully delivered short, sharp, lead-weighted rap-and-slaps, as if his head were a speed bag—beaten so vigorously that he felt he was now sufficiently stunned to sit in the House of Lords. They had been careful in only one regard. They never damaged the incision in his back, where the SID doctors had removed his tag. Decent of them, really. Oddly, his beaters had asked no questions at all, had not even spoken to each other, as if he had just been one of the Nautilus machines. Anyway, all that had stopped a while ago, he was reasonably sure.

Or not.

Time was a relative concept, as either Einstein's or Fyke's very first hooker had once pointed out. Lately, his keepers—three SID knuckle-dragging goons he called *Big Dink, Little Dink,* and *No Dink*—had taken to running the light-and-dark-and-cold thing—keeping the lights on for hours, then turning them off for hours, or days, or ten minutes, there was no way to tell, since he was naked and therefore watchless—by the way, it had been a *lovely* watch, too, an original thirties-era Hamilton that had belonged to a Marine Recon vet he had worked with in Mogadishu—the Skinnies had gotten at him while he was still alive, but Fyke had dropped in on them like the Hammer of God. Killing all the Skinnies hadn't saved the Recon vet, but he did save the Hamilton—it was still on the guy's wrist, although the guy's wrist was some distance from what may have been the rest of him—well, anyway, the Recon vet was longtime dead, and Fyke figured they'd be reunited soon—he found himself humming a bar or two from "Memories" and clapped a stopper over that as soon as he realized it. Perhaps he was completely losing it. For a while now, Fyke had taken to sitting in a corner of the stark, staring, chill-to-the-bone white cell and watching the big, thick door—padded, so he couldn't hurt himself, as was the whole room—watching the door the way a caged cat will watch the door: coiled, ready.

Ready?

Not exactly.

If he tried to stand, he'd fall over sideways. He couldn't go two rounds with Elton John. He scrubbed at his naked arms with the padded cotton mittens—thumbless—that they had strapped on him after he'd tried to pluck out his carotid—an old SID trick to frustrate prisoners who wanted to arrange their own exits; actually, he'd tried it only to freak out Big Dink and get him to say something. On the other hand, regarding the whole carotid-plucking-out thing, and not-withstanding the fact that his old Escape and Evasion teacher at Hereford, a dipsomaniacal Ulsterman named McAvity, hotly contended that he had actually seen it done, Fyke's heart wasn't really in it. Not quite yet, anyway.

He'd check in again on the idea in a few weeks, if he was still alive. At any rate, for all of the above reasons, Ray Fyke was finding his mental clarity harder to locate than Michael Moore's neck.

When he was more lucid—after the last beating?—pain concentrated the mind wonderfully, but not for very long—he had tried to figure out why the SID was interested in him at all. Yes, he had once been SAS, and, yes, he had once been seconded to the Americans at London Station and had got up to all sorts of sticky work with those dashing boyos—he flashed briefly on Kosovo and a hard-faced, pale-eyed Special Forces spook he'd nicknamed the Crocodile because of the snaky way he could slither up on a sentry . . .

Dalton.

Micah Dalton . . . that was his name.

Known as SHRIKE to London Station, one of the famous Birdmen. Actually, Mikey had been a pretty good fieldman, for an American. He'd met him in the Horn and worked on a couple of tricksy ops in Pakistan and then later in Kosovo . . . A very good man—could drink you into a coma, too, which was saying something, coming from an SAS man—and there had been others, other ops and other jolly good toffs to work with . . .

Of course, all of that was *before* . . .

Before his *last* mission . . . before it all went to rat shit in one cataclysmic, self-inflicted cluster fuck. Don't go there, Raymond, old lad. Don't ever go there . . . God, he could use a drink . . . But, for the life of him, he could not get a grip on *anything* that he would have that the SID might be interested in. He hadn't been in the field since . . . *before*.

On the other hand, in the good-news column, he still had most of his teeth, and he still retained the field-issue kit of fully operational male genitalia, which the SID was famous for ripping out right after your Intake because it amused the hell out of them and demoralized the hell out of you, sitting there . . . Cold. Naked. Toothless.

He tried to say "testicleless" out loud, but it was just too damn hard. Anyway, as you can imagine, it was all very depressing. And it all meant . . . *nothing*. Just bloody bad luck. Should have had the Agency tag taken out after he went dark. Never got around to it. And, anyway, the battery had died the year . . . *before*.

He figured that the SID was just rooting around inside his brain on the off chance that they'd come across something intriguing. Just fishing, really. Putting a mixed bag of Intel into their computers—raw data—and then seeing if anything related to other data, cross-checking files and names, that would explain the disorganized and routine nature of his interrogation.

If the SID had reason to believe he was in possession of something truly spectacular, they'd have a team of truly gifted sadists working on him night and day. This felt more like a training mission that Big Dink was running for the edification of Little Dink and No Dink: *Yon Captive Brit: How to Deconstruct.*

Well, anyway, whatever it was they were up to, he was going to die here—he'd heard enough about the SID from everyone in the business—so the idea was to hold up his end and not let these *fucking* Asiatics see a Noble Briton crawl. So, as he was saying, he crouched there naked in the corner and watched the door like a feral cat. And while he watched it, he drifted off a little—the mind becomes a wanderer when the body is in a box—and, this time, it wandered farther away than the walls of . . .

Changi Prison.

Cluster C in Changi Prison. *That's* where he was.

Crikey.

Changi Prison. Three-time nominee for Worst Festering Rathole in This Spiral Arm, by the Venusian Academy of Darts and Fetters. Oh my. Better to close your eyes for just a second and think of your mummy.

So he did. His eyes grew heavy, and he began to slide.

Sleep came in on little cat's feet; his eyes grew heavy . . .

. . . And then he *soared*.

Like an albatross, he soared, high above the concrete bunkers of Changi Prison—high above Cluster C, sailing over the forty-foot-high walls and the motion-sensing cameras and the heat sensors and, of course, the lovely chain-gun towers—soaring higher and higher, leaving Changi Prison far beneath, high enough now to see the airport by the water, then, higher still, the pancake-flat island of Singapore receding wonderfully, and he could see north all the way to Kuala Lumpur and south to the Malacca Strait, and higher, ever higher, until he could look to his left as he flew northward over Kuala Lumpur . . . he could just see Madagascar far across the Indian Ocean . . . and, in the north, at the farthest edge of the horizon, a strip of white sand edged by palms . . . the beaches of Phuket . . . and, beyond those crescent shores, the reptile green, softly mounded domes of the Central Highlands of Viet—

The door slammed open, and they were on him again: Big Dink—a flat-faced, pock-skinned, jaundiced-looking, bald-headed, foul-breathed sweathog in too-tight prison blues—along with his two reptilian sidekicks, a tall, effeminate coffee-colored Hindu—No Dink—and the compact, flexible little rat boy who looked a bit like a Gurkha—Little Dink. Fyke was jolted earthward, as they pinned his writhing body to the greasy padding of the floor. He felt a knee on the back of his neck and his arms being wrenched out of their sockets, as they held him fast . . . and then a sharp, piercing pain in his back. Then . . . *warmth* . . . a river of warm, rushing bliss that began in his skull and rushed down his neck and spread out like the Thames into the broad deltas of his chest and belly and thighs . . . apparently, the light and cold and sensory-deprivation part of the softening process had come to an end and now the SID had taken things to Level 2. His last thought, as the tide of warmth and calm rose up over his head and covered him in blessed sleep, was that a real cat would have been watching the door.

9

The Lido Beach,
Venice

The Carabinieri pursuit boat was shell gray over matte black; long, lean, and fast, with a deep V hull that sliced through the choppy crosscurrents of the lagoon with a hissing snarl. Inside the low-ceilinged cabin, his grim face uplit by red-glowing dials and a small halogen lamp near the pilot chair, Brancati stared silently out at the black night as a beaded necklace of red-and-green lights in the distance grew closer—the gap of San Niccolò by the airport, and, beyond that, the broad Adriatic Sea, roaring and restless in a rising wind, white shark's teeth curling on the tips of long, unsteady rollers. Weather was coming in, a growing bank of green clouds on the radar display. Dalton eyed it from time to time, the way a man might watch the slow progression of a snake across a marble floor, but he said nothing to break the silence in the ship.

Brancati was smoking one of his Toscanos with a closed and brooding expression, his thoughts turned inward, wondering what he was going to do about Dario DioGrazzi, the twenty-four-year-old

Carabinieri clerk they were holding in the Lazaretto right now. As hard as it was for Brancati to accept, Galan's proof was undeniable—a clear videotape of DioGrazzi sitting in a chair at the Café Electro last night, sending the digital shot of Dalton off to an IP address in Montenegro operated by a known associate of Stefan Groz. Dio-Grazzi was being questioned right now by one of their midlevel security people—so far, quite gently—in the early stages of an attempt to uncover how much had been betrayed and for how long.

Why was a matter for later.

The difficulty for Brancati—aside from his murderous anger at the fact of the betrayal—was that young Dario was a distant cousin of his wife's family and had been recruited and trained under Brancati's wing. It was a cold comfort to Brancati that Issadore Galan had not suspected the boy either. Galan had been following another faint scent, looking in another direction entirely, so the exposure of this lad had come as a shock to both of them, if for very different reasons.

Still, what to do with him now was a troubling matter, since the penalty for selling state secrets to a foreign entity was twenty very hard years. So, Brancati was radiating suppressed rage, and the young carabiniere at the wheel was glancing at him from time to time with wary apprehension.

Dalton stood behind Brancati, bracing himself on the chairback, staring out through the windshield at the lights of the Lido streaming past on their starboard rails, his mind as far from here as Brancati's, playing on the immense frying pan full of steaming heat and bustling crowds that was the island of Singapore, and on the northeast part of the city in particular, on the square mile of white concrete bunkers that was Changi Prison.

This uncomfortable silence, heavy with meanings not fully understood, oppressed all three men, carried each across the dark water in a tightly sealed carapace, each man alone in his thoughts. In a few minutes, they had reached and rounded the Lido gap by the airport. The Adriatic took them into its vast, booming dark, and the shop-worn Lido beaches unwound along their starboard side like a string of dirty pearls, half lit in hard, mercury lights, glowing a greasy blue in the dampness, each light surrounded by a distinct halo. Drops of rain began to spatter the windshield and the young captain, glancing nervously at Brancati, finally spoke, in Italian, his voice tight and his lips thinned by stress.

"Sir, Major Brancati, sir—you did not say which beach."

Brancati, looking back at Dalton with a startled air, as if he had forgotten he was there, faced out to sea again and answered the boy in English, a brooding, baritone growl, almost too low to hear over the muted burbling of the boat's Maserati engines.

"Have you no eyes, Rafael? You see the lights! The *bagni comunale,* by the Ospedale al Mare," he said, gesturing toward a low cluster of buildings a hundred yards up an arc of gray sand lit by a string of cold-blue beach lights. In the middle of the narrow crescent of sand, close to the waterline, they could see a flare of brighter lights, hard and yellow, and two police boats, bobbing in the shallow surf, blue lights slowly churning. The pilot brought the boat in through the chop, slowing as the gravel shoals of the long bay rose up under the keel. The tone of the engines dropped, and the stern rose up as their wake caught up with them. The boat surfed the last few hundred feet until the keel scraped on the beach, where it settled and steadied, the waves curling around the hull.

Two men—black figures silhouetted against the lights of the beach—strode out into the shallows and took the prow in hand. Brancati looked at Dalton, gave him a weary smile, and both men climbed out and stepped off the bow and onto the coarse, sandy beach. The air was dank, smelling of dead fish and rotting seaweed. Twenty feet down, the men, gathered around a brightly lit tent on the beach, watched in silence as Brancati and Dalton slogged their way through the sand. Issadore Galan—short, bent, moving un-steadily—detached himself from the group, shuffling through the shale, dragging his left foot slightly.

They met him at the edge of the light cast by portable lamps po-sitioned around the tent, which was actually more of a standing nylon wall pinned to the sand with aluminum rods. Three young men in Carabinieri uniforms and one old man in a yellow slicker stood in silence, watching them. Seven hundred yards out in the Adriatic, Kiki Lujac sat at the wheel of the darkened *Subito,* his attention fixed on the shoreline. The *Subito* was riding on two heavy Danforths, her lines straining against the wind; Lujac had a long Steadicam lens that was trained on the men on the beach. Music was playing softly on the ship's sound system—Pink Martini—and a heavy crystal glass full of Oban sat in a gimballed tray at his left hand. The ship rose and fell on the waves like a dreamer breathing in deep sleep. Kiki watched the men from out of the great darkness of the Adriatic Sea and felt the light-headedness, the short, rapid beating, the rush of blood in his throat, the erotic charge that he always felt when he watched people from a long distance.

Kiki Lujac liked to watch, and this evening he was watching Micah Dalton, had the lens fixed on his hard cheek as he stood in a little group of men, his pale eyes fixed on the face of Issadore Galan. Lujac felt close enough to reach out and run his fingertips gently along the man's jawline. He was truly a beautiful thing, with the kind of natu-ral physical grace you would see in a racehorse or a cliff diver. Lujac hoped he would have a chance to photograph him before he died. And then after. Perhaps even during. That would be a show to start the critics talking. The idea warmed his lower belly, and he ran off a series of telephoto shots just to keep the charge running. Without taking his eye away from the viewfinder, Lujac reached out and turned up the gain on a radio receiver.

The hissing sound of beach curl came from the speakers and filled the cabin of the *Subito,* along with the mutter of idling police boats, and, under that, the muted murmur of men's voices and the droning hum of the portable generator powering the police lights. Lujac turned a dial on the radio set beside him, and the white noise diminished enough for him to make out the voices of the three men standing apart, down at the water's edge. Early in the day, Gospic's man in the Carabinieri had placed a remote-controlled directional mike in the palm line not far from the place Lujac had chosen. Now Lujac watched and listened.

"SHE HAS NOT been in the water long," Galan was saying. "One of the gardeners found her here, a few feet from the water. The gulls have been at her, but not too much."

"Which way is the current going?" asked Brancati. Galan made a gesture, indicating the rolling surf, the dark sea beyond, his black eyes sliding across but not seeing the low black mass far out on the water.

"Out now, more or less. It runs slantwise to the Lido at this time of year, and makes no more than three or four knots at best."

"So she was brought here by the currents?"

Galan shook his head but not with conviction.

"We cannot say. If she went into the water up there"—he indicated the gap of San Niccolò airport—"then she might have been caught up in the flow and brought down the shoreline until she reached the shallows. Then the wave action might have brought her ashore. There is no way to be sure. The tides here are affected by the shallows, by the shoals, so there is no clear stream to judge by."

"And what do you think?" asked Brancati, gently.

"I think we cannot know. It is only a feeling. The current is running out. But she should have been drawn out with the rush and she was not. The season is over, but there are always a few people walking the beach. If she had been here in the afternoon, they would have seen her. Yet here she lies. But there is always ambiguity in this kind of a finding."

"Was she killed here?"

"No. She has no blood in her body at all. If she had been killed here, the sand would be thick with it."

While Brancati considered this, Galan shifted his attention to Dalton.

"Good evening, Micah," he said.

"Issadore."

Galan looked back at the officials standing around the crime scene tent, judging the distance. Then he turned back to Dalton, speaking softly.

"Did you enjoy your talk with Signorina Pownall?"

"I did. Thank you for arranging it."

"Have you reached a decision?"

Brancati was now looking at him as well, his face in shadow. Dalton had assumed that the private room at Florian's had been bugged for the purpose, and the manner of these two confirmed it. They had heard the entire conversation. Dalton had no objection. These men were not his enemies.

"Yes. I'll go. If Brancati here will let me."

Brancati made a noise but said nothing. Galan kept his eyes on Dalton. "And she will go with you? Signorina Pownall?"

"Yes."

Brancati sighed again and looked out to sea. He could not let it go and finally rounded on Dalton, his baritone purr now more of a growl.

"You put yourself in their hands, my friend."

"You said I should try to *come in from the cold,* Alessio."

"Hah! A silly novel. What do I know? And what about Miss Vasari?"

"You've made it plain she's safer without me. I agree."

"She did not go to Firenze, Micah. She stays here for you. To be with you for a time. So you have a responsibility. To her. She will not . . . sever this bond with you. Whatever it is. Whatever the risk. She made this clear to me while you were meeting with Miss Pownall. I argued. I threatened—"

"Cora? That must have been interesting."

Brancati bared his teeth, a flash of white in the dark.

"Yes. She does not threaten well."

"That has been my experience."

Another long silence, with the rising wind stirring the palms in a dry rustle and the sand hissing at their feet. A bat flittered around their heads and was suddenly gone. When Dalton spoke again, his tone was heavy.

"So. I *have* to go to Singapore, then. If we're ever going to have any kind of a life together, I have to go."

Brancati put a hand on Dalton's shoulder.

"Why, Micah? Stay here, in Venice. I would find good work for you, important work. You could be a help to Italy. We have enemies too."

"And Gospic? Will he leave us alone?"

Lujac's belly muscles tightened a bit, as he sat at the long lens. He reached out and touched a button marked RICORDA.

"How will your mission to Singapore protect Cora from Branco Gospic?" asked Brancati, and, in the shadows, Dalton could see Galan's head nodding in assent.

"If I succeed, Cather will help me with Gospic."

"Hah! *We* can protect you from Gospic. Better than your CIA. You don't need Cather."

"No? Will *you* send a man to kill Gospic, then, Alessio?"

Galan's harsh croak came out of the shadow.

"Signores. This is not the place. And the Carabinieri are not assassins."

"No," said Dalton. "But I am."

Dalton held Brancati's look. Brancati moved his head in the dark, his hands rising up, a yellow flame sparking as he held the lighter to a cigar. The tip glowed red. A sea wind shredded the smoke and tore it inland into the palm line by the shuttered *ospedale*. There was nothing else to be said. Galan looked at Dalton for a time, his black eyes still, and then he sighed.

"Well, I suppose we must ask you to look, Micah."

Brancati offered Dalton a cigar, which Dalton took, lighting it with difficulty—the wind was turning into a light gale, and little whirlwinds of dusty sand were skittering in the sidelong light from the arc lamps. Beyond the shoals, the Adriatic churned and tossed, and little flickers of pale light danced across the foaming chop. The sky was black, starless, filled with invisible motion, as the clouds rolled in from Montenegro. Brancati and Dalton pulled their collars up as they reached the little tent. The three guards stepped aside, pulling the old man in the yellow slicker away with them.

They stepped into the hard, yellow light and looked down in silence at the dead woman sprawled on her belly in the sand. She was naked, young, her short blond hair, which had dried in the sea wind, fluttered around her face like cold, white flames. Her head was turned to the left, and her eyes were open, opaque, staring, her blue lips half open. She wore an expression of mild surprise, as if her death had come naturally to her, like an ending she had long foreseen. Her skin was pale blue and veined with purple. She looked as if she might have been carved from marble. Galan stepped delicately into the crime scene and crouched beside her head, pulling on a pair of latex gloves. He reached out and took her jaw, lifting her head so Dalton could see her face clearly.

"Is it her?" he asked, not looking at Dalton.

Dalton bent down to consider her, looking at the thin blue lips, the slightly Slavic cast to her features. He had a flash of red lips twisted in a curse as he stood against the pillared rail near the Bridge of Sighs.

"Yes. It's her."

"You're sure," said Brancati, standing a bit apart. He had three daughters, all young and pretty, as this young girl had been not so long ago.

"I am," said Dalton. "She's the one."

Galan, grunting, pointed to her wrists, where two rings of raw, abraded skin showed around them.

"She was bound, here, with some sort of thin line. We will look for fibers, but with the action of the water . . ." Here, he shrugged. "You see the striations here?" He indicated what looked like stretch marks in the skin, running upward along her forearms. "They make me think she was dragged in the water—through the water—perhaps behind a boat. The bruising meant that she was probably alive, if not conscious, when she went into the water."

"If she drowned," put in Brancati, "what happened to her blood?"

Galan sighed and looked into the dark where the guards waited.

"Carlo, come here. Turn her over."

One of the Carabinieri soldiers came into the light, a fixed expression of mild disgust on his young face, slipping on a pair of surgical gloves. He knelt down and gently lifted the girl. She was as limp as seaweed, as if all of her bones had been crushed. The boy rolled her onto her back and placed her arms by her sides, as if preparing her for a bath. She had been opened from her navel to just above her pubic bone. The wound gaped wide, and loops of yellow-and-blue intestine, coated with beach sand, slid wetly from the cut.

"She had been cut—like this—before she went into the water. She could have lived for quite a while. Many do, even with such a wound."

Dalton, looking down at the ruin of her body, had a vision of Porter Naumann's body—belly opened like this—leaning against the heavy wooden doors of an old Roman church in Cortona. He looked away and saw Naumann's ghost, standing in the outer darkness, a shadow against the line of stunted palms, his hands at his sides, wearing a long blue overcoat, his collar turned up against the wind off the sea, his white face staring back at Dalton, his pale eyes bright with pinpricks of reflected light.

Naumann showed his teeth in a cold, dry smile, lifted a hand, making a broad, sweeping gesture that took in the beach and the police and the ruined woman in the sand at Dalton's feet. His words to Dalton—in Dalton's dream of Cortona, as he lay bleeding from this girl's knife on the steps of the Basilica—came to him as a dry whisper, in his skull:

Grief is coming, Micah. More than you know.

Galan, with difficulty, got to his feet, indicating with a gesture that the young officer should cover the woman with a sheet. The cloth, rippling in the growing onshore wind, had to be held down with beach stones. After they were in place, Dalton thought she looked like a moth pinned to a card. Brancati drew on the last of his cigar and threw the butt away. It arced into the night, a tiny fireball trailing red sparks.

"So, Gospic killed her," he said, watching the butt smolder.

"For failing?" said Dalton.

"And as an example. *'Pour encourager les autres.'* "

"So, he'll send someone else."

"This killing would suggest he already has."

The three men looked at the dead woman on the beach for a time.

"Issadore, I have a question," said Dalton. "Why here?"

Galan shrugged, looking around.

"Why anywhere? The sea does not explain itself."

"Do you think there's any chance she was *deliberately* placed here?"

Galan fell silent. Dalton, who knew his man, waited.

"Of course. Anything can be proposed. It is not impossible. But what would be the advantage?"

"Yes. Why here?" asked Brancati, this time into the wind itself.

Dalton turned slowly, scanning the beach, the palms, and then looking out to sea, into the black vault full of rushing wind and roiling water. Seven hundred yards out to sea, Lujac, watching closely, saw the expression on Dalton's face, the directed intensity of his glare as he searched the darkness beyond the beach lights. Lujac felt the look like the heat from a flame.

Within thirty seconds, he had slipped his cables—leaving the anchors rooted to the seabed—and the *Subito* was heading slowly out into the oncoming swells, making just enough speed to keep a headway against the storm. The *Subito* was almost a thousand yards out when a thin lance of hard-white light stabbed out into the darkness, raking the ocean from horizon to horizon, moving in jerks and fits, cutting crazily back and forth across the water, a tube of glowing pale fire shot through with hard, clear crystals of driving rain. The beam glanced across the stern of the *Subito*—the man behind the searchlight caught a flash of bright gold as the light reflected from the brass letters on her stern—the beam flashed by and on into the empty dark—then back with a jerk, as if hunting for that flash of gold.

But there was nothing there. Only the black eternity of the sea and the storm racing inland across the water.

"What about the radar?" asked Brancati, seated beside Rafael, the cutter's pilot. Rafael indicated the screen, the broad front of storm cloud.

"There are returns, as you can see," he said, indicating a number of small red blips, uneven and faint. "But some are buoys, and this one is a fishing boat called the *Sospiri,* and we have already talked to the captain. These others, they may be boats, or just a flock of birds. This storm is making it very hard to read the returns. Do you want to put a chopper up? Or we can go look for ourselves."

Brancati considered the radar screen, watching the storm mass swelling, thinking it through.

"No. I don't want to lose a chopper—or a patrol boat—in that mess."

"There was that flash of gold."

"I know."

"Maybe a fish leaping?"

Brancati stared out into the darkness and said nothing. He felt Dalton at his back and turned to look at him.

"What do you think, Micah?"

Dalton closed his eyes for a moment, as a wave of fatigue moved over him. His wound was throbbing, and his pulse was too rapid.

"I think I need some sleep," he said, smiling thinly. Brancati studied his gaunt face in the dim red light of the ship cabin and then spoke softly to Rafael in Italian. The patrol boat dropped him off at the Quay of Slavs thirty minutes later. He came into the lobby of the Hotel Savoia and was met by two young Carabinieri guards, who had been playing chess on one of the low wooden tables in the lobby. They rose as he came in through the cut-glass doors, straightening their tunics and blinking with fatigue. It was two in the morning. The small hotel was filled with silence and shadows. Dalton nodded to the two men, who saluted him in return, and then he went on through to the elevator and pressed the number 5.

Cora was in the suite, wearing a cream satin slip, sitting in one of the gilt chairs and smoking a turquoise Balkan Sobranie Cocktail, her long black hair undone, her legs crossed, her bare feet in tiny satin shoes. An unopened bottle of Bollinger stood in an ice-filled silver chalice on the floor beside her long, bare legs. The room smelled of smoke and her rich spicy scent, Eau de Sud, by Annick Goutal. There was music drifting in the background, the Duet from *Lakmé*. Her perfume filled his mind. She had been wearing that scent when he first met her, on the darkened stairwell of her little villa in the Dorsoduro. It had stayed with him ever since, always present, always a goad, desire without any hope. She rose as he came into the room and crossed to meet him. He opened his mouth to speak, but she put her fingertip on his upper lip and shook her head slowly, her hazel eyes wide and her full lips soft, her breath moist and smoky and warm.

"Don't talk, Micah," she said, leaning into him. "Not yet."

10

Thai Airways International Airlines, Flight 919, inbound to Singapore

The 747 was thirty-six thousand feet above the South China Sea, chasing an opal moon through an indigo sky. The ocean far beneath the wing was a savannah of golden light. There was an island—Dalton had no idea which one—passing under the starboard wing; it looked like a black leaf veined in tiny yellow lights, floating on a pond. The first-class cabin was half empty, and the other five passengers—a Buddhist monk in saffron robes; a pair of Japanese businessmen, snoring, point and counterpoint, in their private booth; an attenuated Chinese woman of indeterminate age, with dead-white skin and an expression of general ill will, who tossed and twitched and muttered in her sleep; and a large pink man with a sculpted goatee and a wrinkled white linen suit—all of them gave every impression of travelers wrapped in oblivious sleep.

The Thai flight attendant, a chinabone girl in glimmering red-and-orange silks, was sitting stiffly at her post by the forward bulkhead, head down, long black hair falling around her face, reading a Manga novel by the light of a pencil-thin halogen. The darkened cabin was full of the faint music of orchestral strings that floated over the underlying roar of the airplane's jet engines and the shriek of the wind over its wings. The cabin rocked gently in mild turbulence, rising and falling. Beside him, in their isolated sleeping pair, Mandy Pownall lay back on the reclined daybed and stared out at the ocean below them, her pale hands crossed over her lap.

"Why don't you sleep?" said Dalton, in a low whisper.

She turned her face to him, her eyes shadowed in the downlight from a reading lamp over Dalton's head.

"Why don't you?" she said, giving him a slow smile. She looked at her wrist, realized that her watch was in her carry-on. "What time is it?"

"A little after four in the morning."

"God," she said, bringing her chairback up. "We've been flying for simply weeks. I'd open a vein for a cigarette. What day is it?"

"We crossed the date line. It's Sunday, I think."

"Thank God, we're not doing Narita. I hate that airport."

"So do I. Have you ever been to Singapore?"

Mandy closed her eyes and looked for a moment like a noblewoman's marble effigy on a medieval tomb. Then she opened them again, and that pale inner light she had shone out.

"Once. Years ago."

"Business?"

"They said so, but all I accomplished was a near-fatal hangover and a persistent gastrointestinal infestation that nearly killed me. I hate the Singaporeans. Especially the officials. They're the most sanctimonious, pettifogging, utter and total fucking bores on this entire planet. Except for the Canadians. When was the last time you were there?"

"Years back. After the Horn."

"*Cleaning,* dare I ask?"

"Yes."

"Anyone I knew?"

"Do you remember Sidney Vansittart?"

"That nasty old bugger! How could I not? He squatted on the Sorting Desk at London Station for simply eons, dealing out chaos and calumny measure for measure. Stringy old bird, rather like a syphilitic pelican. Damp, bulgy little eyes, like poached eggs. Story ran, he was going to the prostitute bars on the Patpong Road in Bangkok, ordering up squeaky little ten-year-olds by the bushel basket. Last I heard, he was taken up by the Thai police for disrespecting a Buddha. Tony Crane was his section head then. Caught holy hell for letting the old pederast out of the country at all. Never saw him again after that. Tony said he'd caught AIDS and died in some Southeast Asian cesspool."

"Well, he died in a toilet, at any rate."

Mandy gave him a look.

"Really?"

"Really."

"You're still waters, aren't you, dear boy. Porter always said so."

"Still and shallow. How awake are you?"

Something in his tone caught her ear. She looked at him for a moment and then pressed the CALL bell. The Thai girl floated over and hovered by their booth in attentive silence, her black eyes wide. Mandy ordered two G&T's—Bombay Sapphire, please—which appeared a moment later, frosted over, with thin lemon slices and the ice still cracking. She lifted hers and touched the rim of his glass with a silvery *ping.*

"To business, then?"

"Please."

"And I was so hoping to hear all about your sultry Venetian."

"A genuine interest in another woman's character is unlike you."

"Screw her character. I only want to know the really salacious bits. How was she in bed? Was she worth the punctured liver?"

"Yes."

"Really? Tell me all!"

"I just did."

Mandy made a face.

"God, I wish someone would take a shiv in the googlies for me."

"I'll see what I can arrange."

"You really intend to discuss this here?"

"Rather here than in the rotunda at Changi."

Mandy lifted her head, peered around the dim cabin with a theatrical flair, and then leaned in close to Dalton, placing her right hand on his wrist and filling up his personal space with her perfume and the delightful sensual radiance of a mature and seasoned woman. She was, Dalton had always known, a reflexive and eternal flirt, although— he hoped—quite selective.

"All right." She lowered her voice to a throaty purr. "Last year, in August, we—I mean, Clandestine Ops—had the snake eaters extract three Chinese nationals from the Mexican port of Veracruz. They were on shore leave from a SINOPEC oil-exploration vessel in the Gulf of Mexico, called the *Hao Hai Feng*. They were supposed to be seismic techs verifying a drilling ground, but Crypto City was picking up ultrafast-burst encryptions from the ship that were being relayed to a Chinese satellite we know is tasked for the military."

"What does the Agency think they were looking at?"

"We've got some SigInt and TechInt operating out of Pensacola. Crypto City figured the Chinese were trying to dip into the stream to try to get an outline of what gear we were deploying. And what we were looking at."

"I would imagine the Chinese got cranky."

"They don't know for sure who snatched their lads. They strongly suspect it was us, but, according to the Monitors, they're also shaking trees in North Korea and Venezuela. Apparently, the field unit deliberately left some indications that the techs had been taken in a commercial espionage op in order to claim-jump on future Chinese oil-field developments."

"Clues that pointed to No Dong or Boy Chavez?"

"I would assume. Good to have those two quarreling."

"And now Cather is ready to let these guys go?"

"Yes. I'm told they held the techs at a quarantined site inside Fort Huachuca. All the interrogators were Hispanic. They wore Mexican police uniforms, and the compound was tricked out to look very Third World shabby. So they had no idea they were being held by the U.S., and that amped up the fear factor. They rolled pretty fast, but most of it was stuff we already knew about or suspected. The main idea was to let the Chinese know the Gulf of Mexico was an American lake. Point got made—obliquely—so now it's time to deal the kids out."

"Duly chastened."

"Of course."

"Why would Singapore care enough about three Chinese techies to trade off Ray Fyke?"

"Singapore is worried sick about China—"

"Who isn't?"

"Exactly. So the SID would get the techs, along with everything they told us about Chinese surveillance methods. Bandwidth. Encryption methodologies. Targets. Tactical and strategic inferences could be made from what the techs knew and what they were trying to find out."

"If they're getting all that data, the SID wouldn't need the techs."

"True. We're setting a condition. The SID has to relay the techs straight back to Peking. Unharmed. Intact."

"Why?"

"So the Chinese will finally know who took them. And why."

"They already suspect we took them."

"Yes. But now they'll know. Point made *directly.*"

"Okay. I see that. And we get the undying gratitude of the SID—"

"For a minute and a half—"

"So we're coming in to Singapore as declared agents?"

"No. Undeclared. At least until the trade is confirmed. You'd be playing a freelance broker representing a third-party interest."

"But if the Agency wants gratitude from the SID, they'll have to declare themselves eventually."

"They will. When we've made it reasonably safe to do so."

"We're going in under the Burke and Single legend?"

"Why not? We both know it backward. You and Porter practically invented it, if you recall."

"Yes. But it's a financial cover. Investment banking. That hardly puts us in the way of prison officials at Changi."

Mandy reached into her carry-on and pulled out a large envelope made of pebbled navy blue silk. It carried a red logo and was addressed to a Miss Mandy Pownall, care of Burke and Single, London SW 1. The logo said HSBC: the Hongkong and Shanghai Banking Corporation outfit.

"It's an invitation. To a reception at Raffles. The Home Secretary will be there. The Home Ministry is in charge of prisons."

"Who is he?"

"Chong Kew Sak."

"Don't know him."

"He's new. He just came over from another agency."

She put a slight weight on the word *another.*

"Did he? Let me guess which one."

Mandy reached out and placed her fingertip on Dalton's upper lip.

He felt a rush of memory heat in his lower belly, Cora's body in the half-light of early dawn streaming in through the balcony window, her lips half open and her breasts rising and falling as she slept. Mandy sensed the force of the emotion but not the proximate cause. She took her finger away.

"Yes," she said, unsettled. "That one."

11

Kotor, Montenegro

Branco Gospic was at his carrier-sized teak desk in the old dining hall of his home in Kotor, studying marine charts and punching in numbers on a calculator, when his BlackBerry buzzed at him from the cherrywood credenza behind him, skittering across the gleaming wood like a shiny black cockroach. He stared at it for a while with a look of mild disgust, thinking it might be Stefan Groz calling back yet again to bitch and grizzle and snark about his now-exploded source in Brancati's office. Gospic looked at the caller ID—UNKNOWN—sighed, picked it up, and waited. It was not his custom to speak until he knew who was calling. The caller identified himself as Gianni from Padova—Kiki's alias. Gospic checked his watch. It was a little after noon. The call was twelve hours late.

"Boss, how are you?"

"You are late."

"I know. I got caught in that—"

"Where are you now?"

"In transit. Off the coast. I have some news."

"Yes."

"Saskia says good-bye."

"You gave her my best?"

"Right after I gave her mine. I need your advice, boss."

"Certainly."

"It's about our American friend."

"I assumed this. You gave him our message?"

"Well, actually, not yet."

Gospic said nothing, letting the silence run. On most men, this worked very well, but Lujac had a steely core under his playboy persona and was hard to intimidate. Gospic's control over him was unsteady. This worried Gospic, and he intended to do something about it as soon as Lujac began to disappoint him. Gospic could hear gulls in the background, the churning of heavy waves, a steady wind, and the low mutter of the *Subito*'s engines.

"Aren't you going to ask me why, boss?"

"I don't care why. I made myself clear. You disappoint me."

"It's complicated. He's not alone, and he's on his way to Singapore. Saskia heard you had some kind of thing going on in Singapore, so I figured I better hold off until I talked to you."

Silence then, and Lujac's question hanging. Gospic looked out the leaded-glass windows onto the ragged mountains across the fjord of Kotor. The sky was slate gray, and a steady cold rain was falling. Why was the American going to Singapore? Gospic already knew that the Singapore police were holding this drunken sailor, whom they considered the sole survivor of the wreck of the *Mingo Dubai*. He knew where he was being held—in Cluster C—and exactly what was being done to him, because he had a contact in the local police department, who kept him regularly informed. So, the Prisoner of Changi issue was under control.

But now the American was going to Singapore.

Americans went to Singapore every day. It could be nothing more than a coincidence. He could see no possible connection between Dalton and this drunken sailor rotting in Changi prison. But it worried him, anyway.

It also worried him that someone as unstable as Saskia Todorovich had gotten wind of his *interest* in Singapore. He would have to begin a quiet search for the man who was talking; there were only a few possibilities, but he would check them all.

Had Saskia heard anything about Gospic's plans for the *Mingo Dubai?* Gospic ran his operations as independent cells, but Lujac would already have his suspicions confirmed by this long silence. He would know that his news had left a mark. This was a dangerous breach of operational security, and now Lujac had himself become a threat.

Lujac would have to be handled carefully.

"You allowed this flight to Singapore?"

"I had him at one point, yes. I know. I know. You're pissed. But listen, boss, the guy's . . . interesting. He's making moves. I thought you should know about them. I thought you should have a chance to think it over. Our guy says he had a long talk in Florian's with an English woman—says she's a real stunner who had some kind of mojo with Galan—he says she helped Galan nail a mole inside the Carabinieri—our friend got the idea she was connected in some way to the CIA—anyway, she had a long private talk with our American friend—Galan bugged the entire meeting, but our guy wasn't able to get near the transcript. What he did get was that maybe the American is now back in the club, if you get me. Like all is forgiven? Anyway, the next day he's on a Thai Airways flight to Singapore. With the English woman."

"It would have been more simple if he had not been in a position to take a flight to Singapore."

"Yes. Yes, I get that. But this guy's not a singleton anymore, boss. If he's back in the CIA, then maybe we should stay on him and see what he's up to. Your name was taken in vain, by the by."

"My name?"

"Yeah. By Brancati and Galan and this Dalton guy. They talked about you, about coming after you directly. Dalton, he's a hunter. You can see it in his face, the way he moves. He's got some crocodile in him."

Gospic winced at the mention of Dalton's name but let it pass. He realized that he had been talking on this device—this *wireless* device—for far too long, and now Lujac was becoming . . . careless. The phone was heavily encrypted, but one never knew.

"Is Galan sending someone to Kotor?"

"He said no. Said the Carabinieri were not assassins. Dalton says maybe not, but *he* is. We gotta stay on him, boss. See how big a threat he is, maybe peel him off, get up close and personal with him, and then *a dio.*"

"What about the Florentine *arista?* The Vasari."

"Brancati had her driven back to Florence in an armored limo. She's at the university now, with a couple of Galan's Jew boys riding shotgun."

"So you lost her as well?"

Lujac's voice got tighter. He lost some of his easy charm.

"Look, Branco, my dear friend, I'm trying to do you some good here. This is *my* thing, what I do best. I don't do this for money; I have more than I can use. I'm in this for the charge I get. So what I'm saying is, all you want is to cancel a couple of bad debts; I can do that. Sure. But I took this ball on the hop because sometimes you're your own worst enemy, all this macho vendetta stuff. I'm giving you good info, and your Poppa always said that good info is better than bad blood. But you're pissed off. Okay. Fine. You want me to break off the Dalton thing, daisy on up to Florence and create some lovely splatter, I'll do it. Frankly, it's nuts, but I'll do it."

Gospic held his temper, barely; he never snarled at his people, but he always remembered insolence, and Lujac was insolent. He was also very smart and very good, and he made good tactical decisions. And he had never failed Gospic in any important work. Lujac was valuable and Lujac knew it. Gospic thought about it and decided it might be useful to have a secondary asset in the region, just in case his associates there became . . . what?

Problematic.

"Okay. Go to Singapore. One of our Gulfstreams is in Bari. I'll have Larissa find out where they're staying, and she'll get the details to you in flight. Pick them up in Singapore and stay on them. I want to know where he goes in Singapore and who he meets with."

"I get the idea we got something going in Singapore?"

"No. Nothing."

Lujac sensed the evasion but said nothing. Before Saskia died, he had worked her over for everything she knew about Gospic's operations. In the end, all she had to tell him was that Gospic had sent Emil Tarc to Singapore over a month ago. She had no idea why. Lujac filed the information away, against the day he and Gospic would no longer be friendly. And now Gospic had confirmed her story. Okay, duly noted, and time to back off. Lujac could push Gospic a little because Lujac was good, but Gospic would not tolerate an inquisitive subordinate no matter how useful.

"Okay. One last thing. What about the *arista?*"

"I'll send Radko Borins to deal with her."

"Radko Borins screwed that stunt his last time out. Is he up to it?"

"Yes. He's in Trieste. He can be in Florence in two hours."

"Is he motivated?"

"I gave him a special incentive."

"Yow. Hope he was wearing a diaper. Boss, I gotta ask you . . . why go after the broad? I mean, right now? Brancati knows it was you behind the marathon thing. You really want to start a war with him, just to take out some upper-class *puta*? Galan may be saying the Carabinieri are not assassins, but Brancati made his bones many times over, and he's already pissed at us. You make him mad enough, he'll unload the entire Carabinieri on us, and some of those guys are as hard as anyone we got."

"The woman has a debt. She will pay it."

"Boss . . ."

"No more talk. That is the end of this. You failed to take her, so Radko will do it for you. But, at the end of the day, when I tell you to do it, our American friend will get my message. Am I clear?"

"As megapixels, boss. I'll be in touch. *Ciao.*"

ON THE SEVENTH floor of the giant glass cube at Fort Meade, Maryland, that houses elements of the National Security Agency's global computer systems, a brown-eyed, olive-skinned, heart-attack brunette named Nikki Turrin, one of the Monitors, was sitting at a thirty-inch LCD watching a running scroll of numbers and letters fly over the screen, thinking about her new Great Dane pup's case of separation anxiety, when she got a hit on a flagged target phone that brought her upright. The screen showed a digital packet ID and an adjacent routing number, an indication the mainframe had detected a transmission, targeted at a specific phone matrix, that contained a trigger word or phrase, a voice-recognition hit, or a reference to some person or operation of interest to an element of the nation's Intelligence community. Unlike the paranoid nightmares of the ACLU and

MoveOn.org, the NSA was technically unable to monitor every single communications transmission in all media all over the globe.

Even God would have to outsource that. But they could monitor thousands of *identified* targets. And this was one of them. The digital packet showed only a tag and a reference code—the targeted transmission had been detected seconds ago—and, from the source numbers, it looked like a wireless cell-phone transmission originating somewhere in the upper Adriatic.

The codes did not indicate the content of the packet—Monitors are neither cleared for, nor remotely interested in, content—but the routing code was quite familiar to the tech. This packet—from the size of the file, an audio packet—was to be relayed immediately to Langley, Virginia. Something in the intercept was important to some operation or other inside the CIA. Nikki, a pragmatic but dedicated young woman seraphically free from the chief sin of the career NSA staffer—inappropriate curiosity—hit the requisite codes and the slice of data was duly fired off to a computer in Langley. There, it was received, tagged, and bounced upstairs to another equally pragmatic tech, who transcribed and reencrypted it and fired it through a series of secure channels that terminated in the flat-screen LCD on the desk of a horse-faced, cold-eyed, yellow-toothed, thin-lipped old man in a charcoal pinstripe who was talking on the phone, in his soft, Tidewater Virginia cadences, to a nervous contact in Prague, who had another man in an Internet café across the street pinned in the long lens of a night-vision scope.

The old man, whose name was Deacon Cather, chief of the Clandestine Services section of the CIA, did not stop listening to his nervous man in Prague while he read the transcription of the audio packet, which contained references to *Singapore, Dalton, Vasari,* and *CIA*. Cather scanned the text: someone calling himself *Gianni from Padova* had contacted a Serbo-Croatian mafia don called Branco

Gospic and warned him that Micah Dalton was on his way to Singapore.

Cather knew a great deal about Gospic and his network, but he would dearly love to know much more, which was why he had arranged for the NSA to monitor his communications systems. He was also keenly aware of Gospic's vendetta against Micah Dalton. With half his mind on his agent in Prague and the other half on Micah Dalton and the operation known as Orpheus, Cather weighed the uses that could be made of Gospic's sudden interest in Singapore. Perhaps it would be useful to hear the actual conversation. Much could be learned from a living voice. Cather listened to his feckless agent go on for a time, silenced him with six words of simple instruction that sent the man out into the twilight streets of Prague with twenty thousand euros in a vacuum pack labeled Lavazza Espresso, and then reached out to his keyboard to hit ARCHIVE. The audio packet was then reencrypted in an asymmetric code unique to Cather's Zip drive. The transcript disappeared from the screen, from the system, from ever having existed, and now resided only in a small black steel slab that Cather detached every evening when he left the office, slipping it into his breast pocket, next to a sterling silver case containing Montecito cigars. This being done, Cather leaned back in his chair, crossed his long legs, and placed his liver-spotted hands gently on his belly. Through the tinted window he could see a great deal of rolling Virginia countryside, the tree canopy bathed in a light so pure and clean this could have been the first morning of the ancient world.

He leaned his head back, exhaled theatrically, a thin stream of acidic contentment flowing through his once-powerful frame. The question of Micah Dalton's war with Branco Gospic, seen in the light of Gospic's apparent interest in Singapore, required some careful thought. It was pregnant with tactical possibilities. He slowly pulled his pale blue lips back from his long yellow teeth in a leathery retraction, producing a kind of frozen predatory grimace that stretched the corded muscles of his neck and cracked his blue-veined cheeks into deltas of scaly, sagging flesh. This reptilian display, which his associates had learned to regard with carefully blanked faces, was Deacon Cather's legendary smile.

12

The Celebes Sea

Vigo Majiic, sweat-drenched, reeking of oil and bilgewater, weary beyond belief but unable to sleep with the clamor of the rebuild clanging through the hull, staggered up the gangway and found Emil Tarc out on the open deck beside the gutted bridge of the *Mingo Dubai*. Dawn was hours away, and the heat under the spreading camouflage tarp was brutal, steamy and close and dense with the stink of paint and welding smoke. Tarc was adding to the choking reek with a foul Russian cigarette and watching the small, wiry brown-skinned workers swarming over the floodlit main deck, painting and polishing and scrubbing. Up at the bow, a crew of welders was replacing one of the hatch covers, and the little knot of men was silhouetted in the blue-white flare of a welder's torch. To Tarc's left, a crew of naked, navy-paint-streaked workers was standing on a suspended platform, slathering primer on the side of the hull. Inside the bridge, a team of marine technicians, flown into Sulawesi in a private Lear with the portholes covered and destination unknown, was repairing and replacing the ship's antique electronics and updating the steering hardware.

By Tarc's own calculations, rebuilding the *Mingo Dubai* was costing Branco Gospic around six million euros—and that wasn't covering the cost of bribes to Bittagar Chulalong, the gotch-eyed old villain who was the head of the local chapter of the Babi Rusa Brigade. Tarc turned as Majiic came to the railing, wiping his gaunt face with an oily rag.

"Vigo, you look like goat shit."

"Thank you, Emil. I feel like goat shit. The heat . . . I cannot believe the fucking heat."

"It's not your watch. Go below."

"But who can sleep with all . . . this . . . going on."

"Do what I do. Sleep onshore. There are girls in the village, pretty ones. I have three."

Majiic had gone across to the squalid cantonment of tin huts and prehistoric latrines and wandering livestock that the locals called a village—the young men there had all been forcibly conscripted into the ranks of the Babi Rusa Brigade, and the remaining villagers—leathery old men and women with pinched, hate-filled faces; feral, naked brats, rolling in the muck and the reek; sullen young girls with flat-black eyes—they had not seemed to burn with sexual fire for a scraggy little Serbo-Croatian in dire need of a serious scrubbing. Majiic had once entertained the fantasy of a tropical isle of swaying palms and curling surf and naked Polynesian beauties with laughing eyes and inviting arms. The reality was this stinking atoll and the dwarfish gremlins of this godforsaken island. Majiic had not stayed long enough to exhale twice and was spending all his spare time in the locked steel-walled cabin that had once belonged to Captain Wang. Wang was now lying in three thousand feet of ocean at the outlet of the Strait of Malacca, his skull peeled open like a green banana by three rounds from the Tokarev pistol currently strapped to Emil

Tarc's leg, his body sewed into a canvas duffel bag, along with an ancient Remington typewriter to keep him down. Majiic had no interest at all in risking his manly bits—or his health—in a dubious encounter with one of the *village girls*.

"And what do the old men of the village say?"

Tarc showed his teeth, his leathery skin cracking. Beads of sweat glittered on his unshaven cheeks and his black goatee glistened. The side of his face, lit up by the glare of the welder's torch, looked like pitted sheet metal. He smacked the pistol strapped to his combat pants.

"Bugger the old men of the village."

"Really? How *do* you find the time?"

Tarc's ratlike face contorted in wary puzzlement and then brightened, as he realized that this sullen young pessimist had actually made a joke.

"Vigo. You surprise me."

"I'm not the only surprise you have coming. Have you been watching that man in the blue head scarf, the one sitting on the anchor by the bow?"

Tarc shaded his eyes from the glare of the work lights, squinting into the distance. He saw a small figure squatting by the bow, his bony knees as high as his ears, a home-rolled cigarette dangling from his mouth, his tiny black eyes sharp, his gaze flickering around the deck, watching the work closely. He was wearing cut-off blue jean shorts and a GREENPEACE T-shirt. In his callused hands was a shining steel parang.

Tarc grunted, identifying the man.

"That's Gango. He's Bittagar's enforcer."

"Yes. I know. Do you know what he's doing?"

"Enlighten me."

"He's counting. Counting our men. Counting the days."

"I know. Bittagar thinks he may take the ship."

"That's what I think too."

"It will be ready in a week. So we have some time."

"Time? Time to do what, Emil? Write our wills? Bugger the village elders? There are exactly six of us here, and maybe two of us can use a weapon. Bittagar has sixty men, sitting around in the town and on the hillside up there, smoking bhang and drinking piss-warm Singha and watching the ship. When the ship is ready, Bittagar's men will come down on us like . . ."

"A wolf on the fold?"

Majiic looked at Tarc, who showed his teeth again.

"I went to school, Vigo. I know some poems. Want to hear another one? It will make you feel better, maybe put some lead in your pencil. It runs . . . let me see . . .

" *'I saw a man this morning*
Who did not wish to die;
I ask, and cannot answer,
If otherwise wish I.'

"I can't remember the middle lines, but the rest runs something like

" *'But other shells are waiting,*
Across the Aegean Sea;
Shrapnel and high explosive,
Shells and hells for me.

" *'I will go back this morning*
From Imbros ov'r the sea.
Stand in the trench, Achilles,
Flame-capped, and shout for me.' "

Tarc said these lines in a kind of sacred chant, his eyes closed and his expression as serene as if neither of them were standing on the bridge of a hijacked gypsy tanker surrounded by a jungle filled with pitiless cannibal killers. When he finished, Tarc opened his eyes and smiled at Majiic, who stared back, silenced, his mouth open.

"There. Now you feel better, eh, Vigo?"

The moment had created a cone of airless silence around them. Now the hammer and clang and boom of the rebuilding of the *Mingo Dubai* came surging back, redoubled, an assault on all the senses.

"No," said Majiic, shaking his head. "No, I don't."

Tarc looked disappointed; his face resumed its iron look.

"Okay. Well, how about this? Every one of these stinking ditch niggers we're looking at right now will be rotting in a pit in three days. And we'll mark the grave with Bittagar's head stuck on a stick. Okay?"

13

Changi Airport,
Singapore

Singapore—in particular, the city itself—is a lunatic blend of Mao Tse-tung and Dale Carnegie; a broad, steaming sandbar, as flat as a sewage spill, on which the tyrannical, puritanical government of Lee Kwan Yew, known inside the Agency as "Uncle Harry," has brought forth by sheer force of totalitarian will a postmodern powerhouse of shimmering economic cathedrals and towering spires. These pinnacles rise up out of a hundred little cantonments, teeming with millions upon millions of buzzing little worker bees, all maniacally dedicated to the three First Principles that have always guided the Asiatic mind: never look a cop in the eye; if it slithers you should eat it; and money is the root of all evil only if you don't have any.

The brand-new airport at Changi was conceived as a top-of-the-lungs statement about the New Singapore—acres of gleaming glass and marble, concourses large enough to house the Super Bowl, lounges and bars and shops to rival Rodeo Drive, and enough squinty-eyed, flat-faced, cold-assed little soldier-bots slinging MP5s scattered about the premises to keep Al Gore away from a ham sandwich.

The Terminal 2 concourse was crowded with European and North American backpackers, wearing the trademark uniform of backpackers everywhere: baggy camo shorts; lots of metal bits, sticking out of their lips and eyebrows and noses and chins; butt-stupid, self-inflicted body hair; tattoos; complicated rubber sandals as ugly as cow flaps; and, of course, the inevitable dung-colored hemp T-shirt carrying some vapid political piety—ANSWER (Act Now to Stop War and End Racism), TREES ARE NOT TERRORISTS, FREE TIBET, and Dalton's favorite, for sheer moronic redundancy, WARS KILL PEOPLE AND OTHER LIVING THINGS.

Yes. Wars stopped slavery in America and liberated Europe and put an end to Japanese imperialism and killed Hitler and Mussolini and Pol Pot and Che Guevara and Abu Musab al-Zarqawi. That's why we have them.

Mandy, who was watching Dalton watch the kids, tapped him on the shoulder and said:

"You can't shoot them all, Micah, so we might as well get a drink."

"What if I only shoot one?"

"No. You can't fix stupid. Let's go."

They crossed what felt like an acre of polished tile, dragging their baggage behind them, bone-weary, jet-lagged, and dangerously cranky. A wall of green glass hissed out of their way, and they walked out of the air-conditioned chill of the terminal into the staggering steam heat of a Singapore noon. The muted roar of the city closed in on them and a furnace of heat rose up from the pavement as they reached a rank of long white Cadillac limousines. Dalton saw the one with the Intercontinental logo and was reaching for the handle when two obvious plainclothes cops in shiny, wrinkled black silk suits materialized on either side. Dalton gave Mandy a look and then stepped away from the limo, clearing some room to maneuver if a maneuver was called for. One of them, the older, a frog-faced man with the air of a sleepy lizard, held up his hand and stepped into Dalton's face.

"You are Bulk and Singer?"

Dalton nodded, sizing the guy up; maybe two hundred, and his hands had the callused look of a street fighter. The smaller man, a Malay, went one-sixty, and rode on the balls of his feet.

He looked pale and twitchy, and his eyes were too wide.

"Yes. *Burke* and *Single*. What can we do for you?"

Frog Face glared at Dalton, apparently for having the effrontery to answer his question without genuflecting, or perhaps because he had a face made for glaring and he just liked to use it.

"You are wanted."

"Peachy," said Dalton. "Always nice to be appreciated."

Frog Face worked it out, slowly, and then frowned, not a pretty thing to watch after you've been in transit for twenty hours and can't have a cigarette until this butt-ugly mutt gets the hell out of your face. Dalton was aware of Mandy's presence; still, calm, wary, without fear.

"I mean, my boss wants to see you. Both of you."

"Thrilled to hear it. Have him call me. We're at the Intercontinental."

The short one seemed to feel the need to put his oar in.

"You come now."

Mandy sighed and reached around him to open the car door. The little Malay cop decided to reach out and grab her arm. Mandy did something very quick with her left hand; there was a muffled, cork-popping sound, and the short man was down on one knee, holding his right hand. His index finger was pointing in an impossible direction, and his face was very pale. His eyes now looked sewn shut. Frog Face looked down at his partner and then back at Dalton. The little man began to make a noise like air hissing out of a tire. Everyone was happy to ignore him. Mandy opened the limo door and threw her carry-on into the cool dark of the interior. The driver had the trunk open and was loading in their bags. Frog Face spent a few seconds in quiet contemplation of Dalton's bland, smiling face. Then he bowed.

"I am sorry for this fool," he said, in perfect, British-accented English. "May we begin again?"

"No," said Dalton. "We may not. We're at the Intercontinental—"

"The Presidential Suite," said Frog Face, with a broad smile.

"Exactly. Who wants to see us, anyway?"

"You are Mr. Micah Dalton, of the English banking firm?"

"I am Mr. Micah Dalton, of the desperately-needing-a-cold-drink firm. If you haven't got a chilled flute of Bolly in your back pocket, I advise you to get the hell out of my way."

"My boss is Minister Dak Chansong. Of the Home Ministry. The Minister very much wishes to speak with you both. At your convenience, of course, but as soon as possible. We will send a car?"

Dalton looked at Mandy, who shrugged and climbed into the limo, showing a flash of milky white thigh as she did so. When he looked back at Frog Face, the man was literally licking his lips. Perhaps he had just swallowed a fly.

"We'll be ready at three," he said, disliking the man very much. As the limo pulled away, Frog Face dragged his associate to his feet and subjected him to what looked like a vicious harangue that culminated in a hard backhand across the little man's face.

Mandy, who had found the minibar, had a heavy crystal tumbler in her left hand and an unopened bottle of Bombay Sapphire in her right, gave him an eyebrow lift and a wry smile.

"First find the ice," she said, lifting the glass. "And then the lemons."

"I think you broke that poor little man's finger," said Dalton, pulling open the ice chest drawer, where he found six perfect lemon slices lying in a silver bowl on top of a mountain of crushed ice. Mandy accepted the ice and the lemon slice, and slowly stirred the mixture with her index finger until it looked right to her. She lifted the finger and traced a cold line across Dalton's sweaty forehead.

"I certainly hope so," she purred, leaning back into the leather, crossing her long legs to great advantage and smiling at Dalton over the top of her glass.

"How did you know there'd be lemons?"

"Micah. I handled the hotel bookings. We're at the Intercontinental. It's the finest hotel in Singapore. There damn well better be lemons."

The crowded neighborhoods of eastern Singapore rolled by outside the tinted windows, like a tourist travelogue running with the sound off. Dalton leaned back into the cushioned banquette opposite Mandy and tried not to stare at her thighs. After a while, he gave that up and simply enjoyed the view. A few minutes passed in pleasant contemplation of her stockings and the way her calves were shaped. Mandy leaned forward and set her glass down on the rosewood bar.

"Tell me, Micah, if you can tear your mind away from my legs, why do you think Minister Dak Chansong of the Home Ministry is so anxious to meet with two lowly officials from Burke and Single?"

"Maybe somebody at London Station has been indiscreet."

"No. Nobody's weak at London Station. Remind me, who the hell is Dak Chansong, anyway?"

"Never heard the name. Not in any of the cheat sheets?"

Dalton reached for one of Mandy's cigarettes.

"Not that I read. Perhaps just a polite hello from an overreaching underling, then?"

Mandy lit his cigarette, drew out a turquoise Sobranie for herself, got it going, and huffed at him through the smoke.

"Hah! Not in bloody Singapore."

"I suppose not. I guess we'll hear directly," said Dalton, suppressing a yawn. "Damn, I was hoping to get into bed for a couple of hours."

Mandy inhaled, a red spark flaring in the dim light of the limo. She exhaled slowly, savoring the smoke, and sent him her trademark look.

"If you think you have a couple of hours in you, I'm ready to assist."

"Mandy. Behave. Porter's only been dead a month. Shouldn't you be in mourning?"

"A true gentleman would wish to console the grieving widow."

"Now I'm a gentleman?"

"So this is . . . what? 'Dover Beach'? *'Ah, love, let us be true/to one another'!*"

Dalton grinned, trying to look all sappy mystical as he did so.

" 'For we are here as on a duckling plain.' "

"I think that's *darkling plain.*"

Dalton lifted his eyebrows, looked blank.

"Really? Not *duckling?*"

"Pretty sure."

They traveled for a time, enjoying the cocoonlike silence of the car.

Mandy had been giving the matter of fidelity some thought.

"Tell me, honestly, Micah, do you seriously intend to be utterly faithful to this . . . Vasari . . . creature?"

"I intend to do my utterly best."

"You do, do you?"

Mandy leaned back again, artfully recrossing her legs, looked to her left and smiled at her own reflection in the glass.

"Dear boy. Good luck with that."

Gulfstream A990,
thirty thousand feet

As the jet banked for the final approach to Changi Airport, the sun struck her port side, and six glowing yellow ovals slipped across the damask walls of the passenger cabin. One of the bright ovals slid across Lujac's face as he lay asleep, dreaming of the look in Saskia's eyes as she died. What had she seen, in those last moments? What had she *felt*?

Lujac had spent most of his life trying to understand what it meant to *feel* something. He had often stood in front of a mirror, trying to re-create the expressions he would see on the faces of mourners at funerals, on the faces of the mortally sick as they lay dying, but, no matter how he tried, he had never known a true feeling. He spent his entire professional life—the famous part—looking into another person's face and trying to understand what it felt like to be *other*, to be someone who had the great misfortune to *not* be Kiki Lujac. The light crossed his eyes again, and he came out of the dream. Something was buzzing in his lap, a burring vibration.

He sat up, fully awake, and picked up the phone.

The screen said only PRIVATE.

"Yes."

"Kiki, this is Larissa."

Larissa, Gospic's stepdaughter, brutally disfigured during a rape by militia soldiers in Kosovo, survivor of endless surgical attempts to render her face and body more bearable to herself, and to others; she handled Gospic's books and did all of his critical IT work as well. She was the only woman Gospic trusted and she did not like Kiki Lujac. Not one little bit.

Lujac, who found even the slightest physical defects shiveringly repulsive, avoided her rigorously. He had an oddly atavistic response to her ugliness. It made him afraid of her. He hoped one day Gospic would need to have her dead. He would do the work as a service to beauty. Oddly, she had a lovely voice, a velvety flow, like pouring cream.

"Larissa. *Ma petit chou.*"

"Where are you?"

"Just coming into Changi. Warm and sunny. A perfect day. How is it in Kotor?"

"It sucks. Do you have a pen?"

"I have a recorder in this phone. Go ahead."

"The Intercontinental, 80 Middle Road, in the Colonial district. The Presidential Suite, right at the top. They're registered as Micah Dalton and Mandy Pownall. Dalton is a currency manager and Pownall works in Mergers for the British bank Burke and Single. They're based in London. Daddy thinks the bank is a cover for an Intelligence operation, but he can't find out which one. My guess is the CIA. Only the CIA has that kind of money. They have tickets to a formal ball at Raffles for eight o'clock this evening, your time. Their passports are British, but Dalton is an American citizen. The Burke and Single website says he's a graduate of VMI and Yale, has an

M.B.A from the LSE. Likes to ride, and boxes at a private club in Knightsbridge. Extremely fit. Has a lot of visible scars on his upper torso, which he has attributed to a car crash back in the U.S. Has a reputation for being aggressive and has been known to hurt his opponents. He has title to a flat in Wilton Row, in Belgravia. No mortgage. Salary undisclosed. Very solvent. Solid account at the Bank of Scotland. Not a womanizer, or a creepy bisexual like you. None of your bad habits."

"I consider myself an omnisexual, Cabbage. And you sound like you want to fuck him yourself."

"Jealous?"

"Cabbage, sweetheart, the last time you had an orgasm with someone else in the room was when those Bosnians were passing you around the barracks like a spittoon. Let's don't get personal. You couldn't handle it."

A long silence while Larissa dealt with the comment; Lujac had a reputation for casual viciousness, but every now and then he could take your breath away with a barb dipped in something truly vitriolic. Lujac's day was not now, but it was coming. Her father had made a promise.

"Yes," she said, as if the blade had not gone deep, "I imagine you wish it had happened to you. Being a human spittoon is right up your back alley, so to speak. Dalton has no wife, no kids, no background other than the bio on the website. You can't get a thing about him from any of the databases. His credentials check out, but nothing in between the LSE and coming to Burke five years ago. If he's not a spook, I'm Angelina Jolie."

"Great. Book me there as well."

"Your own name?"

"No. Use the French one. Jules Duhamel. I like being Jules Duhamel. What about the woman?"

"Her background is county, as the English say. Father and mother were gentry, and she went to Cambridge for law. Again, nothing personal. Just her credentials and her position at Burke. If you're contemplating a merger or an acquisition, she's the one who vets the target."

"Are they lovers?"

"I do research, Kiki. I don't do psychic. Do you want pictures?"

"I can go to the website and download them. Can you get me into the ball?"

"You've never crashed a party? Improvise. Use your charm. They'll pee themselves. Do you want any gear? Daddy's man in Bari said you left it all on the *Subito.*"

Lujac was silent, thinking about Saskia's last moments, about staring into her dying eyes. He wanted to be . . . close . . . for this one.

Blade close.

Penetration, he thought, is such a complex word. Like a geode. Crack it open and it reveals all kinds of inner beauty.

"Kiki?"

"No. No gear. Too dangerous in this part of the world. I have my cameras. I'll say I'm scouting locations for a shoot. Matter of fact, I think I will. As for the rest of it, I can get everything I need in the hotel's kitchen."

15

The Intercontinental Hotel, Singapore

The Presidential Suite at the Intercontinental, as is only fitting, took up more room than a carrier's flight deck. It was almost fatally tasteful, in an uncluttered, manly, British Raj sort of way, with lots of exotic woods and brass lamps and green glass walls; three large bedrooms, a formal dining room, a large study, a wall of seamless windows in the living room that laid all of Singapore and a slice of the Marina before the eye of the beholder like an offering. The suite had a resident butler, a genial, older Malay with a Virginia accent named Mr. Dill, who took no kind of offense when Mandy told him they must sadly forgo the pleasure of his services. He withdrew, with a vaguely hydraulic *hiss,* and closed the double doors behind him with a gentle *thump.* Mandy literally fell into the leather sofa in front of the window wall, landing with a sigh, a toss of her hair, and a flutter of linen skirts, kicking her Jimmy Choos off, one, then the other, flicking each across the room with her toe.

"God, this spy stuff is brutal."

Dalton, standing in the middle of the entry foyer and contemplating an immediate bath followed by steak *frites*, smiled at the back of her neck.

"How did you get this past Antonia?"

Antonia was the accounts controller for London Station, a steely young black woman fresh out of Langley, whose gimlet eye, her red pen hovering like a lepidopterist's needle, scanned the expense accounts of the resident agents and support staff, her lips tightening as she closed in on a puffed-up tab or a dubious chit and pinned it to the ledger.

"Not on the books, Micah. I paid for all this myself."

"Mandy! You must be insane."

"Not *literally*, Micah. Actually, we're using *your* credit card."

"Mine?"

"Well. You shouldn't have left it in your flat."

"That's nuts. Nobody asked me for my card. And, anyway, there's no way I had enough room for all of this!"

"No. Burke and Single paid you a quarterly bonus. We just popped it all into your platypus card. You're simply loaded, dear boy."

"How much do we have?"

Mandy told him. Dalton, shaking his head, left to find a bathroom. It took a while. It took longer to figure out the controls for the huge hammered-copper bowl that he eventually realized was a bathtub. A hazy hour or so later, he was floating in a sea of pinkish bubbles, half asleep, working his way through a short, sharp scotch, when Mandy breezed in through the open door, long, lean, and dangerously radiant in a swirly and vaguely translucent little sundress that looked to be made of pale green smoke.

"My God," she said, leering at him. "You look like a lobster in a copper pot."

"Why are you here, Mandy?"

"The car from the Home Ministry."

"The car from the Home Ministry?"

"Is there an echo?"

"It *cannot* be three."

"Alas."

"Dammit! Goddam Singaporean bullshit."

"It could be worse," she said, picking a huge navy blue bathrobe off a brass hook by the shower stall. "We could be in Ottawa."

She walked over to the side of the bowl, held up the robe.

"Come on, Micah. Once more into your breeches."

"They can damn well wait," he said, leaning back into the tub and sipping at the last of the scotch. "By the way, while we're alone, re- member I asked you about Fyke's tag? Did you get anything out of Langley?"

"Yes. I just did. They said the tag still had some power. The med- ics at Changi removed it and took it to the SID offices in the Home Ministry. That's just across the Singapore River from our Embassy. Our people detected a very weak signal, amplified it, and managed to ID the tag."

Dalton considered the story. It was barely plausible. Barely.

"Fascinating explanation. Do you believe it?"

"I'm inclined to. It's far more plausible than the idea that we have a source inside the SID. I don't think they've ever been penetrated. And now, Micah," she said, lifting up the robe again, "we really have to go."

"Turn around."

"No. Ogling your body will be the one bright spot in this whole day."

"I don't want to inflame you. Unbridled lust is dangerous for you older women."

"I'll risk it. Arise."

Dalton arose, dripping.

Mandy stepped back, her expression changing.

"God, Micah, you're bleeding."

Dalton looked down at his belly. A red tint was seeping through the fresh bandages around his torso.

"Christ," he said, touching the wound. "That can't be good."

"You need to see a doctor. I'll call Mr. Dill."

Dalton shook his head.

"No. How do I explain a knife wound? I'm supposed to be a banker."

"What about . . . that? That's a lot of blood."

Dalton looked down at the bandage again and then up at her.

"No," she said, backing away. "I don't do wounds."

"Yes you do," he said, stepping out of the bath and wrapping the robe around his body. "Call Mr. Dill and ask for some Krazy Glue."

"Krazy . . . what do you want glue for?"

"You'll figure it out."

THE CAR WAS a Mercedes limo that had been *militarized*—hardened enough to take an RPG smack-dab in the chitlins and keep on trucking. Mandy and Dalton, now in a cream-colored Zegna suit over a shell pink shirt and a pale blue tie made of raw silk, sat in the darkest recesses of the back, while, in the front, far away, the driver, the same Mr. Frog Face—now identified as Sergeant Ong Bo—silent as a pallbearer, hurtled south down North Bridge Street toward the Singapore River and the Parliament House on its far bank. North Bridge Street is to Singapore City as Sixth Avenue is to Midtown Manhattan. Mandy and Dalton watched as the car flickered from sunlight to shadow and back again as the canyons and towers of the central city loomed and receded.

"Changed a bit," said Mandy, a little awed in spite of her dislike.

"Uncle Harry. He's retired now, but he's still the 'Minister Mentor,' and he sits right beside Lee Hsien Loong, keeping a hand on the wheel. And nobody around here's complaining. Lee took Singapore from a Third World cesspool to the gateway of the East. People are getting rich all over town, and that's the way they like it."

"Still a tyranny, isn't it? Thank God for Stamford Raffles. He put the mark of England on this place. The only redeeming feature. Ever notice that every country that was ever *colonized* by England ended up an economic power and every country under Stalin was—still is—a dog's brekkie?"

"You'd never know it by the way you Brits treated Raffles. He lost four kids to malaria and cholera, his entire collection of flora and fauna sank at sea, and he lost all his money in a bank collapse. The East India Company refused him a pension, and when he died the parish priest in your Old Blighty wouldn't bury him because Raffles opposed slavery."

Mandy gave him a look. Dalton shrugged it off.

"Lonely Planet," he said. "Got it at Marco Polo. Somebody had to know something about the place."

"Let's review. I arrived here only a short time ago, barely three hours, and already I'm hot, I'm hungry, I think I'm getting a heat rash where no sensible girl wants a heat rash, I'm in an armored car with a driver who looks like he catches bugs with his tongue, I'm traveling with a gifted roué who for some demented reason has decided to become celibate now that I've finally got him alone, and we're on our way to see a Home Ministry thug who will quite possibly toss us both in Changi Prison on a trumped-up charge. Am I in Hell? No? Much worse? Then I must be in Singapore."

"You liked the hotel."

"Which I may never see again."

"You're just cranky because I won't boink you."

"The day is young, Micah. Oh jolly. Here we are."

The car slowed as it turned in to a large gated compound in front of a massive stone Victorian pile. A uniformed guard snapped to as

Sergeant Ong Bo rolled up to the gatehouse. The guard leaned into the car to glower at Dalton and Mandy in the backseat and then waved them through to a graveled parking area at the side of the building. Ong leaped out and scrabbled around to open Mandy's door. She gave him a look that should have burned off his eyebrows and managed not to enlighten him any further on the subject of female undergarments as she struggled out of the limo.

"I will take you to Minister Dak," he said, scuttling across to the marble staircase that led up to a set of leaded-glass doors. They entered into a broad marbled foyer done in a chess-set pattern and padded up a curving flight of carved wooden stairs, smelling of lemon and linseed oil, Ong Bo's ample butt remaining at eye level as they climbed. Then down a long, darkened hallway lined with closed office doors, treading on ancient wooden boards that creaked and groaned as they passed, and then delivered by Ong Bo, with a bow, to a stained-glass wall surrounding two massive wooden doors.

"When you are through with Minister Dak, if you are free to go, I will be happy to return you to your hotel or to take you anywhere in Singapore you would wish to go. And may I offer the English lady a small token of my extreme regret for the manner of your reception this morning?"

Mandy looked at him over the tops of her Prada glasses, fixing him in her vast database of unsavory minions encountered in the line of duty.

"Possibly," she said. Ong Bo reached into the breast pocket of his suit and withdrew a small black lacquer box, intricately inlaid in threads of pure jade, tied with a scarlet ribbon. It looked ancient and outrageously valuable. Ong offered it to her, holding it in the open palms of his joined hands in the formal Eastern manner.

Mandy hesitated, and then, with as much grace as she could summon, accepted it. Her acceptance seemed to send a sensual ripple through his large, loose frame. Mandy did not open it, since gushing over whatever tawdry trinket it might contain was going to require more forced charm than she felt able to gather for the cause. She smiled thinly, dropped it into her little Kate Spade bag, snapped the catch shut.

Ong watched the ritual with a closed, passive regard, his eyes narrowed, then he bowed again, his face a little more stony, turned away and knocked twice on the frame. A voice from within, brusque and shrill, barked out a command in Mandarin. Ong opened the door and oiled himself to the side, bowing. The office was very large, very old, and almost empty, with white-painted walls over twelve feet high, ending in fine crown moldings. A large ceiling fan, made of false palm fronds, churned in the still, warm air. On one wall, an antique wooden station clock emitted a dry, clanking *tick* with metronomic regularity. A bank of leaded-glass windows, barred with wrought iron, coated with grime and dust, let a filtered, nineteenth-century light into the room and illuminated a large, threadbare Oriental carpet in tones of plum, gold, and faded blue. The carpet held a large, ornately carved colonial desk, behind which sat a middle-aged Chinese woman, wonderfully turned out in a crisp navy blue suit over blazing-white blouse. Her arms were resting on the top of her desk, seamed and bony hands neatly folded in the middle of the space, a desk which was completely empty except for a Lenovo laptop, an unopened copy of the *Straits Times* newspaper, and a cordless phone. Her expression was familiar to Dalton, although it took a moment to place her. The Chinese woman, asleep on the flight from Milan. He recalled his assessment of her at the time:

An attenuated Chinese woman of indeterminate age, with dead-white skin and an expression of general ill will, who tossed and twitched and muttered in her sleep.

She rose, without smiling, and dismissed Sergeant Ong with a nod.

"Good afternoon. I am Minister Dak Chansong. Please, Mr. Dalton, Miss Pownall, come in."

She indicated a pair of padded leather chairs that had been placed, just so, in front of her desk. Behind her, on the peeling plaster wall, was a large official portrait of Lee Kwan Yew, garishly framed in gilt, and another portrait, much more recent, of his son and heir, Lee Hsien Loong, framed in simple silver. She watched as they took their places, studying them both with that same air of general ill will that had marked her while she was sleeping, an expression that Dalton began to fear might be a mirror of her soul. She sat, offered neither water nor tea—a calculated insult—smoothed her stiff blue suit briefly, and reclined into her chair, still not smiling. Mandy and Dalton, fully aware of the Asian uses for silence, smiled back blandly and said . . . nothing at all. The station clock ticked leadenly, and the scent of Minister Dak's perfume, something floral and bittersweet and expensive, drifted in the still, mote-filled glowing room.

"You recognize me, perhaps?"

"I do," said Mandy, in the same cool tone. "You came in on our Thai Airways flight from Milan this morning. You sat alone in 5A, reading a copy of *The Kite Runner*. You appeared to be sleeping for the last few hours of the trip. When we landed, you got off before anyone else, although, on a second look, perhaps it was only made to appear random. We did not see you at Customs and Immigration, and you were nowhere around when we got out to the Arrivals concourse."

Minister Dak unfolded and refolded her long hands. Her fingers, which looked like bone needles, were tipped in scarlet, and she had a large emerald-and-gold ring on the third finger of her right hand.

"Yes. I must apologize for the Malay. He has been corrected."

"The Malay being the short man?" said Dalton.

"Yes. That is the man. Corporal Ahmed. I am sorry to take up your time, but the matter was urgent, and I needed to see you personally. I know how exhausted you must be. The flight from Milan is long."

"You were in Italy?" said Dalton.

She shook her head. "No. I was transferring. From London."

She paused then, putting an emphasis on the name, but neither Dalton nor Mandy rose to it.

"Yes. From London. Although you are both residents of London, I see you came on board at Milan?"

"Yes," said Mandy, offering nothing in addition.

"You had business in Italy?"

"No," said Mandy. "Just seeing a friend. I don't mean to seem abrupt, Minister, but may I ask you to tell us what matter was so urgent that you needed to see us here this afternoon?"

"Yes. When I travel as an official of the government of Singapore, naturally there is a security element. My work at the Home Ministry is complex. A great deal of travel is required."

"May I ask you," said Dalton, "exactly what your position is here at the Ministry?"

"Oh yes. I am in charge of domestic security."

Sister branch to the SID.

"I see. Rather like the FBI in America."

She lowered her eyes.

"Nothing so grand. Singapore is a small nation. I attend to a number of issues and operate a small staff of no more than five hundred people. Nothing like America's FBI or Miss Pownall's MI5. Quite modest. However, as you can imagine, when I travel, some precautions are taken. We look at possible dangers posed by overflights, communications safety. Passenger manifests. That kind of thing. Quite routine."

Passenger manifests.

"So, you were aware that we were on board?" said Mandy.

"Oh yes. Of course, there was no concern. Your credentials are posted on your firm's website. They were vetted as a matter of course. Everything checked out. But an irregularity emerged subsequently that did cause us some concern. You're aware of our Intourist system?"

"Yes," said Dalton. "Everyone who enters Singapore, on business or as a tourist, is registered with Intourist. Many countries do the same."

Minister Dak inclined her head, obviously not pleased to have her narrative interrupted. Something glittered in her shining black eyes.

"Yes. We maintain a record of incoming passport numbers, visa requests, travel plans and destinations. Hotel registries, naturally. At approximately four in the morning, our time, our Intourist database was unlawfully entered—I believe the word is *hacked*—and certain data were queried directly. We—our technicians—were able to determine that the breach was short and posed no threat to myself or any of our officials, although my presence on our Thai flight from Milan was part of the data obtained by this breach. We determined that I was not a target, and the plane was not diverted. No, the target of this entry seems to be the two of you."

Mandy stiffened in her chair. Dalton leaned forward.

"We were? Miss Pownall and I?"

"Yes. Quite. The information obtained included your passport numbers and your visa details. It also included your registration at the Intercontinental and the time of your arrival. You were the only two people from this flight who had reservations at the Intercontinental. By a process of elimination, extrapolating from the search string, we were able to establish to our satisfaction that the reason for this illegal entry was to obtain information about you and no one else."

"Who would wish to know such a thing?" asked Mandy, her voice a little tighter than it should have been but well within the range of an outraged civilian. Minister Dak nodded in agreement.

"That was our view as well."

"Were you able to identify the intruder?" asked Dalton.

"Not completely. The attack was quite skillful, I am told, and originated in the United States."

"The U.S.?" asked Dalton, now a little rattled.

"Yes. The northeastern portion, we believe. Now, what we are interested in very much is your reaction to this event. Can you tell us why any persons would go to such trouble to discover the itinerary of two business travelers? I must confess, the event has caused something of a stir inside the Ministry, and we are quite concerned to understand the significance. Which now brings us to our most unusual request to have you visit us here. Have you any idea why you have been queried in this manner?"

Mandy said nothing. This was Dalton's game.

"Not off the top of my head, Minister. But it's happened to the bank before. Proprietary information is always of use to competing houses. Burke and Single goes to quite a bit of trouble to protect its interests. Occasionally, determined adversaries get through our systems. To tell you the truth, it's sort of routine in the business. Large amounts of money are in play. Mergers are being considered. Inferences can be drawn even from the movement of our people around the world. And Singapore is a major financial hub, so our arrival here would be of interest to many other investment houses."

"You find this explanation sufficient?"

"I find it plausible."

"You are not concerned for your safety?"

Dalton and Mandy exchanged glances.

"Not really. But if you do find out precisely who pierced your databank, we'd be very happy to have you share the information with us."

"May I ask what is your business in Singapore?"

"We're here to meet with some officials of the Hongkong and Shanghai Banking Corporation."

"Who? Precisely?"

"Mr. Lam, their London operational liaison, and Mr. Hap Ki, their chief Compliance Officer."

She nodded, tapping the names into her Lenovo and striking a key. She waited a moment, her sharp, ageless face lit up by the flickering screen. She narrowed her eyes as something appeared on her screen and then looked back at them.

"We're intrigued, Mr. Dalton, by your background. Specifically, by how little of it there is to be known. We have spent some time this morning trying to get a clearer picture of you and so far we have not been very . . . lucky. Can you explain the lack of ordinary biographical information?"

Dalton hardened up and cooled out fast.

"With respect, Minister Dak, as a citizen of the U.K. and a representative of a respected financial institution, I must admit to you that sitting still for a question like that is not in my nature. If you have some specific reason for—"

She closed the lid of the laptop with a *snap* and turned her gaze upon Mandy Pownall, who returned it with every appearance of cold reserve.

"I wonder, Miss Pownall, if you would mind showing me some identification?"

"You have our passports at the hotel desk."

"Yes. Just a formality. Anything you can show me?"

Mandy sighed, opened her bag, and ruffled around in the interior.

"Excuse me," said the Minister. "What is that?"

Mandy looked confused.

"What is what?"

"The box. May I see it?"

Mandy looked down at the black lacquer box with the jade inlay.

"Of course," she said, handing it across to the woman. "It's from Sergeant Ong. A gift . . ."

Dalton's belly began to tighten as he watched the Minister open the box and extract a long, thin tube, made of green jade, inlaid with delicate golden flames. It was about nine inches long; a cigarette holder. Dak lifted it into the light from the window beside her, turning it carefully. Dalton had all his suspicions confirmed when she raised it to her nose and inhaled. Her face changed. She kept her gaze downward, carefully returning the cigarette holder to the case and then snapping it shut. Hard. The closing *crack* was very loud in the silent room.

"You're aware," she said, locking Mandy in a hard glare, "of our official disapproval of all forms of drug use."

"Oh please," said Mandy, flaring but still controlled, purring in a sardonic Knightsbridge drawl. "I expected rather better of the Asiatic mind."

"You are in possession of a device that could be drug paraphernalia. If we can detect traces of a narcotic substance in this, you'll be charged with possession. We are not English anymore. The New Singapore does not tolerate these vulgar European depravities, Miss Pownall."

Mandy's response would have come as no surprise to anyone who knew her, but it seemed to rattle Minister Dak.

"Bugger the depravities, you poxy old crone. You know bloody well I got this outside your door, from the odious Sergeant Ong. Amateur bloody theatrics. I suppose the whole silly thing at the airport was staged just to set me up for an apology and a gift. My God, woman! You're Chinese. You ought to be able to do *inscrutable* better than anyone."

Dak, whose face had gone white except for two roseate patches, one on each cheekbone, sat upright in her chair and said, "You cannot address a minister of the government in that manner. You will answer—"

Mandy stood up, every inch the British noble.

"Micah. The door."

Minister Dak got to her feet as well, struggling for composure.

"No. I must ask you to wait while I consult with my staff."

"Are we being detained?" asked Mandy.

Dak had herself under control now, and her tone was silk over steel.

"No. Of course not. But if you will indulge me, the matter requires some consideration. I must take some advice."

"How long?"

"Minutes only. Please wait."

She rounded the desk in a stiff-legged walk, passing unfazed between them. The doors opened to reveal two uniformed police officers standing outside and then closed again, leaving them alone in the ticking stillness of the room. Dalton stepped across quietly and gently tried the doorknob and then he shook his head. Mandy, her face now quite white, sat down hard in her chair. Dalton made an inclusive gesture taking in the room—*surveillance, mikes, cameras*—to which Mandy responded with a weary nod.

"Bloody awful Singapore," she said. "It's always the same."

Since speech was impossible, and there was no way out, they both sat quietly in their chairs and radiated righteous indignation to the four walls and the hidden cameras. The palm fan swished through the dead air. The station clock clicked. And clacked. Mandy's right foot began to tremble and her lips were white. The fact that the drug charge was laughable on the face of it might have meant something in England. Not in the East. What a fool she had been to accept *anything*. The gift might as well have been six seeds of the pomegranate because she was now doomed to the underworld. She glanced at Dalton and saw that he was watching her with a look of growing concern. Her wide eyes grew moist and she swallowed, her ivory throat working. *Changi Prison.*

"Here," said Dalton, getting up and crossing to the desk, where he retrieved the unopened copy of the *Straits Times,* "improve yourself."

She took it with a hand that had an almost imperceptible tremble.

"Thank you, Micah."

"Mandy, I have a question."

She waited, a warning in her eyes.

"Who booked us on that Thai flight?"

"Why?"

"We usually fly British Airways. Why Thai?"

She looked puzzled, considering it.

"That's right. We do. I never gave it much thought. I suppose Thai was the first flight out of Milan."

"British Airways flies out of Milan too. We—our firm—have a standing account with British Air."

"I know. Tony Crane puts the flights on his Amex card and then he bills the company."

"Why?"

"He gets the air miles and the points. He's a bit of a miser. His family lost a lot of money after the Great War. He's a bit tight."

"Who booked us on Thai, then?"

"The booking came out of Tony's office. His girl, I guess."

"So, Tony booked it, then."

"Or had it booked."

"Odd?"

She stared up at him for a time.

"Yes. It's odd. A coincidence?"

Dalton said nothing. Mandy studied his face for a while, frowning slightly, her expression inward, and then looked at the station clock.

"How long, do you think?"

She was looking up at him and the fear in her face cut into Dalton. He returned the look, willing her to understand him:

You must not break.

"She said minutes. *Lovely* woman, isn't she?"

Mandy rolled her eyes, said nothing, opening the paper with an angry rustle. She crossed her legs and settled back into the chair. Dalton began to wander around the room, as if admiring the décor, very aware of the microsurette in his forearm, thinking about the infamous SID interrogation protocols and how quickly things can go to hell in the spy business. He turned as he heard Mandy's sharp intake of breath.

She was looking up at him, shocked, white-faced.

"What?"

She handed him the paper, discreetly touching his lips with the tip of her finger, and then pointing to an item in the International section:

SHOOTINGS IN FLORENCE

Three people were killed and two more injured in a shooting at the University of Florence today when an apparent kidnapping attempt was resisted by armed bodyguards. The gunfire took place in the crowded atrium of the Uffizi library. Officials say several shots were exchanged between a single gunman and police officers at the scene. The man was shot several times and taken into custody. He is reported to be in critical condition at the Civic Hospital. Three victims died at the scene and one victim is undergoing emergency surgery. Her condition is listed as grave. Officials are not releasing the names of the victims pending notification of next of kin. The shooter was later identified by local carabinieri as Slawa Radko Borins, a native of Kosovo. Reasons for the shooting are unknown at this time.

REUTERS INTERNATIONAL

Dalton, who got it the first time, read the item three times, controlling any visible reaction, trying to squeeze from the item details that were simply not there. Then he pulled out his cell phone and was not surprised to see the NO SERVICE icon. The room was shielded, of course. He put the phone away and glanced at the landline sitting on the desk. No. Any call was impossible. It would raise questions that could not be reasonably explained. His face, however, was a death mask, a rock face, a killing face, the same one he had shown to Mandy back in that private room in Florian's, a vertiginous glimpse into the *other* Dalton, the one only a very few unlucky people had ever seen. Mandy watched him in horror for a moment and then recovered.

"Too bad, isn't it?" she said, in a reasonably normal voice. "Imagine. In Florence."

"Yes," said Dalton, folding the paper neatly, his hands shaking only a little, setting it back down by Dak's laptop, his throat tight, and a cold fire spreading through his belly.

"Yes it is. In Florence. A damn shame."

16

The Celebes Sea

The gleaming new tanker lay on her spring lines, near but not tightly tethered to the repair docks, rocking steadily in the tidal estuary, her shining navy blue hull set off by two scarlet bands just above the waterline. The bridge, glittering white and glowing in the dappled sidelong light of an afternoon sun that streamed through the dense jungle around her, had a brand-new flag flying from the mast. It rippled in the sea wind, and the sound of it flowing and snapping came down to the pilothouse door, where Vigo Majiic stood, watching Emil Tarc wandering through the mechanical perfection of the new control systems; a million dollars' worth of brand-new radar, satellite communications rig, GPS-connected autopilot, state-of-the-art steering electronics, a polished stainless steel wheel with chromed spokes, new glass all around, and a deck of glowing teak boards. The bridge smelled of fresh paint, ozone, and a trace of Russian cigarette smoke. Beyond the tinted glass of the bridge, the tanker's deck stretched out before them, a five-hundred-foot-long reach of matte-gray steel marked by the black rectangles of the tanker's fifteen holding tanks, each capable of carrying sixty thousand pounds of liquid cargo. At the bow, where the Hindu cook had been slaughtered, there was only a spotless curve of new steel plating and a white-painted rail, beyond which the housings for the bow anchors—also glimmering white—rose and fell gently as the boat lay at the wharf, just under the leading edge of the camouflage canopy. All the scaffolding had been taken down, all the machinery of repair off-loaded onto the dry dock, and no sign now remained of the ruin that the ship had once been. She had been reborn into a new life on the sea.

She no longer was the *Mingo Dubai*.

The papers had been prepared long ago, and the legend created, that would see her safely through the ten thousand miles of crowded shipping lanes and heavily patrolled waters that lay in front of her now. On her huge white stack, a logo had been painted—a massive blue circle containing a large golden star—and it caught the sunlight and flashed out like fire as it moved with the hull. The crew, a carefully chosen group of Bulgarians under the control of a disgraced Bulgarian Marine officer known only as Jakki, had choppered in from Sulawesi two days before. They had seen to the engine room and the operational equipment. Supplies were on board, and she had been ballasted and fueled, enough for the next part of her journey, which would bring her across the Indian Ocean to the Suez Canal, to Port Said on the Mediterranean, where the cargo that would define her true purpose was already waiting. The gun locker now held fifteen brand-new M249 SAWs, along with crates of 7.62 rounds. Her turbines were idling, and the deep vibration of her engines moved through the hull like a heartbeat that Vigo Majiic could feel through the soles of his boots, feel in the wooden frame of the pilothouse door. Tarc, coming to a halt in the middle of the bridge house, looked at Majiic, a sardonic smile twisting his face:

"See, Vigo . . . it is ready."

Majiic nodded and turned to gesture at what lay behind them, a few hundred feet down the estuary, out under the bright sun, cloud shadows playing across the open water.

"Yes. And so is Bittagar."

Tarc came to the door and looked down the river. A huge timber boom had been dragged across the open narrows, secured by massive chains. Behind the boom, and stretching right across the harbor, lay a huge ragtag flotilla of praus, cutters, barges, towkangs, bumboats, and Zodiacs, each one filled with heavily armed men. On a central barge, in the middle of the channel, Bittagar's man Gango and several of his personal followers were standing around a large angular object covered with a ragged tarpaulin.

Bittagar himself was sitting in an old wicker peacock chair in the bow of the barge, wrapped in a plaid sheet, wearing a pair of Ray-Ban glasses, holding an old Royal Navy cutlass in his withered hands. Even from this distance, Tarc could make out Bittagar's gap-toothed leer. Gango lifted a radio handset to his mouth and thumbed the button. A handset crackled in Majiic's tunic pocket. He picked it out and handed it to Tarc.

"You surrender boat," Gango was saying, his voice a thin crackle, his Bugis-accented English almost indecipherable. "We give you safe passage."

"Honest?" said Tarc. There was a silence while Gango worked out the reply.

"Yes. Honest. We not hurt the boat. Only take for the struggle."

Tarc flicked the handset off.

"Vigo, take the wheel. Have the deckhands stand by the spring lines with boarding axes. Tell the engineer to get us ready."

"What are you going to do, Emil? Run them down?"

Tarc didn't reply directly. He lifted the radio.

"Gango, you cannot take the boat without damaging it. Then where will you be? Back at the beginning."

"You no go either way. You dead. We have boat. We build again."

"And do what with it? You don't know how to sail her."

"We have buyer," said Gango, his voice becoming plaintive, a wheedling tone entering, like a trader in a bazaar, buttery and persuasive. "Pay much more than you. Is business only. No make die for only business. Come on *buayo*. No be *lai dat*. No be *kiasu*. No be *kenna ketok* we no greedy take always more better more better take. *Kiasu* no be *lai dat*."

"What's under the tarp, Gango?"

Gango, a tiny figure in the distance, shouted something to the men around the tarp. With a kind of matador's flourish, the men slid the tarp off the thing on the deck. It was an antiaircraft gun, World War II vintage, Japanese, two gleaming ten-foot barrels on a circular track.

The man behind the weapon worked away at two heavy wheels, and the gun swiveled on the carriage, leveling slowly until both long barrels were aimed directly at the bridge. Even from two hundred yards, it was possible to see the black holes of the muzzles. Bittagar's yellowed fangs showed in the hard light, and he raised the cutlass, the blade glinting.

"Very pretty, Gango," said Tarc. "Bittagar's secret weapon."

"Yes. Pretty too much. You a bit the *ah beng* boy, you *ang mor*— you the red-haired monkey, *kambing*. You come down now. Bittagar says you help us take boat to new buyer, we give you some money back. Only fair."

"Very decent of him. Give us a minute."

He thumbed off the set. Majiic, at the wheel, was staring back at him.

"You go along with that, they'll eat us alive."

"I told you, Vigo. You're a worrier. Check the radar, will you?"

"The radar?"

"Yes. See if there's weather."

Majiic looked down at the radar screen. It was clear.

No. It wasn't clear.

There was a single red blob, about a thousand yards out. Bearing 290.

"Boats!" said Majiic. "There are boats out there?"

"No boats," said Tarc, smiling. "Listen."

Majiic listened. The wind off the sea; the new red, white, and blue flag, ripping and popping in a rising wind; the jungle, churning softly; the mutter of the engines deep in the hull; the waves, curling along her hull.

"Nothing. What am I . . ."

Then, in the distance, faint, but growing, a rhythmic drumming sound. Growing stronger and deeper, closing fast.

"What is it?"

"Company," said Tarc.

"Is it a chopper?"

"No. Look at the radar. It's coming in way too fast for that."

"What is it? Is it trouble?"

"Oh yes. It is definitely trouble."

"For who?"

"Watch this," said Tarc. "You're gonna love it."

17

The Home Ministry, Singapore

Mandy and Dalton sat in those two leather chairs in Minister Dak's office for one hour and thirteen minutes, giving every impression of seasoned English patience in the face of stolid Asiatic stupidity. Dalton had managed to stretch the time out between panic attacks about Cora Vasari to almost six minutes, and now was trying very hard not to let himself get angry enough to kill whomever walked back in through those two wooden doors. Mandy had placed a palm over the place in her forearm that held the microsurette and was silently counting her pulse while she watched the sunlight change and soften as it poured in through the minister's decoratively barred windows. She was thinking, off and on, of Porter Naumann and the many ways in which he had been like and unlike Micah Dalton.

Two brothers with different mothers but the same father, she had once thought. Porter she had loved, in the wary, provisional way that smart women love the married men who come into their beds. Mandy liked men, liked their passion and sensuality, but for Dalton she had always felt something much more enigmatic—not love; not even, like, always—but a strong desire to be in his presence, to see him move, to understand his mind. In spite of this, Mandy was too much a loving heart to take any kind of comfort from what had happened, what might have happened, to Cora Vasari in Florence.

Dalton had a ferocious attraction to her, strong enough to risk his life to see her one last time. It was not likely to be love yet—lasting love is hardly ever born out of a terrible shared crisis—but, if it turned out to be as near to love as made no nevermind, then Mandy would yield the game.

Whatever happened, she had liked what little she knew of the woman and wished her to be alive, and, if wounded, to recover without lasting hurt. As for the men behind what had happened to her, all they had left of their futures was the time it would take for Dalton to find them. If any of them were still alive when he found them. Because what she had seen of Brancati and Galan had convinced her that they were quite lethal on their own. So, either way, through the Italians or through Dalton, they had their doom coming.

That is, supposing she and Dalton got out of the Home Ministry in anything other than a SID transport van. If that looked like it was about to happen—and it had happened to an MI6 woman Mandy had known—then she was taking her own way out, on her own terms, and they could dress her remains in the latest Versace frock and prop her up in the Arcade at Raffles. The surette under her palm was in no way visible, but it was a present comfort and a certain help.

Unlike God, who, bitter experience had shown her, was, when your need was dire, nowhere to be found. He'd show up later, though, after the blood had been mopped up and all the tables righted, like a whiskey priest, mumbling vapid pieties and eyeing the Laphroaig.

There came the sounds of heavy boots on boards and muffled voices outside the door. The latch turned and clicked, and the double doors swung wide open, admitting a tall, heavy-shouldered Chinese man in his mid-forties, wearing a bespoke suit in charcoal gray over a dove gray shirt, without a tie. He looked like a man who had arrived in a rush, dressing on the way. He had a broad, blunt face, marked by deep lines around small, cold black eyes. His ochre-tinted face looked weathered by storms and hard living, an aspect weakened by pouty full lips the color of plums and an underslung jaw. He moved well, however, and with authority, paying no attention at all to Minister Dak, who tripped along in his wake with her eyes primly to the floor.

Dalton was on his feet, facing them, before they had covered six feet, and there must have been something in Dalton's look that the man instinctively recognized because he came to an abrupt halt a few feet out of Dalton's reach, turned his body slightly to the right, and lifted both hands up in the beginning of a karate stance. He seemed to realize what he had done at once and dropped his hands again to his side, stiffening, and offering a wary head bob for a bow.

"Mr. Dalton, Miss Pownall. I am Chong Kew Sak. I am the Home Secretary."

He did not have to give his *former* title. He had been the chief of the SID, and the Head Monitor of Changi Prison's Cluster C, until seven days ago. Whatever happened to prisoners in Cluster C happened because he wanted it to happen. Dalton, still on his feet, his hands at his side, tried to put a civilian expression on his hard, tight face and failed. Chong stayed where he was but seemed ready to step back if he had to.

"You're the Home Secretary?"

"Yes."

"The guest of honor at the HSBC dinner this evening?"

"Yes, I—"

"The dinner to which we have been formally invited?"

"Yes, but that is beside the—"

"Are you aware of what has passed in this room?"

"Minister Dak told me that certain contraband may have—"

Dalton stepped in closer.

Chong gave ground and then stiffened again.

"Do you know who we are?"

A flicker in his eyes, a slight glance to the left and then back.

"You are representatives of the English bank, Burke and Single."

"Here for a commercial conference? Visas in order? All papers vetted? Invited by the finance ministry of Singapore?"

Chong opened his mouth and then shut it again.

"Then perhaps you can tell me why have we been treated like criminals?"

Chong found his footing, moved back in.

"I don't understand. There has been no mistake. Minister Dak has"—here he looked at Minister Dak, fixing her like a bug, and then back to Dalton—"has reason to suspect . . . You must sit back down, sir."

"We've sat long enough. I've had all of the local hospitality I can stand. Your minister here has gone to a great deal of trouble to get some sort of leverage on us and there's only one reason I can think of that explains it."

Chong's face did not change in any obvious way, but the muscles in his jaw and cheeks were now tightening imperceptibly.

He's preparing a lie, thought Mandy.

"You will not sit, Mr. Dalton? Please?"

"I will not sit, sir. You're holding a British national. You know him as Brendan Fitch. You have been interrogating him. By you, I mean the SID."

"I know nothing of the SID, Mr. Dalton. And what does a British banker care about some English drunkard in a Singapore jail?"

"I'm going to get right to the point here because neither Miss Pownall nor I wants to spend any more time in Singapore than we bloody well have to. The man you call a *drunkard* is an English citizen. I have been asked—and I suspect that you may already be aware of this—I have been asked by Her Majesty's Government, while we are in Singapore, to open an informal discussion to secure his release. Since we are now in the august presence of the Home Secretary, and the Home Ministry is in charge of prisons, it seems to me that we can cut through a lot of smoke by talking this thing out right here. If you want it to happen, we can be on the next flight out of here, with Brendan Fitch."

"We have held many unsavory British nationals in Changi over the years, Mr. Dalton. It has rarely elicited the personal attention of Queen Elizabeth. Is there some aspect of Mr. Fitch's background that draws to us the compliment of her illustrious regard?"

"I suspect that you already know what his background is."

Chong's face registered fleeting surprise. This admission was not in Cather's plan. But Cather's plan was blown the minute somebody in the cyberworld attracted the attention of the Singapore security people to a pair of ordinary English bankers flying in for a black-tie bun-fight. Mandy should not have accepted Sergeant Ong's gift. Incredibly, she had. They had something on her now, and Chong would have no qualms about using it. It had been done many times before, by every Intelligence agency in the world. But Dalton had his full attention now.

"I see. Perhaps we do," said Chong, feeling his way. "It is true that we have discovered that Fitch was a false identity, if that is your point, Mr. Dalton. Mr. Fitch's real name is Raymond Paget Fyke. He is a former member of the English Special Air Services. He has been, for some years, a contract agent in the employ of the Central Intelligence Agency. This, I think, may explain the elevated attention of your noble Queen, since Britain is now a staunch ally of the United States."

"Fyke's grown chatty, has he?"

"He has become more cooperative of late. As a result, the circumstances of his incarceration have improved. He is being well treated."

"I would like to see him."

"Sadly, he is indisposed. He is in the infirmary at Changi."

"Fell down a flight of stairs? Caught a googly playing cricket?"

Chong's eyes narrowed with a kind of grim amusement.

"Indeed."

"Excellent. We have arrived at the heart of the matter. You admit you are aware of who this man actually is?"

"It's not a question of *admitting*. The man is a spy. I have—"

"You know his real identity. You admit this. Therefore, if you have fully satisfied yourself that his identity is Raymond Fyke, an English national, you are now in violation of your own leader's direct orders."

This seemed to rattle Chong.

"In what manner . . . ?"

"Your revered Minister Mentor instituted the New Cooperative Policy on Intelligence Sharing shortly after the attacks of September eleven. I imagine someone along the way has mentioned this policy to you?"

Chong, like most Singaporeans, didn't enjoy sarcasm.

"This bears no relevance to—"

"Forgive me. I'm informed by the American liaison in London that Mr. Fyke has been the subject of a DSDNI order filed on the twenty-third of November 2002. The Americans inform us that this order—"

"Excuse me, Mr. Dalton. What is this *DSDNI* order?"

"It means *Detain, Sequester, Do Not Interrogate*, Mr. Secretary. Apparently, your own SID people acknowledged receipt of this order the next day, after it was forwarded to all friendly Intelligence agencies through Interpol. That acknowledgment is on file at Interpol and in Langley. Cooperation with exactly these types of orders was mandated by Mr. Lee Kwan Yew's New Policy on Intelligence Sharing. That policy is still in force, is it not?"

"Yes. Of course."

Chong was not enjoying this experience. Mandy, watching it, felt her heart begin to lighten. The power had shifted. Dalton was running the room. She could see Minister Dak's face from where she was standing. Although her face was a mask of humble discretion, a pinkish glow of satisfaction was coloring her throat and cheeks. Mandy thought the best thing Dak could do now was to silently withdraw before Chong realized she was still there, watching Dalton rip him apart. Dak seemed to be of the same mind, because, in a moment, bowing to hide the slightest of smiles, she glided soundlessly out of the room.

"So, we arrive at the logical inference from these facts, which is that at some point in the past few days, when you realized you were aggressively interrogating a man who was the subject of an order that required you, under Mr. Lee's direct orders, to immediately inform the United States Ambassador to Singapore of the fact, you chose to ignore the order."

"These are not matters that I, as Home Secretary, will discuss with a mere civilian, certainly not with one who has offered no diplomatic credentials. And I will not be subjected to an impertinent harangue by anyone, no matter for whom he pretends to speak. Minister Dak has made some very serious allegations against your assistant—"

Here he turned and found to his surprise that Minister Dak had, on little cat's feet, made a clean getaway. Angry now, he glanced at Mandy, and she saw something worse than brutality in his face; she saw carnal appreciation. "And the cylinder that was discovered in her possession has been sent to our laboratory for analysis. Should—"

"Should you work that vein a second longer, I'll see to it that the

U.S. Ambassador here lodges a formal protest with the Prime Minister for your failure to report the unlawful detention—and, I suspect, the sustained torture—of a person under an American DSDNI order. As the former head of the SID and the man who until last week ran Cluster C at Changi Prison . . . that means you personally get to stand up in front of Lee Hsien Loong and explain to him exactly why you have your American allies royally pissed off at you after only seven days at your new post. How's that work for you?"

"You are—"

"I am *tired,* Mr. Secretary. My *partner,* not my *assistant,* and I have traveled several thousand miles to improve commercial relations with your nation, and, I admit, to be *informal* emissaries on a mission of mercy. We have been, since the moment we arrived in Singapore, the subject of insupportable affronts. Affronts to representatives of the world's foremost banking community at a time, I must tell you, when Singapore is reeling from the collapse of its dot-com ambitions and looking at the rise of a formidable economic power only a few hundred miles to the north. Your government cannot *afford* to indulge incompetent ministers and, I assure you, if presented with a complete narrative of these events by an angry representative of the United States, will take action to *correct* them. So here's what I propose. We're taking a cab back to the Intercontinental, where we will refresh ourselves. We must sadly decline the invitation of the HSBC to attend the reception this evening, but we *may*—I repeat, we *may*— not inform the bank of the *true* reasons for our absence, which is our dismay at the way we have been treated by certain officials of the host government."

That one hit home. Chong looked a little green around the edges.

"There, at the Intercontinental, we will await your decision concerning our request to have our compatriot, Mr. Fyke, released without further delay—alive, well—into our custody. Miss Pownall, gather yourself. We're leaving. Mr. Chong, I will not say good day to you."

Dalton did not look at Mandy as he bowed—a short, insulting bow, during which he never took his eyes off Chong's face—he had made an enemy, he could see. But right now, he didn't give a damn. He straightened, and walked easily to the door. Chong turned to follow, his face set and his body poised to do . . . something.

But he did nothing. Mandy breezed by him with a half smile on her lips and her heart in her mouth. The open doorway, where Dalton was waiting with an expression of polite impatience on his face, looked a hundred miles away, and the long hallway beyond it seemed to recede into infinity. No one stopped them at the stairwell. No one stepped into their path at the front gate. They hailed a cab and left the compound. A short while later, leaning back into the greasy vinyl of a lime green gypsy Hyundai, Mandy found that she could actually breathe. She looked across at Dalton.

"Micah, I think I want to bear your children."

Dalton, staring out the window, had already made three futile calls to Venice. Brancati was in Florence. Galan was out. No one knew anything.

"Yeah. I was pretty good."

"Good? You were magnificent. It was like watching Rupert Everett dress down Jabba the Hutt. I particularly liked *insupportable affronts.*"

Dalton's mind remained in Florence. They sat a while in silence.

"Try calling again," she said.

"The battery's dead. Do you have your phone?"

"In the room. Needed a charge. Sorry."

Mandy was quiet again, for a few blocks.

"This cyberhacker thing worries me. It's always the X factor that gets you. This is definitely an X factor. Maybe it's time to get out of Dodge."

Dalton looked at her.

"What, you mean cheese it and scarper?"

"It's a thought. I'm not happy with the idea of being in a cell alone with Chong Kew Sak. Nor am I thrilled with the alternate plan, which involves being dead. My long-term plans did not include being dead."

"Nor did mine. Anyway, we can't scarper. Chong will have sent someone to scoop our passports from the hotel. That's why they held us for an hour and thirteen minutes. They also went through our suite. There'll be taps, bugs, maybe even a camera."

"So we go to the Oriental. Or Raffles."

"No. We're supposed to be English bankers. Moving out of the hotel would kill that cover. Only surveillance-aware people would do that."

"Jolly. So we stay. Where do I shower?"

"I wouldn't."

Mandy shuddered. Dalton could feel her shaking next to him. He leaned in to her, trying to comfort her. Mandy's eyes were shining again. She was a good agent, but fieldwork was not her specialty. Why had Cather sent her along? He always had reasons. What were they? Mandy sighed, seemed to gather herself again, smiled and gave him one of her sidelong looks.

"Micah, we're bloody *spies*, aren't we? We could do something all Matt Damon–ish. Overpower somebody and use our top secret thingy-whatsit to gain entry to the hidden whatsa-hoozit and whisk us all to safety."

"Sorry. The top secret thingy-whatsit is in the shop."

"So we're staying?"

"Afraid so."

"Rats."

"Rats?"

Mandy nodded.

"Right now, rats is *le mot juste.*"

Another interlude; two solitudes of dark thought.

Mandy said:

"About Fyke. Do you think your bluff will work?"

"Chong will either cover his ass with Lee and then have us arrested on some sort of bullshit charge or he'll come back with a face-saving counteroffer. If he does come back, we deal out the Chinese techs."

"Where's your money going?"

"Mandy, I haven't a clue."

Mandy thought that over for a block. They could see the Intercontinental sign looming over a tower. The sky was clouding up. The monsoon season was about to begin. Mandy let out a long sighing breath.

"One good thing, anyway, Micah."

"Yes?"

"Whatever they've been doing to Ray Fyke, they'll stop."

18

The National Security Agency, Fort Meade, Maryland

Nikki Turrin, sitting at an empty table in the Crypto City Starbucks, stared down at the top of her *Vente* mocha-fratte-latte-whatever and tried not to compare it with the exquisite cup of *caffè corretto* she had shared with a lovely young Italian boy on a terrace in Lucca on a Tuscan summer's day that may have happened light-years away. The surface of the *Vente* whatever was sprinkled with a substance the *barista* stoutly maintained was free-trade, shade-grown Brazilian chocolate. Nikki, one of the Monitors and therefore of an analytical turn, had examined the material closely and was coming to the unhappy conclusion that it was actually organic carob shavings. Nikki's heritage was Italian, so she loathed carob as much as she loathed anything even remotely vegan. She pushed the cup aside and turned again to her shell pink Apple notebook, where she had hit PAUSE in the middle of a YouTube video that had her a little troubled.

It was grainy, handheld, a little shaky, and seemed to have been shot from a distance, through a screen of forest growth of some sort.

The camera had been trained on a swimming pool, large, not well maintained, but full of clear water. In that background was a villa of a type she had seen on a trip to Bulgaria a few years back, all pillars and turrets and arched windows, none of them agreeing with anything else. The villa gave the impression of vulgar wealth. In the foreground, a party seemed to be going on, not the kind of party she would have enjoyed. Hookers and thugs, was the impression she got as the video rolled, lots of skinny girls getting naked and being manhandled by beefy, beer-gutted men wearing too much gold.

One fellow stood out: a very large, bald-headed hog of a man with a tattoo that covered his entire chest, perhaps an eagle—an American eagle—with a lance through its chest and some kind of flag or banner attached to the lance. The action unrolled, turned greasy, then nasty, and ended with what appeared to be the horrible choking death of everyone who got into the pool. It had been posted on YouTube by someone who identified himself as YaanMonkey223. YaanMonkey223 claimed to have copied it off an Internet video site in Finland, but in the world of YouTube no serious questions were ever asked about the source or reliability of *content*. What counted was *hits*, how many times it had been viewed, and this video showed some signs of going *viral*, since it had spread as far as her Apple computer in Maryland.

The video troubled her because it wasn't an obvious fake, a setup, as were most of the terminally tedious clips posted on YouTube. This one had a terrible plausibility. Something about it suggested a real place and real deaths. YaanMonkey223 had added a short description of it, calling it a promo tape that had been deliberately leaked in order to create a cyberspace buzz for somebody's upcoming flick. Nikki was not convinced. The deaths looked real, and the quality of the footage—blurry, handheld—reeked of covert surveillance. Before coming to the NSA she had worked for a prosecutor's office in Pittsburgh; she'd seen a lot of surveillance footage during a protracted investigation involving thefts from a container yard.

She played it twice more, thinking it over. Then she copied it to her hard drive, inserted a small Sony Micro Vault into a USB port, and copied the video onto that. She disconnected the Micro Vault and slipped it into the pocket of her jeans. It felt warm against her thigh, almost radioactive.

She left the *Vente* whatever on the table, nodded to some coworkers, gathered up her Apple and her purse, and left the cafeteria.

Somebody needed to see this video.

She wasn't sure who.

She wasn't sure why.

But somebody needed to see it.

19

The Intercontinental Hotel, Singapore

When they pulled up under the portico of the Intercontinental, a liveried doorman had the cab doors open before it had come to a complete stop. A dashing Sikh about seven feet tall gave Mandy a dazzling smile and welcomed her return to the hotel in such convincing tones that Mandy wondered if he was a long-lost cousin. Dalton was left alone to extract himself on the starboard side, almost colliding with a lean, wolfish-looking young man with fine, shoulder-length black hair that shimmered like silk, very tan, absurdly handsome in a hard-cut, slightly Hispanic way, resplendent in a superbly executed navy blue lightweight suit and a crisp white shirt that might have been made by Pink's. Their eyes met briefly, as he stepped back and waited for Dalton to get out of the cab; although he was obviously in a hurry, his open, friendly regard caught Dalton's attention because his eyes were a shade of pale green that Dalton had never seen before. The man—the boy—was slender, looked very fit, and had a kind of hardness under the charming smile that wasn't visible unless you knew what to look for. The man's smile grew wider.

"Forgive me," he said, bowing slightly. "Don't mean to push."

His accent was . . . odd. French, perhaps, but not exactly. Educated.

"Not at all," said Dalton, returning the smile.

Gay? thought Dalton. Decided no. But something was there, a kind of friendly but critical attention, as if Dalton was being appraised by a potential buyer. He yielded the cab, and the man slid into it with an easy, athletic grace, closing the door without another glance at Dalton.

The cab pulled away, and Dalton was looking at Mandy across the empty space. She was watching the cab merge into Singapore traffic with evident interest. She realized he was looking at her and, in spite of her mood, flashed him one of her electric smiles, pulling her sunglasses down and looking at him over the rims:

"Oh my," she said.

"BACK WHERE YOU just came from, please," said Lujac. The driver twisted around to look at him.

"The Home Ministry, sir?"

"Yes, the Home Ministry, please."

The ride to the Parliament grounds took about thirty minutes through thickening afternoon traffic. On the way, Lujac pulled out his cell phone and dialed a number in Odessa, got a beeping tone, hit the pound sign, followed by a nine-character, alphanumeric pin number, and waited. Not long.

"Black Sea Freight Forward."

"Hello, Cabbage."

"Kiki. What do you need?"

"I got into the room. There—"

"How?"

"Pardon?"

"How did you get into the room?"

"How is this your business, Cabbage?"

"If you were clumsy, it will be Daddy's business."

Lujac glanced at the driver. He was—or appeared to be—talking on a cell phone and paying no attention to his passenger. Lujac spoke softly.

"I knocked on the door. I was holding an empty FedEx envelope so that if somebody was in the room, I could ask for the wrong guy and apologize. Just trying to find the right guy to give this to. Somebody opened it. A Chinese man with a face like a frog. Bad suit and heavy shoes. An obvious cop. He looked nervous. I said I was there to assist Mr. Dalton. I asked him to identify himself. He said he was from HSBC. The bank. Like hell he was. I said Mr. Dalton may have left some papers in the room and that I had been asked to retrieve them. He looked at the FedEx envelope and thought about it and then let me in. There was another guy there, a short, ratty-looking Malay with a bruised eye and a bandaged hand. Another cop. They looked like they had been tossing the room. They watched me as I wandered about the suite. Looking for the papers. No papers. There was a cell phone on a charger by the house phone. I pretended to use the phone to call Mr. Dalton. While I did, I palmed the cell phone—"

"What would you have done if no one had been in the room?"

"I have a random-number generator; looks like a Palm Pilot. You stick the slide card in the slot and it unlocks almost every hotel door in Christendom in thirty seconds. Why? Are you taking a night course in illegal entries, Cabbage?"

"Why didn't you wait until there was no one there? Now you've been seen."

"Life is risk. You take it on the hop. I liked the rush, too, with those two cops right there."

"They know what you look like."

"Of course they do. So what? They're gonna call Dalton up, say, Hey, while we were tossing your room, this handsome young blade came to the door asking for you?"

"Aren't they going to be afraid you'll tell Dalton *they* were in the room?"

"This is Singapore. Cops do whatever they want in Singapore. They wanted to toss his room, they tossed it. Maybe they care if he knows, maybe they don't. Frankly, Cabbage, I don't give a shit either way. I'm not here for the waters, am I? I'm here to find out why Dalton came to Singapore and then kill him. Kill him *a whole lot*. This will all be over in twenty-four. The real question is, these are supposed to be two Brits in town for some kind of banking party. Why were the cops in the room in the first place?"

A silence from Larissa's end of the line. Lujac could hear her thinking it through. She was quick. He'd give her that. A monstrosity but quick.

"Something drew their attention. The cops. If I had to guess, I'd say that when we hacked into the Intourist system to find out where they were staying, we left signs."

"That's what I thought too. Did you run a string that would have flagged those two particular names?"

"They were the only ones checking into the Intercontinental. So maybe that would have . . ."

"Not so smart, Cabbage. Now we have cops all over the job."

"We don't know that. There could be other reasons."

"Doesn't matter now. Got to play it out."

"Do you still have the cell phone?"

"No. Of course not. All I wanted was a minute with it."

"Why?"

"Trade secrets, Cabbage. Trade secrets."

The cab was slowing, moving into the gate area of a massive Victorian pile straight out of *Wuthering Heights*. Uniformed guards in bug-eyed sunglasses were tensing up and scowling at the car. Lujac snapped the phone shut without saying good-bye, handed the driver a fistful of Sing dollars and got out of the vehicle, putting a puzzled tourist expression on his face as one of the guards moved forward to intercept him at the gates.

"No get in," said the guard a bit redundantly, given the machine gun and the thuggish scowl, in the pidgin Malay Chinese dialect called *Singlish*. Lujac went for upper-class Brit Twit, one of his favorites.

"Dreadfully sorry. This isn't the Parliament?"

"No *Parla-men*. This Home Ministry. You have note?"

"Note? You mean, appointment?"

"Yes. *Appoin-men*."

"No. Just breezing through Singapore. Thought I'd see the sights. What is this building again? The Home Ministry? Lovely old pile. What does the Home Ministry do?"

Direct questions are considered rude in Singapore, but the guard tried to bear up. He was used to Brit Twits. They were thick on the ground in this part of the world.

"Run all Singapore. Run prisons."

"Prisons? Really. Are there *prisons* in Singapore?"

The guard was a slab-faced, blocky youngster with a unibrow like a big, fuzzy black caterpillar and a deep furrow between his flat-black eyes. Lujac's question made the guard's brow furrow much deeper. He looked a little like Bush thinking. George Bush actually thought pretty well, but it was the bane of his political life that he didn't look good doing it.

"Yes. All prisons run from here. Changi Prison run from here."

"Really. Can one visit Changi Prison? Are there tours?"

"Tours? *Lah*. Go stun now, *ang mor*. You a bit the blur. No tours."

"May I tour this building?"

"No. Private. Must have note. Good day, now. You look-see maybe Arab-town town. Look-see Cheena-town town, can. Good day, *lah*."

The guard turned away, muttering something in Hokkien that may have been a slur on Lujac's ancestors. Lujac waved him off, and wandered a bit, looking for a hawker stand or maybe an open café. He found one not too far away, settled in under an awning, ordered a pint of Singha, a plate of stingray and a bucket of unshucked raw oysters, leaned back into the chair, twitching around a little to get comfortable. He sipped at the Singha—it was chilled delightfully, right down to the core—yawned, blinked, focused his attention on the gates of the Home Ministry.

And waited.

AS SOON AS he entered the suite, Dalton knew it had been tossed. Mandy waited in the front hall, trying not to look for cameras and mikes, feeling that talking herself into this field trip may have been unwise. Dalton went through everything, the entire suite, inch by inch, his motions economical, even graceful. *He moves a little like a crocodile,* she thought, watching him. *Slithery and boneless.* She sat on a chair in the entrance hall, leaden and depressed, and desperately in need of a shower.

But she wasn't ready to go farther into the suite yet.

Just wasn't . . . ready.

Dalton went through the place quickly, his choices based on bitter experience. He came to a halt, like a short-haired pointer, at two distinct locations: a large Zen garden sandbox, complete with ebony rocks, that sat in the middle of the black lacquer coffee table; and, again, in the master bedroom, the long rosewood campaign chest that sat at the foot of the four-poster bed. He came out of the bedroom, his face a little harder than normal, and walked back out to the entrance hallway. He was holding Mandy's cell phone. He held it so that Mandy could see the screen and typed in some text.

2 mks 1 coffee table 1 chest my bedrm
Pretty sure no cam

Mandy took the phone.

Fk pretty sure
B dam sure

Dalton smiled, took the phone back.

Am dam sure
Have a shower
Lots of steam
Fog any lens

Mandy considered it, looking hard at Dalton. She had wanted a shower ever since Chong Kew Sak had given her his dung beetle roll around back at the Ministry.

"I think," she said, trying not to sound theatrical, "that I will have a shower. I'm absolutely beat. Why don't you mix us some drinks? If you want to call the Head Office, use my phone. The phone charges here are ridiculous."

She moved past him down the hall, her shoulders straight, walking like an actress emerging on a stage. She straightened a floral arrangement on the table behind the sofa in the living room, stopped to take in the early-evening panorama of downtown Singapore—the lights were coming on now and the effect was magnificent—she passed on through the living room and slipped soundlessly down the hall toward her own master suite. Dalton watched her go with a certain amount of affectionate amusement.

His face changed as he went into the living room and stood at the window wall, staring out, seeing nothing but the cobblestone atrium and the pillared colonnade of the Uffizi in Florence. He didn't want to make a cell-phone call, even on Mandy's heavily encrypted fast-burst phone.

But he had no choice. The hotel lines were tapped. The suite had been politely ransacked. The signs were everywhere, if you knew where to look. It had been done with just enough roughness to send a message: we've been stamping around in your life and we can do it again anytime we want. Dalton didn't care. They could have ripped the lining out of his suits and shredded his shoes. There was nothing to find but whatever items fit a banker's life. They had learned nothing, and given away everything in the attempt. It was lousy tradecraft, and it made him feel a little better.

He used the remote to turn on the television, got the BBC, spiked the volume up to *stun*, picked up the phone and dialed Brancati's cell-phone number. Venice was nineteen hours ahead of Singapore, on the other side of the date line. It would be the middle of yesterday for Brancati. Dalton didn't give a damn if it was the middle of the night. The line rang three times and got picked up on the fourth.

"Brancati."

"How is she?"

"Where are you? I have been trying to reach you."

"I was in a dead zone. How is she?"

"It's bad, my friend."

"How bad?"

"She is out of surgery. In a private intensive care room. She was shot twice. The first bullet went through her left lung. Collapsed it, but not too much damage. A miracle. The second bullet struck her in the temple. Left side. Traveled around the left side of her head, lodged in the muscle near the base of her neck."

"Spinal?"

"No. Missed the vertebrae. But some bleeding into the brain."

"What kind of slug?"

"Small. Hollow-point. A .32 ACP. From a CZ Model 10."

"That's a Serbian piece, and a close-up gun. How did he get so close?"

"You cannot be on the streets in Florence and not be close to somebody. Florence is made for assassins. I told you this some time ago, when we first met. We told her this also. Many times. You do not control Cora, as you are aware. My men behaved well. Two are dead now. A third will be blind in his left eye. Cora . . . They have put her into a coma, to relieve pressure on the brain. She sleeps now. Her pulse is steady. She is not on a respirator. But her brain function is . . . it is not good, my friend."

"Where is she— No. I don't want to know."

"I wasn't going to tell you. Not on this. Her family is with her. They have come from all over Italy. None of them blame you. Will you come?"

Dalton was quiet for a time.

"She's in a coma?"

Brancati's tone was harder now, the tone you use when you are steeling yourself to share grief. The ghost of Porter Naumann flickered briefly to life in the reflection from the window glass.

Grief is coming, Micah. More than you know.

"Yes. Induced medically. But I must say to you, there is no telling how much time. She may sleep for a month. She may get up and go dancing. She may never awake. She may die within the hour."

Grief is coming.

"Will she know me?"

"Only you can say. What will you do?"

In a coma.

Just like Laura.

His first wife, Laura, had suffered irreparable brain damage after a suicide attempt, an attempt brought on by Dalton's unwillingness to forgive her for the accidental death of their baby girl. She had died more than a month ago, after years in a vegetative state. Now a second woman in his life was lying in a deadly sleep. This was punishment. Karma. Fate.

Will you go to Florence to sit by her bed?

Dalton knew the answer and hated it.

"The only way I can help her is to finish this."

Now the silence was on Brancati's end. Finally, he said:

"That is what I thought you would say." He said it without obvious disapproval, and actually felt none, since a soldier in the field cannot jump up and run home whenever he wants, no matter how terrible the news.

"What about the shooter?"

"He is alive. My men are with him. His world is pain."

"Good. Did you get anything?"

"Did we need anything? We know who he works for. Galan is dealing with that now. If you wish to be in at the kill, you should finish your work there quickly. The Carabinieri are going to make an example of this Serb."

"He's in tight with the Montenegrin government?"

"There is no Montenegrin government. There is only gangs."

"Did you ever find out who did the girl?"

"A male, anyway. She had been raped just before she had been stabbed. We have the DNA. She was dragged behind a boat. Perhaps a fishing boat. We have a record of every craft that was in the lagoon or around the Lido during the time frame. We are checking the owners now. Also, we found a microphone. In the palms, near the hospital. A directional mike. You understand me?"

"We were heard."

"Yes. The microphone?"

"Yes."

"It was one of ours. From our own stores."

"Was it your relative? DioGrazzi?"

"No. He was already being questioned."

"Which means you *still* have a stranger in the house."

"Apparently, yes. Galan always suspected it. When Dario was exposed . . . it was too easy. As if it were deliberate."

"A diversion?"

"Galan thinks so."

"Whoever killed the girl will know where I am now."

"Yes."

"He'll be looking for me here."

"Yes."

Dalton watched a big Bell chopper hovering over the city spires, the last of the setting sun turning her into a fiery red-gold dragonfly. The sound of her rotors came through the glass, faint as a heartbeat in Florence.

"Good."

"It is a reason to stay where you are. I will tell you something, as a friend. To take all this on as your own guilt, it will make you weak. And it is not true. We—I—am to blame for this. I let her go to Florence. I let someone get near her. This is not on your—how do you say?—*your chest*. It is on mine. You do what you need to. We will watch over Cora. No one will reach her again. Have you heard this? Have you understood me?"

"Yes. Yes, I have heard you."

"One thing. When we find out who owned the boat, who do we call?"

Langley? Or do you not trust Langley?

"Me. You have this number?"

"No. It is encrypted."

Dalton gave him the number.

"So, you directly?"

"Yes. No one else."

You do not trust Langley? No. I do not trust Langley.

The Home Ministry, Singapore

The little Malay cop came out of the gate in front of the Home Ministry at nine-seventeen. Lujac dropped some Sing dollars on the table beside the untouched bucket of raw oysters. *Something slimy served in an ashtray*, was Miss Piggy's take on oysters, and Lujac agreed. He had ordered them only because of the very nasty, razor-sharp shucking tool they always supplied with the oysters. He slipped this into his pocket and walked out of the café, his eyes hard on the target. The cop was dressed in too-tight designer jeans, bright red sneakers, and a black-and-white satin team jacket with the logo of the Cleveland Indians on the back. He had on a lime green ball cap—he wore it backward—and what hair was showing under it was damp and slick as if he had just had a shower. From a style point of view, he looked like a two-legged circus wagon. Lujac spent some time looking for any sign of a service piece on the cop, concluded he was unarmed, which corresponded to his information on the off-duty carrying of weapons in Singapore, which was usually only allowed for a few senior officials. Like with most totalitarian states, one of Lee's first priorities had been to ban the private ownership of handguns. An unarmed population is a docile one.

The cop's small, pinched face was downcast, and the bruise around his black eye had opened up across his cheek like a deep-purple lotus. He carried his injured right hand in a makeshift sling made out of a washroom towel. The man looked like he had just finished a very bad day at the office and was now thinking only of a cold beer and the fitful sleep of the been-hard-done-by.

The cop made his way west until he got to the MRT subway entrance on Bridge Street, where he limped down the staircase and merged into a mass of people milling about waiting for the east–west line. Although there were hundreds of people jammed onto the subway platforms, the station was spotless and brilliantly lit. Under the glaring fluorescents, the little Malay's lime green ball cap stood out like a roadside flare so Lujac was able to keep a line on him without getting too close.

A train arrived in a hissing clamor and the smell of ozone. Thirty doors chuffed open down the line; those passengers exiting engaged in a head-down, grunting-and-shoving match with those who wanted in. No voices were raised, no punches thrown, but for a man with some personal-space issues—and Lujac had them all—the Singapore MRT was trial by frottage.

The crowds were clean and not badly dressed. The Singapore style was extremely demure and conservative—if the Taliban golfed, this is what they would wear—but, to Lujac, they all smelled of soy and chili sauce and infrequent bathing, and there were far too many of them.

The doors closed, and Lujac tried to stand as far from everyone else as he could. The atmosphere was wonderfully chill, and nobody talked. Everybody kept their hands to themselves and their eyes on the ground. The Malay cop had found a seat at the far end of the car.

He had his head down and his iPod plugged in, and he was looking at some sort of graphic novel—the pictures could be read from yards away. He favored his right hand, and winced a little each time he turned a page. There was a lost quality about him, and something else, a touching vulnerability, as if he was going through life with a secret sorrow.

That might be useful. Wait and see.

Lujac, sensing a long night, went inward and spent some happy time wondering what it would be like to spend several hours killing Micah Dalton. It would be delicious. The man was so beautiful to look at. Owning him for a while would be something to remember, to savor. The train barreled through the earth, flashing from strobe-lit darkness into flare-bright stations one after the other. The crowds had thinned out quite a bit, and now Lujac was growing a little concerned. He was dressed far better than anyone else in the car and he was tailing a cop.

A cop who had seen him at the hotel, in Dalton's suite, only a few hours before. There was no reason to believe that the man was a bad cop, although Lujac suspected he wasn't a very good one—he had absolutely no situational awareness—but even a bad cop will tumble to a tracker if you whack him about the ears with it.

Lujac got off the car when the train pulled into a stop called Kallang and got back on two cars down. It was a good move, because the next station was Paya Lebar Road, and everyone in the cars who looked like a Malay stood up and shuffled toward the doors. Including the cop.

Lujac waited until the cars had almost emptied and most of the crowds were riding the escalator up to the street exit. He stepped out of the car and followed along, taking his suit jacket off and draping it carefully over his left forearm. He could see the lime green ball cap bobbing along in the crowds about fifty feet ahead. The man never turned around, never looked from side to side. A portrait of morose oblivion. How had he ever been taken on by the Singapore police? Probably a government-forced diversity program.

Hire a Malay: They're fun to watch.

It was full dark now. There was no such thing as a lingering twilight in these latitudes. Out on the street, there was a huge post office, a barbarous, modernist hulk built in the grand tradition of barbarous hulks all over the totalitarian world. The streetscape around this hulk was ratty and run-down, lit by cold-blue streetlamps that made everyone look like a vampire: it was a squalid tangle of badly built stores selling bootleg DVDs, Chinese knockoff hip-hop clothing, Third World electronics, hawker shops lit by bars of fluorescent lights and furnished with card tables covered in cheap plastic and with ugly plastic chairs. Thousands of Malays were out and about on this sultry Asian night, moon-eyed dating couples followed by their squat and surly female chaperones, married wage slaves trailing a line of little brown kids like mallards on a riverbank, all of this gathered into a sprawling shantytown called Malay Village that could only be improved by a typhoon.

A dense haze of steamy air that reeked of fish sauce and chili and raw sewage and fried beans hung over the neighborhood, the sound of Malaysian fusion bands carrying over the rooftops, a type of rhythmic, Asian-falsetto howling that made Lujac think of a castrato in a wheelchair falling down a fire escape. Most of the younger people were crowding the hawker shops and jostling into a large open-air marketplace that announced itself to the world with a large green-and-purple neon sign that read GEYLANG SERAI WET MARKET. *Oooh,* thought Lujac, his stomach rolling, *how yummy.*

The little cop worked his way into this ragtag market, stopping at various hawker stalls to gather together an assortment of ethnic Malayan delicacies—jellied goats' eyes in a vomit reduction, very likely, and perhaps a side dish of pickled dog peckers—the cop got himself a couple of bottles of Tiger beer, fished out, dripping, from a large tin tub full of pee yellow water, took a seat at a long board table and settled in to his repast, hunched over the tray and eating with his left hand, an unhygienic offense that was attracting a great deal of nauseated regard from the people sharing the table.

The cop missed all that, too, sunk deep in his private misery and radiating broadband resentment. *Ripe for the picking,* thought Lujac, watching him chewing a jellied goat's eye with his slack mouth open.

The trouble was, there were damn few *ang mor*s around, *ang mor* being a derogatory Chinese phrase meaning "red-haired monkey"— in other words, Europeans. A few of those wretched backpackers who were all over Italy and Montenegro like a plague of roaches, but they looked nothing like him. Thank God. But if he was going to pick this guy off, Lujac needed to blend in, he needed cover, and there wasn't much of that around.

No help for it, thought Lujac, wondering how this cop thing was going to play out as he stood in the half dark of a side alley and watched his man drain his fourth Tiger, his head back and his throat working. The answer came a few minutes later when the cop set down his fifth bottle of Tiger and made direct eye contact with a young Malay boy sitting alone at a table for two about ten feet away.

The boy was what the Singaporeans call an *ah beng,* a punk-style kid with gelled hair and a row of silver studs punched into both eyebrows. He was wearing a too-large flame-colored shirt with cross-stripes of jagged purple, baggy blue jeans hacked off at midcalf, and oversized black combat boots with the laces flapping loose. His expression was mixed, a kind of thuggish bravado masking an undercurrent of fear. If the kid was over fifteen, Lujac was the Bishop of Rome. The cop was now staring at him—*gunning him,* the Americans liked to say—and the kid was trying to hold up his end by staring right back. The stare down was taking place in a tense silence and in a crowd of totally unaware civilians.

Lujac watched this for a while and thought, *Ahh.*

Now I get it.

21

The National Security Agency, Fort Meade, Maryland

Nikki hit PLAY and sat back, studying her supervisor's face, as he leaned over his Dell and watched the video. His bland pink face was lit up by the glow from the screen, and the image of the video was reflected in each lens of his round tortoiseshell glasses. Under the lenses, his large, wet eyes glistened and his pupils contracted. He drummed a paradiddle—unconsciously, as he always did—on the edge of his laptop keyboard. An overhead vent pushed recycled air through his windowless office, and Nikki shifted in the hardwood chair he had pulled up for her. She kept her eyes on the man.

After a time, frowning, Mr. Oakland sat back in his padded chair, creaking the springs. He interlaced his large pink fingers, turning the knuckles white as he did so, and folded his hands across his broad, white-shirted belly. The shirt strained open in the places between the buttons, showing Nikki three little patches of pink skin covered in pale blond fuzz.

Ask not what your country can do for you, she thought, waiting patiently for Mr. Oakland to deliver a verdict.

"It's real, I think," he said, after a minute.

"I think so too," said Nikki, her heart jumping a little.

"What do you make out of the background?"

"I looked up the trees in our Botanicals database. They're a kind of pygmy Norway white pine. They grow mainly in the Balkans, and as far north as the Po Valley in Italy. I cross-referenced the trees with that chain of low hills in the background—"

"How?"

"I have a friend in Terrain Mapping. He thinks those types of glacial moraine—they're called *drumlins*—and the types of pines we see here, combined, make it likely that the video was shot somewhere in Albania or Kosovo. The rock formation in the foreground looks like sedimentary shale and quartzite schist, so it's a seabed region, which also fits."

"The house?"

Nikki frowned.

"Generic faux Baronial. You'll see this kind of trash castle anywhere from Cali to Malibu to Montenegro. They're mainly low-grade spruce frame, tricked out with gables and columns and all this neo-Romanesque crapola—"

"*Crapola?*" said Mr. Oakland, giving her a shy smile. Nikki blushed a little and recovered. Mr. Oakland was a Mormon.

"Sorry about the *crapola* thing, sir. But you can see, this is basically a vulgar house, and, if we can judge by the people in the video, they're the vulgar people it was built for."

"A reasonable deduction. Anything on the people?"

"So far, no. I needed your permission to do anything more, since doing Facial Recog will chew up mainframe time, and I know we have a lot of more important things to do . . . ?"

She left the question hanging.

So did Mr. Oakland.

"You're still on the Monitors, aren't you?"

"Yes."

"So you've done all this on your own time?"

"Yes, sir."

Mr. Oakland beamed upon her, his fat face shining bright.

"Commendable, Miss Turrin. Quite."

"Thank you, sir."

Promotion? No more boring Monitor work? Please.

Mr. Oakland smiled again, stood up.

"Well, thank you very much, Miss Turrin. I'll take it from here."

Nikki stood up, her face reddening.

"Really, sir, I'd be very happy to—"

"I'm sure. But we really need you on the Monitors right now. That's vital work. National Security work. Protecting our homeland. Vital."

"But . . ."

"I'll make sure the people upstairs know how much you have contributed to this project."

Now it's a project?

"Yes, sir. That would be great, sir."

"Do you have any other copies of this video?"

"No, sir. That's the only one I have."

But it's all over YouTube, you greasy little capon.

"Good, then. Well, the country's at war, Nikki. We can't sit around like a pair of peacenik ninnyhammers, can we? So, back at it, and God bless."

Nikki bared her teeth and gritted out a smile.

"And God bless you too. Sir."

22

The Intercontinental Hotel, Singapore

Since there was nothing to do but wait for Chong to make his move, Dalton and Mandy Pownall waited. They ordered dinner from room service, along with a couple of bottles of Bollinger. They picked at the meal for a time, and together they polished off the Bolly over the next two hours. Mandy—showered, scented, and shining—was now lounging on the sofa in an oversized pale pink terry-cloth robe and watching *Lady from Shanghai* on the plasma TV. Dalton was painfully aware that she was quite naked under the robe, and he was finding it hard to concentrate on the film, which was wonderful. He was keeping his mind off Cora Vasari, too, trying not to allow visions of her body, lying on an ICU gurney, surrounded by beeping monitors, her splendid heartbeat reduced to a jagged green line crawling across a black screen. He was also trying to keep Porter Naumann's ghost from resurfacing in his life; the chemical toxins that had created Naumann in the first place had to have leached out of his tissues by now. But Dalton sensed Naumann's presence in the air around him, saw

Naumann now and then—a fleeting movement out of the corner of his eye, a trick of the light in the darkened hall, a sardonic whisper, a half-open door into an empty room.

Permanent impairment.

Cora had warned him, about the drug he'd been exposed to, in a time that now seemed left behind on the far shore of an onrushing river that had carried him far from her villa in the Dorsoduro, where they had first met. She had been . . . startling . . . radiant . . . a force of nature . . . Her full body and her fine intelligent face . . . Tough-minded and very smart, and sentimental, and gifted with a wicked sense of humor. Sexually, sensually, she was mad, bad, and dangerous to know. The one night he had spent with her in the suite at the Savoia was seared into his libido. She had been demanding and generous, tentative, inventive, shockingly outrageous. And he was beginning to feel that what had begun as a strong physical attraction, in the middle of a hunt for a brutal psychopathic killer, was turning into something closer to . . . love?

Dalton did not do *love*.

Had not *loved* for a very long time. If ever.

Very likely never would.

So why had he exploded into Cora's well-ordered life like a runaway caisson? How did he justify going anywhere near her, dragging his risks and faults and sins behind him like a tattered harness, if he wasn't capable of loving her? His love had done Laura no good at all; had, in an indirect way, killed her. And now Cora Vasari had taken two bullets and was lying on a hospital bed in Florence, deep in a coma from which she might never awake.

Meet Dalton and die.

Porter Naumann had been right:

Grief is coming.

Grief is here.

On the screen, Orson Welles, shot against a shimmering black-

and-white sea, was delivering a silky baritone soliloquy on life and desire and honor. He was lit like a Hurrell portrait, a cinematic monument at the peak of his art, a lock of shining black hair hanging down over one eyebrow. He was now in a grave somewhere in southern Spain, Dalton thought, a gross, bloated corpse rotting in a crypt. Lovely image, that. He reached for the Bolly and saw that Mandy had fallen asleep on the sofa. Her robe had fallen away from her long, well-turned legs, almost all the way to her equally splendid thighs. He got up, a bit unsteady, and stepped softly over to her.

He looked down at her face. In sleep, she looked older, the cold, damn-you humor was gone and the vulnerable woman alone remained. She was as lovely as Cora. He wanted her. He wanted Cora too.

He wanted women to want him.

He'd figure out what to do with them later.

He found a soft, blue cashmere blanket in the hall closet and laid it gently over her sleeping body, turned the sound of the film down a little, and went back to his chair, with the bottle of Bolly and a clean crystal flute, to watch the rest of *Lady from Shanghai*.

Dalton didn't do love.

23

The Fragrance Hotel, 219 Joo Chiat Road, Geylang district, Singapore

The Fragrance rented rooms. Two hours. Twenty dollars. They turned the room around five times a day. The hotel looked like the kind of hotel that did that sort of thing, a concrete-block and corrugated-iron bunker with narrow, badly lit halls and soundproof rooms with soundproof doors. The halls smelled of bleach and looked like they got scrubbed a lot because they needed to be scrubbed a lot. There was a sticky carpet and a concrete staircase, and Lujac covered the ground on cat's feet, gliding along like a navy blue ghost, in and out of the pools of blue light from a row of bulbs overhead covered with wire-frame cases. He knew the room because he had watched the cop and the *ah beng* boy go inside, and then had watched for the light that came on a moment later in a front room on the second floor. He stood in the dark of a side alley and watched as the Malay cop came to the window, staring out for a time, silhouetted in the hard-white light from a single bulb, hanging from the ceiling behind him, his right hand still in the bandage, his baseball jacket unzipped, his cap off. He reached out, the blinds slowly closed, and the little cop turned toward the room.

Lujac was a man of refined feelings and tactful discretion. He knew they'd want to be alone for a time. Get to know each other. He had given them thirty minutes. Now he was right outside the door.

No one had seen him coming, and if anyone saw him go they would not survive the experience. He stood in the dim light outside Room 19 and listened for a while. Low, faint voices, one commanding and the other submissive, and the occasional grunting moan. The door was heavy and well set in a solid frame, but the lock was ridiculous. He reached out, tested the knob. It was always a good idea to check to see if the door was actually locked, nothing made you feel more silly than trying to kick in a door that wasn't locked. Lujac stepped back, took a small Sony digital camera out of his suit-jacket pocket, held it in his left hand. He had the little shucking tool in his right. It glittered in the downlight, a bright curve of silvery steel, a little like a crescent moon. He set himself, breathed out a little, going inward for a moment, and then he lunged forward, his foot up, heel out, striking the door an inch below the knob. The door slammed open, and Lujac was in the dank, half-lit room.

A small twin bed on a bare wooden floor, a rusty sink, a cheap vinyl chair piled with clothes, a bedside lamp made of copper and batik cloth, two figures, both naked and shiny with sweat, frozen in the middle of a tangle of pale green sheets, their positions reversed, head and foot. The camera strobed, running off a series of rapid shots, and each flash lit up the steamy little room like a bolt of lightning, turning the figures on the bed into a kind of jittery silent movie of frantic motion: the Malay cop's wide eyes, irises lit red, as he stared up at the camera. Then blackness, and another flash: cop and the punker boy breaking apart. Darkness, another flash: the boy, caught frozen, fumbling at his clothes; the cop, reaching for his belt, tearing at the pocket. Darkness, another flash: the boy, flying toward the doorway.

Lujac snapped a final shot, slammed the door shut behind him, and kicked the punker boy in the lower belly, hard, catching him in midstride. The kid bent himself around Lujac's leg and slid to the floor, gagging. Lujac heard the sound of metal sliding on metal, a tinny, locking *click*.

The Malay cop, naked, was standing by the bed, holding a small, chrome-plated semiauto pistol in his left hand. His wet face was green in the light from the bedside lamp, his eyes two tiny holes filled with a red glitter, his mouth open. He was gasping, but silently, like a gaffed trout in a boat. He lifted the pistol, pointed it at Lujac, said nothing at all, and fired, a short, sharp *crack* in the room, like a branch snapping.

The round whispered past Lujac's left ear and punched into the heavy wooden door at his back. Lujac went low and exploded at the cop. *Charge a gun, flee a knife.* Another snapping bark, and another round plucked at his coat, burning a ribbon of fire around his rib cage. *Hadn't spotted the little hideaway piece. Should have.* He slammed into the little cop, closing his hands around the pistol, getting a thumb in between the hammer and the pin, bending the gun muzzle up and back, fighting it hard. He heard the little Malay squeal as his trigger finger, trapped inside the guard, was wrenched nearly out of joint. A short, vicious, twisting, writhing struggle; a quick jerk. Now Lujac had the gun.

He straightened, aware of the sharp, red pain at his side, paused for effect, then kneed the cop very hard in the balls, then slammed him across the temple with the side of the pistol as the cop went down. The cop clutched his groin, breath hissing out through his clenched teeth. Lujac stamped him hard in the back of the neck, bouncing the cop's face off the floor. Then he stepped back around the bed and dragged the punker boy to his feet. The kid was still naked. He had his T-shirt in his hand, and used it to cover himself. He stared at Lujac and said nothing. His eyes were like the eyes of a prey animal. He knew what had just happened and why. Lujac reached out a hand; the kid flinched away. Lujac smiled gently, his hand paused in the air. The kid wasn't pretty, but he had something. Lujac decided it was a kind of sweet hopelessness tinged with resignation.

"You speak English, boy?" asked Lujac, soft as sleep.

The boy nodded twice; short, sharp jerks of the head on a rigid neck.

"What's your name?"

"Noordin. Bobby. Bobby Noor*din.*"

His voice cracked on the final syllable, a hoarse croak. There was a slithery sound of sheets being hauled off the bed. The little cop was rolling over, still clutching his groin, and the sheets had come off as he rolled. He was making a low, keening sound, like a lost little girl.

"How old are you, Bobby?"

"Fourteen."

"You have some ID?"

"Yes. It over there."

Bobby made a quick, flicking gesture, indicating the pile of his clothes on the chair by the bed.

"Show me."

Bobby stepped around the corner of the bed. Lujac kept the pistol on Bobby's back as he crouched in the corner, picking through the pile. He straightened, and came back with a cheap black nylon wallet. He handed it to Lujac and moved out of Lujac's reach, glancing across the bed at the cop, and then turning back, his full attention on Lujac. No questions about his rights. No demand to see a badge. In Singapore, what he had been doing with—and for—the cop was a matter for a severe caning and a long prison term. There was no plea to be made. Lujac opened the wallet, checked the kid's ID, saw a picture of an old Malay woman smiling, gap-tooted, into a cheap camera. *A vague family resemblance there, probably his sainted mummy.* Lujac grinned to himself, as he flipped through a dirty bundle of Sing dollars.

"He already pay you?"

"Yes."

"How much?"

"Twenny Sing dollah."

"Okay. Go sit on the bed."

"I please dress?"

"No. Leave the shirt. Go sit."

Bobby hesitated, looking at his clothes. Then he dropped his T-shirt and went back to the bed. He crawled on the bed and curled up against the headboard, covering himself as well as he could. He looked a little like a lemur, big eyes, and a round, open mouth. He began to vibrate like a tuning fork. Lujac liked that. The Malay cop stopped keening.

Lujac stepped around the bed, leaned down, dragged the cop to his feet, and shoved him onto the bed beside the boy. The cop dragged himself upright and got his back against the headboard, keeping some distance between himself and the kid. They did not look at each other. They both looked at Lujac. The cop's black eye was fading a little into green-and-brown tones. His right hand was still bandaged. If he'd been using his right hand to shoot that little pistol at Lujac, Lujac figured he'd be dead now, which would come as a happy surprise to Larissa.

Nobody knocked on the door and asked what was going on. Through the window, they could hear the sounds of the market and the faint echo of distant music. Lujac took a moment to check his ribs. There was blood on his shirt. But not much. He felt his ribs, found a tiny furrow plowed along the flesh. Ruined the Pink's shirt, but maybe the suit would be okay. He hoped so. It was a Brioni.

There was a picture over the bed, a faded color shot of a tropical beach fringed in palms, taken sometime in the forties. On the ceiling, a three-bladed fan turned the smoky air, making a low *whip-whip* sound. The room smelled of sex and sweat, smoke and Tiger beer. Lujac switched the gun from his right to his left hand and pulled out the little oyster-shucking tool. He hefted it in his hand, smiling at the two people on the bed. Neither of them spoke. The cop knew what Bobby knew, what the penalty was for what they had been doing. It would be far worse for him.

He was the cop.

"What's your name?" said Lujac, standing at the foot of the bed and tossing the little shucking tool into the air now and then, catching it by the handle. The blade glittered in the light, making tiny, flashing arcs as it spun and fell. The cop wiped his lips with his bandaged hand and blinked.

"I am Corporal Ahmed. Of the Interior Police Service."

"Out of uniform? A bit?"

"I am"—he searched for the phrase, got it—*"unnah-covah."*

Lujac smiled at that, a bright, open, sunny smile.

"So you'll be happy about the shots, then? Really nails your case."

Corporal Ahmed said nothing, but Lujac could see what he was thinking:

This is Singapore. This European is not a cop or he would have said so. He was in the suite at the Intercontinental this morning. He is some kind of thief. No matter what he says, I can handle it. Except for the camera. Pay whatever. Get out of the room. Get help. Then find the man again and put him into a bare white room at Changi. But first, get the camera.

"I am *unnah-covah*. This boy is prostitute. You have *inna-fere* with official matter. You must—"

Lujac tossed him the shucking tool. It tumbled through the half-light, glimmering like a pinwheel. The cop and the boy flinched away from the tool, and it struck the headboard between them and thudded onto the mattress. They both looked at it. Then up at Lujac. Lujac had the camera in his left hand and the pistol in his right. The pistol was aimed at Corporal Ahmed's left eye, just above the bruise.

"Pick it up," he said.

The cop looked at the boy and then at Lujac's gun hand. He picked up the tool, staring at Lujac.

"Use it," said Lujac.

The boy jerked to the right but stopped when Lujac shifted the gun to him. He saw where he was, and it came as no surprise, but his lemur eyes filled up and he began to sob in silence. The cop stared at Lujac.

"His blood on the floor or your brains on the wall."

The cop shook his head. Lujac fired once. The gun kicked and flared and barked. Chips flew out of the headboard an inch from the cop's ear. The cop made a snaky move with the tool—*snick* and *snack*—Lujac's camera flashed and clicked, flaring out and freezing the moment as the boy's throat was laid wide open from his left ear to his collarbone. Blood gushed out in a scarlet arc, like a spray of rubies, and spattered across the lime green sheet.

Malays are very good with knives. Always have been. Lujac was counting on it. And Lujac caught it all, sixteen frames, a masterpiece of timing. The boy clapped both hands around his throat. Blood pumped out between his fingers. He opened his mouth to scream but no sound came. The cop had cut through his larynx and opened his throat. The kid went blue and rolled off the bed and onto the floor in a tangle of limbs and blood. He lay there, making a faint, breathy gurgle, which mingled with the drumming sound of his blood, spraying, in weakening pulses, across the plywood walls beside his head. Gradually, the line of the blood arc drooped, and, in a little while, the room was very still. There was only the sound of Corporal Ahmed's rapid breathing, the fan blade churning through the air, and the tinny sounds of the street market coming in through the blinds.

"What you *wan?*" asked Corporal Ahmed, after a long while.

"Why, Corporal Ahmed. I thought you'd never ask."

24

The Intercontinental Hotel, Singapore

"Will she die?"

Naumann did not answer. Time passed, and still he said nothing. Dalton and Naumann were standing at the pillared railing around the Piazza Garibaldi in Cortona. It was a warm summer afternoon, and the light across the checkerboard valley far below was honeyed and rich, the timeless light of Tuscany. Naumann was wearing a pale tan summer-weight suit over a soft-blue, open-necked shirt. He seemed to have recovered from being dead, since he now had quite a decent tan and his pale blue eyes were clear. *He looks the picture of health, for a dead man,* thought Dalton. For that matter, Dalton knew many men who were still alive who didn't look half as good as Porter did. Naumann was staring out across the valley toward Lake Trasimeno, apparently lost in thought. Dalton sipped at his glass of pinot for a time, willing to let Naumann be lost in thought. In his heart, he wasn't ready for an answer to his question. Let it be a beautiful day for a while longer. And it *was* a beautiful day. The swifts soared and wheeled in the luminous air, their formation tight and nimble, their wings catching the light as they dipped and rose. The air smelled of cedar and oleander and green vines heavy with ripe fruit. Dalton no longer wanted his answer. But Naumann had not forgotten it.

"Will she die?" said Naumann finally, watching the swifts as they disappeared into the blue distance. "I did warn you, didn't I?"

He held out his glass.

Dalton filled it with some pinot and topped his own.

"Yes. You did."

Naumann turned to look at Dalton. The sunlight lay bright on the side of his cheek, and a single ray of it caught the lens of his right eye, making it shine like a little blue diamond. The left side of his face was in shadow.

"Yes. She will."

Dalton's chest clamped up, and his breathing became difficult.

"You know this?"

"I know she'll die. So will you."

Dalton gave the matter some thought. Asking questions of the dead had its risks. The dead tended to be Delphic.

"Well, we'll all die, won't we? You did."

"Yes," said Naumann, granting the point. "That's true."

"But she might not die from *this*? This attack in Florence?"

Naumann appeared not to have heard him. His expression was remote, his mind elsewhere. He came back after a time, looking puzzled.

"Yes. That's true. She might not."

"Good. Fine. I can live with that."

Naumann smiled.

"Can you?"

"I can. How are *you*?"

"Me?"

"Yes. You're not really *here*, are you?"

"In which sense? Mentally? Spiritually? Ectoplasmically?"

"I mean, you're *absent*. What are you thinking about?"

Naumann's face darkened.

"I'm not sure I'm allowed to speak about it."

"*Allowed*? By whom?"

Naumann made a gesture with the hand that held his wineglass, a wide, sweeping arc that took in all of Cortona. The afternoon sun blazed in his glass as he turned with it, and little diamonds of refracted light—tiny prisms—flickered across his haggard face and glittered in his pale eyes.

"By Cortona, I think. I can't seem to leave here."

"Leave Cortona? But you were all over the States with me. That safe house near Missoula. In Carmel, after Laura died. Now you can't leave Cortona?"

"Yes. Everything's changed. I can't remember how long I've been here. And the clocks are . . . odd. It's always about four in the afternoon. Or late evening. The whole thing is giving me the creeps. You get the idea you're not alone. And things move that should not move. You hear voices. Whispers. Around the far corners. In the empty squares. Down the alleys. You can be in a crowd of people in the square, everyone talking and moving in the light. Close your eyes for a moment, and, when you open them, you're alone. The city is either empty or too damn crowded. Sometimes I know the faces. Other times, they all look . . . inhuman. Dead faces. I'd leave if I could, Micah. If I could figure out how. This place is *old*, Micah. Older than any other place on the earth. The whole mountain is a tomb. I'm beginning to feel . . . out of place . . . here. Resented. But I don't know how to leave. I don't know the way out. Do you understand me?"

"Resented? By whom?"

Naumann merely shook his head, his eyes bleak.

"Sometimes, in the middle of the sunlight, I'm looking at the cobblestones, in the really old part, on the Via Janelli, and I'll see this . . . smoke . . . coming up out of the stones. Gray. You can see through it. But the wind never moves it. It just drifts up into a shape and hangs there. Hangs there and looks at me. I can feel the emotion coming off it. The emotion is *resentment*. Makes no sense. Can't figure it out. Wish I could leave, Micah. Really do."

"Porter, do you *believe* you're dead?"

Naumann looked at him for a while, his face set and stony.

"No. I guess I don't. Do you?"

Dalton stared at him for a while, trying to find an answer. There was a rush of music, a deafening crescendo, that seemed to be coming out of the blue Tuscan sky itself, massed strings behind a liquid, sensuous melody of brassy horns, familiar but without a name. Naumann looked up at the sky, his face changing as he came back to Dalton—a ferocious, warning look.

They're here!

Mandy Pownall was shaking him by the shoulder, her face pale and her hair in disarray. He looked up at her. Her robe had fallen open. He could see her full, round breasts, as pale as pearls, and her erect nipples, a deeper rose color inside an aureole of shell pink; her flat, white belly.

"Micah. The desk just called. The police are on their way up!"

Dalton struggled out of his dream, sat upright in the chair. He was in the suite at the Intercontinental. The plasma screen was rolling the credits for *Lady from Shanghai*. Somebody had turned the theme music up very loud. It filled the room. Mandy stood up and looked down at him, gathering her robe in tight and crossing her arms under her breasts.

"Christ. What time is it?"

"It's four," she whispered, a hoarse croak, straining to be heard over the music, her eyes a little wide. "In the morning."

Dalton got up out of the chair, fully awake. Mandy was watching him, uncertain but steady. She was a tough woman, but she did not need to be here. Why Cather had insisted was still a mystery. But one thing was clear, now that it looked like the bluff had failed and Chong Kew Sak was going to play rough: two agents locked up in Changi was a lousy tactical deployment. Dalton knew there was no way she would have pulled out of the field, if given any time to think about it. But *he* had thought about it. A lot.

"Mandy, I need you to do something for me."

"Yes. Certainly. What?" A hoarse whisper, barely audible over the soundtrack music.

"I need you to scarper."

Doubt flickered across her face and her mouth tightened.

"Now you want me to scarper? Now? Bloody poor timing, Micah."

"Yes. I'm changing the tactics. You need to be on the outside."

"Lovely. And how do we arrange that, with the bloody wolf kicking at the bloody door?"

"Go to your room, Mandy. Get some clothes on. Your bedroom suite connects to the Ambassador Suite next door. That suite's empty."

"How do you know?"

"I'm a spy. Plus I reserved it the morning before we left for Milan and I paid for it when we got here. I like to have an evasion strategy."

"Paid? With what? Your platypus card? The cops will know that."

"No. I used one of the Agency's cover cards."

"Whose?"

"Jack Stallworth's. He's dead, he won't mind. Here's the key card. Get yourself in there. Take the encrypted cell. Plug in the charger and keep the phone charging. Get on the line to the duty desk at Langley and *keep* them on the line. Do *not* get disconnected. You understand me? Stay on that line, and don't open the door to anyone."

"You sure this is Chong?"

"Who else?" he said, looking at the door and then back at her. She had the two small red spots on her cheekbones now, and the glitter in her eyes, the look she got when she was about to dig her stilettos in.

"No. I'm not running away."

"No. You're not. You're staying loose. Operational. They take me, I'll need you on the outside . . . When I'm gone, get Langley to send over someone from the U.S. Embassy. Go straight there."

"No. I'm not leaving the field and hiding in the bloody Embassy."

"You really want to be in a jail cell alone with Chong Kew Sak?"

Mandy worked on it but could not hide the way her irises narrowed, blinded by the incandescent *now*. There were voices out in the hallway, and now a loud, rapid pounding at the main door. The knocking accelerated. Muffled voices in the hall; stern, official voices. The moment was on them. Mandy nodded once, pulled him down and kissed him very hard, put everything she had into it. Dalton felt the kiss burn through him.

Then she pushed him off, her face pale, sent him a last anxious look over her left shoulder and was gone down the hall, her robe flaring wide as she ran. Someone in the front hall was using a boot on the door. Down in his lizard brain, something a little like a crocodile opened one slitted green eye. He felt his blood rising, anger coming up fast. He hit the remote and killed the picture, throwing the suite into an ominous silence punctuated only by the aggressive pounding on the door.

He threw on his suit jacket, glanced around the suite, controlled his aggression, letting it work for him and not against him. He gathered up his wallet and his cell phone, slipping them into his pocket as he walked to the main door, waited a moment with his hand on the latch, lowering his adrenaline, and then pulled it open. Sergeant Ong Bo was standing there, apparently in the same cheap black suit, his rubbery lips pulled tight and his black eyes hard. Two uniformed cops, both thick-necked and bull-bodied and dull-eyed, barely out of their teens, were standing behind him. The little Malay cop, Corporal Ahmed, was nowhere around. Ong was holding up a worn leather badge case, flashing tin, with his best Hollywood war face on. Dalton figured he practiced it in the mirror.

"Mr. Dalton. You must come with us."

Dalton went back to his Brit banker persona, edged it with some steel.

"Bloody hell I will. It's four in the goddam morning."

Ong tried to peer around Dalton's shoulder, but he filled the frame.

"Where Miss Pownall?"

"Out. Hours ago."

Ong had a problem. The only way he could argue this was to admit that they had the place miked.

"Why she move?"

"Why she move? Because you feckless hammerheads searched the entire fucking apartment, including her goddam panty drawer."

Ong, in spite of himself, facing Dalton's rage, stepped back a pace, and then another, until he had backed into one of the uniforms behind him. Dalton was pleased to see it, partly because Mandy was getting the seconds she would need to open the door to the next suite. The loss of face made Sergeant Ong get all hissy.

"She must come too. Where is she?"

"The British Embassy. To file a formal complaint."

It gave Dalton some hope when Ong went a little green at that.

He believed it, or, at least, believed it was *possible*. Which meant their mikes had told them nothing since Dalton had put on *Lady from Shanghai*. It also meant that he'd been right: there were no cameras. And no surveillance in the lobby or on the street, because he'd have known she hadn't left the building. They trusted their mikes. Careless. More lousy tradecraft.

In a word, *mooks*.

Ong was looking a tad downhearted. Not even Chong Kew Sak could get Mandy Pownall out of the British Embassy. This was not going according to plan. But Dalton was still here. That much he could save.

His round, rubbery face, as much as it could, became set and hardened. He turned to the two guards, said something urgent and ugly in Hokkien that apparently meant *Search this pompous asshole's suite right now*. Galvanized, they pushed past Dalton, the muscular boy on the left aiming a hard shoulder butt that Dalton saw coming, steeling himself for it. The kid cop bounced off him and slammed into the wall. He came right back at Dalton, red-faced, boiling with the indignant outrage of a totalitarian cop when faced with the slightest civilian affront; hand up, palm open, a wide, sweeping strike to the side of Dalton's head. This ill-advised action on the part of the kid cop put a variety of factors into immediate play. Dalton's grip on his temper had always been a little slippery. It was four in the morning. He was slightly hungover. Okay. Not slightly. He was a train wreck. The kid was trying to bitch-slap him. Dalton did not like being bitch-slapped. Not one little bit. Plus he was brutally hungover. This may have been mentioned previously, but it bears repeating. So, the situation being what it was, at the end of the day, in the fullness of time, and in the half nanosecond that it took for all these various factors to kick in, Dalton lost it.

In one snaky, fast motion, he caught the kid's incoming right wristbone with his own right hand, jerking him forward and off balance, turning the wrist around as he pulled the kid's arm downward along his right side, using the kid's own momentum, until the kid was almost on his knees, his right arm fully extended, palm twisted sideways. At the same moment, Dalton braced his left hand on the back of the kid's elbow and jerked the kid's forearm upward with his right. This had the intriguing effect of snapping the kid's arm at the elbow joint, which tends to sting a bit. The sound of the joint giving way was a little like somebody twisting the turkey's leg right out of the joint at Thanksgiving, a muffled, sinewy grinding followed by a short, sharp *snap*. The kid's forearm had now assumed an angle in relation to the upper arm that was anatomically quite novel, if not unique. This all happened in less than two seconds. Two seconds that changed the kid's world. The kid's immediate response to having the basic geometry of his right arm radically revised was a contralto shriek, followed by a precipitous upward glissando into frequencies only audible to Nancy Pelosi. A moment later, Dalton not surprisingly, was looking down the black muzzle of Sergeant Ong's Glock service pistol, held out the full length of Ong's arm, the knuckle of his trigger finger showing pink, then white, as he pressed on the blade.

Dalton stared at Ong's wet face over the vibrating pistol, aware of the black hole of the muzzle as it wavered left and right. Stared hard into Ong's right eye at the far end of a long narrow corridor. Waited for the shot, thinking that, so far, the score here in lovely downtown Singapore was Snobbish British Bankers 2 and Pushy Local Noncoms 0, and that, if he had it to do all over again, he would have broken Ong's arm instead.

At Dalton's feet, the kid cop was busily throwing up something lumpy, gray, and apparently inexhaustible on the plush Oriental carpet in the foyer. The other cop was standing out of the firing line, his flat face stunned, waiting for Ong to shoot the *ang mor*. Everybody in the hall was waiting for Ong to shoot the *ang mor.* Hell, even Ong was waiting for Ong to shoot the *ang mor.* Ong did not shoot the *ang mor.*

FIVE MINUTES LATER, Dalton was in the back of the same armored-up limo with the bulletproof glass, sitting alone on the black leather bench seat and looking at Sergeant Ong's rubbery face, shadowy in the downlights from the overhead mood lighting, watching Ong watch him back with a carefully blank expression that did not hide the rage in him. The kid cop with both arms working was driving the limo. The kid cop with the backward right arm that looked sort of funny and didn't work at all was on his way to the nearest military hospital in an unmarked EMS van. Dalton figured the kid was still screaming so loud, the driver wouldn't need to use the siren. Outside the tinted windows of the limo, Singapore unspooled like a long neon hallucination, the streets deserted, the lamps glowing in the damp tropical haze, the tires drumming on the blacktop. The limo smelled of leather polish and Turkish tobacco and the unwashed body of Sergeant Ong. As far as Dalton could determine, they were headed east through the Malay cantonment of Geylang. The last road sign he had been able to pick out of the gloom was Changi Road. Changi Road led, eventually, to Upper Changi Road, which led in its turn to the gates of Changi Prison.

Jolly good work, thought Dalton. *Only on the ground for eighteen hours and already you've found a way to infiltrate Changi Prison.*

The limo rolled on through the steaming Asian night, but it did not roll all the way to Changi Prison. After about a half hour's travel through darkened apartment blocks and shuttered strip malls of eastern Singapore, the streetscape opened up into rolling green space. A few sago palms appeared, and the homes got more expensive; and now, through the palms, Dalton was getting slices of a broad starlit sea. A street sign said NETHERAVON ROAD where they turned, and cruised along through an area that looked and, when Dalton rolled the window down, smelled of the sea. Dalton knew the area, a dense, tree-shaded residential area north of Changi Village, a pricey resort section of eastern Singapore with a view across the channel to Malaysia and Pulau Ubin. In a few minutes, the limo came to a stop under the marquee of a softly lit mahogany-and-teak hotel structure half hidden in palms and bougainvillea. It looked large and pricey and exclusive, more of a sanctuary than a hotel; enclosed, walled, a cloister offering a Zen-like simplicity. The parking lot was empty, and no one was moving around in the grounds. A sign, in fine brass letters, said HENDON HILLS GOLF AND COUNTRY CLUB. Under this sign, a temporary-looking notice had been attached to the wall.

It read: CLOSED FOR PRIVATE FUNCTION.

Sergeant Ong, who had neither spoken one word nor taken his flat reptilian stare off Dalton during the entire trip, grunted a command that Dalton took to mean *Get out*. Dalton tried the door. It was unlocked. Dalton got out, a little stiff, leaving the door open behind him. Sergeant Ong made no move to follow him. He leaned forward, grabbed the interior handle, shot Dalton a look that said *Someday*, and pulled the door closed hard enough to rock the Home Ministry tank a little on its fat, bulletproof tires.

The engine powered up in a throaty rumble, and the limo slipped away into the night, showing a brief flash of taillights as it braked on Netheravon Road, and then Dalton was alone under the low, dimly lit mahogany marquee, breathing in the scent of salt air, his heartbeat gradually returning to sub-myocardial-infarction levels. In the distant south, in the first pale glow of the oncoming sunrise, he could see a silvery plane heading skyward out of a glow of hard-white light that could only be Changi Airport.

He pulled out his cell, considered and rejected the idea of calling the U.S. Embassy and asking for Mandy Pownall. Either she had made it or she hadn't. The absence of a panicked phone call from Langley argued for the former. He flipped the phone shut, extracted a pack of Mandy's Balkan Sobranie Cocktail cigarettes, pondered the color scheme and had just chosen turquoise, when he heard a whispered hiss of wood on steel and a shaft of warm yellow light fell across him. A tall, slender figure, silhouetted in the amber light pouring from the open door, bowed once, and said:

"Mr. Dalton. Please come in. We are ready for you now."

25

The National Security Agency, Fort Meade, Maryland

"What am I looking at here, Oakland?"

Mr. Oakland, who preferred to be called Mr. Oakland, kept his eyes on the monitor, partly because the short and nasty little snuff video held a sick fascination for him that never seemed to weaken, but also because the Assistant Director of Research Analysis was a retired Marine Corps Intelligence Colonel who had been terribly maimed in a roadside bombing in Anbar Province, and now the left side of his face and most of his neck looked like he was wearing the peeled skin of a purple lizard as a kind of half mask. Mr. Oakland, an intelligent and ambitious but rather diffident man, did not want to cause any further offense to the AD of RA by visibly flinching away from a direct look at the injury, which he had done twice already. Mr. Oakland was aware, on a subliminal level, that the AD of RA couldn't give a rat's kidney what Mr. Oakland thought of his face, but this insight never seemed to drill its way through to the surface of his mind.

Mr. Oakland pursed his soft red lips in silent consideration.

"Well, sir, I've had our people do a great deal of analysis on the terrain, and I can confirm that the film was taken in the central cordillera of Eastern Europe, possibly in the northern Balkans or even in northern Italy somewhere. Time of year, based on the vegetation, between late August and early September. It was shot on a Sony digital camera from a distance of about fifty yards, using a five-power digital zoom and a three-power optical zoom. The Internet image is reasonably dense, so we can assume that the camera was pretty high on the pixel range and the original footage was pretty clear. So an expensive camera, and new. Which means the events taking place in the video would be recent, as recent as the fall of this year. I had the techs pull out and enhance facials of as many of the people in the footage as they could. We got negative FR on all the women, but this one individual got a strong positive, the large chap with the tattoo across his chest. The tattoo shows a lance bearing the flag of the Kosovo Liberation Army, and, as you can see, it's depicted as piercing the breast of an American bald eagle. The Face Recog boys"—Oakland liked to say things like "the Face Recog boys"; it sounded so *operational* that he simply had to repeat it—"the Face Recog boys have positively ID'd the man as Dzilbar Svetan Kerk. He's wanted by The Hague for war crimes committed in Kosovo while under the command of Radko Mladic and Slobodan Milošević. Face Recog also made some tentative IDs of two of the other guys"—here, he freeze-framed the video and closed in on two of the beefy guys in too-tiny Speedos—"this guy with the gray goatee could be a KA of Kerk's by the name of Josef Perchak, and this other—"

"What's a KA?"

"A *known associate,* sir—"

"Well, say so, Oakland. I had it up to here with jargon in the Corps."

"Yes, sir. Well, sir, as I was saying—"

"Are you convinced the video's for real? These are actual deaths. Not faked for some fucking sicko movie about to be released? Some PR thing?"

"Well, my people seem to feel the video is genuine. But, of course, absent any real on-site inquiry, we would need to have SOCOM insert a team to pull tissues, samples."

"SOCOM, Oakland?"

Mr. Oakland reddened.

"I'm sorry. I mean—"

"I know who you mean, Oakland. You get anything from our own system on this Dzilbar Svetan Kerk asshole? Or Perchak?"

Oakland seemed to swell up a little. He licked his soft red lips.

"Yes, sir. We certainly did."

"What'd you get?"

"We have HumInt and SigInt. Both confirm that Kerk was last seen in Pristina. At the Grand. In June of this year. The Germans think he's in business with the Chechyns now, trading guns and shape charges for opium base out of Afghanistan. The Taliban are involved. But the really key issue is a rather disturbing digital packet from one of our FISA searches in which Kerk is heard making a reference to a scientist named Vladimir Pasechnik, a microbiologist working for an organization called Biopreparat."

"Jesus. I know what that was!"

"Yes. Biopreparat was the Soviet germ warfare laboratory. Alebikov, the defector, worked there until 1992. After September eleven, he was all over the talk shows, telling everybody who would listen about the things they were working on. Weaponized smallpox. Anthrax spores. After the Soviets fell apart, Alebikov told Sam Nunn that as many as seventy thousand people who used to work there had gone off to places like North Korea and Iraq. That was part of the reason we went into Iraq in the first place."

"Tell me about it. Fucking *Eye-raq*. Fucking WMDs. Far as I'm concerned, WMD stands for *Where's My Dick?* Didn't Pasechnik die under some kind of weird circumstance?"

"Yes. After he defected from Biopreparat, he worked in the U.K., formed his own company, Regma Biotechnics. He was found dead of an apparent stroke, although he had no previous diagnosis. In the FISA packet, Kerk is heard saying that he *managed* the Pasechnik file."

"Who was he talking to?"

"A woman. Unknown. Unknown location too. The call was routed through a microwave tower in Odessa, but it seemed to be only a switch box. We lost the track after Odessa. The Pasechnik case is only part of the picture. Over the next few months, as many as ten more people, all of them involved in Biopreparat or in similar fields of weaponized germ warfare, were killed or died under mysterious circumstances. Set Van Nguyen was working on a virulent mouse pox strain when he died of asphyxia in Geelong, Australia. Two Russians, Ivan Glebov and Alexi Brushlinski—Biopreparat scientists—were murdered in Moscow a few weeks later. Victor Korshunov, massive head trauma, in Moscow. Then Ian Langford in the U.K. Several others, all around the world. All dead in the space of six months. All died violently or were said to have committed suicide. Three more— Avishai Berkman, Amiramp Eldor, Yaacov Matzner—were on a Siberian Airlines flight from Tel Aviv to Novosibirsk. The flight was hit by a Ukrainian surface-to-air missile and crashed into the Black Sea. The Ukrainians denied any involvement, but the investigators decided it had been an *accidental shoot down* by some half-trained Ukrainian soldier stoned on vodka."

"I remember those news stories. Big sensation, and then it all disappeared. The CIA have anything for you? On this Dzilbar Kerk guy? Any other link to Pasechnik or Korshunov or any of the others?"

"Well, since all those leaks to the *New York Times,* we've been a little wary of letting the CIA have everything we find. We try to channel it directly to Defense and State, and let them walk it back to Langley."

"So you haven't asked Langley? Yet?"

"No, sir."

"Don't. Leave them out of the loop. Oakland, I gotta say, I don't like this Kerk guy's connection with a bunch of dead germ warfare people. I mean, what the fuck killed these people in this video? That's no coincidence. That's tactical. Where'd you find this clip, anyway?"

"Ahh, it . . . Well, it first appeared on YouTube, sir."

"On YouTube? How the fuck did it get on YouTube?"

"Thousands of clips are posted on YouTube every day."

The AD of RA gave Oakland a long considering appraisal that Oakland could feel in his boxers. His courting tackle was retracting like the head of a nervous turtle. A very small, nervous turtle.

"The important question here isn't *how*, Mr. Oakland. It's *why*. You follow the Internet closely, do you, Mr. Oakland? Got your own Facebook page? Read all the hot blergs?"

"That's *blog*, sir."

"I'm heating you up, Oakland. Try to roll with it. So you're a crackerjack *Webster's*, are you?"

Mr. Oakland reddened slightly, and his eyes flicked around the room, coming back to rest on a point midway between the second and third button on the AD of RA's shirt.

"I . . . dabble . . . a bit. Of course, I'm not an aficionado—"

"No. Neither am I. Come clean, pal. Some geek kid on your staff bring this video to you?"

"Well, we cast a pretty wide net in my department, of course. All on the same team. All in harness, you know, working shoulder to shoulder—"

"Yeah, yeah, yeah. Who brought this to your desk?"

"Well, I'd have to look at the staffing sheets."

"The *staffing* sheets?"

"Yes. The—"

"You do that. Whoever spotted this clip, I want to meet him. Now."

"Ahh . . . Her, actually. I think. It's coming back to me."

"Yeah?" said the AD of RA, smiling.

Possibly smiling. It was hard to tell with the AD of RA.

"I thought it would."

26

Hendon Hills Golf and Country Club, Changi Village, Singapore

Dalton came through the doors and into the soft, warm light of a long, wood-paneled lobby that stretched away into darkness. The building smelled of wood polish and incense, and music was playing faintly in the air, something lush and full of soaring strings but Asian and rather strange at the same time. Dalton got it in a second. It was the soundtrack to *Memoirs of a Geisha*. Yo-Yo Ma. He had the CD in his flat in Belgravia. Right now, he missed his flat in Belgravia. If he ever got back there with Cora whole and well, he intended to lock the door and rip the phone out of the wall and kill a bottle of Bolly and keep her safe in his bed for a hundred days. The person who had greeted him, a tall, athletic-looking Chinese man in a soft-tan linen shirt and pale green silk slacks, stepped back into the glow of a downlight, studying Dalton the way a keeper studies the big cats, a calm, self-contained, heavy-lidded gaze, his lean face shadowed, and two small points of reflected light in his dark, deep-set eyes.

"I am Mr. Kwan," he said, bowing formally.

"Mr. Kwan," said Dalton, waiting.

"May I ask you if you are armed, Mr. Dalton?"

"You may. I'm not."

Mr. Kwan smiled. His teeth were in excellent condition, but the man himself seemed ageless, neither young nor old. His skin was dry, and although his carriage was erect and firm, he had an air of suppleness and ease of movement. Martial arts, Dalton decided, blended disciplines. Skilled. Could he take him? Yes. Would it be fun? No.

"We will assume you are a man of honor, Mr. Dalton. Will you walk this way, please?"

Dalton stifled the Groucho Marx comeback, sleeplessness and a killer hangover making him a little giddy, and he padded down the long, carpeted hallway behind Mr. Kwan, who appeared to glide rather than walk. Dalton tried to glide too, but the best he could manage was a kind of hip-swinging sashay, which he stopped when he got a look at himself in a full-length mirror at the end of the hall. Mr. Kwan made a left and rolled smoothly off toward a pair of intricately carved wooden doors inlaid with brass-and-silver bars in a pleasing geometric pattern. The doors were huge and heavy, but when Mr. Kwan touched one of them it opened in a silent sweep to reveal a warm, wood-lined, low-ceilinged, amber-lit denlike room filled with comfortable leather chairs. A fire was crackling away in a huge limestone-slab fireplace. A woman was sitting in one of two club chairs positioned by the fire. She was Minister Dak Chansong. She rose as Mr. Kwan stepped back to hold the door open for Dalton. Dak Chansong was smiling. The smile looked unconvincing on her sour face, but it seemed reasonably sincere. Dalton smiled back as he reached the fireplace.

"Mr. Dalton," she said. "Thank you for coming."

"Always a pleasure, Minister. I find Sergeant Ong quite stimulating."

Dak Chansong's smile spread across her parchment face and reached her sharp black eyes, the eyes of a raven or a raptor.

"Sergeant Ong returns the compliment. Mr. Kwan . . . ?"

"Yes, ma'am?"

"May I trouble you for some tea? And then perhaps you would be so kind as to go and see if our guest is settling in. Tea, Mr. Dalton?"

Dalton hated tea.

"Yes, please."

Kwan bowed, withdrew in a glide. Dalton and Dak Chansong sat down in their respective chairs. The fire crackled away tastefully. Dak was wearing a high-necked Chinese jacket in deep plum over a pair of black silk pleated trousers. A ring on her left hand glimmered in the firelight, a large ruby in a gold-wire setting. In the half-light, she looked quite lovely, except for the raven's eyes. Neither spoke during the two minutes it took for Mr. Kwan to return with a large silver tray and a full English tea service, which he set down on a low teak table between them. He performed the classic English tea ceremony in solemn silence, stood up again, and looked down at the Minister with an expression of affection, turned to give Dalton a formal bow, with a rather-less-loving expression, and was gone. Silence, then, and the crackle of the fire. Chinese silence; a kind of contest between two opposing wills. Whoever breaks it loses . . . something. Dalton was never sure quite what.

He sipped at his tea—he still hated tea—and set the cup down.

"The Home Minister," she said, after a while. Then paused.

"Yes? The Home Minister . . . ?"

"Sends his regrets. He was unable to attend. He has been called away unexpectedly. I am here on his behalf. May we set aside the diplomatic protocols for a while and speak plainly to one another?"

"By all means, Minister."

"By the way, I have something for you," she said, leaning forward and offering two navy blue portfolios with the crest of the U.K. stamped in gold on the covers. "Your passports. Minister Chong has *retrieved* them for you."

Dalton took the documents without a sarcastic comment, smiled nicely. She took in a breath, held it for a time, and then relaxed into her chair, crossing her legs at the ankles and folding her hands in her lap.

"We are prepared to give serious consideration to your request. In the matter of this poor British sailor, Mr. Fyke. His case has touched the heart of the Minister Mentor, Mr. Lee Kwan Yew."

Here, Dak Chansong bowed her head slightly, and her tone took on a hieratic purr, as if she were speaking about a deity. Dalton resisted the urge to say something pert and British about "dear old Uncle Harry."

"As well, we are concerned to preserve the excellent relations we have already established with our American friends. You are not everything you appear to be, Mr. Dalton. We are now fully apprised of your connections with American Intelligence, and we intend to honor them."

Somebody talked, thought Dalton. Somebody at the U.S. Embassy, which meant that Mandy had reached it safely and given them a heads-up. Something she would only have done with Deacon Cather's permission. So, the deal to trade the Chinese techs was now in official play. Which meant Dalton's work here in the exotic paradise of Singapore was nearly through and he could catch the next flight to Milan. Minister Dak paused to let Dalton take in the new arrangements.

"Yes. Well, in view of the humanitarian nature of your mission, the Minister Mentor has chosen not to resent the unorthodox nature of your covert arrival. We have confirmed that *your* agency—the Central Intelligence Agency—did in fact issue what you call a Detain, Sequester, Do Not Interrogate order in connection with Mr. Fyke, which was duly noted by our own Intelligence people. The confusion initially arose from Mr. Fyke's attempt to deceive our officials. Naturally, once the identity of Mr. Fyke had been established, we were about to begin the process of notifying your agency when you yourself arrived. In such a . . . timely way."

Dalton smiled, said nothing.

"However, there are impedimenta that must be dealt with before we can release Mr. Fyke into your custody."

"What form would these impedimenta take, Minister?"

"Mr. Fyke was instrumental in a marine disaster which took the lives of twenty-nine men, Mr. Dalton. This disaster took place within our two-hundred-mile limit, and it is therefore our solemn responsibility to ensure that a full and frank accounting of this dereliction of duty be extracted from Mr. Fyke and a condign punishment be decided upon."

"You want to bring Mr. Fyke before a Maritime tribunal?"

Dak closed her eyes, shook her head slightly, and then opened her eyes again, giving Dalton the full force of her official persona.

"No. We are willing to allow your country to conduct an investigation into Mr. Fyke's culpability in the loss of the *Mingo Dubai* and to carry out whatever censure seems appropriate. However, during the period of Mr. Fyke's residence in a secure facility—he was deemed to be a flight risk—he was, unfortunately, drawn into some sort of vulgar prison brawl in the cafeteria, during which he sustained some rather severe injuries."

"Are you about to tell me Mr. Fyke is dead, Minister?"

"No. Not at all. But he will require some form of medical transport if you wish to arrive in America with a living man in your care. It is the Minister Mentor's expectation that you will understand that every possible precaution was taken by our authorities to ensure Mr. Fyke's health and happiness and safety while in our care, and that these injuries which he has suffered can in no way be considered the moral responsibility of the officials of Changi Prison. After all, such incidents are known to happen even in your wonderful American prisons, are they not?"

"They are. Sad to say. Happens every day."

She nodded.

"As I thought. So it will be made quite clear to your government that all the correct procedures were observed and every possible care taken to protect Mr. Fyke's rights and person? That no blame will ever be attached to *any* member or official of the Singaporean government?"

"None at all, Minister. Nor should it be. If Mr. Fyke wants to lie to authorized officials of your government during an investigation into a maritime tragedy and then get himself entangled in cafeteria knockabouts, the responsibility lies solely with him."

"He is—the phrase?—*the author of his own misfortune,* then?"

"Nothing less."

"We have your word?"

"You have my word."

"Sergeant Ong informs me that you were under the impression that some sort of . . . insect that listens? What do you secret agents call it?"

"A *bug?*"

The Minister bared her teeth and shook her head ruefully.

"Yes. A *bug,* was the word. Sergeant Ong said that your associate, Miss Pownall—she is well, I trust?"

"Quite well, thank you."

"She is not with you?"

"No. She had business at the Embassy."

"Really? Was it successfully concluded?"

"No. Turned out not to be an Embassy matter."

"No?"

"No. All a misunderstanding. You were saying? The bug?"

"Sergeant Ong reports that she suspected that a bug of some sort had been placed in her rooms. Does she still believe such a silly thing?"

"Not at all. Turned out to be an iPod. Left behind by a previous tenant."

"An *eye-Pod?*"

"It's a kind of music player. Tiny, no bigger than a cigarette lighter."

"But surely not a listening device?"

"God no, ma'am. We're terribly sorry for the fuss. Please assure Sergeant Ong that we deeply regret the mistake. And I am ashamed to admit that there was a small scuffle between myself and one of his people when he dropped by to pick me up. I overreacted just a tad, and I apologize for any inconvenience I may have caused to his young colleague."

Even Minister Dak found the *inconvenience* line a little hard to swallow, since getting your right arm snapped nearly in two was, even by her own, liberal standards, rather more than an inconvenience. The young officer was still in surgery, a complicated and prolonged effort that *might* restore to him some limited use of his right arm. But she let the word pass with little more than a wry smile.

"I'm delighted to find you such a reasonable man, Mr. Dalton. Now that the matter of Mr. Fyke has been settled, may we move on to another, and not *entirely* separate, matter?"

"Of course."

Here it comes.

"The Home Minister has some concerns."

"About?"

"About what you might wish to call *equity.*"

"Equity? As in financial?"

"No. As in perceptions. It is customary, in matters of interagency cooperation, that a kindness be repaid by a kindness. I'm sure you understand Minister Chong's position? As a matter of national dignity? Of courtesy between sovereign states?"

"I believe I do."

"So, may I assure Minister Chong—and, through him, our beloved Minister Mentor—that you have given the matter of *equity*—a term of art in this context, I admit—given the idea of *reciprocity* some prior consideration? After all, you came to Singapore hoping to secure the cooperation of the Home Ministry. I am sure that, for a man of your tact and experience, the idea of having something in hand with which to *repay* such a kindness would not have been overlooked. Merely as a courtesy?"

Dalton let the silence run until it became Chinese again.

"Yes," he said finally, "we did give the matter some thought."

"Wonderful," said Minister Dak. "Capital. I knew we could rely on the word of an English gentleman. Now, would you like to see our guest?"

Dalton could not keep the surprise off his face. Minister Dak seemed happy to observe it.

"Yes. He is here. Now. We have placed the entire facility at your service. One moment."

She moved her hand, pressed a hidden button. She rose, and Dalton followed her. The doors opened, and Mr. Kwan reappeared in the twilight. "Yes, Minister Dak."

"Mr. Kwan. I wonder if you'd be so kind as to take Mr. Dalton here up to the pool house."

"With pleasure, Minister," said Kwan, looking at Dalton.

"I'll say good morning to you now, Mr. Dalton. I trust your people will be in touch later today to discuss the . . . the courtesy?"

"They will, ma'am. I'll call as soon as it's morning in Virginia."

She smiled then, a more open smile than he'd seen before.

"I take it something specific has been prepared?"

Dalton gave her the sardonic carnivore's rictus he mistakenly believed was a boyishly charming smile.

"Yes. We have something we think you'll appreciate."

"Will it help us with the Chinese?"

An amazing guess? Or something else?

Dalton decided it didn't really matter.

"Do you *need* help with the Chinese, ma'am?"

She laughed then, an open, relaxed, and generally honest laugh.

"Yes, Mr. Dalton. We do. Everybody in the world needs help with the fucking Chinese."

Kwan was holding the door and waiting patiently. Dalton reached out, shook the Minister's skeletal hand. She was a tough, dangerous old pro, and he decided he was glad to know her. She watched him as he walked to the door and called out to him as he was about to leave.

"Do not blame us all, Mr. Dalton."

"Blame you, ma'am? For what?"

"For what you are about to see. It was not done in the name of Singapore. It was not done in the name of the Minister Mentor. It was Chong's work. Chong is a pig. Be careful of Chong, Mr. Dalton. You remember the little matter of the cigarette holder with the opium traces? A *gift* from Sergeant Ong Bo?"

"I remember it vividly, ma'am."

"It was Ong's idea, an old police trick, but Chong allowed it. He seems determined to find a way to put you in Changi Prison, Mr. Dalton. I do not know why. But I advise you to be very careful of Chong Kew Sak."

"I will, ma'am. Good-bye."

"Good-bye, young man."

Kwan led him back into the shaded, shuttered darkness of the empty clubhouse. They went down another long, dimly lit corridor lined with intricately veined teak and hardwoods, stopping at an elevator marked POOL DECK. They rode up in the gleaming brass-and-mirror car to the very top floor. Kwan led them down another corridor until they reached a large security door marked ROOFTOP POOL. Kwan stopped here, with his hand on the bar. A thin shaft of bright sunlight ran the width of the base of the door. Kwan looked at Dalton, seemed about to speak, when Dalton's cell phone rang. Kwan bowed and withdrew to a polite distance. Dalton looked at the caller ID. It was Brancati.

"Micah, where are you?"

"I'm in Singapore. Is it Cora?"

"Her condition has improved slightly. The doctors are encouraged. But she is still in a coma. Have you finished your business there?"

"Just about."

"Good. I have some news, about the girl on the Lido beach."

"Yes?"

"Her name was Saskia Todorovich. She was registered as a student at the Institute in Trieste. But she is a citizen of Montenegro. Her home is Kotor. Which, as you remember, is also the home of Branco Gospic."

"I remember."

"I told you we were going to investigate all the private boats that were in the lagoon that day. One of them was a long white Riva, white over blue. Do you remember such a boat?"

"Yes. It was cruising back and forth by the Isola di San Michele when Cora and I were on the balcony of the Arsenal. You sent a cutter to check it out. Some sort of fashion shooter owned it?"

"Yes. The boat is called the *Subito*—"

"Of course."

Brancati laughed.

"Yes, of course. The *Subito* is registered to Kirik Lujac. Known as

Kiki. He is a professional photographer. Very well known. Very rich. His background is also Montenegrin. His father is a minor member of the Montenegrin royal family. The *Subito* was located by our people two days after we found the body of the girl. It was moored in Bari, locked up and empty. We could not get permission from a judge to search the boat, but we found out that Kiki Lujac had taken a private jet out of Italy the day before. The jet is owned by a company called Minoan Airlines. Galan has traced the ownership back to a firm that has connections to Branco Gospic."

"Let me guess. Lujac flew to Singapore."

"Yes. But there is no record of a Kiki Lujac being registered at any hotel in Singapore."

"He has another identity."

"Yes. We do not know what it is. But we have a picture of him. I think you should see it."

"Can you e-mail it to me, to this phone?"

"I can't. But one of my men will know how."

"You think this Lujac guy killed Saskia Todorovich?"

"I suspect it. If he did, then he is working for Gospic. Which means Gospic knows you went to Singapore and had this man follow you. This means he still intends to kill you. You understand?"

"Fair enough. I still intend to kill him."

"I will save you that trouble. I have already begun. We penetrated his encrypted phone lines in Kotor. We have seized all his assets in Italy. We are rolling up all his people in Venice. By the end of the week, I expect to have his bank accounts located and frozen. Galan has contacts in Zurich and the Isle of Man. Gospic has attempted to assassinate an Italian aristocrat. This assassination, I believe, was motivated by fanatical Muslim hatred of the West. Or, at least, I have decided to think so. I have filed the petition with our Intelligence office to have him listed as a terrorist, which means this is not a law enforcement matter but a matter of our nation's security. So there are no rules. Carlo has sent the picture. Do you have it?"

"Just a minute. I have to get on the Web. Hold on . . ."

Silence at Brancati's end. It was morning in Singapore, which meant it would be the middle of the previous night in Venice. And Alessio Brancati was in his office, hunting Branco Gospic. *Vendetta* was an Italian word. He downloaded an e-mail attachment marked brancati@mil-gov.ita. In a moment, he was looking at a lean, wolfish-looking young man, very tan, absurdly handsome in a hard-cut, slightly Hispanic way, with long, shiny black hair and pale blue-green eyes. He knew him. He had seen him yesterday afternoon, under the portico of the Intercontinental Hotel, in a well-cut navy blue suit; athletic, trim, with a direct, challenging gaze. Mandy had seen him, too, and had then looked over her sunglasses at Dalton and said, "Oh my."

"I've got it, Alessio. He's here. I saw him yesterday, at the hotel."

"Then be careful."

"I will. Thank you. If anything changes with Cora, will you let me know? At once? Whenever?"

"I will. *Ciao,* my friend."

Dalton closed the call but kept Kiki Lujac's picture on the screen for long enough to burn it into his memory. Then he flipped the phone shut. Mr. Kwan rematerialized at his side and continued as if there had been no interruption.

"It is day outside, Mr. Dalton. You may wish to shade your eyes."

Dalton nodded, and Kwan pressed the latch. The door opened onto a wide wooden deck surrounding a huge pool shaped like a lagoon, ringed with palms that swayed in a hot salt wind off the ocean. In the hazy blue distance lay the misted hills and white-sand shoreline of Malaysia and, to the right, the low green island of Pulau Ubin. The roof of the club was on a level with a few distant apartment towers but had a generally unbroken view across much of northeastern Singapore and the island park of Pulau Ubin. Far in the west, the rising sun was setting the towers and spires of downtown Singapore on fire. The light was brutal, hard white and piercing, after the darkness of the hotel interior. Yesterday there had been clouds, the harbingers of the monsoons, but today there was no shade anywhere. Dalton's hangover came back in a sickening wave. Kwan led him across the teak pool decking toward the pool house, a kind of screened lanai fronting a low, rambling wooden structure thatched in dry palm fronds. The building was surrounded by bougainvillea and jasmine and climbing vines. A very pretty young Filipina woman, trim and nicely rounded in green scrubs but wearing those god-awful yellow Crocs, was waiting for them by the screen door that led into the pool house. She was smoking a cigarette and watching them with wary attention as they came up.

"Mr. Kwan."

"Miss Lopez. May I introduce Mr. Micah Dalton."

She inhaled the cigarette, blew the smoke out, unsmiling.

She did not offer her hand.

"You're Agency?"

"Yes. Are you?"

"I do freelance medical escort. For you and the Brits and the Aussies. The times are nasty. They keep me busy. Are you here to see Mr. Fyke?"

"He is," said Mr. Kwan.

Miss Lopez gave Dalton a long once-over.

"Are you a tough guy, Mr. Dalton?"

"Do I have to be?"

She smiled then, a revelation of strong white teeth wonderfully in contrast with her coffee-and-cream complexion. She drew on the cigarette again, exhaled the smoke, her face tightening up again after the warmth of that brief smile. Dalton decided to have a cigarette. She lit a turquoise one for him without comment. They stood together in silence for a time.

"Just as long as you're not a screamer," she said. "I hate screamers."

"I HAVE HIM, sweetie," said Lujac, watching as a tall, supple Chinese man who reminded him of an antelope led Dalton across to what had to be the pool house. "You were right."

Corporal Ahmed said nothing.

He was sitting on the hot-pink vinyl sofa of a vacant apartment on the top floor of a white stucco, Florida-style vacation property called the Changi-Lah Hotel and Suites. The room had gotten the full *Miami Vice* treatment, painted in bilious lime and tedious teal, tricked out in faux palms and, as Lujac had called it when they came in, rickety-ratty-rattan, with faded posters of South Beach hotels all over the walls to remind the inmates of how much nicer the real thing was than this sleazebag, low-rent version, which was all they could afford because, if they were really players, they'd be in South Beach and not Changi Village. Lujac liked the sleazy grunge of the place, but he *loved* the view, five hundred yards straight across the dense forest canopy to the rooftop pool of the Hendon Hills Golf and Country Club. He watched through the tripod-mounted binoculars, as Dalton and the tall Chinese man stood talking to a young Filipina girl in hospital scrubs. Dalton looked tired, rumpled. Hungover.

But, God, he was still gorgeous, thought Lujac. Maybe even more beautiful because he looked so damn weary. So exquisitely *jaded.* Dalton had something of the look of that leathery fellow who played guitar for the Rolling Stones. Dalton had something in his hand, a small turquoise tube. He took a lighter from the Filipina nurse and touched it to the tip of this turquoise thing. It was a cigarette!

Lujac was delighted. A *turquoise* cigarette, with a gold filter. One of those Balkan Sobranie Cocktail thingies. If Dalton wasn't gay, he damn well *should* have been. What a waste.

"Ahmed, how did you find out about this place?"

Corporal Ahmed, who was in Hell, mumbled something vague. Lujac put the glasses down and gave him a hard look.

"Can't hear you, Corporal Ahmed. Can't hear you."

"They move him from Changi yesterday afternoon. Ong make the arrangement. The club was closed for reno, so we just take over the whole thing."

"Did they tell you who the patient was?"

"It the drunk guy who sank that oil tanker. The *Mingo Dubai*."

"What's his name?"

Corporal Ahmed looked sickly.

"Are you sickly, Corporal Ahmed?"

"I don't feel so good."

He was still in the clothes he should have been wearing when Lujac kicked in the door of the room at the Fragrance Hotel. Traces of poor little Bobby Noordin's blood spray had dried black and sticky on Corporal Ahmed's hair, matting it down in tiny clumps and lumps. He needed a shave and a shower. He was supposed to be on duty at the Ministry at noon today. Lujac didn't think he was going to make it.

"Sweetie. I asked you what his name was?"

"He English. Fitch. Brendan Fitch."

"Brendan Fitch?"

Lujac turned around and got the glasses up in time to see Dalton and the Chinese antelope disappear into the darkness of the pool house.

"Corporal Ahmed. What business does our guy have with some poor fucking sailor named Brendan Fitch?"

"Ong says he not really a sailor. And Fitch not his real name."

"What's his real name?"

"Fyke. Raymond Fyke. He supposed to be kind of spy."

"How'd they find that out?"

"They did things to him."

"*Things?* How delicious. What kind of things?"

Corporal Ahmed got even more sickly. Maybe he was afraid he'd give this psycho killer nut bar some fresh ideas.

"I asked you a question, honey bunny."

"Bad things."

"Goes without saying. What bad things?"

Corporal Ahmed told him. Lujac winced.

"Yow! That'll leave a mark."

He watched the rooftop of the country club for a time. Corporal Ahmed sank lower and lower into the couch, his cheeks hollow and his eyes sunken. Lujac was looking at the pool but not seeing it. He was thinking about Branco Gospic, and what the late, lamented, and dearly departed Saskia had been able to tell him about Gospic's plans. Between shrieks.

She knew that Gospic had sent Emil Tarc to Singapore a couple of months ago. And Gospic had confirmed his interest in Singapore by sending Lujac to follow Dalton. And Tarc? Tarc the madman? Tarc the enforcer? Where was Tarc? And what was Tarc doing wherever he was? What did it have to do with this sailor? If it had *anything* to do with this sailor. A tanker had gone down. The *Mingo Dubai*. Was Gospic involved in the sinking of this tanker? If so, why? For what gain?

And what was in all of this that might be good for the Lovely and Talented Kiki Lujac? Lujac watched the rooftop for a while longer, long enough to get the idea that Dalton wasn't coming back out anytime soon.

"Corporal Ahmed."

"Yeah."

"Tell me more about this ship. The *Mingo Dubai?*"

"It just a tanker. Sank in a big storm."

"When?"

Ahmed shrugged, his mind inward, seeing ruin and prison and the cane and a lifetime of unspeakable sexual degradation behind the hanging blankets in Cluster C at Changi. Later events showed Corporal Ahmed that this vision of his future was overly optimistic.

Lujac's razor voice sliced through the fog.

"Ahmed? Don't piss me off."

"Not sure. Maybe three weeks ago? Maybe four."

"What kind of ship was it?"

"Old. Like a scow. Only big. Five hundred feet. Registered in Belize. The owners already got a claim in, for the sinking. They say this English sailor, he the first mate. He drunk, left the wheel in a big storm. Sank the ship when the waves come over the side of it. Now he tell a story about how it was pirates. Nobody believe him. But they find something in him—in his body—that made Minister Chong think he is a spy. So they put him in Cluster C and let the bad boys go loose on him."

"What did they find? In his body?"

Ahmed shrugged again. Ahmed's shrugs were getting on Lujac's nerves. Something would have to be done about Ahmed, but Lujac hadn't decided what that something would be.

"Like a tube. Electric. It say where you are, where you go."

"A GPS locator?"

Another *fucking* shrug.

Try not to frighten him, Kiki. Be patient.

"Okay, a GPS locator. And they went to work on him because of it?"

"Yeah. At first, he don't say anything. Then they use some drugs and later they get the tools out. He say he was a spy, okay, but not anymore. Chong don't believe him, say to really hurt him bad. So they do. After that, he stop saying anything. Just take whatever they do. No more words."

"Okay. He said the ship had been taken by pirates? How did they do it? I mean, how did he *say* they did it?"

"He say they come in a fast motorboat. Alongside."

"Okay. Anything else? This is a big tanker, right? Five hundred feet, that's a lot of tanker. How did they get up the sides?"

Ahmed looked up at Lujac, his face sagging.

He looked ancient.

"He talking nonsense."

"What nonsense did he talk?"

"He say they do it with magic."

"Magic? He said they did it with *magic?* What kind of magic?"

"I don't know. Sergeant Ong only know this from the one of the guards who beat him."

"What—listen to me, honey bunny—what *exactly* did the man say to the guard? What did Ong tell you he said? Get the words as right as you can. Think really hard."

Ahmed gave the matter some prolonged thought. Watching him do it was painful for Lujac, who wanted to help him with the work but knew that once he got going on the kid he wouldn't stop until he killed him.

"The guard say the guy blame magic for the pirates getting on board."

Magic? It made no sense. What the hell kind of . . . ?

"Did you ever see a list of the sailors on this boat?"

"You mean, like a manifest?"

"Yes. A *crew* manifest."

"No list. Too much junker boat for good crew list. Crew from all over. New Guinea. Pakistan. Korea. Never leave ship in port, so no

Immigration fuss. Live all the time on ship. In the beginning, before they find the electric thing in his stomach, Fyke say the names of the men he can remember."

"Do you remember any of those names?"

More hard thinking. More teeth gritting so hard in Lujac's head that the muscles of his neck began to hurt.

"Many Dyak and Malay, I remember. Also some European names."

"Can you remember any of the European names?"

"They were funny. End in *ick*s all the time."

"Ended in *what?*"

This conversation was verging on the ridiculous.

But he felt he was close to . . . something.

"End in *ick*s. Like Buko*vic;* that was one."

"Can you remember any more?"

Ahmed shook his head, his face crumpling as tears began to come.

"What you going to do with me?"

"Look, sweetie, I still have the camera. You've been with me all night. I haven't e-mailed the shots to anybody. I haven't even taken the disk out of the camera. That kid at the Fragrance, he's just another dead bone monkey nobody will ever give a shit about. You help me do my job here, I'll give you the camera. As a gift. You hit DELETE, and life is but a song."

"Who *are* you?"

"I'm a supersweet really nice guy who happens to be burdened with a very short temper. Now, answer the *fucking* question, sweetie. More names?"

"No. My head hurt. Can't think. I need to sleep."

"Sleep soon, darling. Come on. Ends in *ick?* Right. What . . . ?"

Wait a minute. Not magic. Majiic!

Vigo *fucking* Majiic.

Emil Tarc's flunky. Emil Tarc's gofer. Wherever Tarc went, you'd find Vigo Majiic, lurking about in the tall grass. Majiic had been sent somewhere almost six months ago . . . sent to some kind of school. What kind of school . . . ?

He flipped the cell open, punched in the Odessa number. It rang and rang, and then Larissa answered. She sounded sleepy and pissed off.

"Yes."

"Cabbage, this is me."

"It's the middle of the night, Kiki."

"Not where I am. I'm trying to reach somebody, maybe you can help me with it."

"Is it family business?"

"Not really."

"You woke me up for something *personal?*"

Lujac tried to imagine a guy who had *feelings*. How did guys with feelings do regret? They went all sort of soft and whiny, didn't they?

"I know, Cabbage. I apologize. I really do. I wasn't thinking. I know I can be a prick."

"You can't be anything *but* a prick. Like bats have to be bats because they can't be birds. Fine. Now I'm awake. Who do you want to reach?"

"You remember the kid—big, lanky kid—who was always hanging around when we were over in Trieste. Black goatee, chin kind of sunk in?"

"Yeah. Vigo Majiic. Why do you need to talk to him?"

"Things are wrapping up here. I'll be home in a couple of days. I have a shoot in Geneva, for Chopard. My key grips are on a job. I remember Vigo used to work part-time for a photographer in Trieste, a few years back. I figured I'd maybe give him some work."

"When do you need him?"

"Mid-December?"

"Let me see . . ."

Lujac heard some keystrokes, a chair creaking. Behind that, something like a drumming sound. Rain. It was still raining in Kotor.

"No. He's not available anymore. He left the firm months ago."

"Yeah? Where'd he go?"

"Back to school, it says here."

"School? What school?"

"I don't know. I can ask Daddy or Poppa. Poppa sort of liked him."

Dead end. Time to deflect.

"No. Not important. Can you think of anybody else I could use?"

"Now I'm your *employment* agency?"

"Okay. Let it—"

"Wait. We owed him a payroll check. I'll see where we sent it."

Lujac said it wasn't necessary—he didn't want Gospic to know he'd been interested in the whereabouts of Vigo Majiic just yet—but she was already on the computer. A minute passed. No movement on the rooftop deck across the forest. And Corporal Ahmed had just cracked wide open, like an oyster, leaking self-pity. He was stretched out full on the sofa, one arm thrown out and the other across his eyes. His cheeks were wet and he was drooling, and his bony chest was heaving like a damsel's bodice. Now and then, some sort of raspy whimper would emerge from somewhere in his lumpy little throat. The kid was *really* grinding on Lujac's nerves.

"Not here. Sorry. Must have lost it."

"Never mind. If he's not available, it really doesn't matter."

"Okay. How's it going in wherever you are?"

"Just about through here. Can I call your father later?"

"He's been asking."

"I know. I don't want to use his number in Kotor."

"Have you ever?"

"Once. A few days ago."

"Well, don't use it again. Not *ever*. It's not secure. He's setting up another system. He'll call you on that one when it's ready."

"Man. It was deeply encrypted. Branco had it done by a pro from Zurich."

"It's been compromised."

"How do you know?"

"Daddy was on it when someone broke the line and threatened him."

"Jesus! Who?"

"A cop named Brancati."

"Brancati? The Carabinieri major in Venice?"

"That's right. Powered straight through the fire wall and gave it to Daddy right in the ear. In the clear. Daddy was livid."

"What did he say?"

"He said Daddy was *un uomo dentro la marcia funebre.*"

"*A man in a death march?* Did he say why?"

"He didn't have to."

The Vasari woman. Radko must have gotten to her.

"Okay. The phone's a negative. Then how do I reach him?"

"Keep your cell on. He'll reach you."

"Okay. Thanks for—"

"Wait. Four-sixty Alexander Road."

"What?"

"I found where we sent the check. To the school. It was in the personnel file."

"Okay. Four-sixty Alexander Road?"

"Suite 1900. Hey, this is odd. Where are you?"

"Singapore."

"Well, you're in luck. So's Vigo. His mailing address is 460 Alexander Road, Suite 1900, Singapore 119963. You can go see him yourself."

Vigo Majiic is in Singapore. Doing what?

"I have the address on Google. Hold on—"

Lujac held, trying to convey the subliminal impression that he was just being polite, that he really had no special interest in Vigo Majiic.

"It's a school. They have a website. It's the Singapore Maritime Academy. They train people for the Merchant Marine. Vigo Majiic went off to be a sailor."

"Majiic is a *sailor?*"

"I'll bet you *like* sailors, Kiki. All that *blow the man down* stuff?"

"Yeah. *Yo ho!* Thanks, anyway. Bye, Cabbage."

"You keep your cell on. Daddy's going to call."

"Yeah. Look, Larissa. A little favor? Don't let him know I was bugging you for personal stuff. He's a little touchy about that kind of thing."

"Yes. He is. And why should I care if Daddy's pissed off at you?"

"No reason. Sorry I asked. See you around."

"Not if I can help it."

27

The Deck House,
Hendon Hills Golf and Country Club,
Changi Village, Singapore

Miss Lopez checked the patient and the monitors, and then left them alone together. The slatted blinds had been lowered, and a rectangle of barred light lay across the pale green sheets of Fyke's hospital bed. An IV drip stood by the bed, a plastic line snaking into the sheets on the far side of the bed. The room smelled of disinfectant and soap and cigarette smoke. The room was large, floored in aged teak, with bamboo walls and a roof made to look like palm thatch. The pool house furniture had all been removed, and now there was nothing in it but a shiny new hospital bed, a rack of monitors, and three cane chairs arranged around the bed.

Fyke lay on his back, the sheet pulled up to just below his throat. His thick arms lay outside the sheets. His hands were wrapped in white bandages. The bed had been sized for Asian bodies, so Fyke's massive frame overflowed it in all directions. His eyes were closed, and his chest was rising and falling in a deep and even rhythm, his lips half open. He had lost weight since the old days, when they had run through the shattered streets of Pristina, carrying a dead arms dealer and laughing like drunken loons. His cheeks were drawn and pale, and his beard had been shaved off by someone good at the work.

Miss Lopez had told Dalton what had been done to Raymond Paget Fyke, in clinical detail, her anger and outrage only evident in the small red circles on her cheeks and the intensity and clarity of her language. Dalton had taken it in and asked her a few questions about possible remedial surgery, about Fyke's chances of living a normal life.

Her replies had been short and hard-edged, delivered in a quavering whisper driven by withering scorn and white-hot rage.

"He had a full upper denture, which, miraculously, the medics were able to find. But they knocked out a few of his lower teeth. He'll need a full bridge or implants. They went at him with some sort of iron bar. Worked over his torso. From the rope burns on his wrists, they must have strung him up on a meat hook. You follow? Lots of blood in his urine. Cracked a few of his ribs. The medics at Changi are very good at repairing these sorts of injuries. God knows, they get enough practice. I'm worried about his heart. He's ripe for a real myocardial infarct, and when it happens it'll probably kill him. So what could be done for him was done. He's amazingly strong. Tough as boot heels. Otherwise, he'd be dead. It would have been easier on him if he had died early in the process, but they kept a doctor around to prevent the grosser infections and to keep him from a fatal shock response. Kept his blood pressure up, that sort of thing. They even gave him saline and transfusions. Very professional. Very *fucking* professional."

She had stopped there, gathering herself, her black eyes glittering.

"As for the rest, they hit all the standard bases for sadistic asshole jailers. Cigarette burns all over his back and arms. Signs of scorching, in pairs, probably electrical, around the scrotum. The usual device is a handheld Taser. At least he still has all his gear. That surprised me. I guess they were saving that for later—a threat stops working when you carry it out—and then you showed up and stopped the party. It's a good thing you did, because the way they were going they probably would have killed him in another week or so. They get carried away. It stops being about whatever they wanted to know and it just becomes a matter of breaking the man, because if they can't break him they feel like losers, like he's beaten *them*. As for the psychological damage, I'm not qualified to say. I know they used lysergic acid on him, and some other hallucinogens. He's loaded up on Narcan, which is—"

"I know what Narcan is."

She gave him a look but didn't ask the question.

"Okay. Narcan helps. But there could be long-term effects. This sort of drug loads up in the limbic system—"

"I know. I had the same thing done to me, okay?"

"Touchy?"

"Yes. It was about a month ago."

"Oh. Sorry. Are you . . . ?"

"Okay? No. I'm still seeing the ghost of a dead friend."

"Waking or in dreams?"

"In dreams now. Waking? That seems to have stopped."

"Memory okay? Cognition?"

"Cognition normal. My memory is working better than I'd like."

She paused, worked it through, smiled a nice smile at him then.

"I guess, in your line of work, a good memory is a mixed blessing."

Dalton said nothing to that.

She blinked at him and then got back to business.

"Well, psychological damage. In similar cases, and I've seen a few come out of the same wing at Changi—they make something of an art of it there—the post-traumatic reaction sets in over the next few weeks. You'll get rage, grief, hysteria, shame, a burning sense of personal violation almost identical to a victim's response to rape, depression. Followed by a prolonged period of apparently miraculous recovery. Then—not always but often—a few months later, when it all sinks in and the fog clears and the long-term impact really registers, they kill themselves."

Dalton took it all in and thanked her for her analysis in a reasonably steady voice. She had slipped out then, to sit in the sun and smoke cigarettes and get her anger under control. Kwan had tactfully, and wisely, withdrawn, and Dalton was alone in the pool house with what was left of an old friend.

Earlier in the day, in anticipation of his medevac extraction, Lopez had reduced the morphine drip enough to bring Fyke back up to the surface without letting the pain come back too. Dalton watched the cardiac monitor for a while and then saw the number blip from 63 to 79 in a second. He looked at Fyke's face and saw that Fyke's eyes were open and looking right at Dalton.

"Jesus, Mary, and Joseph," Fyke said, in a whisper, his mouth twisting into a leer. "It's the crocodile."

"Ray," said Dalton, softly. "You look like shit."

Fyke's lips tightened, showing white as he grinned.

"So do you. You need to back off the heroin. Where the hell am I?"

"You're safe."

"With you in the room? I bloody doubt it. Are we still in Singapore?"

"For now. They're bringing in a chopper. One of ours. Marines. From now on, you'll be with our people and nobody else. We'll go to Seletar. They've got a Gulfstream there. The crew is ripping out seats to make room for your bed. Miss Lopez is going with us, all the way to Guam—"

Fyke's monitor beeped. His heart rate had spiked to over 100.

"What's the matter, Ray? Should I get Miss Lopez?"

Fyke shook his head, his eyes closed.

"Guam? We're going to Guam?"

"Yes."

"Military?"

"Yes."

"Mikey, they're gonna rip me apart."

Dalton, who knew exactly what Fyke meant, was silent. Fyke opened his eyes and looked across at Dalton, a wild glitter in his watery blue eyes.

"You *know* what I mean. I went dark, took a lot of stuff with me. In my head. They're gonna want to know what I told the gooks. And I don't even *know* what I told the gooks. Before they cut me. After that, I didn't care what they did. No. Don't say it. Lyin' to a sick friend is a mortal sin. Thing is, I don't even know what I'm supposed to know in the first place. Mikey, I don't wanna go to Guam. Can you fix it so I don't?"

"Ray, look at you. You need serious medical help. You need it stateside. Yeah, they'll debrief you. That'll be tough. But, in the meantime, you have to get stitched together. Healed—"

Fyke's chest heaved under the sheets.

Dalton realized he was laughing.

"You don't get *healed* from what the gooks did to me. I told you. They *cut* me. They fed my dick to a dog. Never liked those goddam Dobermans."

"Ray, listen to me, nobody fed your dick to a dog."

Fyke tried to sit up, fell back, his face bright red, his breathing shallow.

"I *saw* it done, Mikey. They used clamps to hold my eyes open. Cut my tackle off with a pair of shears!"

"They didn't cut your dick off, Ray."

"Did too, Mikey. I checked, and it was gone."

Dalton stood up, walked over to the bed.

"Ray, can you sit up?"

"No. Leave me be. I'm not lookin'. I know the little soldier is AWOL."

"I heard your dick was pitiful tiny. You might have missed it."

Fyke gave him a sideways look.

"Who told you my dick was pitiful tiny?"

"When they buried Gordie Hughson in Arlington. You had your full Black Watch on. Your kilt blew up. Everybody in the Honor Guard saw it."

"Shrinkage! That was shrinkage. It was the eighth of December! And there was a stone-cold wind, ripping in straight off the Potomac"

"Okay. Let's find out. Can you sit up?"

A silence while Fyke thought that over

"I can if we do it slow."

Dalton—slowly—gently—raised Fyke up into as much of a sitting position as he could stand. Pain was coming off the man like heat off a radiator, but he didn't make a sound. Dalton pulled the sheet down all the way to the foot of the bed. Fyke had his eyes closed.

He was also holding his breath.

"Open your eyes, Ray."

Fyke shook his head.

"No."

"They drugged you, Ray. Gave you acid. Fucked with your head. Open your eyes."

Fyke slowly opened one eye, looked down at his belly. Exhaled.

The expression on his face would have been funny if Dalton hadn't been so distracted by the damage that had been done to Fyke's entire torso; he looked like a side of raw beef. Fyke opened his other eye, stared down for a time.

Then Dalton lowered him back.

Fyke was quiet for a while.

"Man. I could have sworn."

"You're all there, Fyke. For what it's worth."

"Everything's the wrong color. Have I got gangrene?"

"You never kicked a man in the balls before?"

"Of course. But I never checked on his *fooking* pigmentation afterward. And you're an unsympathetic git, Mikey. Always was."

"I missed you too."

They sat for a time in amiable silence. Whatever had been done to Fyke had not changed the essential man. He was still there. Fyke pressed a button that pumped up the morphine drip a notch. Gradually, his heart rate slowed down to a steady 75.

Time passed.

"Mikey . . . ?"

"Ray?"

"I'm not going to Guam."

"No choice, Ray."

"No. I'm not going to let the Meat Hook lads roast me over a pit at Anderson Field. I've had enough of being beat up. You got any money, Mikey?"

"Yes. I do."

"Ill-gotten, I don't doubt. Can you get me into a private hospital?"

"I'll stay with you, Ray, all the way to—"

Cora. On a gurney, in Florence.

Fyke was shaking his head.

"They won't let you. Soon as we get to Guam, they'll peel you off, and down the rabbit hole I go. Have you got a pistol, then?"

"For what?"

"So I can shoot myself."

"With those mitts on? Not bloody likely."

Fyke raised his hands, stared at the mass of bandages, put his head back on the pillow, blowing air out through pursed lips.

"Christ. I'm a wreck, ain't I?"

"You are, Ray. You are."

"Will *you* shoot me, then? Give me the misery cord, like a good Christian lad? Let me go to my God like a soldier."

"Nope. Won't shoot you myself. Sorry."

"Heartless bastard. Would you give a dyin' man a cigarette, then?"

"You're not dying."

"I am too. Death is in this room, Mikey. I can smell it."

"No it isn't. Your bedpan needs changing"

"Well, give us a smoke, then!"

"Don't have any."

"You're a lyin' Sassenach dog. I can smell them on you."

"I'll give you one when we get to the airport."

Silence, then, and Fyke's cardiac monitor beeping solemnly. His numbers dropped gradually to 67, and looked like they'd stay there. Fyke was SAS, and there is no one in the modern world remotely like the SAS. He was a tenth-century man. Dalton thought he would have been right at home in a Viking longboat, looting monasteries and chasing green-eyed girls up and down the stones of Skellig Michael.

"Ray, can I ask you a question?"

"Fire away."

"Why'd you go dark?"

Something filled the room then, an invisible presence, a force. It felt like grief and bitter shame. Dalton waited it out. Fyke would tell him or not.

"Not now, Mikey. There's a good lad."

Dalton let it go. They'd get it out of him in Guam, one way or another.

"Okay. Subject dropped. You need some more morphine, Ray?"

Fyke shook his head. Another silence while each man dealt with his private horrors. Dalton knew he couldn't leave Ray Fyke to be put to the Question in some soundproof cell at Anderson AFB, but he also knew he couldn't *save* him from it either. *And Cora was waiting in Florence.*

"Mikey . . . I never sunk that ship. I'm not wearing that tag, not for love nor money. I did my duty. I'm a drinker, but I'm not a drunk."

"Then what happened to it?"

"They *fooking* took it, didn't they? Right by the Kepulauan Lingga Lightship. Middle of a storm. Butchered everybody. Dyaks and Malays did it, and they did it for those bloody Serbs."

"Serbs? What Serbs?"

"Majiic. Vigo Majiic and his boys. Some other hatchet-faced hardass, with a prissy little goatee, had an MP5, looked like he was running the show too. The Serbs took my ship, Mikey. You know we saw enough of those bastards when we were in Pristina. Organized. Cold. Took my ship, killed my crew. Poor old Wang. Last I saw of her, I'm clinging to a speedboat in the middle of the South China Sea. Do you believe me, Mikey?"

Dalton spent a while thinking about Serbian mobsters like Branco Gospic and Stefan Groz and celebrity assassins like Kiki Lujac, and how often he and his friends were colliding with Serbo-Croatian thugs these days, in Venice and Florence and on tankers in the South China Sea. The rectangle of barred sunlight had moved across the bed and now lay partly across Fyke's face. His eyes were open, and they glittered in the light like shards of blue glass. "Yes," said Dalton, finally. "I believe you."

"Good. Thank you for that. So the question before us, Mikey?"

"Yes?"

"What the hell are we gonna *do* about it?"

28

The National Security Agency, Fort Meade, Maryland

Nikki Turrin had been summoned to the AD of RA's office. Mr. Oakland had relayed the summons but, being a vengeful little prick, had not told her the reasons for it. So Nikki was following Mr. Oakland's busy, beige-clad, oversized rear down a long and Berber-carpeted corridor past rows and rows of closed doors and through the kind of portentous hush that filled the upper levels of the NSA like incense from a requiem Mass. Nikki had her heart in her throat, and her chest was tight with anxiety, but she was not so distracted that she did not notice that Mr. Oakland's bubbly butt looked like two suckling pigs wrestling in a sack, and that when he walked he took tiny stutter steps instead of the easy, loping stride of an actual human, and his beige Dockers were just a hair too short and he was wearing white ribbed athletic socks and a pair of brand-new Bass Weejuns with double-thick rubber soles to give him some height, and his jacket was a bilious orange-plaid number that may have actually been cut from the kind of bedspread you'd find in a cheap motel in

Bakersfield, if she'd ever been in a cheap motel in Bakersfield, wherever Bakersfield was.

California, she decided, as Mr. Oakland's clenching butt cheeks signaled a rubbery screeching halt outside the double-wide doors that led into the outer offices of the AD of RA himself.

Mr. Oakland turned and looked up at Nikki, his blue eyes bright with envy and malice, his round red mouth puckered tight.

"You'll be going in alone, Miss Turrin."

"You're not coming?"

Mr. Oakland checked his watch, blinked up at her.

"No. I have a prior meeting. Memo me on what's said."

"Yes, sir," she said, looking past him at the doors with a weight in her heart. She refrained from asking him what the hell she had done. Mr. Oakland stepped around her without another word and scurried off in the direction of the elevator bank, fat little legs pumping. He reminded Nikki of the white rabbit in *Alice in Wonderland*. She reached out and pushed against the door and stepped into a plain, spartan-looking anteroom with a secretary's desk, behind which sat, as one would expect, a secretary. She looked up at Nikki as she came into the room, a plain, spartan-looking older woman with shining silver hair swept up behind and sterling silver reading glasses set low on an aristocratic nose. She had a good, strong face and warm gray eyes, and she studied Nikki over her reading glasses, her mouth shaping into a sympathetic smile.

"I'm Alice Chandler. You're Nikki Turrin?"

"Yes. I'm here to see the—"

"Have you ever met him?"

"No. I haven't."

"Have you seen a picture of him?"

Nikki looked a little puzzled. Miss Chandler shook her head.

"He's scarred, Miss Turrin. It gives some people a start. It's okay to start, Miss Turrin. I just thought I'd warn you. You can go in now. Would you like some coffee?"

"I'd love some."

"Black?"

"Yes."

"Okay. Go along now. I'll be right in."

Nikki gathered herself and walked through the half-open doorway behind Miss Chandler's desk and found herself in a shaft of strong sunlight that was pouring in through the slatted blinds of the AD of RA's office. The room was simple and unadorned, but there was a U.S. flag on a staff in the corner—the military kind, with the gold thread trim—bare wooden floors, and a long, low wooden desk, behind which a large, heavy-framed man in a blue suit and white shirt unbuttoned at the collar sat in a swivel chair, staring back at her. He got up as she came into the room, stepping into the shaft of light as he came around the side of his desk with his hand out. Nikki did not start. She took his hand as he introduced himself—his name was vaguely Western, but she only heard his title, the AD of RA, because she was trying to cope with his facial scarring, and that took up a lot of her mental energy. The AD of RA did not seem to notice. By now, he was used to it.

He pulled a chair around and patted the frame.

"Sit down, Miss Turrin. Thanks for coming."

Nikki sat.

"Yes, sir. Mr. Oakland—"

"Screw him. He tried to cut you out of this."

"He . . . I . . ."

The AD of RA laughed; a short, rasping cough.

"You're the one who pulled this video off YouTube, right?"

"Yes."

"Took it to Oakland? Who promptly cut you out of the loop."

"Yes. He did. It was okay. The video seemed to call for something."

"Yes. It did. We've been all over it, and it's got us worried. Has that pompous dickhead told you anything more about it?"

"No, sir."

"Good. At least the little shit knows the *fucking* rules. Sorry. Excuse that. We're giving you a clearance to Indigo, Miss Turrin."

"Indigo?"

"Yes. We've been over your file, and there's no reason why we can't bring you into this. Every reason why we should."

"I'm . . . honored, sir. May I ask what *this* is?"

"Consider yourself sworn, Miss Turrin. May I call you Nikki?"

"Please."

"We've opened a file on this video, Nikki. So far we know a lot about it. Would you like me to fill you in?"

"Please."

The AD of RA filled her in. It took about six minutes. In the middle of the story, Miss Chandler came in with a trayful of doughnuts, along with two cups of black coffee. The AD of RA never stopped the story, thanked Miss Chandler with a smile and a nod, and went back to the narrative, ending with the deaths of the three Israeli scientists on the flight from Tel Aviv. When he was done, Nikki's chest was tight again.

"So, what do you think? What's the first question that pops into your head?"

"The first? I guess, why post this video at all?"

"Yeah. Me too. Why is this thing on the Web in the first place? I mean, it looks like somebody poisoned the water in this pool, killing a lot of people, including this guy named Dzilbar Kerk, who has an indirect but worrisome connection to the deaths of a lot of microbiologists around the world, some of whom were working for Biopreparat in the old USSR. So, anybody has to take what happens to these people pretty seriously, because the thing sure as hell looks like a security threat, and that's what we're paid to look out for. What I don't get is, why take the MPEG and throw it on the Web? Why set off all these alarms? Makes no sense, except it has to, doesn't it? I mean, unless some unhappy underling threw it on the Web just to piss off his boss? Which, based on the video, would be suicidal. You follow?"

"Yes. I understand."

"Yeah. I figured you would. You know this stuff reasonably well?"

"The Internet? As well as most. Better than some. I grew up with it, of course, but, once I got into the Monitors, I really paid attention."

"How do you post something on YouTube?"

"Go online, through your server; go to the website, sign up—"

"You can't post anonymously?"

"No. You have to have an e-mail identity, and it has to be a legitimate one. It all goes through your server—AOL or EarthLink, or whatever—and, since you pay for those services, they have to know who you are. So you need an account to post, and that's an identifier right there."

"What about Internet cafés?"

"That's a loophole. You could sign on to YouTube and post anything from an Internet café, except the posting would be traceable to that particular café. So you'd be vulnerable on that level."

"But I could travel, couldn't I? Take a flight to East Frogfart on the Fen and find a café and post the video from there. Right?"

"Yes. You could."

"And then the video gets picked up and reposted around the world?"

"Not necessarily. It could just sit on YouTube and get accessed. Collect hits. That's how YouTube rates a posting. The number of hits."

"Can YouTube ID where those hits are coming from?"

"What's the point, sir? If your search field is in the millions, where are you? How many man-hours would we have to devote to checking every hit on this video? And why would we? We want to know where it came from, not who looked at it afterward. Right, sir?"

"Right. Good point. You have a flair for this, Nikki."

Nikki smiled. In the sunlight, her smile was dazzling. Actually, *she* was dazzling, a genuine Italian stunner in the classic Sophia Loren style. Her perfume was spicy and complex, not at all floral. He figured it was probably called Ashes of Men. The AD of RA was divorced now, since his wife had found his physical and spiritual wounds impossible to bear, but Nikki was . . . well, who cared how pretty she was. The observation was totally unprofessional, anyway. How old was she? Twenty-eight max? By her terms, he was the walking dead. Not to mention being a grotesque monster. But it *was* a great smile. He found himself smiling back at her, or at least *trying*.

"Anyway, basically, as I told you, we know the video was shot in Eastern Europe, probably the Balkans. The big guy who dies in this video, Dzilbar Kerk—I think you may have heard of him?"

"Yes. I've seen his name on the Monitors' List."

"Well, then you know that Kerk is wanted by everybody, from the FBI to the Sheriff of Nottingham, so he probably had to stay close to home, and we figure home is this butt-ugly gunrunner's palazzo in the video. So if we can find the villa, then we're a lot closer to finding out who made the video."

"Yes. We are."

"So, what's the *second* thing that strikes you about this video?"

"The second thing? I guess that maybe we're seeing what we're supposed to see and maybe not seeing what is really there."

"Good. Great. Like what?"

"Like how do we know it's the pool water that kills them?"

"What do you mean?"

"All we see is some fat, ugly, greasy, hairy thugs drinking some clear liquid out of a vodka bottle, and then they all go swimming and die. How do we know what killed them was in the water and not in the vodka bottles? Or in the air, like a weaponized bacterial spray of some sort?"

"Good. I like that."

"Next, how do we know they *died* in the first place?"

"You mean the thing is faked? It isn't. I wish it had been, but it wasn't. We had every frame blown up and examined by our best forensic pathologists. I mean, super-high-density resolution. Image enhancement. They were even able to get in tight enough on the throats to analyze and time the blood flow in the carotids, got the heartbeats, got a real close look at the kinds of hemorrhaging in the retinas, the inflammation of the nasal areas, catastrophic drop in respiration . . . They went over everything, and they all agreed that what we were watching was real. Those people died, Nikki. And they died *hard*. You follow?"

"I do."

"So, you get it that this is dangerous stuff?"

"I do."

"Good. You need to be ready for that."

"Yes, sir."

"You ever in the field, Nikki?"

"In the field? No, sir. I'm a Monitor. Isn't fieldwork a CIA thing?"

"Fuck the CIA. They're leaking like a used . . . like a used diaper. They're nothing but a *fucking* sedition mill for those goddam treasonous pinheads at the *New York Times*. Pardon my *fucking* language. I don't trust *any* of them. If you go into the field, I can get you some off-the-books tactical support from the DIA. And I do think, Nikki, before you're through, this file might take you outside."

"Yes. Sir. Understood. What do you need?"

"I'm giving you complete access to our NIMA and NASA data banks. Including the military ones. We're going to give you an image of what this villa would look like from straight up, then you can run it through the Balkan and Albanian databases. Look for a match. This is between you and me. No leaks anywhere. This is critical. I want you to put a set of crosshairs right over this stinking pink palazzo. You locate it, and, if we're good, we find something that leads us to the . . . person who made this video."

"And then?"

"And then we, very nicely, ask him why."

"What if he won't tell us?"

"We'll hand him over to people who don't do *very nicely.*"

29

Changi Village, Singapore

Everybody in Changi Village heard the chopper as it came in from the north, heard it long before they saw it, heard that deep bass beat thrumming in the air itself. People in the streets looked up and over the tree line, straining to see what was coming, thinking *Some celebrity flying in from Seletar Airfield. That's where all the stars land.* The thunder of the rotors filled the pool house and sent Fyke's monitor up into the low hundreds again. Five hundred yards away, Lujac stopped what he was doing to Corporal Ahmed and went to take a look out across the canopy. Sure enough, there was a big olive-drab chopper coming in low over the tree line. It was heading straight for the rooftop deck of the Hendon Hills Golf and Country Club. He got the binoculars just as that Chinese guy who looked like a gazelle reappeared on the pool deck, staring into the north, shading his eyes against the sun. The chopper, an old Huey, had big white letters painted on the fuselage—USMC—and a red cross inside a white circle.

"Christ," said Lujac, while he tried to keep the roof deck in his view, speaking to no one particular, sure as hell not Corporal Ahmed, who was on the floor rolled into a naked, sweaty little skin ball and weeping soundlessly. Well, at least he was *soundless,* which was a definite improvement.

"They're gonna medevac the guy out."

Hadn't planned on that. Now what?

MISS LOPEZ OPENED the lanai screen and knocked gently on the wall. Fyke was trying to sit up in the bed, plucking at his covers. Dalton was standing now, looking at Miss Lopez and hearing the thudding shudder of the blades. The rotor wash was starting to kick up dust inside the pool house, and the lanai screens were rattling. Fyke somehow got himself sitting up straight. He swung his legs over the side of the bed and gave Dalton a hard look. "Well, lad, what's the plan?"

Miss Lopez glanced at Fyke and then back to Dalton.

"What does he mean?"

"He means I can't let him go to Guam."

Miss Lopez looked at him, her expression hardening.

"Why? What are they going to do to him in Guam?"

"He has to be debriefed."

Miss Lopez, who had been around the covert world awhile, got it in one. Her pretty young face reddened, and her expression got even stonier.

"Because he's been in enemy hands, you mean?"

"Yeah. Basically."

"He was AWOL, wasn't he? Weren't you?"

Fyke's face reddened, but he nodded. The chopper was right overhead, shaking the pool deck like a cyclone shakes a house.

"Tell me," she said, "will they hurt him?"

Dalton raised his hands, shrugged, his face a mask.

"Then you can't let it happen. His heart isn't strong. They'll want to know what he told them. He's had enough, Mr. Dalton. They'll kill him."

"I do like this girl, Mikey," said Fyke, grinning through his bruises.

"What can I do, Miss Lopez? The chopper's already here."

"You're the CIA, Mr. Dalton. They'll do what you tell them."

"No. To the Marines, the CIA's a bunch of dickless college boys."

"Mikey," said Fyke, his voice hardening. "You were a Special Forces soldier long before you were CIA. Remember that."

The chopper landed, rocking on its rails, the rotor noise subsiding. Within moments, there was a knock at the screen door and then it opened. Mandy Pownall was standing framed in the hard light, blinking into the darkness. She was wearing tailored tan slacks and a military-style tan shirt, perfectly creased, and dark brown cowboy boots. She had a small gray pistol tucked into her belt, from the angular butt some kind of Glock. All she was missing was a highly polished Sam Browne. She looked vaguely dangerous and splendidly theatrical, like Lawrence of Arabia doing lunch at the Savoy. Fyke was obviously delighted by her arrival. She swiveled her head as she took in the scene. It was like watching a gun muzzle track left eighty degrees. She settled on Dalton with an almost-audible click.

"Micah Dalton, you miserable prick."

"Mandy Pownall, as I live and breathe."

"You could have *fucking* called to see how I was."

"A resourceful girl like you? It would have been insulting."

"Who's this . . . medical person?"

"Miss Lopez, meet Miss Pownall. My esteemed colleague."

Miss Lopez gave Mandy a scowl and a short nod. Mandy had that effect on women. Fyke had somehow gotten to his feet, with the sheet wrapped around him like a toga. He looked like Caesar Augustus after a three-day bender. Regal, mind you, but battered. He was weaving slightly, but he seemed to be really enjoying looking at Mandy. That was an HOV lane direct to Mandy's heart. She softened visibly as she looked back at him.

"You must be Mr. Fyke."

"I am. Delighted to meet you, Miss Pownall."

Mandy's appraisal flicked around him like a butterfly, settled lightly on Fyke's bruised face, his broad, predatory grin. She smiled.

"You've been a great deal of trouble, Mr. Fyke."

"He's likely to be more," said Dalton. "It's his MOS."

"We don't have much time. Cather has the Chinese techs inbound from Guam right now. They're about an hour out. We're supposed to take Mr. Fyke to Seletar. We meet the plane there. The techs get off and we get on. We—"

"I take it we're not involved in the trade."

"No. Cather has a team handling that. Howell and Purdy, from—"

"I know them," said Dalton. They were Meat Hookers, from Peary. They'd drop the Chinese techs off and then jerk Fyke right out from under them. There was no way Deacon Cather was going to let Mandy Pownall and Micah Dalton stay on the Fyke case. Their part in this was over.

Mission accomplished.

Medals pending. Hugs all round.

Or not.

"You're trading something for *me?*" asked Fyke.

Dalton started to explain the trade to him, but two medics in Marine Corps uniforms, both wearing Berettas, were now standing in the door. They looked around the room, focused on Dalton.

"Sir, are you Micah Dalton?"

"No, Sergeant. I'm not," he said, in a low growl. "I'm *Captain*

Micah Dalton, A Team, Fifth Special Forces Group, Fort Campbell, Kentucky."

Both Marines stiffened and snapped off razor-edged salutes. Dalton, although capless, returned the salutes.

"What's your unit, Sergeant?" he asked, in a hard, flat voice. Mandy was staring at him. Dalton ignored her. He had just barked out a question he didn't give a rat's kidney about. The real point was to get these Marines thinking about him as anything but another goddam civilian pogue from the goddam CIA, one of the PUNTS, a person of utterly no tactical significance. Both Marines turned to rigid statues, staring into the middle distance, while the First Sergeant barked out their unit coordinates.

"First Sergeant Ryan Hazlitt, sir. Senior Combat Evac Medic, Third of the Third Marines, Okinawa, temporarily assigned to the United States Embassy in Singapore. Captain Dalton, may I present Sergeant Butler Kuhn, Third of the Third, also seconded to Embassy duty."

"You're here to take this injured soldier to Seletar Airfield?"

"Yes. Sir."

"In what?" said Fyke, indignant. "The gooks took all my kit."

The First Sergeant took in Fyke's Roman look, grinned at him, lifted a canvas bag he'd been carrying . . .

"No problem, sir. We've got Marine Corps BDUs and boots. The whole combat field issue, including the plastic razor and the extra socks. We got your numbers from the Changi medics."

"Carry on, Sergeant. Treat him well. He's SAS."

Both Marines stopped, gave Fyke a look. Fyke stood tall, gunned them both back. Miss Lopez stepped in and took his arm, speaking softly to him in Spanish. While they gently disconnected his IV and eased him into the combat fatigues, the Marines radiated the kind of respect bomb-disposal teams show around unexploded 105s. Mandy Pownall stepped in close to Dalton, spoke in a low murmur.

"You're not really going to give him up to Howell and Purdy?"

"No," said Dalton. "I'm not."

"But you can't go with him either, because you need to see Cora."

"I know that, too, but thanks so much for stating the bloody obvious."

Mandy's thin smile was not kindly meant.

She wasn't that kind of girl.

"So, it's Hobson's choice for you, isn't it? Either go flitting off to Florence like a lovesick nightingale and perch by Cora's bed of pain, shredding tissues and weeping salt tears, or stay out here in the field like a real man and try to keep Ray Fyke away from the Meat Hookers."

"Yeah," he said, a hard, cold glitter in his eyes. "It is."

"So what are you going to do?"

"I don't have a *fucking* clue."

"I didn't think so."

30

Seletar Airfield, northern Singapore

It took a while to get Ray Fyke squared away in the cramped interior of the medevac chopper, but they managed it, strapping him into a lashed-down wheelchair just behind the door gunner's post. There was even some room—so cramped it was dangerously close to a sexual experience—for Dalton to ride on the metal equipment bench in between Mandy Pownall and Miss Lopez. The Marine medics— Hazlitt and Kuhn—stayed close to Fyke, radiating an almost-religious awe for an SAS sergeant, possibly the only military class in the world, other than an actual Frankish knight, for whom a Marine would feel that sort of awe, as the Huey stirred up another cyclone on the roof deck, rippling the silken clothes of Mr. Kwan and lashing the water in the pool into concentric rings of white lace, as they rose up into a high blue sky far above Changi Village.

The pilot put the nose down, gained airspeed, and banked hard left—the crowded streets of Changi were filled with upturned brown faces, and the palms were whipping in the downdraft—Dalton looked to the southeast and saw huge white walls and, towering above the walls, he saw the white blockhouses of Changi Prison rising above an open flatland next to a series of hexagonal apartment blocks. He looked away and saw Fyke staring back at Changi Prison with cold murder in his eyes. Fyke felt his look and broke into one of those fierce berserker grins that Dalton had seen so often when they were in the field.

"Payback, Mikey," yelled Fyke, over the shuddering of the airframe and the lunatic howling of the engine, his grin fading. "Coming soon."

Dalton gave him back the grin and then looked to the northwest, past the flatlands and deltas of Pasir Ris, Punggol, and Ji Kayu that lined the Strait of Johor, the border waters between Singapore and Malaysia, northwest toward the open rolling meadow lands of the Seletar Golf Course. In the far north, he could just make out the hills and shores of Malaysia, clouded in blue haze. Deeper into Malaysia, a bank of blue-gray storm clouds was gathering over the mountains, the leading edge of an oncoming monsoon. Up here, at two thousand feet, with Singapore turning below like a game board filled with red-tiled roofs and towers and spires, and ringed by mud-green shoal water, Dalton felt the sea change coming.

It was too loud to talk in the open bay of the Huey. Miss Lopez had gone inside herself, watching Fyke through half-closed brown eyes, her expression a mix of fear and anger and compassion. Mandy, on his left, was staring out at the glittering skyline of downtown Singapore, the wind rippling her military tans and her hair flying, her eyes clouded and cold.

Across the aluminum floor, Fyke sat in the wheelchair, his eyes fixed on the middle distance, thinking about the boys from Langley who would be waiting for him on the field at Seletar and wishing he had a weapon. He had quietly peeled off the large bandages wrapping his hands and now he was flexing his injured fingers and working his wrists, ignoring the pain.

He had stopped the morphine, too, because he needed to be clear. Yes, he was in a world of pain, but it was a world he was used to, and he felt a damn sight better in combat BDUs than he had in nothing but a pale green sheet. He felt like he was home again, in a soldier's uniform, in a military chopper, surrounded by fighting men and pretty women. He was where he belonged. And he was still SAS, by God's holy trousers.

Now and then, he'd glance—briefly—at the little gray Glock in Mandy's belt and then down at the Beretta strapped to Sergeant Hazlitt's right thigh, and then back into the vague middle distance. He was willing to give Micah Dalton some room to work in because he had faith in the man, or, at least, the crocodile inside the man. But he'd do whatever he had to do to stay free. He had a ship to find and people to kill. He could fly a Huey, if it came to it. This Huey, for example. He hoped it wouldn't come to that. The tone of the rotors changed, and Dalton heard the tinny crackle of the pilot's voice in his own headset. His name was Goliad, a Warrant Officer.

"There's Seletar, Captain Dalton. Looks like the CIA is already here."

Dalton leaned to his right, crowding Miss Lopez a little. She shifted away, and he could see the landing strip of Seletar, the tower itself, a few planes scattered about the holding areas, and one highly polished navy blue, silver-trimmed Gulfstream jet parked far off in the celebrity corner, with three black cars and one long white van parked nearby, next to a military Humvee with Marine Corps markings on the engine hood. The Humvee had a big .50 caliber mounted on a swivel next to a roof hatch.

Men in dark suits were standing by the Gulfstream, looking up, their white faces moving as one, hands shading their eyes from the midday sun, as they watched the Huey coming in for a landing.

"Should I put it down by the jet, Captain?"

Mandy was looking at him now. So was Fyke. Dalton could read Fyke's mind, and he had also picked up Fyke's hardening resolve. Fyke was getting ready to do something extreme. Once they hit the tarmac, the decision would be made. Fyke would be in leg-irons and on a Gulfstream headed for an interrogation cell at Anderson AFB in Guam that he would probably never leave alive and they'd be left standing on the Seletar runway with their dicks in their hands. Metaphorically, in Mandy's case. There had been a question in the pilot's voice, which at least meant that he considered Dalton the senior military presence in the chopper, and since, as a Marine Corps WO, he outranked the other three Marines, that put Dalton in command. Dalton gave Mandy a *What the hell* look. She gave it right back.

Dalton pulled his mike in close and shouted over the engine.

"Who's in the Corps Humvee, Goliad?"

"I think that's Major Holliday's ride, sir. He loves that .50."

"Who's Major Holliday?"

"Carson Holliday, sir. Everybody calls him Doc, you know, because of the Tombstone guy? He's the Senior Military Attaché from the Embassy; runs the Embassy Protection Unit too. Force Recon, Third Marines. Combat trooper. Navy Cross. Silver Star. A real hardass. He's here to cover the exchange. One of those limos will be from the Singapore Home Ministry, here to take custody of the . . . I don't know what to call 'em, sir."

"The Chinese prisoners, is close enough."

"Yes, sir. They're in the white van. Where do you want me to land?"

"Holding pattern for now. Patch me through to Major Holliday."

Not a blink. No hesitation at all, as if he'd been half expecting it.

"Aye, aye, sir. Just a minute."

A burst of chatter in his earpiece, then a hard, flat reply.

"Okay, Captain. He's on."

"Major Holliday?"

"Yeah. Who's this?"

A scratchy voice, filled with static and something else.

Suspicion. Resentment. Perhaps Doc Holliday didn't like this mission.

"I'm Captain Dalton, sir. Fifth SFG out of Fort Campbell."

A pause while Holliday took that in.

"What's a snake eater doing in this sorry-ass civilian cluster fuck?"

Dalton wasn't surprised at the Marine's attitude. Holding the CIA's coat while the CIA pulls some sleazy prisoner exchange at an out-of-the-way airfield in Southeast Asia wasn't the kind of thing a Marine Corps combat lifer likes to be seen doing.

"We came to get one of our own out of Changi, sir."

"And you did. Good for you. They tell me he's SAS."

"Yes, sir. He's had a hell of a time. I was—"

"You say your name is *Dalton?*"

"Yes, sir."

"*Micah* Dalton?"

That stopped him for a moment.

"Yes, sir. Micah Dalton," he said, carefully.

"I heard of you. You were in the Horn, your unit was covering an extraction of wounded and KIA. Uadan Highway Strip, near Gesira."

Jesus. That totally fubar *op. Now what?*

"Guilty as charged, sir."

"You called in CAS on your own position. They put a Spooky Gunship in the zone. Laid down chain-gun fire, lit up and shredded about a hundred Skinnies who were trying to get past your unit to put RPG fire into an old Convair Samaritan with UN markings? You were wounded, then you and three guys from your team spent two days being chased all over the AO by the Skinnies until the One-sixty AR managed to pull you out?"

"Yes, Major. Bad times."

"Not for my niece Katie. She was a medic with Charlie Company, First of the Third, working with UNPROFOR Somalia. She was *in* that *fucking* Samaritan. I heard you retired, joined the DIA?"

"Not retired. I'm still Active. Seconded."

"Still Active? Good for you. What can I do for you, Captain?"

"Are there two assholes around, PUNTS from Langley?"

"Yeah. Howell and Purdy. One white and one pink. Coupla limp-dick CIA pencil necks. They brought the Chinese geeks in. I already had the pleasure of their society up to my ass."

"Sir, they're here for my SAS sergeant."

"Yeah. That's what they're saying."

"Thing is, sir, I don't want to hand him over to the civilians."

Silence. Nothing but air rushing past and the rotors pounding and the airframe chattering hard enough to stun. Dalton felt the eyes on him.

"Roger that, Captain Dalton. Why not?"

"He's a good soldier, and I want him in military custody."

More silence. Fyke was watching Dalton. So was everybody else.

"I hear he went AWOL? I hear he's facing federal charges."

"I haven't been shown any *civilian* charges. And if there *had* been civilian charges—federal charges—it'd be the FBI picking him up and not two pencil necks from the CIA, wouldn't it? Sir?"

"The spooks are saying he's a threat to national security."

"With respect, sir, the CIA thought Ronald Reagan was a threat to national security."

"Good point."

He paused then. Dalton could almost hear his gears turning.

"Captain Dalton, is whatever he's charged with a violation under the Uniform Code of Military Justice?"

"No, sir. Not to my knowledge."

"You're missing my point, Captain. I'll say it again. I take it your SAS sergeant was seconded to an operation under American military control?"

"Yes, sir. At one point, he was."

"Then you could make the case that whatever he did subsequent to that falls under the statutes of the UCMJ? Which makes it *our* business?"

"Yes, sir. You could make that case."

"This a big deal to you, Captain? This means we're stepping on civilian turf, taking your man into military custody. There'll be a shit storm."

"Perhaps the Major would lend me a slicker, sir?"

A throaty crackle then, not static. Major Holliday was laughing.

"Goliad, you listening?"

"Sir. Yes, sir."

"Goliad, you dee-dee right now. Get over to Sembawang, put your bird down inside *our* compound. Don't let nobody get near you until I get there. No civilians. No Embassy pukes. Nobody who isn't Corps. Got that?"

"Aye, sir. What about the mission?"

"That *is* your mission. I'll handle the PUNTS. Captain Dalton?"

"Here, sir."

"That thing in the Horn?"

"Yes, sir?"

"It was fucking nuts, Dalton. When I heard it, know what I thought?"

"No, sir."

"I thought, that *fucking* lunatic should have been a Marine."

LUJAC WAS ON the cell phone seconds after the Huey lifted off. Larissa answered, still sounding sleepy but without the attitude.

Instead, she sounded worried.

"Kiki, Daddy wants to talk to you."

"Okay. I'm right here."

"Well, you're on the cell. I told you to wait."

"I need something."

"That's a shock. What?"

"If I give you a cell number and the ID for a brand-new Samsung Katana, can you get me a GPS reading on it?"

"Is this business or personal?"

"Strictly business, Cabbage."

"Is the cell phone on ROAM?"

"Yes. It's a London number. So we can assume yes."

"That could be a problem. Generally, the GPS function only works if the phone is operating locally."

"Then can you track it by the nearest cell tower?"

"That's even harder to do than getting GPS data because you have to hack into the phone company's operating grid. And even if you can do that, the tower number will only tell you where the phone is within a few hundred yards. I'm thinking about the GPS thing. Is the phone in Singapore?"

"Yes."

"Look. Singapore is pretty sophisticated electronically. They do a lot of international commerce there. Lots of trade. The big banks and the global corporations are always worried about having their people kidnapped. They all require that company cell phones and handhelds have their GPS signals activated. It might be possible . . . they might have GPS tracking capacity in Singapore by now, even for foreign phones. I'll have to know the account number. And who the carrier is. And the name of the account holder. And you're sure the phone has its GPS identifier signal turned on."

"It's on. I did it myself."

"What's the number?"

Lujac had it memorized. He was good at that sort of thing.

"What's the carrier?"

"AT and T."

"That's an American carrier."

"Yeah. It's an American phone. Belongs to the CIA."

"Then it'll be encrypted. And if I try to access the GPS system for AT and T locally, it might show up on an alert screen at Langley or the NSA."

"Life is risk, Cabbage."

"I'll have to— I have Daddy on my other line. Hold on."

Lujac braced himself. If something had made Larissa nervous, that something was probably her father.

Gospic was on.

"Lujac. You're *still* in Singapore?"

Saigon. Shit. I'm still only in Saigon.

"Yes. I'm—"

"What have you got?"

"I've got that Dalton and the woman came here to get a man out of Changi Prison. And they did. They just took off in a—"

"Who was the man?"

"Somebody named Raymond Fyke."

A silence. An electric hum. Larissa was still on the line. She was listening in. Why?

"Never heard of him."

"He was going by another name."

"Which was . . . ?"

"Brendan Fitch."

"Never heard of him either. What was he in Changi for?"

"They say he got drunk and sank an oil tanker called the *Mingo Dubai*. In a storm off the Strait of Malacca."

"How could one man sink a tanker?"

"No idea, boss. Maybe he left a tap running?"

A silence. A humming silence, filled with malice.

"Okay. A wasted trip. You still have a line on these people?"

That depends on your daughter.

"Yes. I do. What do you want?"

"It's time. Give them all my greetings."

"All. Including the drunk?"

"Yes. All of them."

"Okay. Right now?"

"Now. Today. Then come home. I have something for you in Florence. Somebody needs to retire."

"Sure, boss. Who?"

"Radko Borins. The Florence cops have him."

"Did he get the job done?"

"Partly. He got the point made. But now he's a problem. Is he a problem you can handle?"

"Sure. Right after I take care of this end."

"Okay. Good work. Be back by the end of the week."

"Looking forward to it."

"Kiki, we're gonna cut you off for now. I gotta have a talk with Larissa. You stay on those people. Get it done."

"Okay, boss. But I think—"

The line went dead.

Thousands of miles away, Larissa was listening to her father's breathing on the other end of the encrypted line out of Odessa.

"Larissa . . . I'm not going to be angry."

"No, Daddy."

"Did Lujac ask you to do anything personal for him today?"

Daddy has my phone tapped.

And probably my apartment too.

"Yes, Daddy."

"What?"

"He wanted to find out where Vigo Majiic was."

"I see. Did he say why?"

"He said he had a shoot in Geneva in December. For Chopard. And he wanted to see if Vigo would be a grip for him, because his other grips were on another job. He said Vigo used to work for a photographer in Trieste."

"And does he *have* a shoot for Chopard in Geneva in December?"

"Yes. I checked with their agency."

"Okay. Fine. And you told him where Vigo was now?"

"Yes, Daddy. I didn't—"

"No harm done, sweet. No harm. I just don't like Kiki Lujac calling my daughter up in the middle of the night, and I *really* don't like him asking you to do personal favors for him. He's an employee. Not family."

"It won't happen again. Sorry, Daddy."

"You don't have to apologize, sweet. Lujac's not a problem for you."

"You should know something, Daddy. He asked me to track a cell phone GPS."

"For whom?"

"A woman named Mandy Pownall. A London number."

"That's okay. That's business. Go ahead and do it. Give him the data as soon as you can. How are you feeling? How are the scars?"

"Healing, Daddy. Getting better."

"Good. Another round coming up in Atlanta, you know?"

"Yes, Daddy. Four weeks."

"I'll come with you. Then we'll have Christmas together. I've booked us into a really nice place in Savannah, Christmas in Savannah, Georgia, in America, Larissa. Just the two of us. Are you happy?"

"Yes, Daddy. Very happy."

"Good. I love you. Bye, darling."

"Love you too. Bye, Daddy."

Gospic rang off. Larissa held the handset for a while, staring into space, seeing but not seeing the rain falling in sheets on the mountains far across the bay. Her cat was up, a muscular tabby, stretching his forepaws and getting ready to shred the couch some more. Radko was in a hospital in Florence, under guard. Daddy didn't need Lujac to go *retire* Radko. The Italians would kill him for shooting the Italian woman. There was nothing Radko could say that would hurt Daddy's business. The Italians were going to torture Radko to death, which was fine with Daddy since it would save him the trouble. So Daddy didn't care what happened to Radko. He just wanted Kiki Lujac to relax, to think he was still in the family business.

So . . .

Daddy is going to have Kiki Lujac killed. For asking about Vigo Majiic. She had no idea why. But Kiki was going to die.

Soon.

Good.

31

USMC Air Unit,
U.S. Embassy compound,
Sembawang Field

Goliad flared the Huey like a combat pro and settled it down with hardly a jolt on the concrete pad with the crosshair pattern, about fifty yards from a group of low, bunkerlike buildings. The Air Unit Compound at Sembawang held another Huey, a big Sea King, a partially dismantled Cobra Gunship, and a couple of fixed-wing craft, including a highly unusual gunmetal gray and completely unmarked sixties-era Lockheed C-140 JetStar, a midsized, four-engine jet transport that had been a favorite of the CIA during the seventies and eighties. Dalton had last seen one—or part of one—in the middle of a burned-out clearing in Colombia, where it had crashed under RPG fire from a FARC patrol, killing eighteen CIA mercenaries. The plane was a dinosaur now, having been retired in the early nineties. So, what was it doing here at Sembawang and why had its markings been painted over? Dalton figured he'd never know.

Holliday had radioed ahead, and an EMS van with USMC markings was waiting by the hut, men in fatigues, standing around by the van, watching Goliad shut the chopper down. The rotors slowed, and the airframe rocked with the descant rhythm. Hazlitt and Kuhn got Fyke onto the tarmac and stood by while the rest of their passengers hopped out as well. There was a moment of silence while everyone tried to figure out what had just happened and what was going to happen next.

Everyone except Fyke.

"Leave off, I tell you," he said. "I'm through being an invalid. Away with you, and my sincere thanks go with you. I'll be needing no further ministrations—I've been hurt worse playing rugby—so I set you all free to walk in the Singapore sun and leave me the *fook* alone."

Fyke stagger-stepped backward, creating some symbolic distance, and then rounded on Dalton, his battered face cracking into a ferocious grin. "Mikey! You old crocodile, I always knew you wouldn't hand me over to a couple of prancing catamites from old Virginny. The Uniform Code! That was brilliant."

Goliad and the two medics looked uneasy, as if they were waiting for the Special Forces Captain to tell them what to do. Was Fyke a guest or a patient or a prisoner? Did he need the EMS van or should they call the MPs instead? Dalton had to keep control of the situation, at least until Major Holliday got here. After that, Holliday would be running the show.

"Goliad, is there a mess facility here? Maybe we could all just take a pew and wait for Major Holliday to get here?"

"Yes, sir." He pointed to a low, aluminum-sided building. "That's the general mess for ground personnel. Mixed ranks. We can wait there."

They all walked across the hardpan together, Fyke struggling manfully, clearly deeply unwilling to be helped by anybody. Miss Lopez trailed along in his wake, looking nervous and trying to figure out where she fit into this situation. The Marines, suddenly released from their transport and medical duties, decided to be relaxed and happy. Mission accomplished: where's the beer? Mandy was drawing a fair amount of attention from the ground crew Marines, but she ignored that, walking beside Dalton, matching his stride. "Okay, so far, so good," she said. "What now?"

"That depends on the Major. This is his turf."

"What are you hoping for?"

Dalton was formulating a reply when her shirt pocket began to shrill. She fumbled at the flap button and pulled out her cell phone, flipped it open, looked at the caller ID.

"Christ."

"What?"

"It's Langley." She held up a hand, put the phone to her ear, listened for a time, managing to get in a couple of faint "Yes, sir"s now and then. Dalton could hear a strong male voice speaking forcefully at the other end. Mandy's face went pale and then pink, and then she looked at Dalton.

"Yes, sir. He's right here, sir. Yes, sir."

She handed him the phone.

"It's Cather. He wants to talk to you. He's not happy."

Dalton gazed heavenward, got no reprieve from that quarter, took the cell, watching Mandy's eyes as he put the phone to his ear. Cather was already talking, a low, purring growl full of quiet menace.

". . . intrigued to hear your explanation, Micah."

"Explanation?"

"Your *reasoning* behind what has just occurred down there. I've just taken a call from Tony Crane in London. He tells me that you have failed to deliver the package to our people and that you have instead entangled the United States Marine Corps in a jurisdictional waltz that may involve the Uniform Code of Military Justice and some strangely named entity he's calling the *JAG's office*. I'm curious to hear your views in this matter, since I'm reasonably certain that Miss Pownall was adequately briefed on the purpose of your mission, the success of which would determine what, if any, relationship you might have with the Cleaners' Unit, and Clandestine Services in general."

"I have some questions of my own—"

"No doubt. And I'd be happy to address them once you've responded to mine. I'll clarify it for you. A little over a month ago, your immediate superior and a dear colleague of mine, Jack Stallworth, was found dead in his greenhouse in the backyard of his residence in Virginia. It appeared that he had contrived to shoot himself several times in the body and once in the forehead, a demonstration of grit, willpower, and heroic dedication to the mission that should shine forth as an example to us all. A shadow fell upon *you* in this regard, and this shadow will remain, until it is dispelled by a directive from this office. So, as I have said, I await your views with an open mind and a sunny smile and the bluebird of hope perched upon my shoulder."

There was a stir at the compound gates as a tan Humvee with a .50 caliber on the roof came roaring up the entrance lane, coming to a sliding stop on the gravel in a cloud of dust. The gates were immediately pulled aside. The Humvee powered in and headed straight for them.

"Sir, you're aware of a man named Branco Gospic?"

A slight pause.

"I am. A Serbo-Croatian gangster. How does this connect with—"

"Is the NSA monitoring his lines?"

"That's classified matter, Micah. And beside the point. We were . . ."

Dalton's attention trailed away as the Humvee pulled to a stop ten yards away. A tall, rangy-looking Marine got out before the Humvee stopped rocking, rigged out in BDUs and wearing a Beretta in a brown-leather shoulder rig. He had a sandblasted face and a long, vulturine beak, and dark eyes that contained a gleaming, crazy spark. He wore his hair in a Marine Corps high-and-tight, and carried the general air of a hungry raptor. He strode, heavy boots coming down hard on the tarmac, to where Mandy and Dalton were standing. Mandy moved in to intercept him while Dalton lifted a hand to acknowledge his arrival, pointing to the cell in his hand. "Major Holliday," he called, "I have Langley here. One minute?"

Holliday frowned and settled, turning his attention to Mandy, who began to talk to him in a low tone, leaning in close, which had the effect she intended, as Major Holliday's fight-or-flirt response kicked in fast. He gave her a large, predatory grin, glancing from time to time over at Micah Dalton with ferocious intensity mixed with curiosity. Dalton went back to the cell phone, speaking with restrained anger and a great deal of urgency.

"Sir, I'm sorry, that was Major Holliday, the Marine in charge here. Let me lay this out for you as I see it. Raymond Fyke's tanker, the *Mingo Dubai*, a five-hundred-foot-long ship, was hijacked by a group of Serbians led by a man named Vigo Majiic. He was the third mate on the ship. I believe that Vigo Majiic may have been working for Branco Gospic."

"And what takes you there, Micah?"

"A Carabinieri major called me this morning. A woman who tried to kill me in Venice was found dead on the Lido beach. Brancati identified her as Saskia Todorovich. Her home town was Kotor, in Montenegro. Branco Gospic is based in Kotor. Brancati thinks the man who killed her was Kiki Lujac, also a Montenegrin. Lujac has followed me to Singapore. He's here now. I saw him yesterday, at the hotel. I think it's plausible, from the connections, to infer that he's here on Gospic's orders."

"Yes," said Cather, evenly, "that's a reasonable inference. I still don't see how this brings us to Mr. Fyke and his *allegedly* hijacked ship."

"If Fyke is right and the ship really was hijacked by a Serbian outfit, Major Brancati says there are only two crime families in the Serbo-Croatian regions capable of mounting an operation like that."

"Stefan Groz and Branco Gospic," said Cather, his voice less remote.

"Yes. That's right. When Fyke and I were together in Pristina, one of the outfits we were trying to penetrate was run by Stefan Groz. We knew of another but weren't able to develop a name. But the DIA opened a file on Groz, and I'm willing to bet that, by now, we've got a FISA warrant on Branco Gospic too. Am I right?"

"That's a security matter. I cannot comment."

"I'll take that as a yes. Have the Monitors picked up anything that connects Gospic to Vigo Majiic?"

"I have no reply to that. But I'm willing to follow your argument for a while longer."

"Did you know that Gospic had sent a man to Singapore? To follow Mandy and me?"

"If I had, wouldn't I have warned you?"

"Sir, you always said that a card is only useful if it's in play. Let's assume you did. Let's assume that you got a packet from your automated surveillance of Gospic's line that contained a reference to Micah Dalton. Why did you pick me to get Ray Fyke out of Changi? And why did you send Mandy Pownall along with me?"

A pause. Mandy and Major Holliday were both watching Dalton now, sensing the tension in his voice. Fyke and the others had gone on to the mess tent. A warm wind swept across the airfield, stirring the palms. It smelled of sea salt and rain. In the north, a huge green-and-black front was moving in. Cather's silence stretched out. Finally, he said:

"I do not admire indiscretion. I trust you have not been indiscreet, Micah."

"If Mandy and I were killed on this mission, that would solve a major security problem for you, wouldn't it, sir?"

Clever lad, thought Cather.

"That's not at all true. At any rate, that vulnerability has been addressed. The asset is being reconfigured—at no small expense, by the way. What once you may have known is now operationally irrelevant. And, I must say, I find it rather stinging that, in order to contain a security breach, you think me capable of sending two fine young agents out into the field in the hope that they might be killed."

"The fact remains, sir, that our knowledge of it can be seen as a problem for the Agency. It doesn't have to be. I had no objection to the program at all. Neither did Miss Pownall. We both approved of it. My interest lay in another direction, a personal one, and it ended when Jack Stallworth died."

"I sense that all this is leading to a request, Micah. What is it?"

"I want you to let Mandy and Fyke and me try to find this missing ship. I want your permission, and I want your help."

"Why would I want to help you in some quixotic and very likely *expensive* quest to hunt a chimera on the word of a drunken deserter?"

"I think Branco Gospic had the *Mingo Dubai* hijacked. I think he went to a lot of trouble to do it. Gospic trades opium base for weapons with the Taliban and al-Qaeda. That's what they *do* in Pristina."

In one detached part of Cather's mind, he was recalling the first time that Branco Gospic had come to his official attention. It was in August 1998; U.S. embassies in Nairobi and Dar es Salaam had been attacked by al-Qaeda and President Clinton had just ordered retaliatory missile strikes on Khartoum in the Sudan and Khost in Afghanistan. Eighty cruise missiles—a *billion* American dollars' worth—rained down on Khartoum and Khost, killing a night watchman at a pharmaceutical plant in Khartoum and five al-Qaeda trainees in Khost.

Sadly, a more effective response was deemed not quite apropos, since the President's moral authority had been rather undermined by a sloe-eyed young *houri* named Monica Lewinsky, who was, that same week, sitting in front of a grand jury and retailing her serial encounters with what Jack Stallworth had described at the time as *the President's staff*. What brought Branco Gospic into it was that seven of the Tomahawks that hit Khost had failed to detonate, and bin Laden later sold five of the most intact ones to China for ten million U.S. dollars, which allowed China to reverse engineer them and thereby establish a solid basis for its own nascent missile program. The other two went to Pakistan and North Korea. Branco Gospic brokered the deal and pocketed fifteen percent. So, yes, he was professionally *interested* in Gospic. Dalton was summing up his case, the passion in his voice ringing out clear.

How brightly the young burned, thought Cather.

"So, I *know* you're on Gospic. That's why you have the NSA monitoring his communications. If you *didn't* have the NSA watching him, it would be a gross dereliction of duty. He's a terrorist, or an ally of terrorists. Now he *may* have acquired a five-hundred-foot tanker. What does an ally of terrorists want with a five-hundred-foot tanker? I think you need to know the answer to that question, sir. I think it's your *duty* to know the answer."

Cather, who had begun his long service to his country in the early years of the cold war, disliked being lectured on *duty* by anyone. His reply was dipped in acid and served on the edge of a straight razor.

"If there is anything in your theory, then the disappearance of this tanker—inasmuch as it may affect the security of the United States— falls within the purview of the counterterrorism unit at the FBI, in New York, and the Coast Guard. Protocol would require me to notify the SAIC at Federal Plaza. Fyke would then become an informant for the FBI, and you would be free to retire to the scented chambers of your little divertimento in Venice."

Dalton, stung, started low and grating, but he redlined fast.

"My *little divertimento in Venice,* Mr. Cather, is currently in a coma in a hospital bed in Florence with a bullet in her head, a bullet put there by Branco Gospic."

He realized he was actually *snarling* at the Director of Clandestine Services. And he was doing it on a cell phone in the middle of a sunny afternoon in the middle of Sembawang Field with a Marine Corps Major and a pale-looking Mandy Pownall staring at him as if his hair had just burst into flames. He was damaging his credibility with the Marine, and with Mandy, and picking a fight with the only man who could help him. It was childish, and, even worse, it was lousy leadership.

"I apologize for that, sir. But you yourself said that the CIA needs to *redeem* itself, sir, and so far the only thing some of our people in Langley have done in that direction is to undermine critical surveillance programs by leaking the details to the goddam *New York Times.* All I'm asking for here is a chance to run down a missing tanker. Let the CIA be what it used to be, an active force out here in the real world and not just another Ivy League think tank, padding its budget and fragging the competition. If I find this tanker and it is a threat, then you can take it to the FBI and the Coast Guard, and I'm out of your life and back in Florence, waiting for one of the finest women I've ever had the honor to meet to either wake up or die."

Cather was quite capable of silence. Indeed, he was only fully alive inside his silences. This was, Dalton realized, Cather's own version of that familiar Chinese silence.

Cather let it run, and then, surprisingly, broke it himself.

"I am told the Chinese personnel have been taken into custody by the Singaporean authorities and will be promptly repatriated to China. So, that part of the mission has been accomplished. I was interested in this—"

Dalton, still stinging from the *divertimento* barb, tried and failed to keep his mouth shut. "Might that be because you've doubled one, or all, of them. Or you've loaded them up with false data in a confusion operation."

There was a long and forbidding silence on the other end. Dalton knew he had gone too far, but there was no way to take it back. When Cather finally spoke, his voice was controlled and cool, but he had *receded*.

"Very byzantine, if it *were* true. Perhaps you should consider a career in the movies. What a charming schoolboy daydream, however, because it would mean that we would have an advantage in our long struggle with the Chinese. Since this is very likely to be the last official communication we will ever have, and in honor of your previous service to the country, I will grant you the *possibility* that getting Mr. Fyke out of Changi *may* have been subordinate to the collateral purpose of this mission, which may have been to create a *pretext* for the plausible reinsertion of three technicians into the electronic surveillance matrix of the Chinese Intelligence establishment. And, further, I will admit that you were selected for this mission because you were both reliable *and* expendable. You have laid the matter before me with all of your usual tact and charm, and now the decision is mine. I take it the Major—the Marine officer; I've forgotten his name—Holliday? Is Major Holliday still in attendance there?"

"Yes, sir. He is."

"Fine. Let me have a word with him."

LUJAC HAD HIS hand on the door of the top-floor room in the Changi-Lah Hotel and Suites, had stopped for a moment to take in the room one last time and make sure it looked the way it needed to look and that nothing he had left in it was going to ever become a problem for him, and then his cell phone rang and *that* became a problem for him because it was Branco Gospic and he had some bad news.

"Larissa got that GPS data for you."

"Good. I thought she was going to call."

"No. She isn't. You want to know where the phone is?"

"Sure, boss—"

"The phone is at a place called Sembawang Field. You know it?"

"I think so. It's an airfield up in the north, near the Strait of Johor."

"Yeah. It is. I looked it up. Part of it belongs to the United States Marine Corps. Guess which part has your phone in it?"

Great. Now what?

"The *Marine Corps* part?"

"Very good. Guess what else? I'm watching the screen right now. Can you look out a window, or something; see that far?"

Lujac glanced at the open balcony doors and out across the forest canopy.

"I think so."

"Then go do it. Do it now."

Something had happened, and Gospic was different. Lujac's nerve endings began to pop, and part of his skin—large patches of it—got crawly and cold. Lujac had been around Gospic when Gospic got like this and Lujac had not liked it. He wished he was still talking to Larissa. He walked across the floor and out onto the balcony, looked into the north.

"What can you see?"

"Forest. Downtown. A golf course."

"Can you see something, small and shiny, going up into the air?"

Lujac tried, could see nothing.

"No. I can't."

"That's too bad. There's a U.S. government plane taking off from Sembawang Field right now. Your phone is on it. I'm literally watching the GPS numbers roll. What are you going to do about it?"

Lujac's throat was a little tight.

"Do you know where it's going?"

"Yeah. Larissa says they filed a flight plan for a place called Kuta. Do you know where Kuta is?"

"Yes, sir. It's a resort town in Bali."

"Kiki, you're not doing real well down there, are you?"

"I'm managing."

"Yeah? Well, I'm sending you some help."

Not good news.

"Not necessary. All I need is the Gulfstream—"

"The people I sent you there to deal with are currently on a plane going to Bali. Maybe surrounded by United States Marines. You're stuck in Changi with your thumb up your ass. You need more than a really nice plane. You need some serious guys with some serious ordnance. Listen carefully. There's a landing strip on the island of Tenggara Barat, next island east of Bali. There's a landing strip there called Selaparang. About sixty miles from Kuta. Are you getting this?"

"Yes, sir. Selaparang. Sixty miles from Kuta."

"Good. The Gulfstream is still on the pad at Changi Airport. Is there anything at the hotel you can't leave behind?"

"No. Some clothes. Some camera gear I took along for cover."

"Any other loose ends?"

Lujac glanced toward the bathroom. The tub was full of ice from the machine down the hall. Plus, he'd run the shower on the kid for an hour, so there'd be no DNA. He'd even scooped out the tub drain, just to make sure. Most of the action had happened in the bathroom, and he'd wiped it all down. This was after he took some pictures with the digital camera in his cell phone and e-mailed them through Gospic's fire wall to the Home Ministry website, just because it amused him to do that sort of thing. They'd paid cash for a month. If he stuck a DO NOT DISTURB sign on the door, turned on the radio, and jacked up the air-conditioning, Corporal Ahmed could last a week.

"No. Everything's cool."

"What's your cover at the hotel?"

"Duhamel. Jules Duhamel. A French passport."

"Don't check out. Leave it all. It'll be safe until you get back."

"Is everything okay, Branco?"

"Okay? No. Everything is not okay. That wop Brancati is fucking with my operation. He's trying to shut down accounts in Zurich; he's rolled up everybody I had in Venice and he's squeezing them until they bleed. He's saying that Radko shot the Vasari broad because she's an infidel aristocrat and he's a fanatical Muslim. He's trying to get the Italian government to declare us a terrorist operation. The Carabinieri has gone to war with us—"

"No offense, boss, but I tried to warn you about the Vasari thing."

"Yeah? Did you? I don't remember. Anyway, fuck Brancati. He's a dead man. Get to the plane, and tell Bierko to fly you to Selaparang. Right now. It's about eleven hundred miles. Put it down there and wait."

"For what, boss?"

"Just wait."

32

Inbound to Kuta City, Bali, the Indonesian Archipelago, twenty thousand feet

Ray Fyke said Kuta, in Bali, was the place to start, and then they all looked expectantly at Doc Holliday, whose rocky face went through a number of changes while he took in all the implications, and then he shrugged his shoulders and ordered up the paperwork that would give them the temporary use of the unmarked Lockheed JetStar—not without an internal struggle, since the plane had been a gift to the U.S. Embassy in Singapore from the collection of the Sultan of Brunei, given in return for confidential Embassy services rendered in connection with an errant nephew—and it was intended as a gift from the U.S. Embassy to the Minister Mentor on the occasion of his grandson's fifth birthday. Which explained why the plane had no markings. It was in the process of being repainted in the Minister Mentor's favorite colors, sky blue and gold.

Cather's request for *any and all assistance* from Major Holliday, reinforced minutes later by a call from Bob Neller, the General in command of the Third Marine Division in Okinawa, got them a full-court press by the ground crew. The Marine Corps in action was a delight to watch. They even sent a couple of MPs to collect all of their things from the Intercontinental. The plane itself was a gem: the avionics and navigation gear were all updated and in first-rate condition—the Sultan of Brunei could afford it—the interior refinishing had been completed the week before, twelve comfortable seats and a well-stocked galley with a full bar, and smelled like a brand-new Cadillac. All it needed was two full wing tanks. Holliday even dug up four brand-new Berettas, and spare magazines; pistols carried on the armorer's books as *failed bench test,* a masterpiece of creative inventory manipulation that only a combat Marine with a master's degree in Petty Pilfering could pull off. They also delivered some additional medical supplies for Fyke, which left them nothing to wish for but a properly filed flight plan. They got that and a clearance from Sembawang air control in five minutes. Doc Holliday flirted for a while longer with Mandy Pownall while they waited for the Marines to get back from the hotel with their luggage. Then he cheerfully wished them Godspeed, and said he damn well wanted his plane back in one piece.

Ten minutes later, with Dalton at the controls, they were climbing, at forty degrees and full thrust, into the increasing cloud cover of a southbound storm system boiling out of Malaysia and Singapore was receding into a green delta, with its core of spiky towers, and the South China Sea was opening up before them.

Mandy Pownall was in the main cabin with a Sobranie and a glass of scotch on the rocks, staring out at the island of Singapore as it rolled away into the west. She felt able to cope with the parting, although the Marines had failed to find—or failed to find the nerve to find—her very expensive underthings, which was going to present some wardrobe problems down the line. No doubt the concierge would FedEx everything to London. It would all be waiting for her, if she ever got back to London alive. Miss Lopez was in the galley, not at all resigned to being the goddam Filipina help, staring at the microwave and wondering what the hell all those buttons meant. Fyke was in the copilot's seat, staring out at the muddy brown shoals at the southern end of the Strait, his battered face solemn.

"Jeez, Ray. Cheer up. You're out of Changi."

Fyke nodded, keeping his hooded gaze out on the broad, green, rippled plain of water. A lone containership was steaming into the east, heading for Borneo, trailing a long white V in her wake. He had a glass of scotch, held awkwardly in his injured hand, but, so far, he hadn't touched it.

"How you feeling?"

Fyke glanced over at Dalton, flashing an oddly shy smile.

"Well, between you and me, I feel like shit."

"Take some morphine."

Fyke shook his big, shaggy head.

"No. No more drugs. I need to stay clear."

Dalton checked the altimeter and leveled them out at twenty-one thousand feet. The plane rose and fell on a current like a sailboat cresting a wave. The engines—four Pratt & Witneys, clustered around the tail section—thrummed a deep, harmonic vibrato right through the airframe, and the cold air whistling over the windshield put beads of condensation around the rim of the glass.

It was a good plane, easy to fly, and he could feel the knots and cords of tension in his back and chest beginning to slip. Even the knife wound in his side had been reduced to an irritating itch, and it hadn't bled in two days. Fyke was getting ready to say something, and Dalton was content to let him get there on his own. Which he did, after an hour, after Miss Lopez had brought them a tray of tuna sandwiches and a pot of hot coffee, which she served without a smile, and, after she had gone, the planet had continued to roll under them, and the green mountains of Borneo had slipped away under the starboard wing, and the long, ragged volcanic archipelago of Indonesia began to unfold along the southern horizon. When he did speak, Fyke's tone was wary and cautious, a man stepping carefully over tricky terrain:

"Mikey . . . I was talking to Miss Pownall . . . ?"

"Call her Mandy."

"Mandy. She says you had a friend in Venice . . . a woman."

"Cora Vasari. She's in a coma in Florence."

"Jeez. What happened?"

"A man named Branco Gospic had a hitter named Radko Borins shoot her in the head."

"Crikey. Why?"

"You never heard of Branco Gospic, Ray?"

Fyke went inside for a time.

"In Pristina, we were looking at a network that we figured was shadowing Stefan Groz. I think the name Gospic came up. That the man?"

"Yes. We never made him at the time, but his name was in the wind."

"Why's he trying to kill your lady friend?"

Dalton looked across at Fyke.

"Mandy hasn't told you about my status?"

"Not a thing. What about your status?"

"Let's say I was on leave for a while there."

Fyke knew better than to ask for details. Questions bounce around, and, sooner or later, you've got your own explaining to do. He let that slide.

"But now you're back?"

"Yes. But while I was off the grid, I had a run-in in Venice."

"With who?"

Dalton told him about Milan and Gavro, the two Serbians who

had tried to mug him near the Palazzo Ducale. Fyke listened without comment until Dalton finished up with the connection to Branco Gospic in Kotor.

"So, now this Gospic character, he's coming after you?"

"No. I'm coming after him."

"And you're saying that this same lad had something to do with the taking of my ship?"

"Yes. I am. Vigo Majiic was a Serb. There are Serbian hands all over this. And there are only two Serbian gangs with the projectable resources to pull off the hijacking of a five-hundred-foot tanker ship in Southeast Asia—"

"Stefan Groz and—"

"Branco Gospic. And I think it's Gospic."

"Did Cather know this? Is that why he picked you to come get me?"

"I think so. But I don't know his whole game."

"Mandy says that Cather pulled you out of Venice to break me out of Changi. In the first place, given how I fucked up and went dark, I can't imagine why that old gravedigger would give a dingo's dangle if I rotted in Changi for a hundred years—"

"Tony Crane was afraid the SID would work you over until you gave up some kind of operational details."

"Such as what? Did they happen to say?"

"Cather wouldn't tell us."

"Now that my head is clear, I'm pretty sure I didn't tell those lads anything but my name, rank, and serial number. I took my beating—God knows, I earned it—and, as far as I can recall, I gave those gooks nothing."

"Cather was afraid of *something*. Any idea at all what it could be?"

Fyke was quiet for a long time.

"Yes. I have," he said, with a sigh. "But it's not about protecting an asset or blowing the cover on a SigInt receptor somewhere. It's more along the lines of one more counterterrorism fuckup being laid at the door of the Agency."

"You care to tell me what it is?"

"I wish I didn't have to. Your good opinion was worth having."

Now it comes, thought Dalton.

"You never asked me why Kuta, Mikey."

"Okay. Consider it asked."

"In Changi, when I was getting beat, I took it like a penance, Mikey, because I think I owed it to God. Like doing the rosary and the Stations, making up for my sins, only this time doing it while hanging from a meat hook upside down and naked, which, leaving out Father Lundigan back at Christ the Redeemer Parochial, was hardly ever required."

"What sins, Ray?"

Fyke sighed, sipped at his now-lukewarm scotch.

"Christ. It was always gonna be Kuta. I could feel it coming."

Dalton said nothing, thinking that Fyke would pick it up again when he was ready. But five minutes passed with nothing further, so he pushed it.

"Ray. Why was it always gonna be Kuta?"

Fyke jumped at the sound of Dalton's voice, as if he'd been a long way gone, which he was.

"Back there, in that pool house, you asked me why I went dark."

"I remember."

"You know what I was doin'? In those days?"

"Sure. You had a trapline laid out along the archipelago, working out of Manado, I think. The Celebes? Now called Sulawesi?"

"Yeah. The mysterious Celebes Sea. You know, that's where Conrad set *Lord Jim.* That's who I was playing. Lord Jim Beam. Had me an office over a bar in downtown Manado. Routine HumInt and

SigInt stuff. Nothing high-level. Just listening to people talk in the towns, Drums Along the Mohawk, I used to call it. I had stringers reporting in all the way from Port Moresby to Jakarta. Pirates. Gunrunners. Opium trading. Money laundering. Corruption in all its inviting forms is the rushing red blood of the East, Mikey, as you well know, and wasn't I deep in the thick of it? Wading belly-deep, with my arms spread wide, and drinking it all in, Lord Jim come among the Bugis, and am I not sending my *com-moon-e-kays* up the line to a zipped-up little prig at the Singapore Station who would, I don't doubt, send what he liked up the line with my station code blacked out and his grubby thumbprints and initials all over it? Scut work, it was, Mikey, because they thought I was a burned-out case, and, I admit, I got tired of it pretty fast, which, lookin' at the outcome, I sincerely wish I hadn't."

"You were better in the field, Ray. Desk work was not your thing."

"Nor yours, I recall. You mind that fat buck we carted all over Pristina, must have weighed three hundred pounds. Up and died on us? What was the name of the club? Where we left him in the toilet?"

"Kozy's Krazy Kit-Kat Klub."

"That was it. Back there, in Changi, I tried to keep my pecker up by remembering all those good times. We were the pair, weren't we, Mikey . . . ?"

He trailed off into silence, losing himself in the past.

"So, what about the trapline?"

"Eh? What? Oh, right. Well, I had this stringer, ran a dry-cleaning service in Kuta, face like a billy goat's scrotum, all wizened up, bright, little black eyes stuck into a nut-brown face, had three teeth up and two down, but he was an old Indochina hand and had seen the Frenchies get butchered at Dien Bien Phu, and a lot more since then.

He was a good source, and when he told me about this guy Amrozi, not connected to farming in any way, a sort of a layabout with ties to a local madrassa, who was coming in to his shop and leaving clothes that stank of fertilizer, he drew the gimlet eye, you see?"

Dalton knew who Amrozi bin Haji Nurhasyim was. And now he knew why Fyke had gone dark. He had always suspected it. But now he knew.

"So, something about this Amrozi fellow and his powdery clothes that are stinking of ammonium nitrate rubs Nguyen Ki the wrong way, so he gets on the phone to me, up in Manado, to tell me about him, wants me to follow up on him, see who his friends are, that kind of thing. This is in early September 2002. At which time, you were where?"

"Wish I could tell you."

"Hah! You were in a cave, looking down on Tarnak Farms, with a Barrett .50 to keep you warm. I got drunk one night and flew to Guam for a break from the fucking gooks all around me. Wanted to see a blue eye and have a genuine Guinness. Ran into Jack Stallworth at the bar in Anderson, and we got stinko together. He's the one told me. Dead now, Mandy says?"

"Yes. Couple months back."

"Heart? He was always a pressure-cooker type of guy."

"Yeah, I hear heart. So Nguyen doesn't like this Amrozi guy . . . ?"

"Not by half. He starts calling me about him, but at the time—you have to remember how warm it gets here in October, so I was cooling my system a fair bit with the Jim Beam. More than a fair bit. I guess you could say . . . Well, I bet you heard the talk?"

"After you went dark, they sent some Cleaners from Cliff Longbow's unit in Okinawa to trace you. Word was, you had gone off the rails."

"Off the rails and into the ditch and up the far side and straight through Aunt Bertie's mudroom. I was dead-blind drunk half the time, and, the other half, I was sorely under the influence. Not my shining hour . . ."

He fell silent then. Dalton didn't push him.

The plane rocked and soared as they plowed through a bank of cirrostratus. Below them, green-and-purple storm clouds, glimmering with internal bursts of pale fire, were roiling over the sea, blanking out entire reaches. Fyke drained his glass, set it down on the console between them.

"Looks like the monsoon down there," he said.

"So it does. We're due for it."

"We are. Well, anyway, I'm drinking a bit, as you heard, and here's Nguyen Ki, trying to get me to pay attention to this guy with the clothes reeking of fertilizer, and I'm listening, with the phone propped up to my ear and a cigarette going, and the no-see-ums are clouding around outside the screens and glowing like sparks under the streetlight, and, all the while, I've got my eye on that tall, square bottle of Jim Beam on the edge of my desk. Long and short of it was, I wrote myself up an action note, full of fine and energetic intentions, which I stuck on a spike and duly forgot about until . . . Well, you'll remember Amrozi's name, I have no doubt?"

"I do."

Fyke laughed, a rueful, humorless grunt.

"So do we all, now and forever, amen. Twelve October, on orders coming from Ayman al-Zawahri himself, a guy named Ali Imron and this Amrozi guy buy a new Yamaha motorbike, which Imron drives to the U.S. Consulate in Kuta and leaves a bomb there, and, just before midnight, he drives two suicide bombers in a white van straight to the club district, where he stops near the Sari Club and tells Bomber 1 to put on his suicide vest and the other one to arm the bomb in the van. The Walker goes into Paddy's Pub, and the other bomber drives the van in a straight line, as it's all he knows how to do, back across the street to the Sari Club, where he waits, and, when the backpack bomb goes off inside Paddy's and all the injured who can still run pour out into the street between the Sari Club and Paddy's, the second bomber waits until they gather all around and then he triggers the big bomb and two hundred and two people die, some of them right away, but a whole lot die later. There were so many burned people that they put them in hotel pools to ease their passing. Victims were mainly Western kids from all over. Eighty-eight from Australia. Imron drove off on his Yamaha and dialed a number on a Nokia cell to trigger the bomb he left by the U.S. Consulate. It went off. Imron had packed that one with his own shit. They traced the explosives through purchase records, and it led back to you-know-who, and they charged Amrozi, along with a bunch of guys, but nobody's been executed yet, and the most a couple of them served was two years before the High Court said their trials had not been 'constitutional.' The Agency pulled one guy, Hambali, in Bangkok, and they've got him somewhere, and I hope to God they're putting it to his eardrums with bamboo skewers every day of the year including Hogmanay."

A long silence, and then:

"So, there you go, Mikey. Why I went dark."

Fyke went inward again, staring out at the gathering dark in the east. Time passed. Dalton could think of nothing to say that wouldn't sound false. He also had a pretty good idea where Hambali was being held: inside the Orpheus system. But that was a thing not to be spoken of to anyone.

After a while, Fyke smiled across at him.

"And that's why I said it was always going to be Kuta. It's a hard truth my mother told me long ago, God rest her. 'Raymond,' she says, 'a man can no more outrun his sins than he can race with the moon.'"

Dalton glanced out the windshield, saw a crescent moon like a Saracen blade, glittering gold through great rents in the speeding clouds.

He nodded toward it.

"There you go, Ray," he said. "We're racing with the moon."

Fyke stared at it for a while. It seemed to be the only thing in the sky moving as fast as they were. He shook his head in wonder, and smiled.

"By God, Mikey," he said, "so we are."

33

The National Security Agency, Fort Meade, Maryland

Nikki Turrin found the AD of RA leaning on the railing that ran around the roof deck of the main building. The sun was going down and the lights of Crypto City were coming on. The sky was the color of a tropical drink, and just as cold. The AD of RA was staring out at the setting sun, and the dying light lay upon his seared and scalded skin, softening the rills and fissures and casting a golden aura around the man. His one good eye gleamed in the light. He was leaning with his hands folded, his forearms resting on the railing. A chilly wind was playing in the bare branches of the trees in the park, and dry leaves were making a skittering-insect sound, as they blew across the pavement far below. He was wearing a dark gray suit, an open shirt under that, and he had a scarf thrown around his neck, a gold-and-navy-blue-striped scarf that looked like cashmere and must have been given to him by a woman. He didn't hear—or didn't seem to hear—Nikki's soft step as she came over the decking to stand beside him.

"Is this a bad time, sir? You told me to get in touch as soon as I had something for you?"

The AD of RA turned to look at her, seeming to come from a very unhappy, if not a desolate, place but warming as soon as he saw her face. The dying light was wonderful for her, giving her a satiny glow, and calling up a pale green fire deep in her brown eyes. She felt his look.

"Not at all, Nikki. Don't tell me you have something already?"

"I do, sir. The villa is in Muggia, a small fishing port across the harbor from Trieste. The precise coordinates are"—she flipped a page on her clipboard and traced the row of figures—"45 degrees 36 minutes 12 seconds north longitude and 13 degrees 45 minutes 34 seconds east latitude. We have an aerial picture of it here—"

Nikki flipped a page and showed him an aerial image extracted from Google Earth.

"It's the house with the blue patch right in the middle, sir. That's the pool. The address is 2654 Salina Muggia Vecchia. Muggia is right on the Italian border with Slovenia. The house was registered in the name—"

Nikki realized the AD of RA was staring at her.

"Google Earth! Sixty gazillion dollars' worth of top secret, state-of-the-art mainframes, and every conceivable database, and a whole city filled with the best data miners in the country, and you found this on *Google Earth?*"

"No, sir. I found it on a vacation-homes-for-sale site for Friuli. Then I looked it up on Google Earth."

"Vacation homes?"

"Yes, sir. I know you wanted me to do a detailed, computerized scan of all the NIMA maps, but I thought, at first, you know, seeing that everybody in the pool had died, it seemed to me that a house like that wouldn't go empty for long—"

"They can still sell a house where nine people died *in the pool!*"

"Yes, sir. I know that. But in the part of the world we were looking at, well, people die all the time, in every way you can think of, and it just seemed to me that I could save a lot of time by—"

"Nikki. I don't suppose I could kiss you?"

"If you want to, sir, but, in the meantime—"

The AD of RA hugged her tight and kissed her hard on the left cheek, a chaste, fatherly smack. She blushed a little but found the experience interesting. His scarred cheek felt like alligator hide, and, God knows, he was terrible to look at, but he smelled of cigarettes and spicy cologne and green apple shampoo, and he was *wonderfully* strong. He released her, beaming.

"God. A *real estate* listing. Deep in the heart of Crypto City, and the kid looks it up on fucking Google. Your generation kills me."

"Thank you, sir. The house was registered in the name of Zonia Sluja Korol, but we did a search of the utilities bills—"

"How did you do that?"

"Actually, I didn't. I had the real estate agent who had the listing do it for me. I told her I was thinking of buying it—"

"Did you give your name?"

"Yes I did. She recognized it—"

"She recognized your name?"

"Not my name personally, sir. The family. My people are from Friuli—there are lots of Turrins around the Friuli region—so it helped that she knew my name, because she was very willing to go the extra mile to sell it to someone from the area, which really paid off. I wanted to know what the utilities and taxes were. She faxed me all the most recent bills—"

"I don't *fucking* believe this—"

"With respect, sir, maybe now that I've let you kiss me on the cheek you could stop saying *fucking* all the time. It undermines your authority—"

"I certainly will. And I apologize. Nikki, you *are* quite a package—"

"Thank you, sir. And the bills were all in her name—Zonia Korol—but there was one bill for an appraisal of the property in the spring of last year, and the appraiser's bill was paid by a check from the personal account of Dzilbar Kerk—I have a facsimile of it, and it shows a signature that matches the handwriting we had on file of Dzilbar Kerk—the house was appraised at one-point-nine million euros at that time, and it is now listed for one-point-one million—"

"Dropped a bit. The deaths?"

"I would think so. I asked her that—her name is Antonia Baretto—and she was pretty straightforward about it. She said there had been some kind of party at the villa, and the caterer had apparently served some oysters that had been contaminated by a bacteria called vibrio. It causes terrible lesions on the skin—similar to necrotizing fasciitis, the flesh-eating disease. At any rate, everybody died—something like nine people. Antonia said the corpses were all cremated to kill the bacteria. And the Carabinieri charged the caterer, who was conveniently a Slovenian—everybody around Trieste hates the Slovenians, unless they marry them. Anyway, they charged him with criminal negligence causing death, and, before they could bring him to trial, the caterer, claiming he was innocent, ran away, back to his home in Slovenia, where he couldn't be extradited. So then everybody *knew* he was guilty, because everybody knows only the guilty run. That was pretty much the end of it."

"Nobody mourned the dead girls?"

"The people who lived there were pretty much hated by the people of Muggia and San Rocco. It's just a small fishing village, maybe five thousand families, kind of sleepy, and these people were loud, vulgar boors, throwing money around and coming on to the daughters and having skanky hookers fly in from Slovenia and generally being utterly and completely obnoxious. So, with God's help, they all died, and everybody was quite okay with that."

"Cold."

"Italians can be quite pragmatic. So now the villa is up for sale—"

"For sale by whom?"

"A corporation registered in Budva, sir. Called ZYKLON."

"Any idea who controls the corporation?"

"No, sir. The company seems to be based in Budva, but all we have are numbers. East of the Adriatic, the records of corporate ownership are pretty sketchy. I guess they like it that way. Sorry I couldn't get more info—"

"She told you quite a bit, for a real estate agent."

"She wants to make the sale. And she doesn't like Montenegrins any better than she likes Slovenians. She wants an Italian to buy it. Even better, I'm Friuliani. So, she's really doing the full-court press."

"Budva? I don't know it."

"Budva is a coastal port not far from Sveti Stefan, which is a sort of luxury resort island connected to the mainland by this narrow causeway. It used to be big in the sixties and then it went into a decline. It's being rebuilt, turned into a hyperluxury resort by this same ZYKLON real estate outfit."

"And now ZYKLON has the villa up for sale too?"

"Yes, sir."

The AD of RA fell silent, staring out at the lights coming on all over Crypto City. The wind was rising, and there was a biting edge to it now. He realized that Nikki was shivering. He whipped off his cashmere scarf and draped it around her shoulders, in spite of her protests. It smelled of his cologne and was warm from his body. She pulled it in tight and smiled at him in a way that was not completely chaste, but his mind was in Italy.

"This agent . . . sounds like you made a personal connection with her."

"She's a professional, and I liked her."

"When you called her, did you use one of our own lines?"

Nikki gave him a look.

"No, sir. And I didn't use my cell either. I drove to a Starbucks in Annapolis Junction. My friend runs it. She let me use her office phone. She's also taking messages for me if Antonia calls back."

"We do have masked lines."

"I know. But Miss Chandler said you were really busy, so I would have had to ask Mr. Oakland to set one up, and he's not too happy with me right now. And he would have wanted to know why I needed one."

"Good. Of course. Nice work, Nikki. How's your Italian?"

"Pretty good, sir," she said, her heart blipping.

"Nikki, I know this is a leap. Would you consider going to Muggia? See the property? If you can, bag some residue samples around the pool? FedEx them back for Forensics? The HazMat people will show you how to do it safely. If we could get a sample of this substance, then we'd have the muscle to make things happen. Force State and the CIA to take preemptive action."

"Sir, I'm completely ready to go, but I'm a Monitor. Not a—"

"I know. Not a Field Agent. Here's the thing, Nikki. I've officially stopped trusting the CIA. Normally, I'd hand what you've developed over to them and let them find sixteen different ways to . . . screw it up. But nine people died horrible deaths in that pool, and one of them connects to the deaths of all those Biopreparat people, and the villa is owned by a corporation with the same name as Zyklon B, which was the nerve gas the Nazis used to kill fifteen million people in their concentration camps. Something's in the wind. I can smell it. If I trusted the CIA not to fuck—not to mess it up, I'd hand it to them. But I don't. But if the NSA or the DIA does it *officially,* we'll need all kinds of formal liaison with the Italians, and that means more risk of blowing the security. You worked for the DA's office back in

Pittsburgh. You know what evidence is. You're in and you're out in less than a week. Would you be ready to do that? Come in quiet, just a potential buyer? If anything looks weird, if anybody gets curious, you split. Would you be ready to do that? And stop calling me *sir*, will you?"

"Yes, sir. I'll try. But will the Director let me do this?"

"Good question. Let's go find out."

"Us? Me? Now?"

"Yeah. Us. You. Now."

34

The Indian Ocean, fifteen miles off the coast of Somalia

Their world was a giant brass bowl overturned on a copper plate that stretched away in every direction, merging with a purely theoretical sky in a band of dirty yellow haze. The sun hung low and burned smoky red behind a veil of ochre cloud. And inside this brass-and-copper chamber lived the *heat*, a blast furnace of heat that scorched their lungs when they inhaled it and seared their lips when they breathed it back out. The thick air was dense with diesel fumes and the salty stink of sea rot, and what little breeze there was flapped in from the west, carrying on its scaly back the fetid reek of some squalid coastal village just below the horizon line. At the wheel, Vigo Majiic watched the compass and the empty ocean all around and felt himself a condemned man doomed to spend the rest of eternity trying to reach a mythical green shore that was always receding into a burning and inconceivable immensity. Emil Tarc, a self-contained man not overly troubled by a hostile universe or febrile intimations of mortality, was out on the flying bridge, staring through a pair of binoculars at two, low sharklike boats that a few minutes ago had been only twin brown smudges out on the western horizon but had now approached close enough for him to make out the faces of the men in the boats and the weapons that they carried.

"I don't believe this," he said, more to himself than anyone else, but Majiic heard him through the headset communications gear they were wearing. He stared through the windshield at the incoming boats.

"What are they?" he asked over the radio.

"Two fast-attack boats, both got twin Mercs the size of cart horses, doing maybe forty knots. Damn. Look at the spray flying around their cutwaters—"

"Customs? Military?"

"No. Civilians. Maybe fifteen men in each boat, no uniforms—they look like jihadis—got those keffiyeh things and their faces covered—loaded with AKs and RPGs. Fucking Somali pirates, is my guess."

"What do we do? We can't let them come aboard."

"All we have are the SAWs. Only really effective out to five hundred yards max. But they can pop an RPG into us from a thousand. And we can't let them shoot the shit out of the hull or cripple the rudder either, can we?"

"What will we do?"

Tarc came back into the wheelhouse, his sharp face rocky and his expression murderous. Through the open door, Majiic could hear the hornet sound of the outboards over the rhythmic rumble of the tanker's engines. The radio hissed and crackled on channel 16, the public frequency, a hoarse, guttural string of Somali and then an abrupt switch to accented English.

"You, on the tanker. We are the Somali Coast Guard! You are in Somali waters. Make full stop. We will board and check your papers. Reply!"

Within a few seconds, the speedboats were less than a hundred yards out, two long, low cigarette boats with rust-stained hulls and huge twin outboards. Both boats were packed with skinny, long-skulled men with chiseled Caucasian features and light brown skin, the distinctive Somali mix of Arab and African blood. One boat cut right in a spray of white curl and headed for the stern of the tanker, taking a position fifty yards off the seething water around the prop and the rudder. A small, bent man in the bow aimed an RPG at the prop, set himself, and waited for the order. The other boat carved a slicing arc left through the water and came up alongside their port side, at a range of less than a hundred feet, where it slowed to match the pace of the huge tanker. The tanker loomed over the cigarette boat like the edge of a cast-iron cliff, massive and unscalable. The ship's radio came alive again, a man barking orders in a hard, snarling tone.

"On the boat. Switch to channel 30."

Majiic looked at Tarc.

"Do it," said Tarc. "Everybody listens to 16. We don't need the damn U.S. Navy coming to help us."

Majiic got on the radio, said, "Roger. Switching to 30."

Tarc was on the ship's intercom.

"Jakki, you there?"

"Yes, sir."

"You see these fucking niggers alongside?"

"I do. You want us to come on deck?"

"No. I don't want the hull marked up. We have to clear the Customs wharf in Aden. Stay below. Get everyone ready. Keep your coms on."

"Yes, sir. Will do. Out."

The radio crackled up again, a hectoring bray.

"On the ship. I am Colonel Mahmud Sia, of the Somali Coast Guard. Lower your gangway, and get all papers ready."

Majiic could see the man who was talking, a tall, skeletal, gray-haired Somali wearing a ragged tan shirt over baggy cargo pants and some sort of British forage cap without any brass badge on the peak. The rest of the men—boys, really, all of them in their late teens and early twenties—looked like feral dogs; unshaven, eyes reddened by the sea wind, dripping with sweat in the blast-furnace heat, wearing everything from basketball shirts and jeans to the shalwar kameez of Pakistan. They were obviously members of some warlord's army, but it seemed to Majiic that they had fallen on hard times. They looked hungry and dirty, and their weapons might have been stored in a litter box. But Majiic knew that you could drop an AK-74 in the sand and drive a truck over it, then pick it up, work the bolt, and light up a platoon. He had seen it done.

"Emil, what am I supposed to tell this guy?"

Tarc had made a decision. The decision scared him a little, that much Majiic could see in his eyes, and that worried him even more, because, if Emil Tarc was going to do something that frightened even Emil Tarc, then things were about to get seriously hairy. Tarc got on the intercom again.

"Jakki, send a couple of your smaller guys up to lower the gangway. No weapons. Tell them to look nervous."

"Aye, sir."

"You're gonna let them come on board, Emil? Jakki and his men could blow those sand niggers out of the water in two minutes."

"And what if we catch an RPG in the rudder and can't steer anymore and we have to get towed to Aden? And they'll get at least one shot off, you can count on that. I can't get this hull marked up. We steam into Aden with a string of AK fire stitched across the bow and there'll be a huge investigation. Everybody'll know we tangled with the Somalis. The U.S. Navy is all over this region. I don't want to draw *any* attention. You follow?"

"You let those niggers on board and they'll kill us all."

"Maybe. Maybe not. We'll have to see."

Majiic stared at Tarc, who gave him back a slate-hard glare for a moment, and then he broke into a crazy grin. He looked like a happy jackal.

"What the hell? Come on, Vigo. It is a good day to die!"

Majiic groaned. During the crossing of the Indian Ocean, the crew had passed the time watching old DVDs on the ship's ancient television. Last night, the feature was *Dances with Wolves*. It was hopeless.

A few minutes later, he and Tarc were standing by the rail with compliant expressions on their faces while the first of the Skinnies came up the railing. Two of Jakki's men—both in mufti and trying to look harmless, in spite of their shaved heads and hard eyes—stood nearby, watching the older one, the gray-haired man in the British cap and the ragged tans, as he stepped down onto the decking, glaring around the ship, the whites of his eyes showing, his ragged teeth bared as he wiped his forehead with a filthy sleeve. Up close, he looked feverish and sickly, and he stank of urine. Was he seasick? Or was it something worse? He had a large Colt .45 in his left hand, and he pointed it at Tarc's head, his trigger finger inside the rusty guard.

"I am Colonel Mahmud Sia. Who are you?"

"My name is Captain Emil Tarc, Colonel Sia. You don't need that gun, sir. We're all unarmed, and happy to cooperate with the Somali Coast Guard. This is my first mate, Vigo Majiic."

Colonel Sia blinked at the two of them, perhaps a little puzzled by their bland, smiling countenances. Could these two unarmed fools actually *believe* there was such a thing as a Somali Coast Guard? Their polite manner had put him off balance. But, then, never before had the captain of such a large ship ever let them come on board. Usually, they'd throw down a valise of cash just to be left alone. Colonel Sia found himself dizzily contemplating an undreamed-of success, actually taking a huge oil tanker that, alas, none of his men knew how to operate. So, for now, no killing.

The rest of his men—thirty-two, by Majiic's count—had clambered aboard and were milling about, staring uneasily at Colonel Sia and waiting for his signal to start the killing. A group of them walked over to Jakki's men and stood right in front of them, glowering, eye to eye, screaming in a rush of Somali. Jakki's men looked straight ahead into the middle distance, stony. Colonel Sia barked at them and they backed away.

"Where are your crew?"

"All below, sir. Too hot to stay on deck."

Colonel Sia frowned at Tarc, as if he had forgotten his name or how he had come to be standing in front of him. Sia was blinking in the heat, his red eyes glazing over. It took him a few seconds to process what Tarc had said. Watching Sia, Majiic felt he was under the influence of a drug. Hashish, or maybe just khat. The man's focus would come in and out, as if he was in a half-world between dreaming and waking. He opened his mouth, wiped his forehead with his sleeve again, and then his focus seemed to return. He snarled out some orders. His men flinched and then they grinned and ran into the gangway doors, clanging down the stairs into darkness, leaving only Sia and, presumably, his bodyguard, a comically short, one-eyed man with a torso too large for his skinny legs and an expression on his face that reminded Majiic of the look that some KLA soldiers had worn when they were getting ready to rape their captives—a wet-lipped, open-mouthed, slack-jawed look. He was holding a short-stock AK-74. He had some sort of native stiletto shoved into his belt. Colonel Sia holstered his Colt, snapping the retaining band over the butt.

He made a hard face and held out a pink-palmed hand.

"Papers!"

Tarc handed him a sheaf of meaningless papers he had hastily scooped up off the plotting table, glancing briefly at Sia's bodyguard as Sia fumbled through the papers. Sia's drugged mind churned aimlessly, as he tried to get an idea of what the cargo was, thinking about where he would sell it and how much he could make on it. And who would buy the tanker itself, once he had killed the crew. But, mainly, how he could avoid sharing the money with these dirty mongrels at his heels, and how *good* it felt to be on the winning side of destiny again after so many years of failure and squalid defeat. He folded the papers up and stuffed them into his shirt.

"I will keep these for our official records."

Tarc pretended to give a damn what he did with the papers, just for the effect, but, since Sia was already a dead man, he didn't really put his heart into it. He had been watching the way the bodyguard was staring at Vigo Majiic, a hungry look on his face, a sideways smile of anticipation.

Tarc turned to Majiic and said:

"Hey, Vigo, I think Baboon Boy likes you."

The guard, who understood English, stepped in with the AK raised, butt first, striking at Tarc's head, which wasn't there because Tarc had gone in under the man's left arm and taken the stiletto out of the man's belt and punched it with all his force deep into the man's lower belly and then ripped up, the man's mouth open but no sound coming out, now on the tips of his toes as Tarc repeatedly jerked the blade upward until he finally felt it grating against the man's sternum. Arterial blood spattered wetly across Colonel Sia's shirt as he clutched at the Colt in his holster, which caught on the holster's buttoned strap and held there long enough for Tarc to jerk the AK out of the bodyguard's hands, pivot on a heel, and drive the butt into Sia's midsection. The bodyguard was staggering back, a look of blank disbelief on his face, as his bloody entrails spilled out over his boots like purple-and-green snakes escaping from a sack. Tarc reversed the AK and fired a single round into the bodyguard's face, exploding it into a red ruin and spraying the deck behind with the contents of his skull.

Sia hit the deck and curled up, retching.

And then it was over, and silence came back in a rush, although Majiic's ears were ringing from the sound of the shot. Tarc knelt down beside the crumpled form of Colonel Sia, tugged the Colt out and handed it up to Majiic, and waited politely for Sia to finish puking, mild disgust showing on Tarc's blade-sharp features. Then he hooked his index finger into Sia's open mouth and dragged him by the flesh of his left cheek into a kneeling position. Sia's chin and most of his left arm was coated in vomit. He knelt in front of Tarc, weaving slightly, his mouth working silently and his bony chest heaving. Tarc stood over him, looking down, waiting.

After a while, Sia found some brave words.

"My . . . men . . . will . . . kill . . . you . . . all."

Tarc grinned, leaned down, wiped his fingers off on Sia's shirt, patted the man's cheek, straightened up and pulled the radio out of his back pocket.

"Jakki? How many are still alive?"

"Eleven. Wait. What? Okay, thanks. We just lost one. So, ten."

"Can they walk?"

"Not far."

"Bring them up."

Ten minutes later, the survivors of Colonel Sia's little armada were standing naked on the foredeck of the tanker, in a tight, trembling crowd, while the crew of the tanker—Jakki's Bulgarian mercenaries—stood around and watched them with blank indifference. Several of the captives had knife wounds, and all had been beaten into bloody submission. They stared out at the men who had taken them, unbelieving. What had happened belowdecks had been a nightmare in a steel maze. Most of them had been taken in grimly efficient hand-to-hand combat, their throats cut or their bellies opened or their backs sliced down the spine. The ones who had survived had survived only done so because they dropped their weapons and begged for their lives, tears streaming down, leaving black streaks on their dirty faces. And now, here they were, on the gently heaving deck of a huge tanker, under a sky of brass on a sea of hammered copper.

Tarc dragged Colonel Sia across the deck plates and stood him up in front of his men. Sia's eyes were bloodred and he was gasping like a man who had run all through the night to escape the terrible thing chasing him only to find that it that had been waiting patiently for him in his room when he finally got back home. Majiic, watching the scene and knowing Emil Tarc as he did, felt a stirring of pity for the old man. Which was ridiculous. He made a face and spat the sentiment out on the deck.

"Colonel Sia?" said Tarc, speaking softly, but loud enough to be heard over the bass vibrato of the engines coming up through the deck. Sia tried to straighten his shoulders and then slumped into limp defeat again.

"Yes. What do you want?"

"Do you know what a black flag means?"

"Yes," he said, after an effort. "It means *no quarter.*"

"So, by the pirate law of the black flag, we can kill you all?"

"We meant no harm. We only wanted a toll. To pass by our water."

"*Colonel* Sia. What absolute bullshit. Colonel, my ass. Have you ever really been the *Colonel* of anything?"

"I . . . I was in the . . . the fighting . . . at Mogadishu. I carried many reloads for the RPGs. Truly . . . Please. I ask you. Let us go to our boats. Let us go home. Be merciful. To the boys. Allah rewards the merciful."

"Ah. So, it's the boys you really care about, is it?"

"Truly. I love them. Me, I am nothing. They are like my own sons."

"Are they? Okay. Tell you what. I'll let you live if you do one thing."

"What?"

He held up the stiletto he had taken from Sia's dead dwarf.

"One by one, as I bring them to you, you cut their throats. You kill all of your *sons* with your own hands, then I'll let you live."

There was a murmur in the crowd of prisoners. It rose in volume until one of Jakki's men chose a boy at random and shot him in the head. Then there was stillness. Tarc watched this and then looked back at Sia.

"See. Now only nine throats to cut. So . . . ? You or your sons?"

Tarc held the knife out in the open palm of his left hand. Sia looked at it for a long time and then he staggered forward and took the knife. Tarc turned him around and kicked him toward the first boy, who was on his knees beside one of Jakki's men, his head down, sobbing. Sia came up to the boy, hesitated, looked back at Tarc, and then he grabbed the boy's hair in his left hand and brought his knife hand around and cut the boy's throat so deep he almost took the head off the neck. The boy pitched forward, convulsing, and died a long minute later in a lake of blood. Sia stepped back from the spreading pool, his right sleeve shiny with blood. He wiped the blade off on his shirttail and looked over to Tarc, waiting for the next boy to be chosen.

"That was a test," Tarc said. "You failed."

Sia's face went slack, and he shook his head from side to side. A hot wind, carrying a scent of rotting fish, crawled over the railing and oiled out across the deck. Shadows lengthened across the steel plates. No one spoke.

"Nail him to the bow of his boat," Tarc said, after a time. "Face up. Point the boat out to sea, lash down the wheel, and send it off."

Sia fell to his knees and held his hands up in supplication. Everyone ignored him. His voice rose into a shriek as two of Jakki's men threw him headlong and dragged him bodily to the gangway. In a few minutes, his shrieks changed to howls, and they heard the thump of mallets thudding into wood. The sound that Sia made then was literally inhuman. They heard the Mercs kick over. A few seconds later, the boat rose up on a white wake and powered out into the Indian Ocean, a skinny black spider splayed out on the bow decking. The roar of the Mercs almost hid the sound of Sia screaming. Then the sounds faded. The tanker's engines muttered quietly. A faint breeze made the pennants flap. They all watched the boat until it was a brown smudge blurring into the yellow haze. Tarc turned to the remaining captives, considered them for a time with a blank face.

"Take them below; have them police up their dead and mop up the fucking mess they made. Then put them all in the boat—naked, no weapons—and send them on their way. After that, will *somebody* please hose down this deck? Looks like we gutted an ox here."

"They'll talk, sir," said one of Jakki's men.

"Yeah. They'll tell *everybody*. And maybe then the *fucking* Somalis will stay the *fuck* out of the Indian Ocean for a while. You think so, Vigo?"

"Yes," said Majiic, trudging slowly back to the wheel. "I think so."

35

Inbound to Kuta City, Bali, the Indonesian Archipelago

Landing a plane at Ngurah Rai Airport in Kuta, on the southern tip of Bali, has a great deal in common with a carrier landing: you come in low out of the setting sun, across a churning sea, the landing strip starts at the shoreline and runs east for not nearly long enough, across a flat, narrow isthmus, and it ends at the edge of a huge swamp on the eastern side of the island. Overshoot it by twenty feet and you're in the swamp.

Dalton did not overshoot it, although the silence in the cabin was telling, as he laid on the brakes, with the tires smoking, while the far end of the runway was coming up fast, like the takeoff end of a ski jump. He hadn't flown a plane this size in a couple of years, and his skills had declined more than a bit. The plane came to a rocking halt—Dalton exchanged some terse words with the control tower—and he taxied the plane around to a circular parking spot some distance from the main building.

There was an odd craft parked in the next circle, a Boeing V-22

Osprey, a chopper-fixed-wing mix that flew a little like a Harrier. It could take off straight up like a chopper and then redirect its turbo-props to pick up serious forward speed. It looked like an oversized Huey with wings attached to the roof and a tail bar with two upright fins. This one, olive-drab and unmarked except for a registration number on her squat, stubby fuselage, looked official, some lucky bureaucrat's government ride. The Osprey was a fairly common plane in the South China Sea, since it provided a lot of the advantages of a chopper but it could carry a lot more troops a lot farther—two thousand miles—and twice as fast as any Huey or Blackhawk could. It wasn't a major weapons platform—the usual armament was a .50 caliber mounted in the rear loading bay—but a .50 could do a fair amount of damage, if push came to shove it up your nose.

Beyond the Osprey, he could see a green Toyota truck heading their way, Indonesian Customs and Immigration. He figured they'd be okay. Doc Holliday said he'd have the Embassy call ahead and say they were just doing a routine flight check before they presented the JetStar to the Minister Mentor. Fyke, still in the copilot chair, was already on the cell phone, speaking an Indonesian dialect and then, after a moment, switching to Vietnamese. Mandy and Miss Lopez were in the rear of the plane, talking amiably to each other while they tried to sort out what Mandy owned in the way of tropical dress that Miss Lopez could borrow without having to go to confession the next time she saw a priest.

The green Toyota came to a stop at the nose of the plane. Two skinny brown men in ODs and lots of enameled brass stepped out and waited while Dalton lowered the gangway. Then they clattered up the steps, heavy boots making the metal ring, and stopped in the doorway, obviously impressed. The aura of mystery money does that in the Far East.

They were gone in ten minutes, with a promise to send along the Cadillac Dalton had reserved. Dalton hadn't reserved a Cadillac, but he didn't say so. Kuta town itself was low and sprawling and ragtag and every bit the palm-fringed, sea-swept, steaming-hot, grease-reeking slacker haven that Singapore was, except there were no skyscrapers, and obviously no dress code in the downtown area, judging by the even more hideous fashion crimes being committed by the local version of the traveling backpacker.

Miss Lopez, who during the flight had announced with some force that her first name was *Delia* and it was okay to use it, was staring out at the streetscape with a homesick expression—Kuta looked a lot like Iligan City in Mindanao, where she had been born what seemed like a hundred years ago. The street kids looked threadbare and wild and she understood how you could get that way if you spent enough time living in the tropics.

Mandy gave the backpackers a sardonic appraisal as the big black Cadillac rolled through downtown Kuta. It was evening now and the lights were coming on, the usual blue-white fluorescent tubes that cast a deathly glow on every face, making the streets look like they were crowded with the living dead, which didn't help the impression the backpackers were making on Mandy. She had an expression of acid disapproval on her fine-boned, English face that could have etched glass.

"God, remind me to have some children so I can drown them," she said, in her best Sloane Ranger drawl, sounding like Helen Mirren after six vodka gimlets. "How long are we going to be stuck in this hellhole, Ray?"

Fyke took the cell phone away from his ear.

"We're a block away from finding out, ma'am."

"Please don't call me *ma'am*, Ray. I'm not your bloody mummy."

"Yes, ma'am. Sorry."

Mandy had already moved on. She was looking at her cell phone, a slight frown showing through her Botox.

"Micah, what's this thingy here?"

She handed him her cell phone. He glanced at it and handed it back.

"It's a GPS indicator."

"I thought so. I did *not* turn that on."

She made a move to shut the indicator down.

"Leave it on, Mandy, if you would."

"How long has it been on?"

"It's been on at least since we left Singapore. And, no, I didn't turn it on. I think it was turned on by Kiki Lujac."

Everyone in the car, including Fyke at the wheel, went quiet. Dalton had filled them all in on Kiki Lujac. Mandy had remembered him from the portico at the Intercontinental, and had taken the news that this wildly attractive young man had been sent to Singapore to assassinate them as a bitter disappointment. What a crying shame. He'd have been such a treat.

"How the hell would he get to my phone? It's been with me all the time—"

She stopped, remembering.

"No. Wait. I left it at the hotel. It needed a charge."

"Yes," said Dalton. "That's what I thought. He got in somehow and turned the GPS indicator on. I noticed the icon at Sembawang, while I was talking to Cather."

"Then why the hell didn't you turn it off?" asked Fyke, with an edge.

"I know why," said Mandy, smiling at Dalton.

"Why?" asked Delia Lopez. "If this guy is as dangerous as you say?"

"You want him to know where we are," said Mandy, "because you're reeling him in, aren't you? You intend to take him. Alive?"

"That's my hope," said Dalton.

"What if he's cloned the phone and monitoring all the calls?" said Delia. "Or he could have put a tiny explosive charge inside it and set it off by calling the phone and then pressing a code!"

Everyone turned to look at her.

She blushed and then hardened up.

"Well, I'm not just the Filipina nursemaid here, you know. I freelance for you Intelligence types all the time. Anyway, I saw it on *CSI.*"

"Don't worry," said Dalton. "I've checked the battery pack. There's no explosive and there's no bug. And the phone's encrypted, so, even if he cloned it, without the algorithm he'd never be able to decipher a call. All he'd hear would be a kind of high-pitched squealing, like a fax."

"But I'm right," said Mandy. "You left it on so he'd know where we are and come after us."

"Yes," said Dalton. "We haven't got time to go look for him, so let him come to us."

"What will you do to him?" asked Delia Lopez. Spending the last six years dealing with the physical and spiritual consequences of torture had radicalized her POV on the subject; she considered it a moral crime on a level with rape. The punishment for rape, where she came from, was death. The look she gave Dalton was a hard one, full of censure. Dalton was about to mount some sort of quibbling defense when Fyke pulled the Caddy to a hard stop outside a run-down, clapboard shop with a long, corrugated-iron roof that extended out over the front of the building. The interior was dim, lit only with a few low-watt bulbs hanging from the ceiling. A hand-painted sign on the glass said, in six languages:

LUCKY HAPPY STAR CLEANER PALACE
Don't let people ruin your clothes by hand.
We do it here by machine.

"We're here," said Fyke. "Why don't you folks get us something to eat while I go talk to my friend."

"*Eat?*" said Mandy, pulling her sunglasses down a bit as she took in the ragtag hawker stalls, garish under the fluorescents, the stalls loaded with overripe fruit and crawling with flies. The streets smelled of rotting fish, durians, and sewage, all of it steaming and stinking in the brutal heat.

"Ray. I'm not even *breathing* deeply. I'm certainly not *eating.*"

"I see a place where we can get some scarves," said Delia.

"Do you," said Mandy, glancing across the street at a pushcart layered with brilliant silks in emerald greens and indigo blues. "I'd love to, and I do believe that's a nice little bar next to it. I trust you drink, Lopez?"

"I do. Shall we?"

"We shall," said Mandy, taking her arm and plunging into the crowds, Mandy giving them a languid, backward wave, as the two of them vectored in on the vendor's cart full of Thai silks and Balinese batik.

"You want me to come in with you?" asked Dalton.

Fyke shook his head, as he extricated himself from the wheel and hobbled across the boardwalk toward the door. Halfway there, he turned his injured knee and went down like a shot bull. He looked up from the pavement at Dalton, wearing the expression of a strong man coming to painful terms with new limitations. Dalton gave him a hand and pulled him to his feet, watching the pain in Fyke's eyes and seeing his own future there.

"Maybe you should come along, Mikey."

"Yeah. Just until you get your legs back."

The shop was hotter than the street, floored in peeling linoleum that might once have been gray, smelling of sweat and cleaning fluid and moldy wood. It was a wide, low-roofed space, with a pressed-tin ceiling and wooden walls. A rickety counter up front separated the entrance from a larger factory space in the rear, where brown-eyed girls in jeans and T-shirts worked at the presses. Along the rear wall, a row of huge, rust-streaked machines churned and rocked, filling the place with the smell of overheated cotton and soap-scented steam. None of the women working the pressing boards looked up as Dalton and Fyke came in, but somebody must have hit a button somewhere because, in a moment, a small, wiry man with a face like a cracked walnut brushed aside a rack of hanging shirts and shuffled toward them, his rubber flip-flops flapping, his damp shirt unbuttoned, showing a torso marked by bony ribs and burn scars and a sunken belly. His black eyes showed nothing, as he reached the counter and stood there, a skeletal dwarf who seemed to be made of old bamboo and dried leather. He stared up at Fyke with a frowning scowl, quite devoid of welcome.

"*Missa* Fyke," he said, after a moment. "You come back."

"Nguyen Ki. This is my friend, Mr. Dalton."

Ki's eyes slipped sideways, took Dalton in without a change in his disapproving scowl, and then slid back to Fyke.

"You still with the Americans, *Missa* Fyke?"

"Not anymore. Freelance."

Ki's expression grew even stonier.

"You go 'way, long time gone. All the people different now. What you want me to do for you now, *Missa* Fyke?"

"Can we have a talk somewhere private, Nguyen?"

"You want maybe bottle Jim Beam, *Missa* Fyke?"

"No. No Jim Beam. A cuppa, maybe."

Ki stood there with his callused hands flat on the worn teak boards of the countertop, looking Fyke up and down in a way that the Ray Fyke that Dalton used to know would never have tolerated. But, then, the Fyke that Dalton had known would never have let a bottle of Jim Beam get in between him and his mission. Nguyen Ki had seen the shades of the coming dead in the streets of Kuta and he had tried to stop that, and Fyke had failed him abjectly. But there must have been something in the way that Fyke stood there and looked him straight back that burned through his sorrow and resentment. His face creased a little, and he showed his yellow fangs.

"Okay—you follow me to back. Mary," he called, and a young girl in a checkered shirt, her hair in a bandanna, looked up from a pile of white shirts. "You take counter, okay?"

"Yes, Grandfather," she said, smiling at Dalton and Fyke, as Nguyen Ki led them down a cluttered laneway between heaps of clothing and stacks of bedsheets toward an open space in the back where he had a kind of office, a spare-looking room with a sagging plywood desk piled high with paperwork behind which sat a battered steel file cabinet. He set a kettle on a small gas burner and shoved a pile of old newspapers off a set of plastic chairs stacked in a corner. He set them out in front of the desk, and busied himself with the tea for a moment, while Fyke looked around the room like a man who has traveled back in time to a place in his past he had been trying hard to forget. Seen in the dim light pouring in through a shuttered window, Fyke looked suddenly ancient, his broad red face marked with lines and fissures. Ki brought the cups over—three delicate bowls in blue porcelain with gold rims—and they sat there for a time, allowing the formality of the ceremony to be honored for a while, as was the Vietnamese custom.

"Okay," said Ki. "You not look good. What happen?"

"I've been in Changi Prison."

Ki shook his head, as he looked Fyke up and down.

"Very bad prison. How long?"

"About a month."

"Long time. Look like shit. Why you in Changi Prison?"

"They said I lost my ship."

Nguyen Ki's face tightened, and his eyes flicked across to Dalton, rested briefly there with a glitter, and then went back to Fyke.

"What kind ship you lost?"

"A tanker named the *Mingo Dubai*. Five-hundred-foot. About fifteen years old. What they call a gypsy tanker. A hull for rent. We made runs from Aden and Chittagong to Burma, through Malacca to Jakarta, all the way to Port Moresby. And then back. About a month ago, we were boarded by pirates at the southern end of the Strait—"

Ki made a face, showing his teeth in a skeptical leer.

"Hah! How pirates board big ship like that?"

"They had friends on board. Serbians."

Ki sipped at his tea, glancing from Fyke to Dalton.

"Once, you with our American friends. Then, after bombing, not. So, after disgrace, you run away to sea, like Tuan Jim?"

Fyke had to grin, although the words bit deep.

"Yes. Like Tuan Jim. Hiding my shame. And then they took my boat and they killed all my friends. And everybody thinks I'm a liar, that I got drunk and sank the boat."

"Yes," said Nguyen Ki, his eyes half closed and his gaze downward at the steam rising off his tea. "And are you liar who sink his boat?"

"No. I'm not. Those bastards took my boat and killed my men."

Ki sipped at his tea again and set it back down. In the silence, they heard the whine of tuk-tuks and jitneys going up and down the alley and the hiss and thump of the presses working. Ki sat back and looked at Fyke for a long time. The old man had that quality they called *gravitas*. It was a little like being in court and waiting for a judge to come to a decision.

"Okay," he said, glancing again at Dalton. "I think you no liar. Boat not sunk. Pirates take it. You want to find out who took it?"

"Yes. And I need your help."

Ki's eyes dropped again, and then he came back up.

"You go 'way long time, *Missa* Fyke. Many of the old names, old numbers, not around anymore. I not work for anybody long time."

"People still talk to you, Nguyen. You still listen."

Nguyen smiled.

"Yes. People still talk. This ship, she a pretty big boat, yes?"

"Yes. Five hundred feet."

"If the Malays take it, they cannot go to China to sell it anymore. China want her own ships, also want much trade, so no more pirates. The China people only steal boat themselves, or turn pirates in to Singapore. So, Malay and Dyak pirates not taking big ships in long time. Singapore Navy patrol the Strait. Even in Sulawesi waters. Indonesian Navy and KIPAM patrol all way from Jakarta to Papua New Guinea now. And the Americans all over too. Very dangerous. Still take small boats and sometimes make toll from big tankers and freighters. So, not the same as before."

He paused, refilled their cups.

"This boat, maybe five hundred feet long. Have white tower at back end? Then, long, low forward, with big hatches all along top? Red on top?"

"Yes," said Fyke, leaning forward in his chair, spilling his tea. Ki nodded, as if Fyke had confirmed something for him, but all that Dalton could see was that Fyke had just described almost every tanker working the seven seas all the world over. Nguyen Ki went inward for a time.

"Okay. You know Bontang?"

Fyke thought about the question.

"Yes. I do. Small fishing town on the eastern coast of Borneo. Maybe two thousand people."

"More now. Big tin mine open up thirty miles north, got conveyor run ten mile, all the way to sea, to fill ore ships. So lots of people live in Bontang until tin runs out. Many young boys from Kuta and Denpasar went up to Bontang for the mine work. Ten days on and ten days off. Lots of money to spend. But after Kuta, Bontang pretty sleepy, eh? Kuta, lots of girls, but Bontang only have hootch girls—number one *Gee-Eye,* all time *boom-boom*—"

Here he broke into a cackle, his eyes shut tight and his teeth bared, as he enjoyed his own joke. Fyke and Dalton let him enjoy it. After a moment, he settled down again.

"So, Kuta boys take company chopper to Diapati. Three hundred miles to Diapati. Lots of *boom-boom* in Diapati. Pretty girls. Clubs. Time back, one boy mother, Niddya Chinangah, she bring in her boy's clothes from three months of mine work. She tells me story. Her boy, Ali Chinangah, take chopper from Bontang to Diapati. Ten boys, all in chopper. Big yellow chopper. They crossing the strait between Borneo and Sulawesi, sun go down so very dark, and pilot say look down there. Down below is a big tanker. Can't see too much in dark, but big white tower like a T-shirt on a hanger"—Nguyen stretched his arms out to indicate the wings of the wheelhouse deck—"and long front deck with lots of big hatches. Big ship."

"Why did the chopper pilot care about it?" asked Dalton. "They must see ten a week in that channel."

"No. Not that many. And all other ship have lights on."

Fyke was listening so hard he was getting a headache.

"This ship was running *dark?*" he said.

"Yes. Running dark. No lights. Nobody on deck."

"And this was . . . how long ago?"

"Three, four weeks."

"Three weeks ago. Thirty knots an hour. Two thousand nautical miles, give or take a few, from the Kepulauan Lingga Light to the Sulawesi channel. They could do that in four, maybe five days. Dammit, Mikey, the timing is right. Nguyen, was there any flag at the staff?"

Ki shook his head.

"No. No flag."

"What direction was it headed?"

Ki shrugged.

"North. Maybe northeast."

"Going *around* Sulawesi," said Fyke, to himself. "Why?"

Ki was shaking his head, impatience flickering across his face.

"No, no. *Lissen.* This not story Niddya want to tell. Like you say, all day boats like that come through Sulawesi channel. This different. Her boy says pilot come around again, maybe see if boat is in trouble, and somebody run out onto deck and shoots at them."

"Shoots at them!" said Fyke. "With what?"

Ki didn't know.

"Just a sparkle-twinkle-crackle from a little chatter gun, all dark against big deck. Never hit nothing, but the pilot he goes up high and gets out of there."

"Did he call it in?" asked Dalton.

Ki shrugged that off, grinning.

"Call in to who? No business. Maybe people on boat think chopper is pirates. Everybody trust nobody in open water there. People can be fisherman one day and pirate next. So, maybe ship captain frightened too."

"No honest ship's captain would let his ship run dark," said Fyke. "He was *sneaking* through that channel. But where the *fook* was he going?"

"Diapati's a port," said Dalton.

Fyke shook his head.

"Mikey, my lad, you can't take a ship that's supposed to be sunk in the Malacca Strait and just steam her all-happy-go-lucky into Diapati with her name painted out. If that was the *Mingo Dubai,* they were headed for someplace where they could change her looks, paint her up brand-new. Get new registry papers. Alter her superstructure enough to disguise her. They'd need a dry dock big enough to hold her. And it couldn't be someplace on the sea-lanes either. Nor any port where there's the rule of law, or a Coast Guard, or a Navy. It would have to be . . . Christ, I have no *fooking* idea. There's no place like that in Southeast Asia anymore."

"Who would?" said Dalton.

Fyke stared at him.

"Who would *what?*"

"Who *would* have a *fooking* idea?"

"*Fooking?* Do I actually *talk* like that?"

"Only when you're speaking. Come on, Ray. This is your turf."

"Nguyen, how much of our old network is still intact?"

Ki shook his head sadly, made a very Proustian *ou sont les neiges d'antan* face, raised his hands to Buddha.

"Only a few here, in Kuta. Diapati, nobody, since Cao Ki died—"

"Cao Ki died? He was only forty. An athlete."

"Big mako shark. Right off shore. Ten feet out. Children watch."

"Jesus. Anybody else?"

"Tia Sally, but she pretty old now."

"So am I. She had a pub in Manado, didn't she?"

"Yes. The Blue Bird. Next to KIPAM, near Sam Ratulangi Airport."

"Kee Pam?" said Dalton. "Who's Kee Pam?"

"Komando Intai Para Amfibi," said Fyke. "Indonesian Special Forces. Snake eaters, just like you, only Marines instead of Army. You never heard of them?"

"Not under that name," said Dalton. "This Tia Sally, she a good source?"

"She was," said Fyke. Ki shook his head.

"Not now. She have diabetes. Lost legs. She sit in wheelchair all day by cash register, smoke-smoke, make sure her people not steal too much."

"She always knew who was doing what in the Celebes, though."

"Yeah," said Ki. "She *lissen* pretty good still. You want I call?"

"No," said Dalton. "Don't call. We'll go up to Manado and see her."

There was a commotion at the front counter. Dalton heard his name being called. He and Fyke came out of Ki's office and saw Delia Lopez standing in the entrance to the shop. She saw them as soon as they came through the doorway, and ran to the counter.

"Micah, Ray—you have to come. It's Mandy!"

"What is it?"

"She's in the bar. I think she might be having a heart attack. I have to go back! Come quick. We've called the ambulance."

They all hit the street at a dead run, weaving through the traffic. A crowd had gathered outside the bar area, tourists and backpackers and Kuta residents, all pressed together in the doorway. Dalton and Fyke went through them like pulling guards, sending people flying into tables. The interior of the bar was crowded with customers, most of whom were gathered around two young Balinese women who were crouched beside Mandy, who was kneeling on the floor, breathing hard, her hand on her chest, her eyes wide. There was a Thai silk scarf on the floor by her left knee, lying in a tangled heap of fiery oranges and brilliant scarlets.

Delia crouched down beside her. Mandy was looking at Dalton, a terrible fear in her eyes, her breath coming in gasps, each shorter than the last. She was trying to speak. They could hear sirens in the distance, coming closer, closing in fast. Dalton knelt down beside Mandy. She reached out and pulled him close, forced out some words he could not understand. He leaned in closer. Her body was hot, and she was coated in perspiration. Mandy tightened her grip on Dalton's shirt.

"Bitten," she managed to say. "I put the scarf on . . . I think something bit me!"

"Are you in pain?"

Mandy's brief sideways glare was truly killing, one of her very best, and she gritted out her answer through clenched teeth.

"Do . . . I . . . look . . . *happy?*"

"She was bitten," said Dalton, looking across at Delia Lopez. "She thinks something was in the scarf."

Lopez immediately pulled up Mandy's sleeves, tore her blouse open. A large brown spider scurried across the upper swell of Mandy's china-white breast. Dalton saw a tiny red dot with a drop of blood on her skin. Mandy saw the spider and screamed, slapping at her torso. Delia caught her hands: "No! It will bite again!" The spider was incredibly fast, darting for the cover of Mandy's shirt. Dalton snatched the spider off her skin; felt a sharp stinging sensation in his palm. Delia threw a bar glass toward him, saying, "Don't crush it—we need to know what kind it is!" Dalton slapped the glass over his palm and turned his hand over, dropping the spider inside. It immediately began to climb up the side of the glass again, feelers twitching. Dalton turned the glass upside down and slammed it down on the floor.

Men in blue were all around him now, and Fyke was pulling him backward away from Mandy. In a moment, she was surrounded by paramedics. Fyke picked a menu up from a nearby table, slid it under the glass on the floor, and held the glass up to a light. His face changed as he watched the spider scuttle around the interior of the glass.

"Do you know what it is?" asked Dalton.

The spider was about an inch across including legs, dark brown, with a smooth hide and an odd marking on its back. To Dalton, it looked like a violin, and as soon as he realized that his left hand began to pulse. He looked down at it and saw the same kind of mark that he had seen on Mandy's breast. *Spiders,* he thought, remembering Venice.

Why does it always have to be spiders?

"Yes," said Fyke. "It's a brown recluse. A female."

"Jesus. I thought so."

Necrotizing wounds the size of dinner plates. Renal failure. Coma.

Fyke looked down at Dalton's hand, saw the lesion there, a tiny red mark with two bright drops of blood, glittering under the light like tiny rubies. Dalton stared down at it. There was pain, not bad yet but building.

"Boyo," said Fyke. "You and Mandy need to get to a hospital. Now."

36

Selaparang airstrip, Tengarra Barat, sixty miles east of Kuta City

For once, Kiki Lujac did exactly what Gospic told him to do. He had Bierko fly him to Selaparang airstrip, sixty miles across the channel from Kuta, and he waited there. And he waited alone. Bierko took off again in a few minutes, telling Lujac that he had orders from Gospic to get the Gulfstream back to Bari right away. There was nothing Lujac could do about that, other than shooting Bierko in the knee with the late Corporal Ahmed's little semiauto—he'd kept it as a memento of their brief but memorable affair—which wouldn't have helped, since Lujac couldn't fly a jet. So, here he was, and if this place wasn't Hell then it was the place where people who didn't have the pull to get into Hell right away had to wait around for an opening.

The airstrip was a narrow, pitted stretch of blacktop, unmarked, carved out of the scrub bush all around, and used mainly by local transport services and a few private planes owned by some of the mining interests in the region. A squalid cantonment of tin huts and wooden shacks was clustered tightly around the strip, fighting a losing battle with the encroaching jungle. There seemed to be no young people, only a few emaciated ancients, stumbling around in the gloom under the forest or sitting slumped over on their porches, staring blankly out into the mist and nursing bottles of lukewarm Singha. There was a large cinder-block building at one end of the strip, tucked into the edge of the tree line, roofed in corrugated iron, with a neon sign in one gun-slit window—TIGER BEER SOLD HERE—and it served as a kind of ticket counter, Laundromat, penny flop, whorehouse, latrine, and wet bar to whomever was unfortunate enough to have to spend any time here, which, in this case, happened to be the Lovely and Talented Kiki Lujac, who was leaning against the pitted wooden countertop and staring down at the surface of his beer, where a tiny winged creature was struggling to stay afloat and looked about to lose the fight at any moment.

There was no one else in the bar area except an elderly woman with Bugis tattoos across her cheeks and one gotch eye as round and yellow as a pickled egg. Her job, as far as Lujac had been able to define it, and he had plenty of time to work it out, consisted mainly of manning the cash register and keeping the beer cold and the mattress turned on the greasy cot at the far end of the hall, next to the filthiest, foulest, and fetidest unisex latrine in all of Southeast Asia.

An undernourished Bugis girl, who looked no older than she needed to, lounged on this stained mattress on the cot at the end of the hall, clacking a wad of gum loudly. And repeatedly. She had an iPod on her belly and was flipping idly through a well-thumbed Manga book, using it, from time to time, to smack another insurgent cockroach into crunchy yellow paste on the wall beside the cot. If the stains were any guide, the cockroaches were losing a lot of good men.

Over Lujac's head, a broad, flat sail-like device made of woven reeds swept back and forth, stirring the steamy air and annoying the clustered bats trying to get some shut-eye under the bamboo rafters. It was raining hard now, and had been raining for quite a while, the rain drumming on the corrugated-iron roof and making an infernal, monotonous din.

There was a card table in one corner with an old fifties-era Seabreeze record player on it, next to a pile of—God help us all—Wayne Newton albums. So far, Lujac hadn't succumbed to the siren call of "Danke Schoen," but if the scrawny Bugis pop tart at the far end of the hallway didn't stop smacking her gum like that pretty damn soon he was going to take one of the Wayne Newton LPs down there and saw her head off with it.

Time passed, during which a lot more bugger-all happened in various deeply forgettable ways, but Kiki Lujac had stopped paying close attention and had sunk into a kind of a lizardlike torpor, during which he entertained a series of lurid fantasies involving Micah Dalton and a rubber dropcloth and a variety of everyday objects one might find around the house. He had conceived an intense resentment of Micah Dalton by this time, because, if Micah Dalton hadn't been such a tricksy and unpredictable target, then he, Kiki Lujac, would be sitting on the fantail of the *Subito*, in the harbor at Santorini, sharing a deep-dish, ice-cold mojito and a hammock with some pliant hard-bodied Grecian youth seraphically free of those pesky gag reflexes. But, no, here he was, in Hell's lobby. So Dalton was going to pay.

Then he was going to find out what Vigo Majiic was doing with Emil Tarc and what it had to do with some drunken ex-spy and his missing tanker and how it could all be handled in a way that would end up with Kiki Lujac on top of the pile and everybody else either dead or wishing they were. The old Bugis woman behind the bar sat up on her bar stool and cocked an ear at the ceiling. A few seconds later, they both heard the sound of a rotary craft coming in low across the forest canopy. The beating of the rotors rattled the corrugated sheets above, drowning out the drumming of the monsoon rains. Outside the open door of the bar, the weeds began to lash around wildly in the downdraft. Lujac pushed himself off the bar and stepped out into the twilight as a very strange-looking aircraft, with a vertical propeller at each wingtip and a body like an oversized Huey chopper, flared out and settled heavily down onto the tarmac a hundred yards from the blockhouse.

It was a Boeing Osprey, a hybrid between a fixed-wing plane and a chopper. Lujac had seen them on the deck of a Grecian aircraft carrier in the eastern Med. They had a range of around two thousand miles, and were used all over the Indonesian Archipelago. Although this one was painted olive drab, it had no military markings, just a registration number painted on its side. Still, it looked pretty official, and that gave Lujac a bit of a jolt in his lower belly. The rotors slowed, rocking the airframe as they cycled. A door popped open on the crew chief's side, and a squat, plump figure in a cheap black suit more or less flopped out and landed flat-footed on the rain-soaked tarmac. He looked up at the low charcoal gray clouds with an expression of reptilian disapproval on his sallow, thick-lipped face and deployed a very British-looking black umbrella, which was promptly shredded by the prop wash. He glared across the tarmac toward the open door where Lujac was standing. Lujac recognized the man around the same time that the man recognized him. Lujac's belly went cold and did a slow roll. He had last seen the man in Dalton's suite at the hotel back in Singapore.

He was Corporal Ahmed's partner, Sergeant Ong Bo.

37

Ronchi dei Legionari
Airport, Monfalcone, Italy

Antonia Baretto was waiting for Nikki Turrin when she walked out into the pale, watery light of Friuli in late November. She was nothing like her voice, which was rich and buttery and had the earthy tones of a mature woman. Antonia Baretto, leaning against her soft-green Alfa Romeo convertible with her arms crossed and a bright smile on her handsome young face, was a Nordic-looking water sprite no older than Nikki. Walking toward her, Nikki felt they could not be more than a couple of years apart, but where Nikki was a tall, elegant brunette with an hourglass shape, Antonia Baretto was slight, slender, pale-skinned, and so white blond she looked almost albino. She stepped forward as Nikki came up and offered her hand—a cool, dry, firm grip—smiling brightly as she did so. Her eyes were clear and blue, filled with good humor and cool intelligence.

"Signorina Turrin. How lovely to see you. The flight was good?"

Nikki rolled her eyes and smiled.

"Milan was a mess. But the flight here was very nice. Thank you for arranging it. I could have driven."

Antonia waved the comment away, as she opened the passenger door and took Nikki's carry-on bag, a large red leather item she had bought at the market behind the cathedral in Florence. In a few minutes, Antonia had the Alfa rolling smoothly through the flat farmland around Monfalcone, heading for the coastal highway that would take them down the bay, through Trieste and along the curve of the sound to Muggia, a distance of around thirty miles. Antonia drove well, with none of the stunt-driving lunacy of the typical Italian driver. The day was cool, and there were rain clouds hanging low in the mountains to the east. Antonia slipped a CD into the player—Paolo Conte, to Nikki's surprise, a singer who usually appealed to much older people—and settled into the leather seat, glancing across at Nikki with a bright smile.

"You look younger than I expected," she said.

"So do you."

Antonia laughed.

"I have to show my card just to get a prosecco. I'm actually thirty-three. Nobody believes me. I suppose time will fix that. I'm looking forward to showing you the villa. I know the history is a little odd, but I think you'll like it very much. And the sellers are—*come se dice?—ardènte.*"

"Motivated?"

"Yes! *Motivadissima!* Your Italian is very good. Have you been very much in Italy?"

"I was here last year, in Tuscany. We stayed in a villa near Arezzo, and then went to Florence, Lucca, San Gimigniano—"

"All those towers! Such a silly place. Did you like Florence?"

"I drove. Got there on a Saturday evening. Got lost. Panicked."

"Yes. Me too. I never try to drive in Florence. Where did you stay?"

"At the Lucchese."

"Near the Uffizi. My God. Did you hear what happened there just a while ago? People were shot. Two men and a *professori*, of *psicologìa*, she was shot there too."

"Oh no—killed?"

"No. She is in . . . *una chioma?*"

"A coma?"

"Yes. They say it was terrorists. The woman was from an old family, aristocrats. The Vasaris. Very wealthy. The Carabinieri are very angry. They have one man"—here she gave Nikki a significant look—"a Serb, of course—they are as bad as the Slovenians—and he is being questioned. But that was in Florence. We have little crime up here, except for the docks in Trieste, where there are too many foreigners. What do you do, in America?"

"I work with an IT company?"

"*Eye-Tee?*"

"Information Technology. Computers, that sort of thing."

"You must be very good," she said, accelerating around a curving ramp and powering onto a road marked SS14. The sea along their right was just visible under a bank of wet fog. Winter was in the air, and it looked like a rainstorm was coming in from the mountains. The coastal plain here was flat and level, and Antonia had the Alfa up to two hundred kilometers in thirty seconds.

"Very good? I suppose so," she said, thinking about the way the AD of RA's scent had stayed in her mind on the long Alitalia flight from D.C. to Milan. He had booked her in first class and handed her a black Amex card with a fictitious corporate ID under the name NIKKI TURRIN.

Then he had kissed her good-bye, his damaged face visibly moved and filled with sudden anxiety. She had kissed him back, on his scarred cheek, partly to stop him from changing his mind and partly because when she was in close like that it was all about how he smelled and his warmth and how strong and sweet he was and there was nothing about the damage.

"We have a good company," said Nikki, watching the sea on her right.

"You must, to be able to look at a million-euro villa."

"My family has some money. They may help."

Her family had about as much money as Nikki did, which was nowhere near enough to buy a cottage on the Chesapeake let alone a villa in Muggia. Nikki felt guilty, leading the agent on, but then that's what they meant by *covert* and *clandestine*. She realized she was now a kind of spy, and felt a combination of shame and exhilaration at the idea. Antonia seemed to find the explanation sufficient and did not press her again.

The traffic, which had been light all the way from Monfalcone, began to get heavier as they passed through the outskirts of Trieste and into an industrial area near the docks. Antonia found an off-ramp and got onto the Via Flavia, racing past the dockyards and the factories toward the port of Muggia. The air smelled of smoke and traffic but, up ahead, soft-green hills rose gently upward, and, as the Alfa climbed into the tangled streets above the little harbor, Nikki could see how pretty the town would be in the high season. The hills were heavily treed and here and there they passed an olive grove or an orchard.

As they climbed up the twisting roads in Antonia's agile sports car, the private yards turned into estates and the little homes into villas. Antonia braked hard into a right turn marked SALINA MUGGIA VECCHIA and traveled down a long winding road covered with terra-cotta shards until they came to a stop in a large, secluded parking area in front of a massive iron gate, intricately worked, set between two tall stone pillars, each pillar supporting a bronze statue of some sort of raptor, wings outstretched, talons extended. Antonia set the brake, glanced over at Nikki, rolled her eyes theatrically.

"Slovenians love their stupid eagles. If you buy the place, we can get some marble urns and put some flowers there. Come on, I have the keys."

They got out, Nikki feeling a dizzying sense of unreality as she stood in front of the same gate that she had seen in an enlargement of the video. It had been barely visible in the distance beyond the pool, a purely theoretical locus somewhere out there in the wider world. Now it was right in front of her, and it was the scene of a multiple murder.

She felt her throat tightening. She was a long way from Pittsburgh.

"Nikki, are you okay? You look cold."

Nikki nodded, pulling her cashmere scarf—*his* cashmere scarf—around her shoulders. "I am, a little. The wind is stronger up here."

Antonia used a large brass key to work the lock in a box by the gate. The gate swung slowly back on electric motors, shrieking like gulls. They got back in the Alfa and followed the drive as it curved around and up through an avenue of small evergreens. Beyond the curve of the lane they could see the villa at the crest of the hill, a sprawling neo-Romanesque monstrosity, with meaningless turrets and gables and domes stuck on at random intervals across the roofline. The lawn had run to seed, and the place had a general air of ruin and decay. Antonia made no excuses for it as she pulled the Alfa to a stop under the entrance portico, the tires crunching in the terra-cotta gravel.

"I know what you're thinking," she said, as they got out. "The place is a disaster. But, really, it isn't. Under the stuck-ons, it has good bones. Two weeks and a good carpenter could have the place smoothed out very nicely. Come, let me show you inside—all the furniture is gone; of course, it was terrible stuff—so you can see the place as an empty canvas."

She dragged one of the heavy double doors open and waved Nikki inside, searching for a light switch, as they stood in the great, gloomy hall before a set of curving stairs that rose up in a helix toward the second floor. The front hall had been inlaid with black-and-white marble in a herringbone pattern. Open doors on either side led to a large reception hall on the one hand and what looked like a wood-paneled study on the other. Antonia was right; the vulgarity was all on the outside. She followed her through the rooms and out into large open space at the back of the villa, the kitchen and the dining area, and a wall of leaded glass that overlooked the deck and the pool itself.

"See," said Antonia, spreading her arms out. "You can see the bay from here. Isn't it splendid, Nikki?"

"Yes it is," said Nikki, seeing only the half-naked girls and the beefy men choking and dying in agony in the water and on the marble decking.

"Are you not well, Nikki?" asked Antonia, coming close and putting a hand on Nikki's forearm. Nikki put her hand on top of Antonia's. Her skin was warm, and she smelled of lemon soap.

"I think I'm a bit tired from the flight."

"Of course. I should have taken you to lunch first. We can go now, if you like. And come back tomorrow. I have a wonderful room for you at Stella, right on the water. And my mother has invited you for dinner tonight. You will come, won't you? She wants to hear all about your family. She thinks we may be related. Of course, she thinks everybody in Friuli is related to everybody else. But, you will come?"

"Yes. I will. But let's do a quick look around now. Then, after lunch, maybe we can come back?"

"Certainly. Let me make a call. I can get us a table at Stella for lunch, if I call now."

She flipped her cell phone open, frowned.

"My battery's low. I have a car charger. I'll plug it in and call from there. I'll be right back. You go look at the view."

Antonia walked quickly off down the hall toward the front section and the main doors. Nikki's heart began to beat a little faster. She had the little HazMat kit in her purse. And the pool—the focus of all her analytical attention for days now, the entire point of this mission—was just beyond the glass doors on the far side of the dining room. She drew a breath, stiffened, and walked across the inlaid-wood flooring, her heels striking hard and the sound echoing off the bare walls. The place smelled of cigar smoke and funeral flowers and would have to be aired out before . . . She smiled at that. She wasn't going to *buy* the place. She was here to do a job.

The deck curved around the entire back of the villa, a shell-shaped cascade of semicircular levels covered in pale pink marble. A small Romanesque temple, with what looked like a bar and a stove, had been built at the shallow end of the pool. The pool itself was very large, mainly square, but with a broad, curving edge at the deep end. The pool had been drained, and scrubbed until the tiles gleamed. It was deep, and the walls were straight and high. Empty, it looked like a large pen designed to cage bears. The bottom of the pool, in which a small puddle of water remained, a few dead leaves floating in it, had an inlaid pattern done in tiny squares of dark malachite and pale turquoise and lapis lazuli—a massive shark, with a muscular curve to its body and a flat, sinister head.

It was very well done and looked almost alive, seeming to quiver with terrible life, as Nikki stood at the edge of the pool and looked down at it. She looked back toward the glass doors. There was no sign of Antonia.

Do it now, Nikki. Don't wait.

She took the little HazMat kit from her handbag and knelt by the edge of the pool, pulling on a pair of latex gloves. Her heart was hammering against the side of her ribs. The kit contained a series of cotton swabs and some sterile vials, along with a few small plastic bottles and a rasp. Working quickly, her breath coming in short, sharp gasps, she worked her way along the edge of the pool, covering those areas where she remembered seeing people die, dying right on the marble squares under her feet. In a few minutes, she had filled several vials and had a bottleful of scrapings. She stood up and looked back at the house again.

Where was Antonia?

She looked at the pool again. A ladder had been lowered into the deep end, left there by the workmen who had cleaned the pool. She did not want to go down into the pool; not at all. She walked over to it, slipped off her shoes, and climbed down into the pool anyway. It was deeper than she thought, almost fifteen feet at the deepest. By the time she reached the bottom the sky had been reduced to a square of gray cloud framed in white tiles. She bent down and ran the tip of a swab over the malachite mosaic around the shark's snout and dipped a vial into the standing water near the drain. Her feet were damp and her knees ached from kneeling. If Antonia came to the edge and asked her what she was doing, she would say she was—

"What are you doing?"

Nikki looked up. A small boy, with a pinched, narrow face and long shaggy hair, was standing at the edge of the pool, staring down at her. He was wearing a wrinkled gray silk suit. With a vest. The outfit looked ridiculous on the boy, who could not have been more than nine or ten. The boy's expression was sullen, and his dark brown eyes had no light in them.

"I'm checking out the pool," she said, with an edge. "Who are you?"

The boy shrugged, stuck his hands in his pockets, and began to walk along the edge of the pool. Nikki glanced at the ladder, feeling suddenly vulnerable. She looked down to what she had thought of as the shallow end of the pool. The edge was at least ten feet off the bottom. Essentially, she was in a bear pit. She walked quickly over to the ladder and put her hand on it. The boy was standing next to it, but he had his back turned to her, his attention somewhere else.

"She is in the pool, Father."

A voice, in the distance, coming closer, an old man's voice.

"I know, I know."

Nikki began to climb up the ladder, looked up and saw that an old man was now standing beside the little boy, his hand resting on the boy's head, a stiletto of a man with an air of dissipated elegance, blue-lipped, of indeterminate age, wearing a beautifully tailored gray silk suit. His face was like a skull and his lidded eyes had a pale glitter.

"You are the lady from America?" he said, in a voice like a dry branch scraping against a window in the dead of winter.

"Yes. I . . . I was checking the pool out."

The boy found this amusing. He was missing teeth in the front of his mouth. His laugh was high and sharp, a yelp, like a jackal or a fox. The old man smiled down at her, and patted the boy's cheek, letting his fingertips slide along the boy's skin in a way that seemed more sensual than paternal.

Nikki found that she disliked him extremely.

"Where's Antonia?" she asked.

The boy showed his teeth.

"She is in the house."

"May I ask, who are you?" she said, as she began to climb the ladder. The old man said something in Croatian or Serbian to the boy. He stepped to the top of the ladder and put his hands on it. Nikki's stomach tightened, but the boy only stood there, staring down at her with a look on his face that might have, on an older boy, been a sexual leer. She pulled the top of her blouse tighter, and began to climb again. When she got to the top, the boy held his hand out and helped her onto the deck, his lips half open, his eyes moving over her body in a way that made her feel like kicking him. The old man waited a little way away, his hands at his side, his expression cool.

"I am the owner of the house," the gray man said, in an accent Nikki could not quite recognize. Croatian or Serbian. "This is my stepson, Vladimir. You are Miss Nikki Turrin, I am told."

Nikki turned to look at him.

"I was under the impression that the house was owned by a corporation."

"Were you?" said the gray man, walking a little behind her. They reached the glass doors. Nikki saw Antonia Baretto standing at the long kitchen counter, staring through the glass at her. Her face was bone white and her expression fixed. Three small boys stood in a semicircle around her, looking up. Nikki pushed the doors aside and came into the large, empty dining area, her shoes clicking on the intricate parquet flooring.

Antonia's eyes followed her as she came across the room. The little boys had turned around and were staring at Nikki. They looked like brothers, small, pinched faces and the same dead-brown eyes. They were all dressed like schoolboys, in slacks and shiny black shoes and baggy white shirts. They had sallow skin and looked underfed and hungry. They all had the same air of leering contempt mixed with a kind of greasy adolescent sensuality. It was clear from the expression on Antonia's face that she did not like them very much either.

"Nikki, this man is the owner of the villa," she said, in a tight voice. "I did not expect him to be here."

"No, she did not," said the gray man. "But when I heard you had come all the way from Maryland, I decided I wanted to meet you."

Nikki looked around at the little boys, wondering why they were here and why they were not in school. The gray man seemed to sense this.

"These little boys are my . . . *pupilla* . . . I am their guardian."

Nikki tried a disarming smile on the boys. They looked back, unblinking, reminding her of stray dogs, watchers, devoid of any emotion other than a vaguely predatory air. They gave her the crawling creeps, actually. She looked over at Antonia and saw her feelings mirrored there.

"Are you all right, Antonia?"

She nodded once—a sharp, jerking motion—her hands tight around her purse. Her cell phone lay on the counter in front of her, open. The gray man came and stood beside her, staring across the counter at Nikki.

"Signorina Baretto tells me that you have come from America to look at my villa. I am honored. It is true that a corporation owns it, but, I must say with humility, that I own the corporation. My name is Stefan Groz."

Nikki smiled but did not offer her hand. The name was spoken with a degree of formality, as if he expected her to know who he was. She did not, but the atmosphere in the house was vibrating with tension, a tension that he had brought with him, he and his little coyotes, but she could not understand what the tension arose from. Even Antonia looked remote, her expression blank and her eyes wary.

"Tell me, Miss Turrin," said Groz, "how you learned of the house?"

"My family is from here. I have always wanted to buy a home here. So, I always look at the listings. I saw this house. I called Antonia—"

"Yes. She told me that on the phone. From Annapolis Junction, in Maryland. Is that where you live, Miss Turrin?"

"Yes. But how—"

"How odd that you seem to live in a Starbucks coffee shop? The price for this villa is rather high. You must be very wealthy."

"My family has some money."

"Yes. They must. You were interested in the pool, I see. You have a little testing kit, so my boy tells me. You are concerned about the pool water? Mold, perhaps?"

"Yes. Well, no . . . There were . . . issues about it. The pool."

Groz nodded his head, his eyes never moving from Nikki's face.

"Yes. The sad history of the pool. Everyone knows about it. I can understand why you were worried. Such a terrible thing. Of course, I have had the pool area bleached and chemically sprayed and power-washed. There would be no trace of the virus—"

"Antonia said the problem was a bacteria called *Vibrio vulnificus*. That's not a virus; it's a bacteria."

A flicker of annoyance crossed his face.

"You are correct. At any rate, the testing kit . . . I am curious about it. Would you be so kind as to show it to me?"

That was the end of that, as far as Nikki was concerned.

"Look, to be honest, I really don't like your attitude and your questions, and I think I'm not going to buy this place after all. Antonia, perhaps you could take me back to the airport?"

Antonia nodded, her face gaining some color as she saw a chance to get away from this bloodless old man and his terrible little homun-culi. She reached for her cell phone, but Groz placed his hand on top of hers and held her there. She closed her eyes. A tremble ran through her slender body. Now the malice in the man was out in the open. When she opened them again, her eyes were bright with fear.

"Before you go, can you indulge me? Do you know what interesting place is not very far from Annapolis Junction, Miss Turrin? A place called Fort Meade. Fort Meade is said to be the home of the famous National Security Agency. Do you know this place?"

"Everyone knows about it. Antonia—"

Groz reached quickly across and pulled her purse from her hand. He turned it upside down and poured the contents onto the countertop. There, amid the clutter of makeup and credit cards and airplane tickets, lay the HazMat kit, a small, rectangular box made of clear plastic.

A label on the front of it said:

HAZARDOUS MATERIAL
If Found Do Not Open / Return To:
Environmental Matrix, 2260 Laurel Way
Annapolis Junction, Maryland

Groz picked it up and looked at the various swabs and scrapings that Nikki had collected. He set it down carefully and looked back at Nikki, saying nothing, apparently waiting for her reaction. There was a short, sharp sound, like something punching through glass, followed by a distant, rolling crack. She blinked. When she opened her eyes again, Stefan Groz was standing in front of her, a look of intense puzzlement on his narrow face. There was a small red hole in the middle of his shirt, about an inch below the folds of ancient skin around his throat. He reached up and touched the hole, pulled away a fingertip coated with blood, and then he looked back at Nikki. His mouth opened, as if he were trying to share with her his confusion about this strange phenomenon. Then the glitter went out of his eyes. He seemed to see something of great interest in the middle distance, was still for a moment, and then dropped down below the countertop like an empty suit. The boys backed away from his body and were now staring up at Nikki as if she had somehow killed the old man with a magic spell. The boy in the silk suit—Vladimir— reached into his pocket and pulled out a little silver pistol. There was another sharp crack and a hole appeared in the middle of his forehead, snapping his skull backward, sending him sliding across the bloody tiles, coming to a stop at the feet of a figure standing in darkness at the end of the hall.

This figure came forward into the light, a bent old man in a rumpled brown suit and heavy cordovan brogues. He looked down at the body of Stefan Groz and, briefly, at the child who had also been shot, and then at the other boys, who had backed away into a corner of the kitchen and were staring up at the man as if he had just materialized out of the parquet tiles. The man sighed, reached down and plucked the little pistol out of the boy's hand, studied it for a moment, and then set it down on the counter next to the pistol Groz had dropped. He looked at Nikki and Antonia, shook his head, and softly said: "*Una giocattolo*, a toy. *Tal demenza.*"

Then he sighed again, lifted a handset, and spoke into it:

"*E morte, Carlo. Due. Grazie. Venga.*"

He put the radio away and came over to the counter, leaning his hands on it and breathing deeply, as if he had run some distance, which he had. His rough skin was lined and seamed and his features seemed to have been crowded into the center of his face. His hands were bent, gnarled, as if his fingers had been broken long ago, but there was kindness in his weathered face, although in the eyes there was an essential coldness.

He turned around and smiled at Antonia Baretto and then at Nikki.

"I am Issadore Galan, of the Carabinieri. I apologize for . . . for this," he said, making a gesture that took in the kitchen, the carnage, the entire ugly encounter, "but we have monitored the phones of Stefan Groz for some time. He is the subject of a very large operation—*one* of the subjects, at least—but we have not until now been able to have him come to Italy and, because our judges are idiots and the Montenegrin judges are criminals, we could not obtain permission to go to Budva or to attempt to extradite him. Signorina Baretto, we heard you on his phone, saying a woman was coming from America to look at the place, and we became interested. So—*che fortuna*—we watch as he crosses the border with Slovenia and drives to Muggia. He becomes aggressive, seizes your purse . . . We intervene. Signorina Turrin, may I ask who is your employer? Is it by any chance the National Security Agency?"

Nikki hesitated, uncertain what she should do.

Galan saw this and shook his head sadly.

"We are not the enemy, signorina. But I think that you and I, we may have the same enemy."

Nikki studied his face for a while. Men in navy blue tactical uniforms bearing the crest of the Carabinieri arrived and began to police up the scene. Galan waited patiently, his expression full of sadness and sympathy. After a while, she told him everything she knew about 2654 Salina Muggia Vecchia and nothing at all about the NSA, which he seemed to not only understand but to accept as, for her, the right decision, if not the only possible decision.

38

Sam Ratulangi Airport, Manado, northern Sulawesi

They flew through the night, a thousand miles northeast from Kuta, crossing the coral atolls and volcanic islands of the Celebes Sea on a warm, cloudless tropical night under a blade-thin moon that cast a rippled golden light on the open water far below their wings. The islands were black shadows marked here and there with tiny constellations of pale lights; remote villages deep in the coconut palm jungles, fishing ports, now and then the brighter clusters of open copper and tin mines. Dalton was at the wheel, his left hand burning with pain, a round, blue open sore in the middle of it. His hand was wrapped in ice that Fyke would change every hour or so from a bucket in the galley, sprinkling the bite with hydrogen peroxide while the bandage was off. Dalton was loaded up on extra-strength Advils, popping them like cinnamon hearts. Neither man had much to say. They sat there, side by side, in the cockpit and watched the forward horizon rolling toward them at five hundred miles an hour, the four turbofan jets at the tail making a muted, whistling roar.

They had left Mandy Pownall in an emergency-ward bed back at Madame Suharto Municipal Hospital, Delia Lopez at her side. The doctors at the hospital had confirmed the bite of a brown recluse spider—not too difficult, since they had the venomous little bitch in a bottle—agreed that it had very likely been asleep inside the silk scarf—they were common in closets and around clothing—and had done all the usual things—ice, painkillers, monitoring her vitals and her renal functions. She had been awake and talking, the pain under control, still pale and tight with anxiety, when Dalton kissed her good-bye.

A young intern in the hall told Dalton and Fyke, with a worried look back toward the door to her room, that he did not expect but could not rule out extensive renal damage, and, if the wound on her breast became necrotic, there could be a large spreading sore, the dead tissue would have to be excised—there was the possibility of terrible scarring, a need for extensive cosmetic surgery—and, although in this case it seemed unlikely, there was always some danger, with a bite this close to the central nervous system, of coma. And death.

Dalton listened to this painful talk of scarring and a coma and death about yet another woman whom he loved and reached the private conclusion that he was in a hell of his own devising, doomed to atone for all the damage he had ever done in this world; and, if Porter Naumann's experience was any indicator, there was worse to come in the next.

Fyke, sensing his mood, stopped at a hawker stand on the way back to Ngurah Rai Airport and bought three bottles of Bombay Sapphire gin, because sometimes all you can do about the everyday wounds of life is to resort to multiple applications of internal anesthetic and hope for a better day tomorrow. Now they were airborne and inbound to Sam Ratulangi there were eight hundred miles of rearview mirror separating them from the recent past. Dalton got a radio call from the air traffic controller at Sam Ratulangi, gave him his numbers, and settled back into the pilot seat, his face shadowed and uplit by the instrument lights. The JetStar drove through some turbulence, the airframe shaking, rattling the glasses on the tray at Fyke's feet. He leaned down, lifted up the bottle of Bombay Sapphire, looking quizzically at Dalton.

"One for the ditch, Mikey?"

"How many have I had so far?"

Fyke considered the bottle.

"Three. Small ones."

"And you?"

"Three. Large ones."

"I could use some coffee. We'll be on the ground in thirty minutes."

"The field is open?"

"They have a night crew for emergencies. I told them we were having trouble with the GCA radar. They'll light up the field for us."

"Okay . . . Not true, is it? About the GCA?"

"No. It's fine. Coffee?"

"Coming up."

Fyke was back in a couple of minutes. Right at the edge of the forward horizon, dark against a field of stars, was a large, low black mass, with a small cluster of lights, in a concave curve around the edge of a broad seacoast. Fyke handed Dalton a cup of rich black coffee and strapped himself back into the copilot's chair.

"Manado?"

"That's my hope."

"Can I ask you a personal question?"

"Sure."

"Mandy was telling me about this ghost you've been seeing."

"Has she? Our Mandy has a little problem with discretion."

"Was it a secret? She didn't think so. You told Delia about it. See-ing a ghost. This Porter Naumann fellow. Did I know him?"

"He knew you. He worked out of London Station, but you were with Tony Crane. Porter and Mandy created Burke and Single."

"Burke and Single? That's one of ours?"

"Yes."

"I never knew. And how did Porter Naumann become a ghost?"

"He died. That's pretty much a prerequisite."

"Don't be flip, Mikey. You know what I'm asking."

"Don't you already know the answer?"

"I've been making a few educated guesses. It has something to do with how you're no longer working for the CIA."

"We're working for the CIA right now, aren't we?"

"Yeah. But it feels like freelancing, doesn't it? But, then, it always did. Nobody like us ever really belongs to the Agency. We're all part-timers and casual labor, as far as the Agency is concerned, unless you're Deacon Cather. My point is, what happened to Porter Nau-mann, was it your fault?"

"No. Not that part of it, anyway."

"But you then set out to do something ghastly to whoever killed him?"

"Yes."

"And in the doing of that, other people got hurt. This lady in Venice?"

"Yes. Indirectly."

"But the mainspring, the core of it, you didn't start all that, did you? You just did what you could do along the way. How's Porter doing now?"

"Last time we talked, he was trapped in Cortona. He couldn't leave. And there were things he was seeing in the street; looked like black smoke in the shape of . . . demons, I guess. Coming up out of the stones, and they were hissing at him. He was worried."

"Jesus. I don't blame him. I'd pee myself. He told you all this?"

"Yes."

"What did he do? Just slide down a moonbeam and pop into your room?"

"No. Porter wasn't a moonbeam kind of guy. I was dreaming."

"So you never see him when you're awake?"

"Not anymore."

"But you used to?"

"Yeah. I got a face full of some kind of powdered drug. Peyote and datura, they said. That's when I started seeing Porter."

"Peyote and datura? That stuff will stay in your skull forever."

"Thanks. And on that cheerful note—"

"So, Naumann, he really was just a hallucination? His ghost, I mean."

"The phrase *just a hallucination* doesn't quite catch the impact of having one follow you around most of the American Southwest, does it? Anyway, he didn't think he *was* a hallucination."

"You talked it over with him?"

"Yeah. He was pretty convinced he was a real ghost."

"Were you?"

"He made a great case for it. Jury's still out."

"Have you seen him since you left Italy?"

"No. I haven't."

"So he was telling you the truth? He *is* stuck in Cortona. At least, his ghost is. You gonna help him with that?"

"How would I do that?"

Fyke thumped the controls in front of him.

"My point *exactly*. You see, I know what you're thinking, Mikey."

"Do you?"

"You're thinking about the essential evil horrible awfulness of you."

Dalton said nothing, staring out at the lights of Manado.

"See? I thought so. Some free advice, Mikey?"

"Is it worth it?"

"Every *fooking* penny."

"Okay."

"It's not you."

"What's not me?"

"Something happens to *everybody*, Mikey. Even to ghosts. To take on the weight of every bad thing that happens is a mortal sin. The sin of pride."

"You took on the weight of Kuta."

Fyke sipped at his coffee, fumbled at a pocket, pulled out one of Mandy's outrageous colored cigarettes, lit it up, exhaled softly, sending a plume across the instrument panel. He offered one to Dalton, lit it too.

"Yes. I took on Kuta. And am I not setting it right even now? The great thing about being a Catholic, Mikey . . . you *are* a Catholic, aren't you?"

"Nope. Not anymore. Episcopalian."

Fyke made the sign of the cross over Dalton.

"*Ego te absolvo a peccatis tuis in nomine Patris et Filii et Spiritus Sancti*. You are now officially shriven of the crime of being an Episcopalian and have become an honorary Catholic. So, Mikey, lad, the great thing about you now being a Catholic is you get forgiveness."

"Forgiveness from whom? The people you hurt?"

"Jesus no. Hardly ever. Most people are miserable, surly sods who wouldn't forgive you for a lukewarm martini. Mainly, you get it from God."

"Yeah? How can you tell? He sends you an e-mail?"

Fyke touched his chest.

"You feel it in here. Not right away. After a while. It comes to you."

"You really believe that, Ray?"

Fyke was quiet for a while, watching the smoke drifting in the cockpit. He tapped his ashes into his empty coffee cup.

"I have come to believe it, Mikey. But I have come to it very slowly."

"And you think I can?"

"What you're doin' now, how's that workin' for you?"

There wasn't much to say to that.

They were on the ground at Sam Ratulangi forty minutes later, a single-strip airfield ten miles northeast of the mangy little coastal town of Manado, in the middle of low, rolling hills and fields of co-conut palm and copra farms. The Immigration counter was closed. One sleepy guard blinked at their passports and waved them through to the taxi stand, staring fixedly at their backs as they walked away. He was on the phone a few seconds later.

They hired a large old Mercedes, painted bright pink, and gave the young female driver—a very handsome Chinese girl with a six-hundred-watt smile who gave her name as Tangerine—instructions to take them to Tia Sally's bar. She gave them a look but started up anyway. Within a few minutes, she had them cruising through the low, dark hills and narrow country roads lined with coconut palms, with the lights of Manado a pale glow on the southwest horizon line. Fyke was asleep in minutes, but Dalton sat there, awake, his left hand aching brutally, staring out at the passing scrub brush, the occasional village, closed up for the night, flitting by his window in a blur of shutters and cinder-block walls, his eyes heavy with fatigue.

He closed his eyes.

Someone was flashing a red light in his eyes. He opened them up and saw that the interior of the taxi was full of flickering red light. Tangerine's face was reflected in the rearview mirror, her eyes glittering with the red flaring lights that were pouring in through the back window. Then they heard the short, sharp klaxon sound of a police siren. Fyke snapped upright, blinking into the glare, straining around to look out the back window.

"Who the *fook* are they?"

"KIPAM," said Tangerine. "I know the truck."

"The commandos? What do they want with us?"

"I don't know, sir, but I have to stop."

She pulled the big Benz over to the side of the road and rolled her window down. Steamy scented air poured inside the car; frangipani and car exhaust and the earthy smell from a nearby stand of copra. Black shadows flicked across the rear window. A cone of hard-white light pierced the side windows, and someone smacked the glass beside Dalton's head with the tip of a baton, hard enough to make him jump, and waking up his temper.

Dalton rolled down the window and squinted into the beam of a halogen flashlight, seeing a vaguely military figure behind the light. The man had a steel ASP baton in his other hand. He leaned down into the window and put the light on Ray Fyke, who blinked back steadily.

"You come in plane?" barked a high, Chinese-sounding voice.

"Take that light out of my face," said Fyke.

"You come in plane?" the soldier barked at him, smacking the roof of the taxi with his baton and sending a sharp lance of pain through Dalton's skull, which, in turn, woke up the green scaly thing that lived deep down inside Dalton's brain. Then he did it again.

"You betta answer, boy! Get you outta car!"

Dalton glanced across at Fyke, who was now grinning back at him.

"Why are these kids so pissed off at us?"

"No idea. Let's find out," said Fyke, an edge in his voice.

Dalton sighed as the kid banged the roof a third time—he looked forward and saw Tangerine flinch every time the stupid kid dented her roof; the scaly thing that lived in his lizard brain now had a migraine—Dalton popped the door open, forcing the young soldier to give ground as he got out onto the roadway. They were now standing in the headlight glare of a vehicle that, from what Dalton could make out, looked like an armored Humvee with a big CIS .50 MG on a roof-mounted swivel. The soldier, an extremely muscular and apparently neckless young man with a military high-and-tight, wearing a starched and pressed Indonesian Marine Corps uniform with MP markings, backed away a little more and held the halogen light up in Dalton's face, effectively blinding him. Fyke was out of the car and on his feet on the other side, a second soldier in front of him, almost nose to nose if the kid had been a foot taller. The soldier facing Dalton had his ASP raised, the tip near Dalton's face, since he was using it to point at Dalton. Which was stupid, since Dalton could rip it out of his hand in less than a second if he wanted to. Which he didn't. Yet.

"What plane are you talking about?" said Dalton, trying for a placatory tone, trying to cool the situation down.

"Night Officer at Sam Ratulangi call. Say plane just land. No markings. You fly that plane? Come in at night. No papers!"

"Yes. I fly that plane. It has no markings because it's being repainted. And I showed the guard our papers. What the hell business is it of—"

"Unmarked plane? Why no markings?"

"It's being repainted. What are you so goddam angry about?"

"No angry *me*," screamed the kid, waving the ASP around in Dalton's face and tugging his pistol out with his left hand. "You big trouble! You under arrest! Get on knees now!"

He heard the other cop yelping at Fyke in Chinese and Fyke's calm, measured answer, also in Chinese, which Dalton did not speak. At least the kid in *his* face could speak English. Dalton tried one last time.

"How about you put the sidearm away and just tell me what the trouble is?"

The kid's eyes were huge in the headlight glare. He looked like he could be stoned on something. Probably adrenaline. And steroids, judging from his build. He put the pistol on Dalton, his finger inside the trigger guard: "You under arrest. You kneel down! Kneel down!"

Dalton lifted his hands up in front of him, palms out.

"Look, Corporal, if we can just—"

The soldier tensed, and, in a sharp, quick move with a lot of force in it, swung the ASP at Dalton's temple, a killing blow if it had landed. It didn't. Dalton caught the strike with his left hand—the spider-bitten hand—and a bolt of blue fire ran right up his arm all the way to his shoulder.

He heard a blow, and a strangled yelp, from the other side of the car. Fyke was not a yelper. He and the MP both turned to look. But they were committed now. Dalton caught the muzzle of the MP's pistol in his right hand, forcing the barrel up. The MP triggered a round, but the slug went zipping away into the night—he heard Tangerine screaming something in Chinese—and Dalton ripped the pistol out of the Marine's hand and slammed him across the cheekbone with the muzzle. The kid's head snapped back, and a ribbon of blood flared out in the glare of the headlights. The kid went down. Dalton booted him in the belly, just to make his point. From the huffing sound on the other side of the taxi, Fyke was doing roughly the same thing to the other MP. Fyke straightened up, panting a bit, laid his left hand on the roof, and looked across the car at Dalton.

"Kill the lights on that Humvee, Mikey."

Dalton ran across the gap, jerked open the door, and shut the Humvee down. When he came back, the lights were off on the taxi as well, and Fyke was leaning on the trunk, his arms crossed, his chest heaving.

"Another fine fix you've got me into, Stanley," he said. "What was that all about?"

The sound of rolling thunder cut off Dalton's reply. They looked up as a set of red lights appeared in the sky, riding a thudding, booming sound.

"A Blackhawk," said Fyke. "What do you want to do?"

"What the hell do they want?"

"No idea, lad. But make up your mind, because I have the strong impression that KIPAM won't give us much of a chance to explain."

"Can you run?"

Fyke shook his head.

"I can stumble a few yards, throw up, and pass out. Will that help?"

"Not much," he said, turning to the driver.

"Tangerine?"

She stuck her head out the driver's window, her eyes very wide.

"Can you drive with your lights off?"

"Yes, sir."

"Then get the hell out of here!"

"Yes, sir."

The tires churned up gravel and dust, and Tangerine's pink Mercedes was a memory in a few seconds. About a half mile out, she braked to take a curve. In the distance, the chopper veered suddenly off course to follow her taillights. It boomed right over their heads, a big Blackhawk with a red skull face painted on the hull. Fyke had already dragged his MP into the tree line. He stopped, breathing heavily, watching the chopper as it thundered by at two hundred feet.

"KIPAM Marines, all right. Jesus, I hope they don't shoot up Tangerine's taxi. What *have* we done to irritate those boys?"

"No idea," said Dalton. "How'd they miss the Humvee?"

"They won't next time," said Fyke, pointing to a second chopper, coming in from the same direction, a spotlight flickering around crazily as it skimmed the canopy.

"Things go to shit in a hurry in this corner of the world, don't they?" said Dalton, shaking the sting out of his left hand. It had come into play during the fight, and now it felt as if he had driven a spike through the middle of his palm.

"That they do," said Fyke. "The Humvee has one of those CIS .50s on the roof. You feel like a last stand, Mikey?"

The light from the Blackhawk lanced overhead and arced into the south, following the highway into Manado, tracking the receding lights of the first chopper.

"Maybe it has a radio too," said Dalton.

"Let's go see. What about these lads?"

"Cuff them to a palm trunk. Bring their pistols and their radios."

"Done, Captain."

Dalton dragged his man over to the nearest palm trunk, plucked his Streamlight out of the holster, jogged back over to the Humvee, tugged open the driver's door, using the MP's flashlight to check out the contents. The cramped interior held a suite of command-and-control electronics, most of which Dalton was pretty familiar with— the Indonesians got most of their gear from U.S. suppliers like Motorola and Microsoft—and there was a rear rack with two spotless M4s and a large box of ammunition. Behind the driver's seat was an open hatch, with an ammo case right under it and a belt of big Browning .50 caliber MG rounds rising up through the hatch to feed the roof-mounted machine gun. The Humvee was armored and looked like it had been fitted with bulletproof glass. They could do some damage, if it had to come to a fight, and if the Blackhawks didn't have anything other than the usual pintle-mounted light 7.62 MGs in the doorways. A few .50 caliber rounds in the right spot will take almost any chopper down, even an Apache gunship, which Dalton devoutly hoped the KIPAM did not have—please, God—because the problem with taking on a Hellfire-equipped Apache with a .50 caliber is roughly the same problem you encounter when you bring a butterfly net to a bear hunt.

Dalton did a quick battle-readiness assessment and concluded that if they made a stand right here, right out in the open, the best of all possible outcomes had them both chopped into Baco-Bits in two minutes or less. He needed to get some distance, lose that chopper, find them a place to go to ground, cool everybody out, lower the tempo, and get these lunatic KIPAM cowboys to please just *explain* themselves.

Fyke reached the passenger door with the pistols and the radios just as Dalton got himself settled in behind the driver's wheel. Fyke scrambled through the gap and stood up in the hatch, beside the .50. There were no keys in any U.S. military vehicle, and this was no different. He hit the START button, the diesel powered up, he tugged the wheel hard left, and powered the Humvee straight into the jungle, crashing through thickets of bougainvillea and scrub brush and swerving around tall, slender trunks of coconut palm. It was still dark under the canopy, but, in the breaks through the palm fronds, he could see a pale pink light spreading out across the sky.

He took the Humvee up a low hill, crested the hill, and roared down the other side. Fyke was up in the gunner's hatch, shining the way with the dim beam of the MP's halogen flash, hiding the light with the palm of his hand.

They had covered perhaps ten miles of mixed, open ground and sparse stands of coconut palms when the narrow cone of hard-white light flickered across a large metal shed, a smaller cluster of buildings—all dark and deserted-looking—and then settled on another low, shedlike structure made of bamboo and thatched in dry palms.

He leaned his head down into the cabin and shouted at Dalton.

"Shut her down, Mikey. Let me do a recce."

Mikey shut her down. Fyke loped heavily off into the darkness. Dalton had no idea how much pain the man was in, and Fyke was pretending he was just fine, which was SOP for the SAS. Well, Dalton was doing pretty much the same thing. He'd been *shivved in the googlies,* as Mandy had so elegantly phrased it, and yet here he was flitting about the jungle in Southeast Asia just as if he were still a sprightly young lad with a stellar future and no serious communicable diseases. Fyke was back in a few minutes.

"Looks like a deserted copra farm. Stick it in the barn."

Dalton drove the Humvee through a stand of overgrown copra plants, their leaves whipping at the windshield and leaving streaks of white sap across the glass, bounced twice, as the wheels jumped a low cinder-block fence, and slid across the threshold and into the darkness of the thatched barn. He shut the engine down again and leaned his forehead on the wheel, cradling his left hand in his right palm, his chest heaving. Fyke was lurching around in the dim, dappled interior of the barn, apparently looking for something. He stopped, staring, steadied the flash on something bulky, and stumbled into a shadow, emerging in a moment, dragging a long black hose. He stopped in front of the truck, aimed the hose at the windshield, and pressed the nozzle. A blast of water struck the Humvee, rocking it. Dalton sat inside the vehicle while Fyke hosed it down, from grille to tow bar.

He was cooling it off, lowering the heat signature, because those KIPAM Blackhawks would probably have infrared sensors fitted. He was quick, but, then, if recent experiences were anything to go by, Ray Fyke was harder to kill than herpes simplex. Fyke dropped the hose, came back to the driver's door, popped it open, and flopped back inside. He put his head against the headrest, blew out some air and sucked it back in again. In the silence, above the ticking of the engine and the pounding of their own hearts, they could hear the faraway sound of chopper blades thudding in the steamy night air. The sound got fainter, and then it was gone, and all they could hear was the *chirrup-chirrup* of crickets and nightjars and the sighing of the wind in the rafters. Something slimy struck the windshield of the Humvee.

"Bat shit," Fyke explained. "Barns are always full of them."

"The technical term is *guano,*" said Dalton. "And shouldn't they be out and about, not hanging around the rafters in the dead of night?"

"*Oot and aboot,* don't ye mean?" said Fyke, his teeth showing white in the dim light. He checked his watch, read the luminous dial. "Most of them are. But morning's coming, and they'll be done for the day. Hearth and home, and a jolly old bang at the missus. You got any smokes, by the way?"

Dalton pulled out a couple of Mandy's Sobranies, gave Fyke the pink one—it was hard to tell in the dark—took a blue one himself, lit them up.

"What do you think got those lads all stirred up?" said Fyke, after a while. A soft-pink light was showing in the rips and cracks of the barn roof, and they could see more and more of the interior of the barn as the morning opened up around them.

"Well, why don't we ask them?"

"If you turn on this comset, it'll send out a GPS identifier."

"Excellent point. How's your cell phone?"

"They can triangulate on a cell phone too."

"Not as easily. Only to the nearest tower. They already know our general area."

Fyke fumbled it out, flipped it open.

"Deader than Di and Dodi. Yours?"

Dalton flipped his open.

"Got a bit."

"Did you bring Mandy's? The one your pal Kiki is tracking?"

"Yes."

"You still got the GPS turned on?"

"Yes."

"So Kiki can sneak up on us and murder us all in our beds, is it?"

"That's the plan."

"Well, bringing that darling lad into our sea of troubles strikes me as kind of redundant now, don't it? I mean, we got an entire regiment of Komando Intai Para Amfibi hunting us down, and, if I recall correctly, you had a glass knife shoved into your gizzard only awhile ago and now you've got a spider bite on your hand that's probably, even as we speak, sending a horrible, incurable poison into your brain, so, any second now, you're gonna go into agonized convulsions and die screaming out Sassenach gibberish while peeing all over yourself, and I've got scorch marks on my balls and broken ribs and a bunch a teeth missing, and Delia says I have a bad ticker and am like to fall down dead at any moment, if the syphilis don't kill me first. What would you call us, Mikey, giving us all that?"

"Reminds me of the ad for the lost dog: 'Missing, one white-and-brown Jack Russell terrier. Three legs. Blind in one eye. Neutered. Got the mange. Right ear bitten off—'"

" 'Answers to Lucky'?" said Fyke. "I heard that one."

They had a good laugh at that, but Dalton turned the GPS off anyway. On a computer screen in Kotor, Montenegro, Branco Gospic saw the icon blip off and picked up his phone. Larissa answered. She had a short conversation with her father, and then called Kiki Lujac's cell phone. There was no answer. She left a message. On a screen at Crypto City, in Annapolis Junction, a Monitor picked up the signal and hit RECORD/NOTIFY. Three floors above him, the AD of RA was staring out the window at a grim November evening, thinking about Nikki Turrin and waiting for a phone call from a Major Alessio Brancati in Venice. In Washington, Deacon Cather was out to dinner with an old family friend, one of the Georgetown Harrimans, who had served with Allen Dulles. They were having osso buco—made with cream and not tomato sauce—and a very dry pinot grigio. His beeper went off. He glanced at the screen, saw the notification, and put the machine back in his pocket. The pinot was suspect. Cather thought that it might be corked. He raised his skeletal hand and called for the sommelier. In Kuta, Mandy Pownall was sleeping, sedated, dreaming of Cortona. The night nurse, who believed it was a help against spider bites, brought in a candle scented with eucalyptus oil, lit it, and set it on the bedside table. Delia Lopez thanked her, and went back to watching Mandy's chest rise and fall and silently chanting the Sorrowful Mysteries of the rosary. In Cortona, where it was raining hard, the ghost of Porter Naumann was sitting at a table in a medieval square near the Via Janelli, watching plumes of black smoke that stank of the grave rise up, hissing, from the ancient cobblestones. A strong wind, carrying the scent of crushed eucalyptus leaves, came rushing over the jagged stone walls and poured down into the square, shredding the plumes into wisps, and in a moment they were gone. In Florence, Cora Vasari opened her eyes and gasped softly. A nurse came into the dim room and put a cool hand on Cora's forehead, speaking gently, smiling down. *"Eucalypto,"* said Cora, *"fior del finocchio?"* The nurse said something soothing and pressed a button on the wall behind Cora's bed. In the coconut palm jungle six miles northwest of Manado, in the cockpit of a stolen Humvee, Micah Dalton was staring down at Mandy's cell phone and frowning:

"You wouldn't happen to know a phone number for KIPAM?"

Fyke blew some smoke out and shook his head.

"Try Information."

"You're kidding. You worked this region for years and you're telling me to call Information?"

"Have you got a better idea?"

"You know, I could have left you in Changi."

"Fine with me. I rather liked it there. Three squares. Lots of exercise."

"They were beating you bloody every day. Like clockwork."

"Sensible people take great comfort in routine. Phone Information."

Dalton did.

The operator told him that number was restricted.

"Restricted?" said Dalton. "Restricted to who?"

"*Whom,*" said Fyke.

"To people in the Army," she said, primly.

"Wouldn't people in the Army already know the number?"

"Yes. They would."

"Okay. I'm in the Army. You can tell me."

"If you were in the Army, you'd already know the number. Sir."

"I forgot it."

"You have a nice day, sir."

Dalton flipped the phone shut, gave Fyke an *I told you so* look. Fyke reached into his shirt pocket, pulled out a business card, handed it to Dalton.

PINK ELEPHANT TAXI

Tangerine Kwan, Owner

66-38-364-700

"You got her card?"

"We might need a cab again. Anyway, she's a pretty girl," said Fyke.

"Ray. She's what? *Eleven?*"

"I'd be like a father to her."

"Yeah. Father Rasputin."

Dalton punched in the numbers, waited. The line began to ring. It rang three times and a man answered, a hard, barking phrase in Chinese. It sounded very coplike, and Dalton made the intuitive leap that it probably belonged to a cop.

"I'm looking for Tangerine Kwan."

"You the American?"

"Yes. I'm the American. Who's this?"

"You come in the plane last night?"

"Yes. I'm also the man who almost had his head taken off by one of those steroidal assholes you're passing off as MPs. Who are you?"

"Mikey, you're a silver-tongued devil, to be sure," whispered Fyke.

"I am Major Kang Hannko, officer commanding First Brigade, Komando Intai Para Amfibi. You will tell us where you—"

"Major Kang, I'm Captain Micah Dalton, A Team, Fifth Special Forces, United States Army, out of Fort Campbell, Kentucky."

A pause.

"You are not a soldier. You show no soldier ID."

"I think this is all going pretty well, don't you?" said Fyke, who could hear both ends of the conversation.

"Can you work a phone, Major Kang?"

"Phone?"

"It's that electrical thingy you have in the hand that doesn't have your dick in it. The phone is bigger, and it glows in the dark. That's how you can tell them apart. I want you to call Sembawang Airfield in Singapore—"

Kang was skeptical.

"That is the American Marine Corps base—"

"Yeah. And ask for Major Carson Holliday. Officer commanding."

Muffled voices in the background at the other end of the line. Then a string of commands in Chinese, and then Major Kang was back on the line.

"You resisted arrest. You injured my men."

"I put your kid to sleep, Major Kang, because he tried to take my head off with a steel rod. How's he doing?"

"He's in the brig. Both in brig."

"Good. They need to be. Got your—"

"Wait. Don't hang up."

"Sure. Got all day."

More fast Chinese chatter in the background. Three minutes of this, then Kang was back, marginally less irritating.

"We wake him up. He is not very happy. Major Holliday say to ask you if you have any idea where York Hunt is?"

"York Hunt?" said Dalton, trying not to laugh. Fyke, however, was on the floor of the Humvee. "Well, that's a secret Marine Corps password."

"He also say you have . . ."

It was clear that Kang was listening to another phone at the same time.

"He say you have a . . . cranio-rectal inversion? What is this?"

"It's a way of looking at the world. Everything goes really dark."

Muffled talk, then Kang again, a slightly more polite version.

"Maybe we need to talk, Captain Dalton."

"Maybe we do, Major Kang."

"You will come in. Bring back my Humvee, too, maybe?"

"We can talk just fine here. Why the hard-on last night?"

"Hard-on?"

"Why the aggressive takedown. We flew in from Kuta—filed a flight plan and ID'd ourselves to the TC at Sam Ratulangi. Showed the duty guy our passports and papers—"

"You arrive in an unmarked plane."

"Yes."

"We are having some trouble with intruders. Airplanes. Choppers."

"What kind of trouble?"

"Not on this cell phone. You come in. Show me some ID. Then we maybe can talk about this trouble. Where are you?"

"Reasonably close. Why?"

More background chatter, and then Dalton and Fyke could hear a chopper in the distance but getting closer. Kang came back.

"You are maybe in the old copra farm, about ten mile east of highway?"

"What makes you think that?"

"I know the farm. Bats live there. Many bats."

"Okay."

"Many bats. They are flying around in cloud right now, thousand bats in a big black cloud. Maybe they do not go back in barn because KIPAM Humvee with two men is already in the barn."

Dalton and Fyke exchanged glances. Fyke shrugged.

"Maybe you're right, Major."

"Yeah. Maybe my dick's bigger than my phone too."

39

V-22 Osprey,
airborne over the Celebes Sea

A pale rose fire was lighting up the crest of a large storm front that seemed to take up most of the eastern horizon. Lujac stared at it through the right-side porthole, and shifted in the hard-frame seat. Across the aisle, Sergeant Ong Bo was snoring loud enough to be heard over the hammering drone of the two big props churning away on either side of the fuselage. Up front, the pilot, a taciturn Malay with a tight slit of a mouth and facial scarring that looked tribal, was staring out at the northern horizon and chewing what Kiki thought might be khat or coca leaves to keep him awake. In the rear, beside a large bulky shape wrapped in a tarp, a young Chinese boy in civilian clothes and a very military haircut sat with his back against the weapon, reading a weapons manual by the red glow of a bulkhead lamp. Beyond him, the tail section of the plane, the floor of which could be lowered down as a ramp, rattled and chattered in the wind stream. A few cracks could be seen around the edge of the ramp, letting in a rush of damp, chilly air. The entire craft rose up and shuddered, and settled on the air currents like a tugboat butting through a rolling sea.

Lujac was not enjoying the ride, and recent events had given him a great deal to think about, none of it pleasant. He closed his eyes and went wandering off to where it had started, back at Selaparang airstrip.

Sergeant Ong had walked across the tarmac and come to a stop in front of Lujac, who had the little silver pistol in his right hand, hanging down by the side of his leg. Sergeant Ong's face was slick and wet, and his thick lips were slack, but his eyes were cold and black, and had a tiny yellow glitter in the pupils. The rain was coming down harder, and the rattle of the drops on the tin roof had almost drowned out Sergeant Ong's words:

"You Mr. Lujac?"

"Yes."

"I know you."

"Really? How delightful. I am afraid I can't say the same."

"I am Sergeant Ong Bo. Of the Singapore Police Department."

The Osprey pilot had not shut down its engines. They rumbled and churned in the gathering dusk and blue exhaust fumes rose up into the evening sky and spread out across the jungle canopy.

"You must be so proud. How can I help you?"

"You know a man named Micah Dalton?"

"I know him, yes."

"Yes. You were in his room at the hotel. You know where he is now?"

"Last time I checked, he was a few miles from here, in Kuta."

"Yes. His plane there now. We come from Kuta to find you."

"Find me? Why?"

"You have evidence for us."

"I do?"

"Yes. Little pistol there in your hand."

"This?" said Lujac, lifting it up.

"Yes. That belong to Corporal Ahmed."

"I don't think so."

"Yes. I know that pistol. We found Ahmed. In Changi hotel."

"Really. By *found him,* you mean he was . . . hiding?"

"No. He was dead. We find him because man who killed him sent digital pictures to Home Ministry to show him. Dirty pictures. Filthy. We figure out where he was from pictures. Changi-Lah Hotel. Top floor."

"Okay. And this concerns me how . . . ?"

"We have reason believe Mr. Micah Dalton kill him. You have way to follow him. Cell-phone GPS. So you come with me and we go find Mr. Dalton together, and we do justice to him."

"You think Micah Dalton murdered your Corporal Ahmed?"

Ong smiled, a sight Lujac could have easily forgone.

"At end of day, Mr. Lujac, everybody think so. Ahmed was a criminal. Pervert. No one miss Corporal Ahmed in Singapore. Dalton will be blame. If we have Ahmed's gun to find. And digital camera to leave."

Lujac looked at Ong for a while.

"Just how did you know to find me here?"

"You have bags?"

"I have one."

"You go get."

Ong bowed, turned toward the idling Osprey, began to walk back across the tarmac. Lujac followed, caught up to him, stopped him with a hand. Ong's arm was padded with fat, but underneath was real muscle.

"How did you know where to find me?"

"Mr. Lujac, we working for the same man."

"We? Who the hell is *we?*"

"You. Me. Mr. Gospic in Kotor. And Minister Chong."

That shut Kiki up for a moment.

"Chong Kew Sak? The Home Minister? He's in on this?"

"This is his plane. The Osprey. Belong to Home Ministry."

"What does Chong get out of this?"

"Same like all. The money."

The pilot sounded a klaxon horn, and revved the rotors.

Sergeant Ong's face closed up.

"Enough talking. Time to go."

They had taken off in a few minutes, banked, and headed north. Hours later, as the dawn was tinting the eastern sky, they were at six thousand feet and following the Sulawesi coastline eastward, passing the clustered lights of Diapati. Manado was about a hundred miles along the coast. Lujac had no idea what Ong and his companions planned to do when they got to Manado, but he figured it had something to do with whatever was under the tarp in the back of the plane. Nobody was talking about it to him, anyway. He flipped open his phone, saw that it had shut itself down when the battery got low. He had a spare battery, switched it out, and turned the phone back on.

Amazingly, he had a signal. And a message notice.

He hit PLAY and heard Larissa's voice.

"Lujac, this is me. The GPS indicator for the phone got shut off just a few minutes ago. So now we can't track him. The last indicator put him a few miles northeast of a place called Manado, in Sulawesi. There's an airport there, called Sam Ratulangi. Call me when you get this message."

Lujac checked the time the message was sent.

Less than thirty minutes ago. He put the phone away, reached out and tapped Sergeant Ong on the shoulder. Ong came awake immediately, sitting up and blinking, as he tried to recall where he was and why.

"What problem?"

"Dalton's cell phone. He just switched the GPS off."

Ong's face did not change. He stared at Lujac for a full minute, and then he got up and walked through to the cockpit, leaning down to say something to the pilot. The pilot nodded.

Ong came back to his seat, belted himself in. The Osprey banked, and the tone of the props changed, powering up, as the plane turned in to the rising sun. They were obviously now going to someplace other than Manado.

"Where are we going now?"

"We going to overfly airport near Manado. Sam Ratulangi. If the plane is still there, we set down and wait. Sooner or later, he come back."

"And if he doesn't?"

"He will."

"Tell me, Sergeant Ong. Why's Dalton in Manado in the first place?"

"We think he looking for something."

"Do we know what it is he's looking for?"

Ong blinked at Lujac for a while, clearly unwilling to let him in on the larger picture.

"Yes," he said, finally. "We know."

"Is he close to finding it?"

"Yes. Very close."

"And if he finds it?"

"It would be bad."

Lujac sat back and looked at Ong for a few moments. Ong looked down, so Lujac could not read his expression. Ong knew more about Gospic's operation than Lujac did, and it was pretty clear that Ong wasn't going to fill him in. Which meant that Ong figured Lujac didn't have much of a part left to play in it. Lujac suspected that his usefulness to Ong and to Branco Gospic had come to an end when Dalton shut his GPS indicator off. He still had the stainless Colt pistol. Ong had a large Glock tucked into his belt. The pilot had a Beretta strapped to his thigh. The boy at the back did not appear to be armed. Lujac could not fly an Osprey any better than he could fly a Gulfstream. To summarize, Kiki Lujac was a dead man.

"I have a suggestion."

"What?"

"Your whole plan depends on Dalton coming back to this plane of his. If he doesn't, we're screwed. There's only one other way you can play this."

"Okay."

"We go to whatever he's looking for. Wait. When he gets there . . ."

Ong closed his eyes, and, for a time, looked profoundly weary. Lujac didn't blame him. When this was all over and everybody else was dead, he was going to take the *Subito* somewhere warm and sultry and stay there until he forgot his own name. Ong opened his eyes after a moment.

"Okay. We go there."

"Is it far?"

Ong closed his eyes again, put his head back, folded his hands.

"Wait. You will see."

40

KIPAM Marine Blackhawk, airborne, one hundred and eight miles east of Manado, northern Sulawesi, the Indonesian Archipelago

Major Kang turned out to be a serious combat leader whose grasp of the English language simply needed some polishing. A rocky-faced old lifer in his mid-fifties, with a touch of the thousand-yard stare in his eyes, he was clearly adored by his men, and the little KIPAM base seemed orderly and well run. Kang had listened carefully to Dalton as he explained, in simple terms, leaving out volumes, why they had come, in the middle of the night, on an unmarked plane, on a mission to Manado. Kang had asked a couple of acute questions and listened patiently to the answers.

"So you think a stolen ship might have passed through the Celebes Sea. Maybe right by Manado?"

"Yes, sir."

Kang sat back at his desk at the KIPAM base, looked out at the perimeter wire and the low, palm-covered hills beyond the base. A pair of Blackhawks was sitting on the pad, being worked over by ground crew. A platoon of T-shirted young Marines was running cadence on a soccer field at the far end of the drill ground. The sound of their chant came across the hardpan, faint but clear, the insistent, rhythmic pounding of the words sounding like home to Ray Fyke and Micah Dalton, sounding like an old familiar song sung in an unknown language.

"We patrol these waters all time, Captain Dalton. Not likely to miss very much. Also, we keep radar sweep. Pirates are a big problem in these waters. So our eyes always open. Ships go by, yes. Busy channel. Some tankers, yes."

"Do you check the papers of these ships?"

Kang made a gesture, taking in the tiny base.

"We are not . . . equip? Too many jobs. Anyway, ships that do not stop in Diapati or Manado are not our problem."

"Did you see a tanker, like the one Mr. Fyke has described to you, did any of your air or sea patrols pick up on a tanker like that?"

"Boat you describe, this could be any tanker. Yes, we see a few—maybe nine or ten go through the Celebes Sea past Manado every week. Far offshore, because this is shoal water, very hard to navigate. But this ship, the *Mingo Dubai*? I remember a notice. It sank. Cleared Malacca Strait, and then break in two in big storm. One survivor. They put him in Changi jail."

"That ship never sank, sir," said Fyke, with some heat.

"But report says they do a sonar scan of the seafloor there. Lots of big iron down there, east of Malacca. Ship is down there, not in the Celebes Sea."

"With respect, sir," said Fyke, controlling his anger, "the Japanese lost a lot of shipping in that channel during the war. There's no way to tell one hull from another. And I give you my word as a soldier, Major Kang, the *Mingo Dubai* did not sink. It was hijacked by pirates."

"You know this, Sergeant?"

"Yes, sir. I do."

Kang looked as if he'd like to ask Fyke why he was so sure. But something in Fyke's eyes suggested that it might not be wise.

"Why would pirates take ship through the Celebes Sea. Most pirates take a stolen ship to China, or maybe Mindanao."

"No idea, sir."

"Major Kang," said Dalton. "This trouble you were talking about. What kind of trouble was it?"

"What kind . . . ?"

Kang went quiet, looking at the two men sitting in his office.

"You two are not just soldiers, right?"

Fyke did not react, but Dalton nodded.

"We're looking into the disappearance of this ship because we think it might pose a security threat to the United States."

"So you are CIA?"

"We're sort of freelancers," said Dalton.

"Okay. But for the CIA?"

"In effect. Yes."

More contemplative regard from the lifer. Steel wheels spinning.

"Tell you what. I will show you *my* trouble, you will tell me what you see, maybe then we can talk about your trouble. How does that sound?"

"Sounds like a deal, sir," said Dalton.

Kang picked up the phone, ordered up a KIPAM Blackhawk, and they were airborne, heading east into the sea green channel between Sulawesi and Papua New Guinea an hour later. The sun was coming up out of a storm bank over Papua, and the Celebes Sea looked like a sheet of etched green glass. They flew high and fast. A Blackhawk can do around one-eighty, so they were hovering over a tiny tropical island called Pulau Maju forty-five minutes after they lifted off from the KIPAM base.

The island, which was shaped almost exactly like a shark's tooth, was a coral atoll that had formed around a volcanic cone thousands of years ago, like most of the islands in the Indonesian Archipelago. Four miles deep and five miles wide, it had a peak in the center, jagged, like a broken tooth, and the land, sloping away from this conical peak like a green felt skirt around a Christmas tree, was ridge-backed and rocky and coated with dense jungle, dotted with stands of coconut palms and bamboo groves.

It looked like difficult terrain to Dalton and Fyke, ground you would not want to have to fight in or over. Major Kang was leaning out the open side door of the Blackhawk, staring down at a village he had called Pasirputih, the only village on the island.

The KIPAM pilot brought the Blackhawk to a hover about five hundred feet above the village, which was not much more than a large cluster of cinder-block and tin buildings around a long, narrow inlet that ran into a long fissure, or gap, in the volcanic base of the island. It was a unique feature, almost a fjord, about two thousand feet long and a couple of hundred feet wide. Halfway up the fjord, the channel took a hard left turn. Beyond the turning, at the closed end of the fjord, there was the burned-out wreckage of what might have been at one point some sort of cannery, now nothing more than a tangled heap of charred poles and caved-in tin roofing and the remains of a great deal of bamboo scaffolding.

The village itself looked deserted, and several of its main buildings also looked as if they had been either burned or torn down by hand. No dogs ran in the ruins, no cattle wandered through the glades, and no villagers looked up at them as they drifted across the site, the downdraft kicking up dust devils on the packed earth, and flattening the sea grass.

"What are we looking at?" Dalton asked, shouting over the roar of the engines. Major Kang shook his bald head slowly, his expression grave.

"We are looking at a massacre."

He spoke into his headset, and the pilot banked the chopper, flared it out, and set it down on the beach, fifty feet from the water-line. They hopped out—Fyke, with some help from one of the two young KIPAM Marines who had come along; Dalton and Major Kang; and the pilot, a lean and lanky kid, quite tall for a Chinese man. Dalton had been warned by one of the two Marines in the escort detail that the MP Ray Fyke had taken down a few hours before was the pilot's younger brother. Which probably explained the pilot's stony manner and hostile silence. Kang led them up the beach and into the main area of the village.

"We clean up the bodies. All over here, and in the hills. Four hundred sixty-two people. Boys. Girls. Old men. Women. May be some still in the jungle, but nobody alive here. Also place was set on fire. What you call *accelerant*—gasoline. Anything bamboo or wood. We think at first a terror group call Babi Rusa Brigade. They like pretend they are Abu Sayyaf, Jemaya Islamiya, like that—al-Qaeda wannabe—but really all they do is pirate stuff and extort money from villagers."

He got onto one knee, dug down into the sand, and came up with five or six spent shell casings, held them out for Dalton and Fyke to look at.

Fyke picked one up, turned it in his fingers.

"Seven-six-two. NATO."

Kang nodded,

"Yes. How many shell casings like this you think we find?"

Fyke looked at Dalton, shook his head.

"I'd have to guess, couple of hundred?"

"So far, we find more than ten thousand rounds. Just in the village."

"Ten *thousand?*" said Dalton.

Kang nodded again, his expression hardening up as he recalled what it had been like to walk through this village a few hours after it had been wiped out.

"M134," said Fyke. "Had to be."

"Yeah." He looked up into the sky, then past the booming surf to the broad plain of glimmering green sea. "Came in airborne."

"Had to be in a chopper. M134. Six barrels. Made by General Electric. Thing weighs forty pounds loaded, and vibrates like crazy. Rate of fire, over five thousand a minute."

"Not a chopper," said Kang, who had given the matter a lot of thought. "Too far to come. Most chopper range less than three hundred miles. Had to have a base inside that perimeter. And it was not one of ours. And not from Papua either. We work with them all the time. All accounted for. Had to be a plane."

"Ten thousand casings in this sector. ID any more areas?"

"Yes. Up there," he said, nodding toward the open end of the long, narrow bay. They walked along the beach and reached the mouth of the inlet. The water here looked much deeper, as if the floor of the cut had been dredged out. Dalton stood at the edge and stared down into the deep green water. There was something down there.

Boats, rafts. Tangled wooden structures.

He shaded his eyes and saw that there were perhaps fifteen or twenty small craft scattered around the bottom of the lagoon.

And something else—a large, angular object with two long tubes . . .

"That's an antiaircraft gun," he said. "Looks like something the Japanese left here."

"Yes," said Kang. "Also down there we find over sixty men and boys. All had weapons. Over here"—he walked around to a depression in the ground; the sand looked like it had been bulldozed into a heap and then plowed back—"here we find a pit. Maybe every-body in village. Men. Boys. Old women. Young girls. All had been shot many times with this bullet. This seven-six-two NATO. There was a . . . ?"

He made a gesture, indicating a spearhead.

"A lance? A stake? On it is stuck a head. Old man named Bittagar Chulalong. He was headman of Pasirputih. Somebody cut his head off and stick on this. Leave him there. In that water, maybe thousands of shell casings. Too many to bring up. We find most in the sand. There will be more up there."

He pointed to the jungles covering the sides of the cliffs.

"Were the casings scattered all over, or concentrated in these fire areas?" asked Dalton. Major Kang had to work out the meaning, but he was quick enough.

"No. Many in one spot. More in another."

"But not a trail, one after the other?"

"No. All in heaps."

Dalton looked at Fyke, who nodded.

"Had to be a chopper, Major. Planes have to strafe. Choppers can hover. That's how you get all those casings in one area. People were concentrated there; the shooter comes in, hovers, lights them up with his minigun. Drive motor is electric, operates so fast you can't see individual rounds. Just a buzzing sound, and everything in front of it just disintegrates. He could lay down twenty thousand rounds in five minutes. The spent casings would shower down while he raked the crowds. A gun like that, you can kill everybody in a sector in five minutes. Major, are you sure it couldn't have been a chopper?"

"Pretty sure. Like I say, short range. We searched for a base from Diapati all way to Papua; all the little islands too. No chopper."

"What was up at the end of the valley here?"

"Come on. I will show you."

They walked in single file along the edge of the inlet. The hills rose up sharply on both sides until they were in a shaded gorge. After about a thousand yards, the trail took a sharp left turn into a narrow valley, bounded by volcanic cliffs thinly covered in jungle greenery and stubby palms. Dalton stood at the edge of the gorge and looked down into the water, which was not the right color.

"This channel. It's deep. Even this far from the shore. Must be fifty, sixty feet down."

"Yes," said Kang. "They used to have cannery here. Many years ago. Russian company. They bring in barge and dredge out the channel so they can bring in big boats right to loading dock.

"How long ago?" asked Fyke.

"Maybe twenty years. All gone now. Just ruins."

"The factory looks like it was blown up."

"Yes. Fire too. All fresh."

Dalton and Fyke stood there, looking up the cut at the tangled heaps of bamboo and rusted iron about five hundred feet away.

"Where's the canning machinery?" said Dalton.

"Sold for scrap by Bittagar. Long time. Nothing there now but rusted conveyer belts and boilers. Anything too big to move."

Something was fluttering in the undergrowth a few feet away. Dalton climbed up the hillside and saw a piece of cloth, shredded, singed, in tatters. He held it up to the light. A woodland camo pattern was still visible. The thing was made of nylon netting, strong but light. And it was new. He stood there on the hillside, staring down at Fyke and Kang, and then letting his eyes travel along the inlet, from the sharp left turn to the charred wreckage at the end of the channel.

"Ray, how long is this part of the inlet?"

Fyke ran a practiced eye over the ground.

"Five hundred feet. Give or take."

"And wide?"

"Two hundred feet here. Maybe a hundred and fifty at the far end."

Dalton slid down the hillside and handed the piece of camo netting to Fyke. "There are scraps of this stuff all over that hillside, Ray. The camo net must have been huge. Major, do you have any way of finding out who the people were who ran this cannery? You said they were Russians?"

"There would be records in Manado. Many fishers there took their catch to Pulau Maju. I will find out."

"Thanks. Ray. Do you see what I'm seeing?"

Fyke stared at the cut for a while.

Then he had his Gestalt moment.

"The tanker. They brought it *here*. Hid it under the camo netting. So no satellites or planes could spot it. What's up there is what's left of the dry dock. They brought the *Mingo Dubai* right here."

Kang was watching the exchange.

"The ship? *Mingo Dubai?*"

"Yes," said Fyke, his face reddening as the implications sank in. "The *Mingo* was five hundred feet long. A beam of ninety feet. She drew almost thirty feet of water fully loaded. This channel has been dredged out to sixty feet. It would have been perfect. A hundred miles from anywhere."

"These the same people killed all the villagers?" asked Kang.

"I think so," said Dalton.

"Who are these people?"

"Serbians. From Montenegro."

"You know this for sure?"

"Pretty sure."

"But where'd it go from here, Mikey?" Fyke asked.

"I don't know. How many tankers like the *Mingo* are there?"

"Worldwide? Maybe five hundred, maybe a thousand, in her class. She's one of the smallest types, a Seawaymax. Obsolete now. Too small."

"How much can she carry?"

"Sixty thousand metric tons. Why?"

"Branco Gospic had the ship taken. Who does Gospic trade with?"

"Terrorists. The Chechyns. Taliban. Al-Qaeda. Iran. North Korea."

"If they got hold of a tanker, what do you think those assholes would do with it? Turn legit and go into the shipping business? Or fill it full of ammonium nitrate—or something worse—and sail it into a U.S. port?"

"Jesus."

"Exactly. How many ports in the United States?"

"Why just the U.S.?"

"Because that's who we work for, Ray. We'll let everyone else know, alert all their agencies, but we're concentrating on the U.S. How many?"

"Hell . . . maybe a hundred and fifty."

"What are the major ones? I mean, ones that could handle a mid-sized tanker like the *Mingo?*"

"Got to be at least eighty. Port of South Louisiana. Houston. New York and New Jersey—"

"New York? Christ. They're gonna have to go to red, bring in Homeland Security, the Navy, the Coast Guard—"

"Major, can you patch us through to a landline from the chopper?"

Major Kang nodded.

"Sure. Come with—"

Two things happened at once.

The Major's radio set beeped, and they heard the sound of a plane closing in. The sound seemed to come from all around them, echoing and reechoing up and down the inlet. Kang picked up his radio and thumbed the CALL button, barking out a question in Chinese.

The reply was a tinny crackle. Kang issued some orders. He was putting the radio back in his belt and reaching for his pistol when a large aircraft flew straight across the cut, blocking out the sun, a twin-rotor Osprey, olive-drab, without markings.

They all looked up as the Osprey, in hover mode, hammered down the gorge toward the KIPAM Blackhawk parked on the beach. The rear loading ramp was open, and there was a figure in the bay, a young Asian boy, in jeans and a bomber jacket, standing behind a tripod-mounted weapon. An M134 Minigun. Beside the gun mount stood a crate with a belt of ammo running up to the gun. The kid on the trigger was looking east toward the beach and did not seem to notice them.

"Jesus, Mary, and Joseph," said Fyke, staring up.

The Osprey disappeared behind one of the hills, banking. Kang was on the radio, speaking urgently. They heard the sound of the Blackhawk's engines starting to turn over. Then they heard a sound, like a silk curtain being ripped apart, but insanely loud and close. Kang and Dalton looked at each other. There was a popping sound, return fire—Kang's two Marines had M4s—and the pilot had a Beretta—then the ripping sound returned, a terrible rising-and-falling sound, with a machinelike whirring chatter under that, like a chain saw cutting through lumber. It cut off abruptly.

They heard the rotor pitch changing, getting louder. The Osprey was coming around again. The three men looked for cover. There was only the tangled wreckage at the far end of the gorge. Nothing had to be said. They ran for cover, stumbling along the rocky edge of the channel, Kang out front, Dalton staying close to Fyke, Fyke laboring, limping, breathing hard.

They were almost there when a black shadow crossed the green hillside about a hundred yards down from their position, and a moment later the Osprey thundered ponderously across the roof of the gorge, coming to a stop midchannel, turning slowly as the pilot searched the ground.

The ruins of the cannery were fifty feet, thirty feet—the Osprey was coming around slowly, sunlight glinting off the windshield, the rotors two disks of spinning light. Dalton, looking back as he ran, could make out the sharp brown face of a man sitting at the controls, and someone else, a round, flabby face, a face he knew, leaning into the window next to the pilot, also scanning the cut. Kang had stopped at the edge of the wreckage, staring up at the Osprey, his face hardening. He jerked out his Beretta just as Dalton reached him.

"No, Major. He hasn't seen us yet—"

Kang paid no attention. He lifted the piece up, aimed. Fyke and Dalton stumbled past him and burrowed into the ruins behind him. It stank of gasoline and death. The beams of the old cannery had tumbled inward, tenting a space beneath them; hard, stony ground, littered with spent shell casings, slivers of bamboo, spilled oil, and bits of pulpy material that were probably decaying human flesh. This cave-like opening led back to a larger area, cut into the hillside, some kind of storage room.

Dalton and Fyke, on their hands and knees, scrambled toward the area, with no thought other than to get as much solid matter as they could between them and that minigun. They heard the Major's Beretta as he fired—single shots, carefully aimed, measured, one after the other, reaching to nine before the minigun opened up on him. Again that terrible zippering sizzle.

A hard rain of rounds chattered across the ruins. They couldn't see what had happened to Kang. They didn't need to. Bits of Kang were splattering against their backs as they ran. Fyke fell hard, slamming his knee into a jutting stone. His face went white with pain. Dalton reached him, tugged him across the last ten feet into the little open area at the back. They came to a full stop up against what looked like the curved side of a huge steam boiler, set right up against the face of the cliff.

They could go no farther. Fyke pulled himself up, set his back against the boiler, pulling out his Beretta, breathing in short, sharp gasps. The space was coal dark and smelled of burned flesh. Thin shafts of sunlight pierced through gaps in the ruins in front of them, blades of hard-yellow light, with motes of dust drifting inside them. They could hear the thrumming sound of the Osprey; the pounding of her rotors seemed to bounce off the rocks behind their heads. A huge black shadow cut off the thin beams of sunlight. The vibration of her rotors and the hurricane wind of her downdraft drove clouds of dust up into their eyes, choking them. The Osprey hovered overhead for a moment. Dalton and Fyke were holding their breaths, looking up; their pistols were useless. There was a moment of stillness inside the cascade of wind and the pounding beat of the rotors. They distinctly heard a metallic snap, the gunner pulling the lever, and then the fire rained down again, for a full minute, six thousand rounds, each round the size of a lipstick tube. The minigun was literally shredding the wreckage, the gunner methodically sweeping the muzzle back and forth, pouring rounds down on the ruins, brass shell casings tumbling out of the loading bay and falling down in a cascade, the casings tinkling as they fell like coins through the cracks and fissures, some of them dropping right in front of Dalton and Fyke. The firing seemed to go on forever, a terrible, drumming impact. Fyke had his hands over his ears; Dalton was staring out at the open ground, watching the rounds drilling in, stitching an exploding trench right across the stones and coming closer. Closer, stone chips flying, stinging their faces. Then the firing stopped.

THE OSPREY HOVERED for a time, turning slowly in the sunlight, the gunner staring down at the smoking ruin below him and thinking that nothing could have survived that. Sergeant Ong came to the open bay, looked down. The boy watched him, his brown eyes wide and his hands slightly numb from the high-frequency vibration of the weapon.

"If there's anybody there, Mr. Ong, they have to be dead."

Ong looked down at the tangle of steel and wood for a while, and then turned and looked back into the darkness of the interior. Lujac was standing there, staring back out at him.

"No," said Ong. "We have to make sure. We put it down on beach. Come back on foot. If Dalton alive in there, we burn him out."

Lujac could barely hear what Ong was saying over the roar of the engines and the ringing in his ears. But he got the general idea. He came forward to the open bay and looked down at the smoldering ruins a hundred feet below him. Then he looked over at Ong, smiled brightly, and shot him in the middle of the forehead with Corporal Ahmed's little popgun. Ong tumbled out of the open bay, falling awkwardly, arms flailing, and slammed into the wreckage, hard, splitting open like a mango. The boy at the gun station was staring back at Lujac, his mouth open, a shy, nervous smile playing around the corners of his lips.

Lujac glanced back, saw the pilot craning around to look toward the back of the plane, unsure of what had just happened. Lujac patted the cute little gunner boy affectionately—perhaps more than affectionately—on the side of the face and then walked back through the interior to the cockpit. Lujac put his silver gun in his pocket, lifted his hands up to show he was harmless, and sat down in the copilot's chair.

"And what's your name?" he asked, unfurling a broad warm smile.

"Sam Bobby Gurlami."

"I suggest you get us the hell out of here, Sam Bobby Gurlami."

"Why?"

"Because you just shot the shit out of a KIPAM Blackhawk and killed a whole lot of Marines, and I'm willing to bet at least one of them got to his radio before he died. They will resent this. Extremely. People will come."

Sam Bobby took this in, and then he powered the Osprey up and hit the button that closed the rear bay. They were at a thousand feet and climbing when he brought the nacelles forward and turned the chopper into an airplane. He had it up to three hundred miles an hour a few minutes after that. Sam Bobby got the Osprey settled down and then looked over at Lujac.

"Why did you kill Sergeant Ong?"

"Because, my dear Sam Bobby, he was going to get us all killed."

"How do you know that?"

"Recently, I have been making something of a study of our Mr. Dalton, and I have learned a few lessons along the way, one of which is not to crawl into a long, narrow pipe when there's a crocodile at the other end."

"Okay. I can see that."

"Did you know what this was all about?"

"No. All we knew was that when we got the call we were supposed to come to Pulau Maju and shoot the place up. Kill everybody on the island."

"And did you?"

Sam Bobby gave him a large, wet-lipped leer.

"Rock and roll! Like killing bunnies with a ball-peen hammer."

"Tell me, was there a ship here when you arrived?"

"Yeah. Big oil tanker. Five-hundred-foot at least. Brand-spanking-new."

"Did Ong tell you anything about that?"

"No. I asked. He said to shut the fuck up. So I did."

"What the story on the kid back there?"

"He's my son."

Lujac looked back. The boy had the minigun tarped and was sweeping up some stray shell casings. He had his iPod turned on, and was dancing a little two-step while he worked. Lujac figured the kid was a psycho, which was fine by him. The lovely thing about psychos was they were reliable, hardheaded people who were not easily panicked and did not get all gummed up with pointless emotions such as sympathy or guilt.

"How did you get this Osprey?"

"Ong requisitioned it. It belongs to the Home Ministry."

"Ong said this was Chong's plane. I didn't believe him."

"Ong's a fucking Sergeant. Nobody hands you one of these Ospreys if you're a Sergeant. You have to have some pull."

"So you figure Ong was right. That Chong is in on . . . whatever it is?"

"Sure. Has to be. We were gonna be rich. Now I don't know."

"What was your cut?"

"Ong said we'd each get fifty thousand."

"Fifty thousand is rich to you?"

"Damn right. We were going to get into the landscaping business."

Lujac figured what Ong had planned for Sam Bobby Gurlami and his kid was a chance to get very deep into the landscape itself, and stay there.

"But you had no idea what, exactly, the . . . the game . . . was?"

"No. But there was a lot of money in it. Ong was going to buy a resort in Phuket with what he got. If it was enough to turn Minister Chong, then it has to be millions. In Singapore, you cheat or take a bribe, they kill you."

"So I've heard. Tell me, Sam Bobby, do you like money?"

Sam Bobby showed his teeth, very white against his walnut hide. "Yeah. Sure I do. It's all about the money."

"Then you are about to earn a whole lot of money."

"More than Ong was going to give us?"

"Sergeant Ong was a fat, cheap prick. I mean, did you *see* that suit?"

41

Royal Air Force Lockheed P-3 Orion, nine hundred miles due west of Diego Garcia, the Indian Ocean

They were on a routine shakedown flight, training up some new people cycling in from the Reserves. The newbies were all back in the main cabin, learning about the surveillance and listening gear that had just been installed. The Orion was a four-engine patrol plane, maybe twenty years old, and had spent most of its service life flying these SigInt operations out of the airfield at Diego Garcia. The pilot, W. O. "Bingo" Binnings, two years away from retirement, was wondering how he would adjust to a life far less vivid than this one, and his copilot, a young East Indian woman named Audrey Singh, with three years of flying, was staring out at the vast shimmering expanse of the Indian Ocean and thinking of her upcoming physical—she was pregnant and had told no one about it, especially not her husband, for reasons we need not pry into here—when she saw something like a small black speck, floating in the middle of a field of shifting light, two thousand feet below her wing.

"Bingo, do you see that?"

Binnings, an older man, wore glasses and did not like to admit, even to himself, that his eyes were beginning to fail him.

"Where are we looking, Audrey?"

Singh pointed down and to her right.

"Down there, bearing one-nine-one. Small black thing. Do you see it?"

Binnings could make out nothing in the sidelong glare of the setting sun, but he had faith in the girl's young eyes.

"Shall we go down, take a look?"

"Yes. Please."

He put the plane into a slow bank and went back along their route, bringing the plane down to five hundred feet off the chop. He banked again and retraced their route, slowing their airspeed as much as he dared. Singh was leaning forward in her seat, frowning out at the seascape, using a pair of binoculars to scan the sea, as they raced over it at three hundred and fifty miles an hour. Something black was bobbing on the horizon. They were on it, over it, and thundering past it in a few seconds.

"What was it?"

"It was a boat! An open boat."

"We're a thousand miles from anywhere, Audrey. Are you sure?"

"Go 'round again, Bingo. Please."

"As you like it, my dear."

He did the circuit again, and as they came back on the line he handed her a digital camera.

"Get a shot, if you can."

"Okay."

Once again, they were moving far too fast to get a good look. But it was definitely an open boat, some sort of twin-engine cigarette boat, adrift in the water, rolling madly in the swells. There was no one in the boat, but something black and vaguely manlike was lying on the bow. A gull was sitting on its chest. The gull fluttered heavily off when they flashed by again. Singh snapped a string of pictures, and then she flipped the display panel open and hit REPLAY. She stared down at the images for a few seconds, and then he heard her slow intake of breath.

"Oh my God," she said. "It's a man."

She handed the camera to Bingo, who shaded the screen with his hand and held it up close. She was right. Spread-eagled on the bow of the speedboat was a tall, skinny black male—probably male—wearing what was left of some kind of tan uniform. He was shoeless, and it looked like the birds had been at him, because there were holes ripped in his shirt and pants and dried blood clots all over him. His face was a nightmare, most of the edible flesh already torn away by gulls, and his eyes had been thoroughly pecked out as well, nothing left but two gaping black sockets full of crusted blood.

"My God," said Bingo Binnings. "Note the bearings and the GPS, and call the base. I'll make one more run, and we'll drop a beacon. They'll have to scramble one of the Ospreys."

WHICH THEY DID. But night comes down like the lid on a coffin this near the equator, so it was the next day before they managed to find the boat again. The pilot hovered the Osprey over the drifting boat, and a rescue diver rappelled down to the deck; very hazardous duty, what with the wind, and the downdraft from the rotors, and the sea building so that the boat was leaping and bucking about like a hog in a gate. But the diver got himself safely down and knelt beside the half-eaten figure on the bow.

He keyed his helmet mike.

"Bloody hell," he said, into his mike. "This man's been nailed to the bow. Bloody nailed!"

"Say again," came the voice of the crew chief, leaning out of the open bay, held in by a safety strap.

The diver looked up at him.

"He's been nailed to the bow. Through his wrists and ankles."

"Yow! Must have pissed somebody off," said the crew chief. "See if he's got any ID on him."

The diver gritted his teeth, held his breath, and patted the man down. He felt something in his shirt pocket, tugged it out, a sheaf of papers, bloody, folded, and crumpled. He managed to get one open, held it flat against the body's chest.

"It's a bill of lading."

"A what?"

"A bill of lading. A cargo manifest."

"Does it say what ship?"

"Hard to read. The *Mingo* . . . something. *Mingo Dubai*, I think."

"Well, stuff it in your vest. We'll go through it. Can you un-nail him?"

"Not without doing some damage."

"Well, he's dead, isn't he? He's not going to care."

"Look, Frank, why can't we just leave him be?"

"What? Nailed to a boat? Left to drift? He's an affront to the bloody senses, you manky Scots git, not to mention a hazard to fucking navigation. We can't just leave him here."

"Can't we sink the boat? I mean, he's . . . all nailed down."

"Don't be such a pantywaist. Pry him loose and strap him up. We'll haul him back to Diego and give him a decent burial."

The diver shrugged, cursed the crew chief silently, pulled out his pry knife, went to work on the body's left ankle. He heard something like wood creaking against wood, looked up and saw, with a thrill of pure horror that stayed with him for the rest of his career, that the body was moving: the neck stretching out, growing rigid, corded sinews rising in the sun-scorched skin. The lipless mouth opened slowly, the fingers twitched weakly, and, from the gaping, toothless, and tongueless mouth, came a faint but terrible rasping moan. The diver jerked back, dropping his pry knife into the deep.

"Christ on a fucking crutch!"

"What?"

"This poor bastard is still alive."

42

Airborne,
inbound to the USA

No KIPAM Marine had gotten to a radio, and the M134 Minigun had chewed the Blackhawk to tiny ribbons of aluminum and chips of plastic. It had also shredded Major Kang into a kind of pulpy pink paste with boots on that was more or less located around the edge of the cannery wreck. His radio—at least, many of its constituent bits—was visible in this material. And there was, as predicted, no cell-phone signal. Dalton and Fyke—both stunned, dazed, in mild shock, but otherwise, amazingly, unhurt—walked away from the wreckage and looked around them, hearing nothing but the booming of the sea and the wind rustling through the palms. They were considering trying to make a raft out of bamboo when they heard the sound of incoming choppers. The KIPAM base air controller had heard the panicked cross talk, had listened to the buzz-saw sound of the minigun, a short warning yelp—and then a profound silence.

He had drawn the appropriate conclusions and scrambled every available air asset to hunt down whatever aircraft could have been near Pulau Maju, while dispatching a Blackhawk and two Apaches to the island to see what the hell had happened. Dalton and Fyke were airborne in their Lockheed JetStar two hours later. It was four o'clock in the afternoon, local time.

Fyke got on the radio to the Duty Desk at Langley and filled them in on the theoretical threat posed by the *Mingo Dubai*. Langley got everything they had to give in a few short exchanges, rang off, and contacted the Director, who got on to Homeland Security and the President, and the massive grinding machinery of the United States security system lurched into inexorable motion over the next forty minutes.

Dalton had the plane on the ground in Guam, sixteen hundred miles east of Manado, a little over three hours later. They refueled, took on some supplies and a change of clothes—this time U.S. Air Force Special Forces blues—and covered the 2,194 miles from Wake to Wheeler Air Force Base, on Honolulu, in a little under six hours. A two-hour overlay at Wheeler for a refit and an engine check, and then another twenty-six hundred miles to Fort Lewis, Washington, where an Agency Gulfstream was waiting on the tarmac.

It had been fitted out with cots and came equipped with a shower. Dalton and Fyke were shaved and shining and sound asleep by the time the Gulfstream was at twenty thousand feet over the Rockies and the Great Plains were opening up under its wings like a broad green carpet. It was a little before midday mountain time and they had covered eighty-three hundred miles, from Manado in the Celebes to the cold blue sky far above Butte, Montana, in a little less than eighteen hours. It was eighteen hundred miles from Butte to Washington, D.C. The jet was at thirty thousand feet over La Crosse, Wisconsin, when the pilot got a patch-through call from Langley. Deacon Cather was on the phone.

"They're asleep, sir," said the pilot.

"I know," said Cather. "I'm afraid it will be necessary to wake them."

"Certainly, sir. Captain Dalton or Sergeant Fyke?"

"Captain Dalton, if you would."

In a few moments, Dalton was on the line.

"Mr. Cather?"

"Micah, I have a person on hold here. I think it would be useful if you were to talk to her yourself?"

"Yes, sir. Of course."

"I'll stay on the line, if you don't mind."

"Not at all."

"Thank you. Go ahead, Maryland."

"Captain Dalton?" A woman's voice, young, a little nervous.

"Yes?"

"My name is Nikki Turrin. I'm with the NSA?"

"Pleased to meet you, Miss Turrin. How can I help?"

"Well, it's complicated."

"I have nothing but time."

"First I have to give you a message from a Major Brancati, of the Carabinieri. He's been trying to reach you for several hours."

Grief is coming.

"Did he say why?"

"Yes. He said to tell you that Cora Vasari woke up yesterday. That she's going to be fine. That she was asking about you."

Dalton found that he was staring through the porthole at the eastern part of the United States—a field of lights and water—while an immense fatigue settled over him, a wave of relief that was almost hypnotic. He closed his eyes, pulled in a deep breath, let it out slowly.

"Thank you, Miss Turrin. You have no idea how happy I am to hear that news. How did you meet Major Brancati? Is this the complicated part?"

"Yes it is."

Nikki gathered herself, told the story of 2654 Salina Muggia Vecchia, from the YouTube video all the way to the incident at the villa and the death of a man named Stefan Groz.

"Groz is dead?"

"Yes, sir."

"Anything on Branco Gospic yet?"

"Only that Major Brancati says the two were connected. Mr. Cather tells me that you've been hunting for a tanker?"

"Yes. We still are."

"Well, we've put a lot of things together—my boss and I and the analysts at the NSA, and then with Mr. Cather—and we think that what happened at the pool and the missing tanker might be connected."

"They are. Through Branco Gospic."

"Yes. Of course. But what concerns us is the bacteria we found at the villa in Muggia. As I said, it was a strain of *Vibrio vulnificus*. It usually only grows in host tissue, like shellfish, oysters."

"So far, I think I'm following you."

"Well, we found some traces of this bacteria in the decking around the pool, probably splashed up when the people were dying. The thing is, it was still active. Still multiplying."

"But I thought it couldn't grow without a host?"

"Yes. That's true. But this strain seems to be different. It seems to be able to replicate in water. It may not need anything else."

"How fast does it grow?"

"We don't know. We only have a tiny sample, and that's degraded. But if it were healthy, our people at the labs estimate that the growth rate could be exponential. All it would need to thrive would be fresh water."

"Exponential? Means exactly what?"

"I mean—well, the lab people think it could infest an entire water system within a few weeks. It could find hosts in freshwater fish. If it were able to survive in ordinary water, it might even infect people who used the source for drinking water. Our main concern is, what if Branco Gospic has found a way to keep this culture alive in something like a tanker ship?"

Sixty thousand metric tons.

"You're saying you think the *Mingo Dubai* might be carrying this vibrio culture?"

"Yes. All you'd have to do would be to take on fresh water and then introduce the bacteria. It would take several days, but, if this theory is correct, then by the time the tanker got to a U.S. port it could literally be full of active *Vibrio vulnifucus* in this mutated form. If it were to be introduced into a body of fresh water, the results could be . . . severe."

"What kills it, if anything?"

"Salt water."

"Nothing else?"

"Of course. Bleach, that sort of thing. But mainly salt water. Have you been able to find this tanker yet?"

"Not yet. But we've just started looking."

"Micah, this is Cather."

"Yes, sir."

"Have you got any timeline on this ship at all?"

"Yes, sir. It was moored in a cut on an island one hundred miles east of Sulawesi two weeks ago."

"I think we can add some detail to that. An RAF Orion spotted an open boat adrift nine hundred miles west of Diego Garcia. They sent out a Search and Rescue plane and got a survivor off the boat. At the time, he was still alive. He died a few hours later. He was unable to talk—actually, by the time they found him he was very likely insane—I won't go into why—but there were papers in his pocket that appeared to have come from the *Mingo Dubai*. They were old records, a cargo manifest dated several years back, but somehow they ended up in the shirt pocket of a Somali adrift in the Indian Ocean. So I think we can, for our purposes, infer that the *Mingo Dubai* has already passed through the Suez. NATO and the Italians are looking at all similar ships in the Med, but so far no hits. I mean, they all have legitimate papers. And I am afraid we can assume this ship, in its new incarnation, will also have a perfectly convincing pedigree. We don't have the resources to stop and check the cargo of every tanker making calls in American ports. We get over forty thousand port calls every day. How fast can these tankers move, Micah?"

"Fyke says, with a light load and good engines, and in calm weather, the *Mingo Dubai* could do forty nautical miles an hour."

"Multiplied by twenty-four hours a day—"

"They can cover nine hundred miles—"

"So, in two weeks, that ship could travel . . . ?"

"Nearly twelve thousand miles, sir."

"It's about five thousand miles from Sulawesi to the Suez—"

"That's five days and some, sir. Another four to get through the Med."

"How far from Gibraltar to our eastern ports?"

"I can answer that," said Nikki. "About thirty-six hundred miles."

"Which means, it might be closing in on one of our ports right now."

"We should stop all tankers inside our two-hundred-mile limit, sir."

"Which we *cannot* contemplate, Micah. The effect on our economy would be disastrous. Not to mention lawsuits from shipowning firms, suppliers whose cargo is delayed, international outrage. We're already the most unpopular nation on the earth—"

"Only with our enemies, sir—"

"We need to narrow down the search parameters. We simply can't check every tanker—"

"What are we going to do, sir? Wait until one tanker does something hairy and then jump on it?"

"Effectively, yes. We monitor all tankers of this type approaching any of our ports, especially the large ones: Long Beach, Houston, New York and New Jersey, Corpus Christi, Mobile. My God . . . the logistics—"

Nikki Turrin broke in.

"Excuse me, but I think we can ignore all those ports, sir."

"We can?" said Cather. "I'm riveted, Miss Turrin. Please go on."

"I mean, we can ignore them only on the basis of the scenario we've come up with. A tanker filled with a mutated form of vibrio—"

"Because," said Dalton. "Salt water kills it. All of our ocean ports are saltwater ports. Including New York, Hampton Roads, Long Beach, Corpus Christi . . ."

"So, where is it headed?" asked Cather. "Where would it go to do the most damage to the United States of America?"

A silence. The jet shuddered through some turbulence, the muted roar of her engines a soothing murmur. The lights along the eastern seaboard were coming on as night swept westward out of the North Atlantic.

"My boss and I have talked this over with the analysts—"

"Who's your boss?" asked Cather.

"The AD of RA, sir?"

"Ah yes. I knew him before he . . . Well, never mind. How is he?"

"He's *worried*, sir."

"Of course. I'm wandering. And your conclusions?"

"That there was only one U.S. port where a ship like this could do the most irreparable damage to the heartland. If the bacteria behaves the way—"

"And what port is that?" Cather asked, cutting her short.

43

The Port of Chicago, southern Lake Michigan

The city filled the entire starboard horizon, a shimmering curtain wall of towers and spires, glowing with financial energy and all the arrogance of an imperial global power. It was early evening, the sun was going down behind the center of the city, setting the western sky on fire. The ship was steaming slowly south, slipping past the downtown shoreline, heading for the Port of Chicago harbor at Lake Calumet, twelve miles down the shore. For literally miles and miles, they had churned their way along the shoreline of Lake Michigan, and, for all that way, there was nothing but city lights.

The metropolis and its suburbs stretched far into the distance to the south, curving around the southern end of Lake Michigan into an indigo haze, a necklace of glittering beads that went all the way around the Indiana shoreline and gradually faded into the darkness. To Vigo Majiic, who was cursed with imagination, it reminded him of the scene in *Close Encounters,* when Richard Dreyfuss walks up the ramp into the starship, looks up and sees a universe of lights, an entire city, inside the ship's sphere.

Sailing the *Mingo Dubai*—now reborn as the *Maersk Empire*—with a Russian flag on her staff, into the heartland of America like this was, Vigo had to admit, a great achievement, although his participation in it had been generally reluctant, frequently grudging, occasionally craven. But they had done it, largely thanks to Emil Tarc's fanatical determination. They had come many thousands of miles, from the Strait of Malacca halfway around the world to the Port of Chicago. All that remained was to finish it and go home.

He watched as the downtown core of Chicago moved slowly by on the starboard side, its scintillating mirror image reflected in the placid waters of the lake. It was a lovely night, starlit, calm, with a bite in the air that carried just a breath of the hard Midwestern winter that was already gathering itself up in Minnesota and along the Canadian Rockies.

They had been stopped three times by ICE boats and once by a Coast Guard cutter. They had been boarded and inspected for contraband and explosives, but all they were carrying was fifty thousand metric tons of condensed soy milk, bound for a processing plant in Gary, Indiana. They had papers to prove it, and the processing plant was actually expecting their shipment. They had even opened some of the liquid holds for a visual inspection. Condensed soy milk; it would have been hard to find a more innocuous and wholesome cargo. The inspectors left shortly afterward, almost visibly bored.

Other than these routine stops, the trip had gone by without incident. They had loaded their soy—it really *was* soy milk—at Jakarta, where soy milk was a major industry, crossed the Indian Ocean, amused themselves with some Somali pirates, sailed up the Suez to Port Said, where they took on a thousand fifty-gallon drums, sealed and welded shut, which had been shipped there from Gospic's bottling plant in Budva. The drums had been marked RAPESEED OIL and loaded on the ship by dockworkers who had no idea what they were handling. Once out into the North Atlantic, they had—carefully—introduced the vibrio bacteria into the tanks containing the soy milk, and then they sealed the hatches, leaving the bacteria to do its work as they crossed the Atlantic and came down the Saint Lawrence Seaway.

By the time they reached Chicago, according to Gospic, the bacteria should have multiplied exponentially. When it was released into the waters of the Port of Chicago, at the head of the Little Calumet River, it would bloom like a terrible, invisible tide, spreading from the Little Calumet to the Calumet, intersecting with the Chicago River Ship Canal, and, from there, within a few days and weeks, it would spread down to the Illinois River, and from the Illinois to the Mississippi, infecting, if all went well, almost every river system in the American Midwest. When word of the contamination reached the global public—and Gospic was going to make sure it did—the consequences to the American agricultural and industrial life along the Mississippi, and throughout the heartland, would be . . . immensely satisfying.

Not to mention personally rewarding for Vigo Majiic, who was, to be honest, only in this for the money. Tarc was different. Tarc had been in Kosovo when NATO pilots bombed the Pocket, siding, as he put it, "with those Muslim mongrels in the villages and killing better men than they would ever be." Clinton had been President then, but the pilots were American, and now Tarc was taking a great deal of pleasure from knowing that America would feel the Serbian blade sinking deep into its underbelly.

The wind was cutting cold now, and, in spite of the magnificence of the view, Majiic went back inside the wheelhouse. Tarc looked up from a picture laid out on the navigation table, tapped the photo, a Google download. You had to love Americans: if you wanted to plan a terror operation, Google Earth would cheerfully provide the maps.

"Vigo, where's Jakki?"

"In the wardroom, with the rest of the guys."

"What are they doing?"

"They're talking, Emil."

Tarc made a face.

"Griping, you mean. They're getting on my nerves."

"They thought they'd be getting off the ship at Manitoulin Island in Lake Superior. That was five hundred miles ago."

"So they get off in Chicago instead. What's the difference?"

"Jakki says Manitoulin Island is in Canada. Chicago is right in the middle of America. It's a lot easier to avoid a few Nanooks of the North on snowmobiles than the entire United States Homeland Security grid."

"And how were we going to moor up at the berth with only you and me on board? We steam in without a crew, you think that wouldn't get the attention of the Master of the Port?"

Vigo had no good reply to that.

Tarc was silent.

"They going to be a problem?" he asked, after some thought.

Majiic didn't answer right away, partly because he had no intention of goading Emil Tarc into a confrontation with Jakki and his razor-blade companions. Tarc would lose, and, without Tarc, Majiic was pretty sure he'd be over the side and in the water, swimming for his life, about a second later. Tarc should have kept his promise and paid Jakki's men off at Manitoulin.

"No," said Majiic, finally. "Jakki has them under control."

Tarc was staring out at the city skyline, his face as closed as a fist.

"You been watching those choppers?" he said.

Majiic followed Tarc's gesture, saw the lights of the helicopters, three sharp-nosed black silhouettes low against the lights of the Chicago waterline.

"No. What are they?"

"They're Apaches. Gunships. Chain gun. Hellfire missiles. I've been watching them through the binoculars. They've been cruising back and forth along the waterfront, all the way from Navy Pier down to Calumet, and then back again."

"This is America after nine-eleven," said Majiic, shrugging it off. Tarc was a paranoid. If the Americans had any idea what the ship was carrying, they'd have sunk her off Saint-Pierre and Miquelon, back at the mouth of the Saint Lawrence.

"We've been boarded and inspected three times, Emil. Let's just cruise into the harbor, moor up in the turning basin, set the soup a-dumping, and go have some dinner somewhere. Job done. We all go home by different routes, like we planned, and Gospic pays us for work well done. Don't hunt grief."

"Grief?" said Tarc, his tone sharp. "I'm not hunting grief, Vigo. I'm here to make an impression on America. Why are you here?"

Majiic shrugged.

"Honestly? The money."

Tarc was about to say something when Jakki opened the wheelhouse door and walked over to Tarc. He was dressed in civilian clothes—jeans, a leather jacket, cowboy boots—but he looked like an artillery shell anyway.

"The guys want me to ask you something."

Jakki's attitude was cold but clear. He was not hostile, but he was close to getting there.

"Okay. What is it?"

"They want to know why we have to go inside the port. Why can't you just cruise along the shore here and open the vents? Lake Michigan flows into the Chicago River, which goes into the Illinois, and the Mississippi. What's the difference?"

"The difference," said Tarc, patiently, "is concentration. We want the stuff contained by the walls of the canals. The river current flows west, yes, but it's slow, and it wanders all over Illinois, mainly at no more than five or six miles an hour. We want the effect to be as strong as it can be."

Jakki gave the answer some thought.

"I'll tell them. Another thing. We want to get paid now."

"You get paid when we're alongside the berth and moored."

"That wasn't the deal. The deal was we got off at Manitoulin. This is not a request, Emil. We want to get paid out now. That's how it is."

"Fine," said Tarc, angry. "Tell them to get their gear—"

"We're already packed. We want the cash. Now."

"Okay. It's in the safe. Tell your people to go to the wardroom, have some coffee. I'll come down in a few minutes and we'll share out."

"You'll come down in five minutes."

"Yes. Okay. In five."

Jakki sent Majiic a look, turned and walked away. For a heavy man wearing cowboy boots, he moved like a cat, soundless and supple. Tarc watched him walk away with an unreadable expression on his face. Once the door had closed, and they could hear Jakki's boots clanking on the metal stairs as he went back to the crew deck, Tarc picked up the binoculars again and focused them on the three black insectlike shapes that were floating along the waterline, less than two miles away. As he watched, they flared in a tight formation, rose up, reversed direction, and headed back up the shore toward the downtown core.

Tarc took the binoculars away, handed them to Majiic, and said: "Keep an eye on those birds. We're about four miles out of Calumet. Radio Port Control, and tell them we're the *Maersk Empire* and we're coming in for our berth on schedule. We're not booked to off-load until the morning. See they remember that. I'll be right back."

Vigo watched him go, verified the Autohelm, and stepped back out onto the wing deck to clear his mind and settle his nerves. A thousand yards away, inside the pilothouse of a small Coast Guard cutter running with only her navigation lights on, a surveillance technician watched through a tripod-mounted telescope as Majiic stepped to the ship's rail, took out a cigarette, and lit it. They were shadowing the ship, had been ever since it had come inside the Tactical Perimeter Boundary that Homeland Security had set for all Seawaymax-class tankers bound for the Port of Chicago. This ship, the *Maersk Empire*, had already been boarded three times, according to the Operations computer in the Port Authority office down at Lake Calumet, and its papers had been verified by the International Marine Registry in Marseilles. It was carrying a load of condensed soy milk and was en route to a berth that had been duly booked with the Harbor Master two weeks before.

So, no real urgency with the *Maersk Empire*, but it was a Seawaymax-class boat, and the technician had been present in the Ready Room when a CIA agent, with something of the crocodile about him, had stood up in front of a roomful of Homeland Security guys, FBI agents, Coast Guard sailors, Port Authority cops, and assorted spooks from what the FBI was calling OGOs—Other Governmental Organizations—and when he filled them in on the Seawaymax threat the tech sat up straight and listened hard.

He had the lens, and the guy with the cigarette, so he snapped a shot with the attached digital camera—ran off a string, as the guy took a few quick puffs; he looked nervous, even at a thousand yards— and downloaded the shots to a disk, which he handed to his partner, a serious young blond woman who was the captain of the cruiser. She slipped the disk into her MDT and e-mailed it to the Collections Data clerk at the Port Authority office in Lake Calumet, who uploaded the shots and posted them on the large LCD display in the center of the room, where the movement of every ship in southern Lake Michigan was being monitored in pretty much the same way as airplanes are monitored at O'Hare. The shot, a digitally enhanced telephoto, was tagged:

UNKNOWN SHIP'S OFFICER

Bridge of Maersk Empire

Registry # MDE2665-DWT60-SWMX 2036

Back on the wing bridge of the *Maersk Empire,* Vigo Majiic finished his cigarette and went back into the wheelhouse. He was on the radio to the Harbor Master a few minutes later, giving the clerk their ETA, when Tarc came back on deck. He walked over to the wheel, looked down at the bearing. His face, lit up from below by the greenish glow of the compass screen, had what looked like freckles all over the left side.

"You've got something on your face," said Majiic.

Tarc put a hand up, touched his cheek, looked at his fingertip.

"Oh. Thanks," he said, taking a cloth from the tool drawer and wiping his face off. Majiic realized that what had looked like freckles had actually been blood spray.

"How did it go with Jakki?" he asked.

Tarc gave him a look.

"How do you think it went?"

Majiic looked out to the lake again, his chest tightening.

"What are you going to do, Emil?"

Tarc walked over to the navigation table, picked up the Google Earth shot, spread it out on the console in front of them.

"This is the harbor mouth here. There's a tall steel bridge that crosses the canal. That's not our problem, because it's a real high bridge and we can go under it at speed. Here's the problem. It's eleven hundred meters from the harbor mouth to a swing bridge, where a street called South Ewing crosses the canal. You see it here, the road marked 41. It's too low to get under, just a lift bridge; comes up in two sections, so we'll have to have enough headway to crash right through it if we need to. We're expected, so it should be open, but when they see us coming in so fast—I figure thirty-five knots will do it, but more is better—they may drop the bridge to try and stop us."

Tarc's attention was on the photo, so he wasn't seeing the look on Vigo Majiic's face. Tarc's eyes were wide, a kind of heat was coming off him. His voice was high, tight, his breathing short and rapid. Majiic thought about how far it was to the Very flare gun in the signals cupboard. If he could get to that and fire a rocket right into Tarc's chest . . . ?

"So, you'll have to have her moving at forty knots when we enter the mouth of the canal, Vigo. As soon as we're in the canal, I'll start venting the holding tanks. Then—you see here, where the canal turns to port?—we have to keep up our headway, even as we swing around this bend. No matter what, Vigo, I'll be counting on you. We have to be at full speed, and you need to take that curve at speed. And you'll have only another five hundred meters before we hit the second lift bridge right here, where East Ninety-fifth Street crosses over . . . We have to take that out, if they won't open it, and we have to assume they won't. There's a rail bridge up next, but it's a high bridge, too, so all we have to do is cover the five hundred meters from the Ninety-fifth Street bridge to the Chicago Skyway, where Interstate 90 crosses over the river. Our only problem, then, is to bring the ship to a complete stop under the Skyway—we set her on fire and she blows, the bridge is gone. You'll have to go full astern as soon as we've taken out the bridge. It might be a problem—"

"Why do I have a *problem* at all?" asked Majiic, who was miles ahead of Tarc and busily figuring out how to jump ship at the first opportunity. "Why are you even thinking about this? This is *fucking* nuts!"

"Look, Vigo, for this whole thing to work we have to make an impression. We can't just steam gently into Calumet Harbor and quietly piss ourselves empty like some *fucking* cockapoo. We need to make some real noise. Otherwise, the Americans will just spin some bullshit story about red tide or algae bloom, and nobody will know we've hit them hard."

"I thought Gospic was taking care of that."

"Sure. But the U.S. will just say it's typical terrorist bullshit. How serious is anybody taking that fairy bin Laden these days? No, we need to hit them and be *seen* to hit them. A big event that Gospic can point to. So—"

"You saw those Apaches up the shore? If you do what I think you're going to do, they'll come in and light us up like it was New Year's."

"Which is an event, then, isn't it? The boat blows, the cargo gets dumped into the river. Mission accomplished."

"We'll *fucking* die!"

Tarc took out his little MP5, laid it on the counter beside the Google shot.

"You *might* die later or you *will* die now, Vigo. I told you all about this back on Maju Island, didn't I? Achilles? Flame-capped? It was always going to come to this. You want to burn out or fade away, Vigo?"

"I want to get old and die in some pretty girl's bed."

"Well, you may yet. Look at it this way. This is America. You live through it, they'll give you some celebrity lawyer, take ten years to try you, get a hung jury, and you sell the film rights to Columbia Pictures. There are the buoys and that string of lights is the bridge over Calumet Harbor. Now, fire her up and turn her into shore. I'll be right here beside you"—he lifted the MP5 and pointed it at Majiic's head—"so let's make this happen."

Vigo Majiic stared into the muzzle of the MP5 and only saw a black hole large enough to eat the sun. He spun the wheel around, the huge ship heeled over, white water curled from her port side, the compass swung madly around, the old hull creaking and groaning like the iron gates of an ancient castle. In the hull, sixty thousand metric tons of condensed soy milk shifted in fifteen separate holding tanks. The lights of Calumet Harbor moved from the starboard side to the starboard bow and slowly came into line with the white bow light on its standard, five hundred feet away from the wheelhouse.

Vigo Majiic pushed the throttles forward and the entire ship's frame shuddered as the prop dug into the cold waters of Lake Michigan. White water began to curl back from the steep prow, feathering out into a widening wake. Five hundred feet of steel and iron and liquid, driven by eight huge diesel engines, pushed forward by a massive steel prop that stood thirty feet high and weighed a hundred tons, came up to speed and aimed itself at the mouth of Calumet Harbor. They had three miles to cover. At forty miles an hour, they'd be in the canal in less than five minutes. The *Mingo Dubai* was on the last three miles of her long career.

In the Port Authority office three miles away, right next to the tall steel gateway that marked the entrance to Calumet Harbor, Ray Fyke came back from a long cigarette break and looked around the room, crowded with agents and sailors, saw Micah Dalton, leaning back in a chair, staring back at him, smiling, sipping a cup of steaming black coffee.

On the situation screen behind Dalton, Fyke saw the listed details of the next Seawaymax-class tanker scheduled to arrive—the *Maersk Empire,* carrying a load of condensed soy; she was the ninth Seawaymax-class tanker they had marked for surveillance today, and the twenty-fourth since they had set up shop in Calumet—and, beside it, he saw a telephoto shot of a man with an underslung jaw and shaggy black hair. He was leaning on the wing deck railing and smoking a cigarette. He looked worried.

He fooking *well should be,* thought Fyke.

"Mikey," he said, quietly, "that's Vigo Majiic."

Then the radio set beeped. It was the Coast Guard surveillance craft they had tasked to shadow the *Maersk Empire,* discreetly, into the harbor.

"Port, this is Whiskey 6. We have a problem here."

THEY WERE ALL gathered around the radar screen. It was easy to pick out the incoming tanker. She was moving faster than any other tagged blip on the screen. She was now a half mile out. She'd hit the canal entrance in four minutes. The Harbor Master had seen to it that the South Ewing bridge and the Ninety-fifth Street bridge were down and locked. Armed cops had taken a position on the decks of the bridges, and more men were on the rooftops of the buildings that lined the canal. The Harbor Master turned to the Homeland Security man next to him, tapped the screen, and said:

"Bring in those Apaches!"

"No," said the Homeland chief. "You can't blow the hull."

"Well, we better do something fast," said the Harbor Master.

"We are," said the man from Homeland.

THERE WAS SILENCE on the bridge. The ship was vibrating like a church organ, a deep, thrumming energy that seemed to rise up from the deck plates and pour out from the bulkhead walls. The lights of the harbor were sharp and clear through the windshield, less than a mile away and getting larger by the second. Vigo had set the course and locked it in. There was little to do now but to brace himself against the wheel and hope to survive the impact with the South Ewing bridge.

If he was still standing after that, if they hadn't blown the ship out of the water with one of those Apache gunships, he'd try to swing the ship to port and get her bow around in time to take the Ninety-fifth Street bridge. Five hundred feet of iron moving at thirty, maybe forty knots. He didn't have a chance. But if he didn't try, or if he grazed her bow or hung her up in the bend, Tarc would kill him.

Tarc was standing by the wheel, his attention fixed and rigid, his mouth half open, a witch light in his black eyes. He was paying no attention at all to Vigo Majiic. He had his hand on the VENT switch.

Gospic had given instructions that all fifteen holding tanks could be vented from below the waterline. Venting sixty thousand metric tons of condensed soy would take quite a while. But, once it had started, the process could not be stopped. Mainly because, once he pressed that VENT button, he was going to shoot the console to pieces. The wheelhouse was suddenly filled with the klaxon sound of an alarm.

Tarc looked at Majiic.

"What's that?"

"Proximity alarm. It computes our speed and bearing and combines it with the radar returns. It's a collision warning."

"Can you shut it off?"

"Emil, we're gonna be in the canal in thirty seconds. I can try."

"Try!"

Majiic hurried over to the signals console behind Tarc, opened the door, reached down and pulled out a large Very flare gun. He lifted it up and aimed it at Tarc. Tarc was not there. Tarc had seen Majiic's reflection in the wheelhouse glass.

He was a few feet to the left. He smiled at Majiic, triggered the

MP5, and stitched six holes up Majiic's belly and into his chest. Majiic went back and down. Tarc stepped over to Majiic's body, looked down at it, shaking his head. "Poor, dumb—"

A slamming boom that echoed around the wheelhouse walls and the front of his chest blew outward in a spray of bone and blood. The deck came up like an onrushing steel wall. Tarc hit it hard, rolled over onto his back, staring up at the wheelhouse roof. A face appeared in his rapidly shrinking field of vision, a battered Irish face, missing a few teeth.

"Raymond Fyke," the man said. "Pleased to meet you."

"Ray," said Dalton. "How do we stop this thing?"

Fyke came to the wheel. The entrance to the canal was five hundred yards away. Fyke hit FULL ASTERN and turned the wheel to starboard. The lights of the harbor entrance began to slide slowly—very slowly—from dead ahead to a degree to port; there was a large empty field on the northern side of the canal, and a low stone breakwater. Fyke had the wheel hard over; the entire hull was groaning and creaking, a grinding sound of steel plates bending; the engines were howling, and the prop, reversing now, was churning up a pillar of white water and foam at the stern. Slowing . . . slowing. The canal entrance had slipped a little bit farther to port. The hull was vibrating like a struck gong, the windshield was full of lights, the proximity alarm was braying loud enough to stun. They saw the chopper that had dropped them onto the roof of the wheelhouse rise up and get out of the way; they saw the red-and-blue flickering of police lights all along the canal sides and crossing the South Ewing bridge—

"Mikey," said Fyke, standing by the wheel, "you better grab something solid because we are going in."

Dalton did. Fifteen seconds later, the *Mingo Dubai* struck the nine-foot stone breakwater at the northern edge of the Lake Calumet canal, traveling at a speed of approximately sixteen knots. Her forward stabilizer crumpled like eggshell and broke wide open. Momentum carried the tall, flaring bow up and over the breakwater wall. With a shrieking, grinding sound, with sparks of steel flaring out across the earth, the steel plates of her hull slammed through the stone wall like boxcars hammering over a railroad crossing. The ship drove on into the field, fifty, a hundred, a hundred and fifty feet, slowing, her lights flickering. The area had been cleared of civilians, but the rooftops and canal sides were packed with federal officers and Coast Guard people and they stood in stunned silence, watching this mountain of steel grind its way slowly into the deserted field. And stop. The ship had almost one-third of its length on dry land now. The big prop was still churning in reverse. The hull settled, rocked, and settled some more. There was a long, stunned silence, filled with the sounds of distant sirens and the slow chuffing of the ship's engines. Fyke killed the engines, and the prop froze in the water. He looked over at Dalton.

"Jesus, Mikey, that was a—"

There was a huge, rending sound—steel breaking away, girders popping—the hull gave a final, convulsive shudder, and the *Mingo Dubai* snapped itself completely in two. Everything that was in the ten holding tanks that were in the part of the hull that was still in the water gushed out in a pale gray torrent. Forty or fifty thousand metric tons of condensed soy milk went into the Calumet harbor canal, and there wasn't a damn thing anybody could do about it but stand around and watch.

TEN MINUTES LATER, they were still doing that—standing around and watching—when Dalton's cell phone rang. It was Mandy Pownall.

"Mandy, where are you?"

"In London. They tell me the ship just hit the fan in Chicago."

"It did. We're fucked."

"Tony Crane and I have been watching something develop at Burke and Single. In the U.S. commodities market."

"Like what?"

"No time now. I need to talk to someone named Nikki Turrin. The girl who found the video on YouTube. Do you know where she is?"

"Why her?"

"Micah, just tell me where she is."

"Far as I know, she's at Fort Meade."

"No. She booked off at the end of the day. The Duty Desk says she's off until eight in the morning. She's not answering her cell. I reached a woman named Alice Chandler. She works in the office of the AD of RA—"

"What's that?"

"Micah, you're beginning to wear on me. He's Nikki Turrin's boss. Retired Marine officer. Alice Chandler was evasive. I got the impression that Nikki Turrin and her boss have started up one of those office romances and Chandler's covering. I think she knows where they are, but she won't—"

"Try Langley. Cather knows him."

"Okay. You hang on—"

"I will."

Fyke was at his side.

"What is it?"

"It's Mandy. She's been watching the commodities market. She thinks there's something happening."

"The *American* commodities market?"

"Yes."

"Crikey. That was fast."

"What do you mean?"

"We know Gospic, you and me, as well as anybody. He's no *fook-ing* fanatic. This stunt, he did it for the money. That's all he cares about. What happens if this *poison* he's come up with, what happens if it really does go all the way down to the Mississippi, Mikey? And the word gets out?"

"The Illinois and the Mississippi water half the farmland in the Midwest. If a panic started—"

Mandy was back on the line.

"Micah?"

"Yes. Here."

"I got her. She was thinking the same thing."

"Which is what?"

"Why the video? Why put it out in the first place?"

"No idea. Gospic's a sick—"

"Maybe. But he's not stupid. We've seen a lot of proxy buyers on line. Out of Odessa, Russia, all over Eastern Europe. They're locking down bids all up and down the U.S. commodities market. If it crashes, these buyers will make—God—billions—"

"Only *if* there's a panic."

"Of course there'll be a panic, Micah. When word gets—"

"That's my point. Have you got Nikki Turrin on the other line?"

"Yes—hold on."

"Hello . . . Mr. Dalton?"

"Nikki. Is your boss there?"

A brief hesitation.

"Yes. He's right . . . right here."

"I need to talk to him."

Muffled words, then a deep vibrato voice.

"Dalton, this is Hank Brocius. I'm the AD of RA. What's up?"

"Sir, can the NSA monitor a whole sector of the grid? Everything going in or out?"

"Depends on the grid."

"This would be Eastern Europe, the entire Adriatic seaboard."

"Yeah, we could. We have that area pretty well covered."

"If I could give you a list of specific grids—particular locations and websites and commo nets—could you lock them down? Nothing gets in or out. Their world goes dark."

"How big a region are you talking about?"

"Maybe a city. Like Odessa. Kotor. The entire region."

"That's almost an act of war. That would need a presidential order."

"How long would that take?"

"God. Maybe two hours. Maybe less."

"It has to be done *now*. Right now."

"I don't have the authority—"

"I know. But do you have the power?"

"Yes. I mean, it could be done. The SURGE program could do—"

"Will you do it?"

"It'll mean my job. Maybe prison. I'm gonna have to know why."

Dalton told him.

44

Kotor, Montenegro

Branco Gospic, a heavy-bodied, slope-shouldered bull of a man, with cold gray eyes and a bald skull distorted into a chestnut shape by a near-miss mortar round, was sitting stiffly upright—his bullet-pocked belly would tolerate no other position—on an iron bench on the pillared balcony of his villa overlooking the Montenegrin coastal village of Kotor. The night was coming on, a cold, bleak night, with snow on the peaks and the cutting Bora winds ruffling the waters of the sound. Rain was misting the air. The lights of Kotor were on far below his balcony, and long rollers, driven by the Bora, were crashing into the breakwater that, in the summer, would be full of pretty girls and tourists. Tonight it was empty, as was the large old mansion behind him.

He had sent Poppa away. The old man was failing, and the recent troubles—the loss of much of their fortune, and the growing coldness between Gospic's people and the Montenegrin officials who were his usual allies—had brought Poppa low. He had sunk into a confused state, and spent much of his time in a wooden chair, wrapped in a blanket, and staring out into the fjord, singing scraps of old songs from his youth.

So, Gospic sent him to Odessa, to stay with Larissa, while Gospic rebuilt his empire, which had been effectively dismantled by that . . . cop, Brancati. Gospic was winding it up here in Kotor. The place had become inhospitable. He had a lot of money still, freighted away in Geneva and with the Jews in New York. He had been forced to break his promise to spend Christmas in Savannah with Larissa. It was not safe for either of them in America. The stock market crash that he had expected to take place after the delivery of the poisoned soy milk to Chicago had not taken place. Although he had used his resources in the cyberworld to spread stories about the poisoning of the American heartland, the panic had not taken hold. And the Americans were saying . . . nothing. There had been no public response, no official denials.

It was as if the event had never happened.

It puzzled Gospic, and he would have to do something more—

"Mr. Gospic?"

He turned around, saw his old housekeeper standing there, her winter coat on, her bag in her hand.

"Yes, Irya."

"I'm leaving now. Will you be all right?"

"Certainly. You go along."

"The house is all closed down. Everyone has gone."

She looked out across the bay, at the tall black peaks and the troubled water of the fjord, at the lights of the town, pale and watery in the rain.

"Will we come back here, Mr. Gospic?"

"I don't think so."

"Where will we go?"

"For now, you go to Odessa, to be with Larissa and Poppa."

"Will you come?"

"In a while. I have some things to do."

She hesitated and then turned away.

"Good-bye, Mr. Gospic."

"Good-bye, Irya."

She was gone. Gospic waited a while, watching the night take hold of the fjord. Then he got up and walked over to the edge of the balcony, looking down over the city. It had been a good place.

But there were other—

"Long fall, isn't it?"

Gospic turned around. There was a man standing in the darkened entrance to the mansion, a hard-faced man in a long navy blue overcoat, his hands by his side, his long blond hair whipping in the wind off the harbor. Gospic reached for the pistol he kept in his jacket pocket, and felt a hard blow, like a punch, in his belly. It knocked the wind out of him, his legs went rubbery, and he sat down hard on the bench. The stainless Colt he had been reaching for slipped out and clattered on the stones at his feet. He looked across the balcony at the man in the long blue coat.

"You're Dalton," he said, through pale lips, and fighting the weakness that was rising up from his legs. The man walked over, looked down at him. He was holding a Beretta pistol in his right hand.

"Yes," he said. "She lived, you know."

"Who?"

"The Italian woman. Cora Vasari."

Gospic nodded. His eyelids were heavy.

"I heard. Everything went wrong when I went after her."

"It went wrong before that."

"Maybe. It should not have. There should have been a panic."

"I know. The NSA picked out your buys. You shorted the commodities market worldwide. You stood to make billions in the panic."

"Yes. But there was no panic."

"No. It was the video. You shouldn't have done that. It made no sense, unless there was no mutated bacteria at all. All you needed was the fear."

"How did you know . . . ?"

Dalton made a gesture, taking in the night sky.

"The hills have eyes, Branco. In Muggia people watched. Men came every week to respray the decking. Why?"

Gospic shook his head. His belly was on fire but the rest of him was very cold. He made no sign. He would not give the man the satisfaction.

"To keep the vibrio alive," said Dalton. "Every week, you had the deck sprayed with fresh bacteria. Otherwise, it would have died. That was why the vibrio was still active when the NSA got there. You put out the video knowing that the Americans would pick it up and investigate. When it comes to national security, we overreact. We do too much. One man runs through a security gate and the entire airport gets shut down for twelve hours. One accident in Long Beach and the economy slows for a month. How did you kill the people in the pool? It wasn't the vibrio."

Gospic stared up at the man, smiled a bloody smile.

"We have our secrets, we Serbs. Someday you will get your answer."

Gospic closed his eyes. Opened them again.

The man was still there.

"Are you going to wait until I die?"

"No," said Dalton, lifting the weapon. "I have better things to do."

45

The *Subito,* Santorini, the Aegean Sea

Lujac came out onto the fantail with the drinks and found Marcus lying back on the lounge chair, smoking the colored cigarettes that Kiki had taken a fancy to after his long and memorable sojourn in the South China Sea. Marcus was beautiful, slender as a fencing foil, tanned, but with pale blue eyes in a rough Slavic face. His mouth had a hard turn to it that Kiki found very attractive. He was getting tired of the lazy, languid Greek boys who were always drifting around the Aegean Sea. They were like gazelles and gazelles bored him. He now found that he preferred the crocodiles.

Marcus was definitely a crocodile.

Marcus also liked it rough. Actually, Marcus made Kiki a little nervous, which, lately, was a feeling Kiki had become addicted to. Micah Dalton had eluded him—or he had eluded Dalton—and the money thing had come to nothing. But Kiki Lujac was still very rich, and he was still the Lovely and Talented. He gave Marcus his mojito, sipped at his.

The lights of Santorini Harbor were all around them, like a necklace of golden beads, and the air was warm, full of the scent of retsina and olives and salt water. Soft music was playing in a cantina, the sound of a tango drifting across the water. Marcus finished his drink and set it down.

"Kiki, let's go inside."

"Now?"

"Yes. Before you get drunk again."

Kiki stretched himself, turning like a cat, sighed. He had the patience for another game. Soon Marcus would be sound asleep, and Kiki would have all night to do whatever he wanted to do with this wonderful young crocodile, because he had drugged the boy's last mojito with Rufinol.

"Okay," he said, draining his mojito. "Youth must be served. What do you want to do?"

"I want to tie you down."

"Really. With what?"

"Your scarf."

It was Italian silk, indigo, very long.

"I had a scarf like that once," said Marcus.

"Did you," said Kiki. "How nice. Come inside."

They want inside. Soon, Kiki was wonderfully bound—throat, wrists, and ankles—in the indigo silk scarf. Kiki was naked, helpless, deliciously in the crocodile's power, and very ready. Marcus stood beside the bed, weaving slightly, feeling a little dizzy, looking down at him.

"I had a scarf like that once. But I gave it away."

"Really," said Kiki, with a teasing flirtatious smile. "To a lover?"

"No," said Marcus. "To my sister. Her name was Saskia."